HIDDEN PEARLS

The Skull

I0598761

Jo Del Chat

PARNASSUS PRESS
PUBLISHING

Parnassus Press
8165 Valley Green Drive
Sacramento, CA 95823
www.parnassspress.net

First Edition: March 2018

Published in North America by Parnassus Press. For information, please contact Parnassus Press c/o Marcus McGee, 8165 Valley Green Drive, Sacramento, CA 95823.

Library of Congress Cataloguing-In-Publication Data
Jo Del Chat
Hidden Pearls: The Skull/Jo Del Chat– 1st ed
p. cm.
Library of Congress Control Number: 2010943502
ISBN – 978-1-941859-73-5
1. FICTION / Action & Adventure. 2. FICTION / African American / General. 3. FICTION / Thrillers / General. 4. RELIGION / Ethnic & Tribal. 5. BODY, MIND & SPIRIT / Goddess Worship

10 9 8 7 6 5 4 3 2 1

Comments about Hidden Pearls: The Skull and requests for additional copies, book club rates and author speaking appearances may be addressed to Jo Del Chat or Parnassus Press c/o Marcus McGee, 8165 Valley Green Drive, Sacramento, CA, 95823, or you can send your comments and requests via e-mail to jochat4@gmail.com.

Also available as an eBook from Internet retailers and from Parnassus Press

Printed in the United States of America

I dedicate this book to my husband, Claude, and to my sons — Lazarus, Jarred, Exiever and Nicholas.

Thank you for giving me the drive to strive for better life, and always having an open mind to hear my ideas.

To my husband — your insights and witty wisdom on the directions I should take, the long hours, sitting at the table, rooting for me to finish the next chapter made all this possible. Thanks for the love and support!

In life, you can accomplish anything when you have great people in your corner!

To Porshia, Jordan and Shawn'Nashia Kirkpatrick — thanks for listening to my crazy ideas and encouraging me to put them down on paper.

Joanne Costello is a scientist with unstable nature. She feels most men are chauvinists who think they are the dominant species and woman are sex objects. When Joanne crosses paths with Marlon Celestin, he is a possible fatal distraction to her research.

Marlon Celestin sends a wicked desire through her body that becomes alive beneath his masterful hand, but will she allow his methodical tactics to penetrate her heart, even if her body cries out for him!

PROLOGUE
SOMEWHERE IN NEW JERSEY

"Aahhhh! You fucking bitch! I'm going to kill you!" he screamed while in pain, receiving another blow to the head from the heel of her boots.

"Ahhhhhhhh! Stop! Please stop! Untie me! I won't hurt you! I promise."

Bang! Bang! Bang!—three more blows to the head.

"Ahhhhh!" he yelled, delirious, bleeding from his mouth. Crouching, he crawled under the car to protect himself from more abuse.

Joanne continued her assault, grabbed his gun under the driver seat and smashed it across his face, knocking him to the ground. She dragged him from underneath the car, pulled him up and slammed him between the driver side doors of his Lexus. She kneed him in the groin and kicked him in the head one last time.

"You think you can put your hands on me? Hurt me and get away with it! You son-of-a-bitch! The answer was "No!" with another forceful kick to his head.

"No! If you were the last man on this earth, it will still be 'no,' Asshole!" she yelled, seeming deranged, as she caught a glimpse of herself in the side mirrors.

"Ouch… please stop hurting me! I'm sorry for putting my hands on you," Andre cried out in pain, thinking of all the ways he was going to enjoy killing her.

"Putting your hands on me is the least of your problems, motherfucker," she repeated. "You tried to rape me!" she screamed in his face.

She came to an abrupt stop as she heard sounds coming toward them. She scanned frantically for his bodyguards, who were posted not too far away. She quickly adjusted her clothes, put on her boots and stood over him, observing the position of his body on the ground. Andre's face was severely bruised, and he was bleeding from his scalp. His left hand cradled his ribs, which had been kicked too many times.

Joanne was not in her right state of mind, due to being nearly-raped. She held the gun to his head and tried to pull the trigger, only to realize the safety lock was engaged. She cocked the gun and was ready to try again, but she was halted by flashes of light coming towards her.

One of the guards pulled up to the side of Andre's Lexus. Joanne quickly put her knee on his throat, shutting off his vocals, preventing him from screaming out, pretending that he was orally pleasuring her.

Seeing only their boss' head on the side of the car, the guards laughed, poking fun at Andre's expense, his muffled cries appearing to be sexual.

"Yo, boss, I thought you said, you didn't eat cat!" one of the guards yelled across the parked cars.

Joanne gave them an annoyed look, pretending to be disturbed by the interruption. She stared at them until they took note and controlled their laughter, assuming the lovebirds wanted to be left alone. They pulled off, leaving Joanne to continue torturing their boss.

Eyes swollen, red and throbbing from Andre's earlier punches, she whacked him with the butt of the gun again and continued assaulting him until he lost consciousness.

She dragged his body to the car door, sat him in the passenger seat, and driving around the dirt field, she found a nice ditch and kicked him out of the car. His body rolled in the ditch on the side of the empty field he owned. She drove off with his car, simultaneously blowing the horn and blowing kisses for the guards before streaking out of the front gates.

Joanne drove through South East Jersey and dumped the Lexus at a junkyard near Red Bank. She wiped the car clean with Clorox bleach wipes from her purse, walked out and shot one of the car's tire with Andre's gun. She hurried to leave to area, concern that someone may have heard the gunshot. She made her way to Sarcomere Avenue. near the food mart and called her father. He picked up on the fourth ring.

Julio Costello, a successful biochemist and archaeologist, settled in New Jersey twenty-five years earlier, along with his wife Cathleen and daughter, Joanne, who was the apple of her parents' eyes.

From an earlier age, Joanne showed incredible strength and beauty. She was knowledgeable about many things and understood the world around her. She had a natural ability to heal and was a perfect, well-behaved child who make her parents proud.

After her fifteenth birthday, this well-mannered child began to show signs of being irrational, authoritative, temperamental, reacting to other people's emotions and attitudes. She acted territorial towards her parents and personal things and developed a powerful hatred for the opposite sex to show her superiority.

Aware of their daughter's wayward and impulsive behavior, her aggression, bad-temperament and her hate for authority figures, they made a strenuous effort to get family therapy to help her cope with everyday problems and dealing with males. Mr. Costello was concerned about his daughter's behavior and about the type of undesirable man she attracted. Many men became dumbstruck with admiration, wanting her for beauty and strength.

Although Joanne worked in the same field as her dad and graduated at the top of her class, she was not interested in any man, especially the ones that work with her father. Her therapist suggested for her to try something new, to go on a date. Andre was one of those guys, as per her father's request, the son of his latest project.

Andre Voltaire a ruthless tyrant, a self-centered chauvinist pig who saw Joanne having lunch with her father, claimed he was in love begged her father to introduce him. After much protest from her father, Andre threatened he would have his wealthy father pull all investments from Costello and shut down the current project if Andre didn't get his way.

Having no choice, Julio gave in and convinced Joanne to go on the date. He had been on edge since arranging for his daughter to go on the date with Andre. He was unable to sleep and paced the room for hours after she left, waiting for her to walk through the doors.

The sudden ringing of the phone didn't sit well with him at all! Deep down, he knew something went wrong. He's been coaching Joanne all week, encouraging her not to let things get to personal on the date. He urged her to ignore Andre's male chauvinist comments or his machismo.

He took a deep breath and answered the phone.

"Hello," he said in a flat tone. Hearing nothing on the other end, he switched ears, adjusting the receiver. All he could make out was static on the other end. He held the phone to his other ear and listen to things in the background.

"Jo-Jo! Is that you? Hello, Joanne!" He raised his voice, trying to make sense of the whole situation, panicking as he thought the worst.

"Daddy! Help, please!" Joanna cried into the receiver. "I think I killed him!

Hearing the alarm in her voice, the color drained from Julio's face.

Joanne kept repeating the same fraise over and over; in a deranged state of mind.

"I killed him! I killed him!"

"Okay, sweetheart! Where are you? I need to come and pick you up."

"Daddy! I'm scared,"

"I know, Baby. Just tell me where you are?" he said, fearing for his daughter's life.

"I don't know. I don't know what happened, Daddy. Help!"

"Look around and tell me what you see," he said, reasoning with her as she repeated the same words. He was having hard time at getting her to cooperate with him to discover her location.

"Try, baby! Where are you calling from? he whispered with sorrow in his voice. The line was quiet for a moment as he waited for her to response.

"Uh…. Umm, I'm in a supermarket, near the train tracks and a Dunkin Donuts, on the corner.

"Sweetheart! Ask someone for help. I'll need to come and pick you up." He thought he could hear Joanne talking to someone before coming back on the line.

"Daddy, I'm in Red Bank, near the tracks."

"Okay. Stay in the store and I'll be right there."

Mr. Costello reached his daughter in record time. After Joanne explained all that had happened on the date. he instantly wanted to hurt Andre for putting his hand on his princess.

They sat in the car for hours, thinking on their next step. Knowing that Joanne couldn't go home because of the incident, he had no choice other than to send her to Miami. The police and the Valbrune family would be looking for her.

Julio's brother, Albert, lived in Miami with his wife and kids. Joanne could stay with them until the matter was settled. He would report her missing for a while.

"My wife is not going to like this at all!" he whispered to himself, wondering about how Cathleen would feel about him sending her daughter out.

"Jo, you have to leave, baby girl. Tonight! And tomorrow I'll report you missing. I want you to go to Uncle Albert in Florida and fly to Haiti on Monday morning. Maybe I should wait until your safe in Haiti before I fill a missing person report," he mused, assessing the situation.

"I'm going to call your mother to meet us at the airport with some of your things," he said, trying to reassure his daughter.

"But daddy! That's mean! I could never come back," Joanne pleaded between cries.

"Don't think negative. I was thinking of moving to Haiti in a couple of years. Now, I have a reason to finish my research there. I have great connects in Gonaives," he laughed nervously, trying to lighten the mood.

"You can start my research department for me in Port-Au-Prince. Stay with your uncle Emilio on the top floor of the family home. Don't forget all the other family you have. I know you are very close to Fabiola, so I think this move will be good for you."

Plan concluded, Mr. Costello hugged his daughter and walked away to call his wife.

Joanne cried her heart out as the Costellos sat in the airport terminal. Cathleen couldn't hold back her tears as she realized she could have lost her daughter to the maniac who attacked her. Now her baby would have to move away from her loving home and with people who wouldn't understand her or protect her. Cathleen buried her face in her husband's chest.

It was 7 a.m. when Joanne glanced up at the clock, waiting for the nine o'clock flight for Miami. She was seated in a waiting area of the terminal when Channel 12 News flashed the image of the Lexus and a picture of Andre. She touched her father's arm, directing his attention to the monitor as they listened intently.

"Earlier this morning, police were called to this empty field behind me, where they discovered the gruesome scene of a man, beaten and left for dead. The victim was identified as Andre Valbrune of the Valbrune family, a family with known mob ties in the tri-state area. Sources close to the family believe this attack might start a war with a rival family or families," the reporter stated, glancing up from her notes.

"Andre is a twenty-three-year-old male with has a long history of violence and arrests. He was on trial for murder just last year, though he was acquitted on all chargers. Police are trying to piece together the events leading to the attack, which left him in critical condition at St. Jude's Hospital. The evidence is still sketchy on details relating to why he was in this field, though there is a report that he was on a date with a young lady. No word yet on this companion, who police are say is missing in action. Valburne's vehicle was found four miles away from the crime scene. Again, police are asking anyone with information regarding this horrible beating to contact their crime tip hotline immediately to help solve this crime."

Joanne strangled on her attempted words and looked in the opposite direction.

"I can see the CIS crew just entering the crime scene. I'll keep you posted about any new developments. I'm Sandra Blake, Channel 12 News. Back to you at the studios."

The broadcast ended, living the Costellos in bewilderment.

"Okay, you're going to catch the next plane to Haiti. Forget Miami! It's only a matter of time before the police figure out that you were the woman on that date with him. Let's go!"

Mr. Costello changed the ticket, paying in cash for a ticket to Haiti that would leave at 9:30. He kissed his daughter "good-bye." As he and his wife held hands as they watched their daughter's plane ascent, taking her off to a new life.

CHAPTER 1
Port-au-Prince Haiti

JOANNE

At 2 p.m., the "fasten-your-seatbelt" signs glowed red, indicating that I'd reached my destination. The flight attendant's voice echoed throughout the plane, giving passengers instructions as we descended. I rested my head by the window and admired my home, my paradise, with its wide mountainous view of exotic flowers and palms trees blooming on overgrown hills that spread across the Island.

The splendid view of the of the coastline golden sands met with transparent turquoise-blue and neon green-waters that softly crashed onto the sand. A ringing sound in my ears popped as the plane descended on to my new home. The overflowing soft waves revealed the many colorful coral reefs that lay along the ocean floor. I took a deep breath, enjoying the natural landscape as the runway appeared.

Walking along the paved white tile hallways, I was greeted by vibrant collections of art that decorated the walls, and by live musicians, playing authentic *twoubadou*. Exiting the airport, I looked for my family, and leaving the air-conditioned building, I felt the hot sun kissing my cheeks as the cool winds eased its affect. Standing on the sidewalk, searching for a familiar face in the sea of people behind a gate, waiting for their loved ones, I spotted my uncle and waved as airport personnel helped me with my luggage.

Our welcome was brief, as my uncle ushered me to the awaiting vehicle. I noticed all the *tap-taps*—various vehicles used for public transportation, ranging from taxis to minivans to 4x4 pick-ups, all modified to take passengers to many destinations throughout the island. Each was unique, inside and out, with vivid, vibrant colors, reflecting the personalities of the driver. I sat back and took in the atmosphere of the busy streets, lined with palms trees that separated the smooth, paved surface en route to my family's home. All along the roads were more colorful splashes in vibrant art and painting, reflecting the personalities of vendors who sold handcrafted arts and goods on every corner.

A few hours later, after I settled in, I was in the mood to explore my new world, and standing at the balcony, I took a whiff of the many red *choeblacks* (hibiscusus) covering the entire area. The streets in the city were filled with activities as the locals got ready for the nightlife in Port-au-Prince. The young got dolled-up, leaving the elders to gather on the corners for fun and laughter.

On my first day back, which was after a long absence in the states, my cousin Fabiola took me around town to meet some of her friends. I looked around as we walked down Rue Avenue Miller, noticing how different life was in Haiti. The houses were made of bricks, with sheet metal attached, to keep the sun and the rain away (though not so much the heat!)

After reaching upper-class towns, like Kinscoff or Bellevue, Mountagne Noir, Labadee and Petion Ville, I realized those places looked like Bellaire or Miami Beach. There was so much that Haiti had to offer. I was glad to be home for good and wished many more of my people would make the decision to come home permanently, working with the younger generation at rebuilding this paradise!

As my cousin and I strolled around town, someone walking in our direction flagged her over.

"Yeah, Carl. What's up?" she asked the young man, who wore a NY Yankees hat, acting like he was the coolest guy in the block. He stared at me, licking his lips, while carrying on a conversation with Fabiola.

"Nothing, but who's that with you?" he asked, still licking his lips.

"Oh, that's my cousin. She just flew in from The States. She's staying here for a while." She turned to me, and made the introductions.

"Joanne, this is Carl. He's a friend form school. He's kind of cool," she said in a nonchalant manner.

Carl flexed his muscles while making eye contact with me. There was a weird expression on his face—like he wanted to eat me on the spot. I ignored his face as he extended his hand.

"If you need anything, beautiful, just call on me. I'm at your service," he said, trying to look extra sexy, which was a turn-off!

From the distance, I heard a strong voice calls out to Fabiola to get her attention. I turned to Carl.

"Well, thank you for that. I'll keep it in mind. So, are there any good parties tonight?" I asked.

"Hell yeah! There are few. It's Friday night!" he said with a big smile on his face. "Disip is playing at club Plezi Mwen. After that, Carimi will be at Bull's-Eye, chilling all night with the owners. If you'll be my date tonight, I can get you both into the party. I'm pretty tight with the owners."

He reached out for my hand, like I was supposed to be impressed by his declaration, and then a sharp voice rang out.

"Carl! Carl, get in here!" a woman's voice called to him. I thought it must have been his mother.

"Hold on, Mom. I'm coming," he yelled through the entranceway to his house.

"I'll be right back, beautiful. Think about me when I'm gone?" he whispered before running inside.

I located Fabiola, talking to a group of guys—at least fifteen—sitting in front of a boutique store, laughing. As I looked around the street, I notice all the expensive cars lining the corner of the store. For a poor county, these people really knew how to show off!

Fifteen vehicles, all brand-new, from Mercedes to Jags, Hummers, BMWs. I recognized four of them and a two-door Bentley. The cars looked so out of place.

Carl came running back. "So are you ready to party?" he asked, awaiting my answer. Before I could turn him down, Fabiola came from across the street.

"Joanne!" she announced, excited about the invite. "You're VIP tonight at Plezi Mwen—*special guest to Shoty!*"

Carl looked at Fabiola and sucked his teeth. On hearing her words, he groaned and walked away upset. I looked over at Fabiola.

"What's up with him?" I asked. She shrugged her shoulders, giving me a perplexed look. "Your friend just asked me to go with him before you interrupted," I said. "I was trying to let him down easy. He seemed sweet—not like most of the crazy ones I attract."

"Joanne, he's is small compared to Shoty," she laughed. "That's why he walked away. In this area, A15 rules," she said. "That's your first lesson since you're living in this country now!"

"Well, that's all good, but I'm not ready to be with anyone like that," I answered. "So go tell him 'no, thank you—that I'm not interested.'"

"Joanne!" Fabiola cringed, horror written across her face. "Shoty *runs* this sector. You can't decline him!"

"Look, it's my first night, and I have a lot of unpacking to do. I don't want to get involved or have people looking at me. I just want to be left alone."

I walked away, leaving Fabiola talking to herself.

"Shoty is not going to like this. What am I going to do?" she sighed.

"He's your friend. Deal with him! I'm going home to finish unpacking and go to bed early. My head still hurts from last night."

As I navigated my way back to the entrance; I felt someone's eyes on me. I looked at the crowd. All were sexy men, but one in particular stood out: he was at least 6-feet-tall, with bronze skin, a muscled body and the sexiest lips I'd seen on a man. He leaned on a black Bentley and smiled as we made eye contact.

When he made a sign for me to come to him, I kept walking. He reminded me of a younger version of Laz Alonso, the actor. If I had learned anything in this world, it was to never trust a handsome man with money. He looked like he was both. I didn't need that kind of drama in my life!

Chapter 2
SHOTY

On Friday afternoon—on one of the hottest days in Haiti, I drove around the block to meet with the guys regarding a problem with a businessman who wanted to take over one of our properties?

"These people are a pain in the ass," I sighed in frustration, pulling to a stop on the corner of Avenue Miller and Grand Avenue.

All the members of our A15 crew were already assembled, waiting for me. The streets were lined with array of vehicles from our showroom. My comrades were sitting on the steps as I approached Riffle, who was arguing with Simi about who had "the baddest chick last night."

As I scanned the block, I saw an old lady crossing the street and a group of young girls jumping rope on the sidewalk. I noticed Fabiola, talking to a neighbor. I thought his name was Carl, or something.

Next to her was this long-haired, thick beauty—with face and body to match. She was light-almond, with rosy, pink lips. My dick got rock-hard just thinking about what those lips could do to me.

"Damn, I like that!" I said out loud.

"I guess... if you like them that big!" Simi commented.

I looked at his stupid ass. "Man, shut up—with those *toothpicks* you date!"

"Hell, yeah! I like to pick them up and carry them all over the house while I'm fucking," he retorted, as if he had just won the "Mr. Wonderful" contest.

Simi came over and watched Fabiola's friend for a minute and nudged me. "What are you gonna do with all that booty?"

"Don't worry about what I'm going to do! Just worry about what Rachelle is going to do to you when she catches you with those toothpicks all over the house you pay for!" I teased.

Riffle, Magnum and the rest of the guys laughed at the expression on Simi's face upon hearing Rachelle's name. Rachelle was the so-called "future wife" who had claimed him as "her man" five years earlier. She was only fourteen when she met him for the first time, and she decided to move into his villa, which had the effect of him to staying away from her... and his mansion.

I motioned for Fabiola to come over to me, and she crossed the street, leaving her companion in deep conversation with Carl, who was probably trying to make a date. *Sorry to rainy in you parade, amigo*, I thought to myself as Fabiola approached. Cage's security team stopped her before she could reach me.

"It's okay, Jock. She's good!" I said, waving him off.

"So Faby, what's up? Who's your friend?" I asked, still unable to take my eyes off the young woman.

"Well hello to you, too, Shoty. How are you doing?" she replied sarcastically, rolling her eyes at me. I gave her a hard look, waiting for her to compose herself.

"That's my cousin from The States," she said reluctantly. "She'll be staying in Haiti for a while. Why you ask?"

"She's beautiful! Bring her to the club tonight as my special guest." I turned to Mag. "Yo, Mag—VIP for my friends tonight."

"Sure man," he confirmed.

After I finished my conversation with Fabiola and sent her back to her cousin, I noticed Simi, still examining my new "beauty" across the street.

"What are you thinking about?"

"Yo Shoty!" he said, shaking his head. "That girl eyes are cold, man. You need to stay away from that. You promised 'no more psycho chicks.'"

He was reminding me of the variety of women I had dated in the past—women who caused me a lot of issues. But I had to laugh at that, coming from Simi.

"No more psychos—no more than Rachael, cuz Rech takes the cake for that title," I said.

"Why you bring her up for? You're always doing that shit! I haven't talked to the girl in two years," he complained.

"Then keep your psycho comments to yourself, brother," I said. "Besides, you haven't met her yet! Give her a chance."

"Good luck with that!" Simi said, shaking his head.

I sat back, watching that big booty bouncing down the street. I was looking forward to that night. I couldn't wait to get my hands all over that booty!

Chapter 3
SHOTY

As the clock struck 3 a.m., the club was winding down, thought there still were a couple of drunks on the dance floor. Some people were hooking up for their private parties, while others were making their way to the exits. Riffle came over.

"Your girl didn't show up?" he asked, amused.

"Yeah. I don't know what happened. I can't even get Faby on the phone," I laughed, surprised because I couldn't remember the last time my order was ignored.

"Do Faby know that was a direct order?" he asked.

"Yeah, she's been around me long enough to know. I can't believe how hung up I am about meeting this girl. I don't even know her name," I said, remembering how her thick booty jiggled in those tight pants she had on.

"How come you never hook up with Faby?" Riffle asked jarring me from my thoughts. "It's clear she has feelings for you."

"I never thought of her that way. Besides, we grew up together. She's like a little cousin, or sister even."

"Yeah, a little cousin who has a big crush on her big brother."

"What? Man, you make no sense!"

"You said you thought of her as a sister or cousin…"

"Riffle—shut up!"

"I'm just pointing out," he insisted, "that your 'little sister or cousin' was a little upset because you asked about her cousin… and didn't even bother to acknowledge her."

"I've never given her any notion that our friendship was anything but what it is," I answered. We're good friends—nothing more, and she's married!"

"Be careful with that," Riffle said. "I agree with Simi—your new-found love interest has that 'I'm a crazy bitch' look, but then again, you like them like that! See you in the morning."

Riffle walked away, leaving me with my thoughts. I didn't care. I still wanted to meet her—crazy or not.

The days turned into weeks, and the weeks became two months, providing no opportunity to meet Faby's cousin.

"Why? Can't I get this girl out of my mind? Damn!" I sighed. As I walked around town, I found myself in Rue Monsieur Giue, the area of Fabiola's family home. I paid close attention to the house with the pink balcony. As I walked up the block, it seemed luck was on my side. There she was—standing on the balcony, watching the activities of the ins-and-outs of the town. I waved 'hello.' She turned and walked into the house, as if she never saw me.

I was stunned and confused. *No female has ever ignorer me like that!* Now she had me talking to myself! *Maybe I'm the crazy one!* Shaking my head, I looked up at the empty balcony in disbelief. An old man who lived on the block saw the whole thing and approached me.

"Boss man," he whispered. "Please excuse her. She's not a happy person. She really doesn't talk to anyone—not even to her family," he explained. "Her cousin, Fabiola, been out of town for a couple of weeks now. All she does is go to work in the morning and come home late at night. No boyfriend, boss."

"You're a very observant person," I remarked. "How did you know I wanted information on her?"

"You have that look in your eyes, the look of a man wants a woman who's hard to get," he answered.

"You think she's hard to get?" I asked.

"Oooh, I *know* she's hard to get. You're dealing with a oneness not form this world," he warned, rubbing his chin. "She's beautiful, intelligent, strong by nature, and from what I'm told—a bit irrational and impulsive." He recalled a conversation with her uncle, who was concerned about his niece. "Boss man, they don't make women like her anymore, and she's a fabulous cook. You're not the only one sniffing around here after her. She has many admirers."

The old man stared off at the balcony dreamily, with visions of his younger self-courting her. "But I think you can handle her," he said, nodding. She needs the kind of man who'll take control."

As I observed the old-timer, it seemed he hadn't eaten anything for days, and he needed bath.

"So what else can you tell me about 'Miss Attitude, not from this world?'" I probed.

"Well, Mr. Shoty, sir," he continued.

"Aaahhh, you *do* know who I am?" I asked.

"Yes sir, everyone around here knows who you are. You're a success story to us. We watched you grow into what you are," he said proudly.

"All except one very beautiful—what did you call her? 'Oneness?'" I asked, glancing at the balcony one last time.

"She lived in the U.S. all her life until a few months ago," he said. "Her parents sent her here to live with her uncle after an incident back there. From what I hear, she beat up a guy, putting him the hospital. Her parents were scared for her life! The person she beat up was a well-known gangster. She stayed to herself and had no friends. All she do is work!"

"Do you have a name for me, old-timer?"

"My name is Pierre," he said, laughing, "but hers is Joanne."

"Joanne?" I whispered. "Nice!" I pronounced, liking the way the name sounded. I pulled out a couple hundred-dollar bills.

"So, this is your first payment to keep what's mine safe. Do we understand each other, Pierre?" I made direct eye contact. "She will be mine!"

"Boss man—you might have some problems there," he said, his face serious, "because from what I'm told, that girl is impulsive. Just remember that this a small neighborhood. We can't be held responsible for her actions. This block can't take A15 heat!"

"Thanks for the warning, but I want her!" I insisted.

After Pierre took the money, I motioned for him to look up at me again.

"Let all those admirers of hers know who she belongs too."

"Boss man, I'll pray for you, so God will keep you safe."

Pierre walked up the alley and entered a brick house on the corner. As I headed back to my car, I spotted the person I'd been looking for coming around the corner.

"Fabiola!" I called out. "Where have you been? I've been searching for you."

She looked up at me, stunned that I would be looking for her—we had been friends since childhood. My parents owned the store on Avenue Miller, and all the neighborhood kids went there for the free candy I sneaked out of the store.

I had become a millionaire eight years earlier—after joining the A15 crew. After that, Fabiola and I grew apart and I only saw her when I came to the neighborhood.

FABIOLA

I had wished for a romantic relationship with Shoty. He never saw anything but friendship in me, but now he wanted to get with Joanne. That did not sit well with me for two reasons: one, Joanne is a bit insane; and two, they would never get alone because he was demanding, and she had a bad temper. I felt I would always be in the middle of their mess.

"You've disappeared on me," he said, walking up. "What happened that night?"

"Ooh… Joanne didn't want to go, and I had to leave in the morning for Jeremy," I answered. He noticed that I was looking around frantically, avoiding eye contact.

"Look, you don't have to make excuses for her. I already know she can be difficult. I like your cousin and I want to get to know her. Can you help me with that?" he asked.

"It's not that simple, Shoty," I explained. "Joanne is stubborn. If she doesn't want to do it, you can't force her."

"Don't worry about all that. Just get her to me, and I'll do the rest." he said confidently.

As I stared at him, he looked like he just won a war that hadn't yet begun. I just shook my head, making the sign of the cross sending up a prayer for him.

Shoty didn't know what he was getting into!

JOANNE

I walked back onto the balcony after walking away from the guy who invited us to a private party at his club. I had refused, not wanting to encourage his attempt at being friendly. He reminded me of all the qualities I did not want in a man. I refused to be distracted by anything that was not work.

My plan was simple: help my dad build his lab for his Theology research. Beginning on my second day in Haiti, I worked from sun up to sun down. I would work until my parents were able to join me in Haiti, and we could be a family again. Missing them was hard on me. I wished I could have just ran back to them. Mom and Dad always knew how to make things right.

The last eight weeks were the hardest, not being able to speak with them. It was the first time I had been away from them in all my life. Two weeks earlier, Fabiola went away to visit her side of her family on the mountains and to get her merchandise ready for the spring sale.

NARRATOR

Joanne completely threw herself into her work at designing the lab from sun-up to sun-down every day, except on Sundays. She attended her Sunday church service at 4 a.m. and used the rest of the day to relax with her favorite book. Her nights were full of loneliness, with no companionship.

It was Thursday that Fabiola was scheduled to come home. Joanne was on the balcony, waiting for her cousin's return, when noticed her cousin's friend, looking up at her. Finally, her cousin came up the alleyway toward the family home. Within minutes, they met on the balcony.

"So, you're back. How was everything?" Joanne asked, giving Fabiola a hug.

"Good. Everyone is fine—kisses and hugs for you," she muttered as she circled her cousin, noticing she had lost weight.

"You're not eating," Fabiola scolded.

"I haven't had much of an appetite."

"You have to try and eat. I know you miss them." Fabiola seemed sad for her cousin and decided to change the subject. "How do you like your new job? I heard you haven't been home much."

"It's all right. It's a lot of work!" Joanne answered. "Keeps me busy, which I need right now… or I'll go crazy thinking about my parents."

Joanne noticed that her cousin was nervously pacing the room, tense and uneasy. After a long silence, Fabiola grabbed Joanne's hand, looking into her eyes.

"Look Jo, the guy I talked to you about before—he really wants to meet you."

"What guy?" Joanne asked, confused. "The one that I spoke to? Carl?"

"No. The one who invited you to the club? He really wants to meet you," Faby answered, releasing her cousin's hand.

"He can want something, but that's doesn't mean he's going to get it," Joanne said as she walked toward her room to get ready for bed.

"Oooh, Jo-Jo," Fabiola said, distraught. "You don't understand. Shoty *wants* you. He will stop at nothing until he gets you."

"You make it sound like I don't have a choice in this!" Joanne snapped as she gathered up her bathroom essentials. "I can date anyone I want, and right now. I don't want anyone."

"Here in Port-Au-Prince, A15 rule!" Faby insisted. "Not the Government. The Police can't even touch Shoty and his crew. So please, Jo, just meet with him."

Joanne stuck her head out the shower to answer her cousin.

"And you want *me* to meet with this guy? With the history I have with men? Let me ask you something. Is he paying you to do this?"

Faby cast her eyes to the floor, avoiding Joanne's eyes.

"No payment," she replied, "but I know Shoty. If thing don't go his way, or if he feels I played him—I might lose my post and my permit to sell. These are serious people. They don't play around."

"You want me to get involved with these people?" Joanne asked, exiting the shower, drying off. "Don't you remember that I escaped with just my life?"

"No, I didn't forget, and I wouldn't ask you to do it if it wasn't serious," Faby said in a grave manner, sneaking a peek at Joanne's round derriere that jiggled as she walked.

"It's not me who got you involved. It's that *booty* of yours! He wants it!" Faby teased as she walked out the room.

CHAPTER 4
SHOTY

It had been a whole week since I talked to Fabiola about her cousin, and I still saw no plans for us getting together. A new idea popped in my head, so I picked up the phone and dialed Faby's number. She answered on the third ring.

"Hello," she said, sleepy.

"Hi Faby, what's up?" I asked.

"Who am I speaking to?" she asked.

"It's Shoty, Faby! Wake up. We need to talk."

"Yeah, it's only 1:30 in the morning, and I'm in bed with my husband! Why you calling me? Can't it wait until the morning?"

"No, it can't wait," I insisted. "I need you to set up a little gathering at your place for about 15 of my friends… and invite your cousin."

"Shoty!" she groaned into the phone, "you're putting me in a bad situation with both you and my cousin. Joanne already accused me of being paid by you. I don't want any parts of this!" She sighed, frustrated. "Look, I know how you operate, and this thing can get very ugly. Please forget that you ever saw her and find a girl who can make you happy. Jo would be a thorn in your side. This whole thing is ludicrous!" Hearing only silence, she continued. "My cousin is not the kind of woman you date. She will *fight* you and your crew. So yes, I'm afraid for her… and you. She's had bad experiences with men like you in the past, and the outcomes were not good."

Though I heard the fear in her voice, I listened without interrupting.

"My uncle sent her here because the guy she was dating—not evening dating, it was just a date—he tried to force her into sex," she explained, breathing heavily into the receiver. "Joanne snapped—beat him up and send him to the hospital. Hello?" she said to confirm I was still there.

"Yeah, I'm here, finish your story," I said, intrigued.

"Well, when he came out of his coma, he put a contract out to kill Joanne. Her parents thought Haiti was the safest place for her… until she met you, Shoty. I don't think she will be safe when things get ugly between your two!" She paused for moment, which gave me a moment to collect my thoughts, like *what kind of fucker would put out a contract on a woman because she said no? I'm really going to kill this motherfucker!* My mind drifted, feeling angry. Finally, I responded.

"I understand your concerns, but I still want her. You don't have to worry. I'll take good care of her. I promise! Now, can you plan the party? All expenses on me! It will be your party, and I've just invited my friends." I waited for her to respond.

"You and fifteen of your friends in my house, Shoty? I'm poor and you're millionaires. I can't entertain fifteen millionaires in my home," she scoffed.

"Seventeen, actually, but it's okay. We're still friends from back in the day, so don't think of my friend any differently than you think of me, okay. So you'll do it?' I asked.

"You leave me with no choice. It's my husband's birthday next week. I guess I could say it's for him."

"See what happens when you put your mind to do something? It gets done. I always loved that about you!" I said, smiling ear to ear, envisioning myself with Joanne on my lap.

"This is the last time we're discussing my cousin," she protested. "I'm not going to help you with any crazy scams after this. If this doesn't work, you're on your own."

"Good, now I get to meet your husband, too! And Faby—he better come correct! See you on Friday."

JOANNE

Friday morning. As I woke up, the sun was already high on the horizon, making the room hot and humid. I didn't have to go to work that day. Fabiola wanted me to help her throw her husband a birthday party that night. She asked for my help in preparing the food. I hadn't cooked since I moved there, but cooking helped me collect my thoughts, so it was a good day.

She had created a big menu, serving *giot, polet fruit,* peklize and rice and beans, plus *hors d'oeuvres* for sixty guests. It seemed she had an unlimited ATM card for the party. At 7:30 p.m., I finished cooking the food and helped put up the decorations. When it was time to get ready, I went up and took a shower.

I had brought an outfit, so I could get dressed at Faby's house. I stood there, admiring myself in the mirror, wearing a light demi mini-skirt that insinuated my curves. It also had a baby-blue, deep, V-cut shirt to show off my triple-Ds. Satisfied with what I saw, I walked out the bathroom in search of Fabiola.

By then, I noticed that some of the guests had started showing up, so I went to Faby's husband, Erick, and wished him his fifth "Happy Birthday" for the day.

I pulled Faby back into the kitchen to help me with some of the food. As the party got going, more people showed up. The turn-out was great. I hoped there was enough food for everyone. After a few minutes greeting Faby's friends, I wanted some time to myself, so I walked along in the garden in the front of her home and sat on the patio, putting my feet on the lawn chair while I sipped rum and coke.

I heard voices coming from the entrance of the house, and when I looked up, I recognized the guy who Faby said wanted to meet me. He was talking to her and Erick, but his eyes were searching for something else the whole time—they were resting on me, staring at me. He was smiling.

I ignored him and continued with my drink, but I noticed he was meeting and interacting with many of the people at the party—he brought 15 guests with him who were spread about the small balcony. After a while, Mr. "I-want-to-get-to-know-you" came over and sat opposite me, staring, making me uncomfortable.

"Didn't your mother ever teach you that it's impolite to stare at people?" I asked.

"Yes, she taught me not to stare," he answered, "but she never said anything about staring at my wife."

"You're a cocky-ass niggah," I retorted.

"You'll find out soon enough just how cocky I can be!" he laughed, winking. "But I'm not a niggah," he warned, angry. "Don't ever use that term with me!"

I rolled my eyes as I imagined kicking him to a faraway place where he might never come back.

"Okay, you wanted to meet me, and now we've met. If I didn't know any better, I'd say you set this all thing up!"

"Seriously?" he laughed. "You think I would go to all this trouble to meet a woman? Please! You're not all that!" he said, dismissing me with a wave of his hand.

"Guess we aren't going to meet," I said, standing to leave, but then he extended his hand to me.

"Hi, I'm Marlon," he smiled. "My people call me Shoty."

I glanced at his hand and rolled my eyes as he waited for me to shake it, then I walked away.

"Yo! Beautiful—you are going to be that rude and not shake my hand?"

 I turned and looked into his eyes.

"I'm not all that!? So, you go find you're 'all-that' girl! Let *her* shake your hand." I said as I turned to walk away.

"I don't *like* this dude!" I said, talking to myself. "He's arrogant and full of himself. I hate the way he keeps looking at me! 'Looking at his wife?' Man, please! That damn line can work on other females, but not me. I want nothing to do with him!" I was head for the bedroom I was using. "Why am I letting this guy get to me? He's not that cute—with his big head, and his nose isn't small either. He wants to call me rude? He don't even know the meaning of the word!"

Headed back inside, I ran smack into Fabiola.

"Faby—that asshole who you call your friend is really an ass! He just said, I 'wasn't all that!' Bitch-ass—he really pissed me off!" I didn't give her a chance to respond. "What kind of man would tell a woman she 'isn't all that' and then try to shake her hand!" *I wanted to punch that cocky smirk off his face.*

"Joanne, take it easy," Faby said. "I'm sure you said something that he thought wasn't very nice. Just give him a chance. He might surprise you. He's very nice man, you know."

I looked up, spotting him as he made his way to the kitchen. He was confused as he seemed to be searching for Faby.

"Well," I said, "your 'Mr.-Nice-Guy' is trying to get your attention!"

She tried to convince me to talk to him, but I walked away, headed to the stove for some more *hors d'oeuvres*. As I occupied myself with getting the rest of the food out of the oven, I sensed his presence at the doorway. He stood there quietly, watching me work, while I pretended he wasn't there.

I couldn't tell if it was the lighting or the change in his demeanor, but suddenly he didn't seem so bad. If I hadn't been annoyed with him, I might have said he was the sexiest man at this party.

"Can I help you with that?" he said in a low voice, behind my neck. I felt his breath and inhaled his cologne, while my body responded to his nearness. No guy ever had that effect on me before. I had goosebumps all over my arms and butterflies in my stomach. My pussy jumped for joy. I couldn't explain the feeling that came over me for this man who had worked my last nerves. I turned to face him.

It was as if time came to a standstill and I was seeing him for the first time. He looked more sincere and caring—not at all like the cocky son-of-a-bitch from moments earlier. But then I remembered his true nature and realized I had to stay away from men like him.

"No, thank you. I don't need any help."

"Just trying to be helpful," he said, throwing his hands in the air.

"You can go sit with the rest of the guests," I suggested.

"Did I do something to offend you?" he asked, looking into my eyes.

"Well, what do you think? When you tell someone they're 'not all that...'"

"Oh, that! You are upset about that? Let me ask you this," he said, nearing, our noses inches apart. My body was betraying me, wanting him to touch me.

"Were you as offended when I called you beautiful?" he whispered in a low hoarse voice that sent chills through every fiber in my body. His breath smelled of the minty gum he was chewing. As he came closer, our lips were just a brush away.

"Cuz I've been calling you beautiful since I first saw you," he said, staring deeply into my eyes.

I couldn't look away. My limbs were numb as his gravity pulled me toward him, overwhelming my impulse to take a step backward. The closer he got, the harder it was for me to move away. I forced myself to close my eyes, remembering all the boys who taunted me as well as the ones who wanted to force themselves on me. I took a step backward.

"Faby said you were a nice guy, but not for me, so let me save you your time and energy. You're not my type, okay?"

I tried to move past him, but he blocked me with his body. It seemed as if this man had never been rejected before because he seemed confused. Taking a deep breath, I wanted to make sure he understood that I was not interested.

"If you want more explanation, I would be more than happy to break it down for you."

As he motioned for me to continue, I noticed how his personality had changed from our earlier conversation. He took a few steps back and leaned against the wall, crossing his arms over his chest, attempting to intimidate me with an intense stare, waiting for my explanation. I cleared my throat and counted to three.

"You—you're a man of money. You think everything is like the money you possess. You take control of a person, and they can't breathe. That person becomes your domain, your possession. You seize and won't let go. I'm an independent woman. I make my own decisions. So, Mr. Marlon, I'm not your type. Excuse me!"

Before I could walk away, he grabbed my arm and pulled me toward him, holding though not restraining. I could have escaped his grasp if I wanted, but his strength and restraint impressed me.

"First, you need to know me before making that assumption," he said. "Second, I love an independent woman who does for herself—someone who isn't trying to get with me for my money. Third, if I have an attraction for a female, I do what it takes to get to know her. So, I'm sorry if my money and my persona offend you."

After he released my arm and left the kitchen to join his friends, I stood there, staring at his back. He seemed angry as he interacted with the people around him, and I was turned on by his aggressiveness.

After all the food was out, I returned to the garden and sat opposite him, finishing my drink and glancing out to the street. I heard one of his friends making jokes about "psycho bitches." That was really getting on my last nerve! Mr. Marlon said nothing.

"Yo, Shoty—I'm telling you, your new chick is psycho," one of his friends said. "Just look at the way she's focused on the street. I swear—

you always find the crazy ones! She looks like she can chop you up, man, and feed the remains to your family."

I studied the man's face as he came closer to me, mocking me.

"Excuse me, Miss," he said. "Can I ask you a question? Are you always so cold and distant to human beings?" I could smell the alcohol on his breath. "Do you even like men?" he continued, "because I tried telling my friend Shoty over there that you might be into women, and that's why you don't like him. Am I right uh… huh… huh? Men don't do it for you?" he taunted.

I don't know what came over me. I just felt like choking that asshole, so I did! I put my hands around his neck and brought him down to my level.

"Don't you ever in your miserable life fuck with me!" As my hands squeezed his neck harder, he just laughed at me.

"Yo Shoty—get your girl. She's bugging," he strained out to his friend.

As I looked around the balcony, everyone had grown quiet. They were waiting to see what would happen next. I noticed the red dots that began appearing all over my body, glowing amber red, though I couldn't quite determine what they were… not until my choking victim and Mr. Marlon simultaneously waved their hands and the spots disappeared.

Frozen in position, all Shoty's friends stared as Fabiola frantically apologized to them. Yet all eyes were on me.

"I am so sorry. Please excuse her," she kept repeating.

"Shoty! Shoty, get your psycho girl off me!" his friend called out between breaths.

"Fabiola!" Shoty shouted. "Is your cousin clinically insane? Or is she on medication, and forgot to take it today?" he asked, never losing sight of me.

"No, no, no! She's not on medication or clinically insane, but, but she might be a little crazy— which I already told you!" Fabiola explained.

"Look! Take your hands off my friend!" he shouted, sending most of the guests to take cover. "…before I take it personal! I get it! I'm not your type."

We gazed at each other for a long moment.

"Joanne, take your hands of him now!" he roared.

At that instant, I could tell he wasn't a man to fuck with. My whole body trembled at the force of his command. My nipples tightened, and an electrical charge surged to the core of my body. As I stared at his angry face, all I want to do is kiss it. Never would I have believed I would find a man who could excite me sexually. I released his friend. He stood and fixed his clothes.

"Damn, girl, you have super strength for a girl!" Shoty's friend joked. "You really was choking me, like a dude!"

"Let's go!" Shoty barked out, and the whole crew got ready to leave.

Fabiola tried to reason with him as they made their exit. She approached me with a frantic look.

"Joanne, what have you done? I told you these people are dangerous! You attacked Rocket of all people," she screamed at me.

"Then why'd you bring them here?" I screamed back. "You wanted me to know this motherfucker, even after I told you I didn't want to see him. Why is that? Did he pay for this party?"

Instead of replying, she walked over to her husband. "I have to talk to Shoty! This thing isn't over." She buried her head into his chest. I watched her horror-stricken face as her husband tried to console her.

"Don't worry about it! It's my problem, I'll deal with it!" I offered and went into the house.

I grabbed my belongings and started to walk home. As the events in the kitchen replayed in my mind, my body still craved to be near him. I savored his smells, the sound of his voice, the way he controlled his anger, and the respect others had for him.

Every time I replayed our encounter in my mind—him leaning on the wall with that stern expression on his face—I envisioned being in his arms, kissing him, making love to him. He stole my heart in that kitchen. I couldn't breathe, couldn't think without him on my mind. *He is all I want, and I must have him. I'm going to get him*, I vowed!

As the days passed, and Fabiola was frantic with worry, not knowing what to expect. She refused to call her friends, for fear that they might turn that incident on her. She worried that she would pay the price for Joanne's attempt on Rocket's life.

The cousins hadn't spoken since then. Joanne mainly stayed to herself and in the lab. Fabiola only came over to see her dad when Joanne was at work. She felt Joanne could have handled the situation better, because she had been warned her about the crew. The residents of the block were on the lookout for any type of retaliation from Shoty's crew.

Meanwhile in the kitchen at Blanc Villa, Rock explained the choking incident to his friend, Madeline.

"I tell you, Maddy, this girl is insane. She has super-human powers. If she had held a little longer, I would have been in trouble."

"Wow! All this happened while I was gone." Amazed that someone besides her had gotten the best of Rocket, she held her side and giggled.

"I would *love* to see you being choked, Rock," she said, laughing, with tears coming out of her eyes.

"You got choked by a girl? I thought I was the only one who could best you. I have to meet this 'psycho chick' you keep talking about!"

"No, you won't meet her," Rocket replied, his face grim, "cuz Shoty say he's through with the crazy. I've only been seeing him with nice, stable girls this week." Madeline just laughed harder as he complained. "You know one look at me makes grown men run for their lives, but you just laugh at it." Looking at her face, he started laughing too.

"That's because I have a devil on speed dial," she reminded him.

"Yes, you do, and on that note, I'll let you go to bed before he gets after me for keeping you up." Just then, Cage walked in through the door.

"I should have known you were keeping her from me. I swear, if it's not you, it's Shoty," he said in his low-key voice.

"Why? Afraid of a little competition? Worried you might lose your Maddy?" Rocket joked, smiling.

"Never," Madeline objected as she hugged and kissed Cage. "There's only one devil I want. No one else compares."

Many called Cage by the title of "The Devil's Son," and he was feared by everyone but Madeline. They met at the villa two years and half earlier, the result a prank gone wrong. The crew thought Shoty, who had been the first to chase her, was in the shower, and they sent in Madeline with towels, but Cage emerged naked from the shower and instantly fell in love with her. Shoty noticed the effect Madeline had on Cage and stepped aside for his friend's happiness. They had been together for two years, during which Cage had been to hell and back with her, but he loved it.

CHAPTER 5
JOANNE

Four o'clock in the morning, and I couldn't sleep again. I saw him every time I closed my eyes. I remembered his cologne and how my body reacted to his nearness. I tried to use my vibrator, but it didn't relieve the emptiness I felt. My body screamed for his touch.

It had been two weeks since the incident, and I hadn't seen or heard anything from them. I didn't know how to get those urges out of my system. I had to do something.

"This dude is driving me insane!"

SHOTY

Saturday night at the club, I waited for Riffle and Roc to show up. Kadanse was playing, so the line extended around the corner. It was only 10:30.

Rocket walked in with two beautiful girls on each arm.

"Yo, you want one? They're cleared, no crazies," he joked, referencing Joanne and the way she manhandled him.

For a whole week, it was all he talked about. The girl was really a nut-case. She had attacked Roc in the presence of Simi, Tech and Cage—even with lunatics Riffle and Cage there, not to mention the rest of the Crew.

A15 had never walked away from a situation like that before, and she didn't even want me. That was a new experience to deal with. Guess you can't win them all. The club opened at nine to the club-goers who were getting ready to party. At 11:15, Roc came running to me.

"Shoty, the crazies are out tonight!" he said, pointing at the entrance.

There she was—a vision in blue. I was dumbstruck, glued to the entranceway. "Damn, she's beautiful!" I whispered.

"She's looking for something… or someone," Roc observed. "Does she know that this club is part of us?"

"I'm sure she does!" I replied. "Her cousin's been here."

"Is she meeting a guy here?" Rocket asked while trying to turn me away and divert my attention. I gave him my hard look.

"Don't look at me like that!" he objected. "That is not exactly a clubbing outfit. That dress is for a special someone…" he said, still following her every move. "Oh, I think she spotted you, man! She spotted you man," he whispered without looking from his cup. I didn't look up either. I just focused on the crowd in front of me.

"She's walking to you my friend," he warned.

I turned, and yes—she was coming my way. Every fiber in my body tensed with the anticipation of just being near her.

"Guess you're right," I whispered.

I put on my mean face, but that didn't stop her. She walked right up to me, threw an arm around my neck and gazed into my eyes. Soon, her lips were on mine, kissing me—those kissable lips I'd been dreaming about were on me, kissing me, and the soft sound of her honeyed voice vibrated deep in my soul.

"I'm sorry! I'm so, so sorry," she repeated between kisses. She held onto me tight and pressed her body close to mine. I maintained my mean face, willing myself strength as she continued to apologize.

"If you still want me, I'm yours," she whispered in my ear. Her nearness was affecting me in a major way, as my fingers itched to hug her big, bouncy derriere.

"I can't stop thinking about you. I couldn't sleep or eat for the last two weeks. You did something to me the night in the kitchen!" she complained. "My vibrator doesn't do anything for me anymore. My body is screaming for your touch. I need you!"

I looked at her, baffled by what she had said, and watched her turned to Roc, who too was in shock. She leaned toward him and kissed his cheek.

"Sorry for choking you." she whispered.

I closed my eyes as she returned to me with her apologetic affection. "I was so mad at you for saying all those things. Please accept my apology," she said, batting her eyes, looking like the most innocent creature on Earth.

At a loss for words, Roc glanced over at me confused, while I was trying to keep my dick in check. Her touch was affecting me in a big way! She smelled so damn good as she continued her caresses, kissing my neck before moving back to my lips again. I noticed that the crew, too, was paying close attention to what was going on.

She gazed into my eyes, disappointed that I wasn't responding to her.

"Do you want me to leave?" she whispered between kisses.

It took everything for me not to crush her to me and enjoy heaven. Instead, I pried her body away from mine, reflecting on the two months of chasing her and her refusing all my attempts.

"How do you know I'm not here with someone? Maybe I picked up a wife?" I said coldly. I watched her imaginings play on her face. Embarrassed, she pulled away from me.

"Oh... no! I'm an idiot! I'm sorry again. Forget you ever saw me!" she blurted out and hurried out the club.

"Damn! Between you and Simi, I don't know who gets more pussy," Roc grumbled.

"Shut up, Roc! You're the one fucking two women a night," I reminded him.

"I know! That's why I said, you and Simi..."

CHAPTER 6
JOANNE

I ran out from the club. I couldn't believe I just did all that! I had never throw myself at a man before, or had strong feelings for one. I cried all the way home.

This guy was cold, but he turned me on. Damn! What was I going to do? I still wanted him. I cried, feeling empty, those few minutes in his arms felt wonderful. "Look Joanne you're a strong woman, you can do this, you can forget him. He is just a man, like all the men around the neighborhood." I tried to come to terms with the situation. I arrived at home about 11:55. I undressed and went to bed, with Marlon on my mind.

There was a bang at the door that woke me up from my sleep. I looked at the clock; it read 4:00 a.m.

"Who is knocking at my door so late?"

"Faby is that you?"

No answer. The sound continued

Knock! Knock! Knock!

"Faby?" I repeated, rolled out of the bed. Still no answer. The knocking got louder

"Look. You have to say who you are, I can't open this door," I yelled through the doorway.

"Open the door!" Came this deep masculine voice, and my heart stopped. That was *him* at my door, at 4:00 in the morning. It took me a minute to find my voice, as I panicked not know what to do as the knocks continued.

"Ooh… I'm sorry about earlier, but Faby didn't tell me, I didn't know you were married. Now I'm upset for not being told he was married and wondered why was he chasing me? I paced the room, my mind running a mile a minute and I needed to put an end to this. "I'm not trying to create a problem for you, Sir. I wasn't told of your status! A thousand sorry, for throwing myself at you. It won't happen again!" I stuttered on the other side of the door.

"Open the door!" His hoarse voice echoed again.

"Sir please go home to your wife, I'm sure she's waiting for you to come home." I tried reminding him of the wife he claimed to have.

"I'm with my wife, if she opens the door so I can go to sleep, then I will stop banging on it!" he roared. "Jo, I'm tired. Open up," he demanded

"No Sir, you have to go home to your wife. Standing at my door at four in the morning is not good, what will the neighbors think, and won't that go back to your wife?" I tried to reason with him.

"Jo! I'm giving you to the count of three, to open this door, so I can make love to you, declare you as my woman, and go to sleep. Or if you want I can also break the door down and do all that anyway," he threatened.

I never had anyone dared to talk to me in that tone before, like I'm supposed to jump because he said so! Yea Right!

"Good night, Mr. Marlon, have a nice life. Maybe I'll bump into you in the street or even meet your wife in the near future," I said and moved away from the doorway, when I heard his low-key voice while he began to count.

"One, two, three!"

He took in a deep breath, and the whole door came apart. I stood there with my mouth wide opened. Looked at the frame in his hand as he filled in the doorway.

"What did you do?" I screamed as he walked in.

"I said open the door, you refused, so I broke the door." He explained his arms reached out to me grabbed my waist, pulled me to him. I felt his hand palming my booty and I stared at him.

"Now where did you leave off earlier?" He raised his head up trying to recall our earlier conversation. "Oh yeah! you were saying something about being my…" he paused for a moment to collect his thoughts, and looked deep into my eyes.

"That's if I still wanted you." He cracked a smile. "Well! I still want you, and your mine," He declared, kissing me on my neck. His body was affecting me and clouding my mind. I closed my eyes, taking on his scent the whiffs of liquor. Remembering his statement from earlier.

"No! No, I can't be with you, you said you had a wife, at the club," I tried to get away from him by pushing on his chest that was hard as a rock!

"What I said was. how do you know I didn't have a wife? He used his low bass voice that's creating sensations that are alien to me. He continued to worship my neck as his lips tickled every fiber of my being. "you're the one who came in on a mission. Did you think I was going to sit by and wait until you made up your mind, on whether or not you want to get involved with me? Uh, uh… speak!" he said, looking deep into my eyes. Then he kissed my nose and bit my bottom lip. Adding more to his explanation.

"I don't chase pussy, never have and never will" I had already forgotten you," he whispered in my ear.

"You brought all that desire back, when you were kissing me at the club, I mean you came up, and just started to kiss me like that." He tried to pull me closer to him. His cologne was intoxicating. I closed my eyes and gave in to the effect of both the cologne and kisses on my neck. The sensations grew more intense and I didn't want it to stop.

"No, you are married, and I can't get involved with you, and you're also too demanding. It's not going to work, even though you are so sexy, but no. I don't want to be with you. You're married!"

"What is it going to take to convince you that I'm not married?" he said.

I don't know, but you said it yourself, and I believe it."

"Okay, okay here," he took his phone out of his pocket, and handed to me.

"Call anyone on this phone and ask them, or better yet, hit conference call, and everyone that matters to me will be on the line with you. Go head I'm getting ready for bed," he stated in a sensual tone and kissed the tip of my nose. "And for you!!!"

He continued to rub my derriere and hips, pulling me closer to his engorged erection that was hard and ready, making my body and mind weak.

God! Is it possible, to fall in love so quickly? I don't even know him! He feels so right, like we are part of the same coin that became whole.

I hit the conference key.

"Yo, I thought you would be deep in making love to that psycho chick in blue tonight. What's up?" a voice asked through the speaker.

"Maybe the psycho chick kicked his ass, yo we might have to move, he could be bleeding somewhere. Are you okay man? I'm on my way, and where the hell is security?" Another voice shouted.

"Sic, calm down. Joanne just wants to ask you a question. And Riffle, stop calling my girl a psycho," Shoty said, interrupting their outbursts. He stared at me.

"Go ahead, ask them," he encouraged.

"Uh, um I just wanted to know if your friend here, Marlon—"

"Shoty!" fifteen voices repeated.

"Shoty, right... so is he married?"

"Yeah! To you," one of the voices said.

"Sic, come on man this is serious, she's not playing around. I can't even take my shoe off," he complained.

"Why are you hanging on to this psycho chick. I thought you would have moved on by now, man? Remember our motto—we don't chase pussy. The hell with her!"

"Rocket, chill. I don't think calling them was a good idea."

He tried to take the phone from me, which I hid behind my back.

"No, this is interesting. I want to hear more about this motto of yours. But Rocket, you seem to be a very forward person. So just tell me, yes or no, is he married?" I asked again.

"No, he's not married, and he won't be any time soon!"

"Why do you say that?"

"Are you a virgin?" he asked.

"What's that have to do with him being married?"

"His wife needs to be a virgin! And not of a psychotic nature. I don't understand why he's putting so much effort in trying to fuck you."

"Which one are you, asshole!!"

"The one you choked, and kissed, trying to apologize to earlier."

"Okay, no more talking to Rocket, guys. I'll check in the morning." He came to me and wrapped his arm around me.

"Sorry, Rocket is Rocket, but he's my right hand. Enough of this, I want you, and I know you want me too, so I'm going to say this for the last time: I'm not married! I'm not involved with anyone. I mean, I do have friends and women I sex, but no committed relationship with anyone. Okay, it's done! I want to finish what I came here for."

I closed my eyes and prayed for guidance, and embraced that magnificent man embodying my existence.

CHAPTER 7
SHOTY

I was standing in the middle of the room, watching Joanne collect her thoughts, loving the way she downcast her eyes and bit her lower lip in deep concentration. I scanned her body from head to toe. With her low-cut booty shorts, and a matching white beater, a deep cleavage line making her triple D's spill over. My mouth watered at her erected gumball nipples, poking out of the pink shirt. She was thick in all the right places.

Her stomach was flat, with her voluptuous hips and ass I couldn't get my hands on. I kept rubbing her—god's gift to me. My hands traveled all over. I ran my finger down her exposed cleavage and teased a nipple with my four fingers. She smiled and looked away, like she was fighting to give in'

"Do you want me, Joanne?" I whispered in her ear. "Do you want me to stop, cuz if you say no, I'll leave," I offered, before things went too far and I couldn't hold back.

I noticed the effect my words had on her. She made eye contact with me. I stopped cold turkey, waiting for her to make a choice.

"You would do that for me? You would wait and not have sex?" she asked in a small voice.

I took that moment to really look at her as a woman, a very beautiful sexy light-brown Haitian woman with a face of an angel, soft honey golden skin, kissable pink lips and long black hair that she put high in a pony tail. I saw myself growing old with this woman. Looking deep into her eyes, I liked the life I saw with her.

"Yes, I would wait for when you're ready for that! But remember, you came to the club looking for me. I thought you wanted to be mine, which I'm willing to consummate our life together," I said, running my finger to the side of her face. She lifted her head, resting on her chin, to look me in the eye.

"I will do only things you want me to," I kissed her lips, worked my way down her lower jaw line and nibbled on the apex of her neck.

"Ooooh... Shoty, I do want you," she whispered in a sensual manner.

"Just know this: if I have you tonight, it's not for a few months or a few years! You will be mine until the day I depart from this earth," I said seriously.

"All I want is sex! Remember, I have a vibrator.

"You have to crush the mood, uh! No more vibrator, I'll be your vibrator," I said in a sexual tone, kissing her neck.

"We'll see about that. I have to see the energizer bunny at work first, then I'll consider it!" she replied with a smirk on her face. She better not let me see it or I'll break that shit in half.

"No more!" I roared. "Now! Back to what we were discussing, I'm very demanding and challenging! I always get what I want, no questions asked. That's me. There is no median. I'm Haitian—it's in my nature, can't change it."

"What are you getting at?" she said with her hand on her hips, ready for war.

"I'm just saying that I'm the man and I alone wear the pants. I'm just letting you know from jump what kind of man you're getting."

I don't want a man, just sex!" she repeated. I chose to ignore her statements, continue on with my declaration.

I'm very demanding," I mumbled, kissing her lower lip.

"Arrogant," I said continuing to kiss her chin. "Probably a lot of other things you don't like in a man," I finished, holding her close to me.

Joanne eyed me for a long moment, considering getting involved with a man like that but I could see my kisses were distracting her thoughts and she wanted more.

"Well you're a stubborn Haitian man, and I'm a stubborn Haitian woman—a match made in heaven! Now shut up and kiss me."

She pulled me by the collar and kissed me with all the passion she possessed, I couldn't help but draw her closer to me and give her what she wanted.

CHAPTER 8

All was quiet as the two lovebirds stood in the middle of the room. Shoty embraced the woman he wanted to claim as his, but he was having a difficult time defining the appropriate role for her. In his mind, knowing Joanne was not a virgin; he wondered if she would be content with just being his woman.

"God baby, if you were a virgin, I'll marry you tonight," his thoughts ran through his head. He kissed her long and hard. His hand traveling down her body, cupped her one breast, slid between her cleavages, gave it a firm squeeze then bent down and kissed a nipple.

Shoty, being the conqueror, placed his other hand between her legs, feeling the warmth of her sex. Joanne, not expecting him to be so bold, gasped and took two steps back, eyed him warily and held her breath. She tried hard not to compare him with the low lives in her past. She grabbed his hand in an attempt to stop him, which he ignored. Using his fingers lightly, he started a rhythmical dance on her bud.

"Sssssssss, ahhhh… Umm!!" Joanne hissed at the sudden contact. He nipped and nibbled on her lower lip, backed her against the wall. His other hand played with a nipple through her tight shirt.

"Ohhh, you feel better than the vibrator," she moaned, closing her eyes, enjoying the feel of a real man, for the first time in her life. Shoty smiled and slid down the length of her body, knelt on the floor and pulled her shorts down, exposing her pussy, and took his time to admire her thick meaty sex.

"Pretty, he looked up at her I like it!" he whispered.

Parting her legs wider, he used two fingers inside her, concentrating on her bud, and continued his dance. Shoty stood back up and pinned her to the wall, let his fingers do their magic.

Joanne rested her head back felt the solid frame behind her, wrapped her arm around his neck for support. A wave of sensation took over her body. With anticipation of something wonderful to come, loving the fiction of his fingers

Shoty enjoyed making her weak, and wanting. He noticed the change in her breathing. She clutched on to him tighter, her body jerked and shuddered in his arms.

"Shotttttttty;" Joanne's scream formed a powerful release.

"Mmmmmmm… Ohhh, my," she continued to moan, holds on to him, stares in his eye. He kissed her then removed his hand to rub her voluptuous booty, bringing her closer to his hard rock member, pressing her against the wall.

"Can your vibrator do that?" He asked and watched her taking deep breaths to control her racing heart.

"No! Not like that!" she said between breaths. "Never like that!" she confessed, kissing him back.

"No more talk about that again, understand," he insisted.

She shook her head yes. Shoty still held her against the wall, moving his hands to cup her breast and nibbling on her neck, then bent his head and put a giant nipple into his mouth, while palming the other.

His tongue flicking on one nipple brought it hard and aching. He lifted the other breast until they were pressed together, going back and forth wetting each one at a time, making slurping sounds, over and over again!

His mouth created such a magical wave that Joanne couldn't help but convulse in his arms again.

He smirked in a cocky and arrogant manner, watching her try to regain control again.

"That's two in less than ten minutes, and I didn't even take my pants off yet! How's your battery now?" he teased, laughing, walking away to leave her on the wall.

Shoty took off his shoe and pants, sat on the bed unbuttoning his shirt.

"Come here, beautiful," he signaled for Joanne to join him. She took a moment and admired his five-foot-nine muscular frame, bulging biceps, and flat six-pack abs. On his upper right chest. there was a tattoo of a shotgun, with a smoking barrel that had the letters M.I.C.H. coming out of it.

Joanne gasped at the sexiest man she'd ever seen, sitting on her bed. She made her way to him, stood right in front of him, straddled his body, wrapped herself around him and kissed his lips.

"I have to tell you something," she said. Summing up the courage to talk about her personal life, she wanted to explain why some people thought she didn't like men, or why she always wound up beating them up. Andre wasn't the first man she hurt.

Joanne never discussed those feelings with her parents or doctor. She never liked boys before Shoty. Not that she liked girls, but she had a natural hatred for men, could not stand to be around them! She took a deep breath.

"I never been with a man before, you're my first!" she blurted out.

CHAPTER 9

His heart stopped from hearing her breathe those words. Uncertain if he had heard her right, he tightened his hold while she sat on him.

"What do you mean?" he asked, searching her eyes, seeing the truth. But he needed to hear it from her lips again.

"It means, you're my first," she said, taking a deep breath, nervous about the whole ordeal.

"I haven't been with any men before you. Many have tried, but they just end up in the hospital," she shyly explained.

Joanne wrapped her arms tighter around his neck, studied his expression from the news

"You're not happy that I haven't been with anyone? "She asked as he stared at her in disbelief and drifted in his own world.

Shoty took a deep breath as he realized he found his virgin, his wife and best friend. He looked deep into her eyes and saw the innocence of being sheltered, but confused on somethings

"Why! Why are you using a vibrator?"

"Hmm?"

"Don't *hmm* me! You started to explain, so finished."

"Um, my doctor suggested that I needed some kind of release, for my pent-up anger toward men. A friend of my mother brought me my first vibrator, and I've been using them ever since. But I was warned to never penetrated it inside of me. Apparently, it's a gift for my husband to enjoy. I'm not getting married!" She stated firmly, looking deeply into his eyes. Shoty chose to ignore her and pressed for more important matters.

"What's up with the anger with men?"

"Well, that's a long story," she replied.

"Does it look like we're going anywhere?" he asked, holding her tighter on his lap.

"It's the middle of night! Can we do this another time?" She begged, not willing to go down memory lane, with those taunts she had to endure.

"Nan, I want to know why!" he persisted.

She closed her eyes, took two deep breaths and continued with her story.

"It started when I was in middle school. A group of boys used to tease me because I was taller and stronger than them. They called me a lot of names." She raised her head and looked into his eyes.

"That's why I choked your friends," she said, confirming her earlier actions.

"Okay, continue!"

"When they saw I was able to block them out, they got physical, pushing me around, knocking my books on the floor, a lot of little things like that. That lasted until I reached high school." She looked up at him again and downcast her eyes.

"In my freshman year, I joined the wrestling team, so all of that stopped. Then they tried being my friend because they were tired of going to the hospital. They couldn't tell their parents that they were beaten by a girl," she said, watching his reaction to her story.

"You know, if I ever see any of these men today, I'll kill them!" he stated with vengeance.

"I beat them enough in school, even gave them a couple of broken arms, and some head injuries. Where they would never forget me." She smiled as she saw the effect that had on him, changing his hustle demeanor.

"Okay, later for body injuries, now I want to make love to my wife." He sings putting soft drops of kisses on her lips.

"I'm not getting married," she reported, returning his kisses. He just smiled at her while his hands traveled around her body, took hold of her hands then stated. "We can go down memory lane tomorrow. Put your hands around this!" he whispered in her ears guided her hands to his dick, which was hard and ready.

"He's wanted to come out and play since he saw you at the club."

Joanne used her hand slide it up and down the length, admiring it, loving the feel of it in her hands, amazed by how hard and soft it was.

"I love that dress you had on. It took everything in me to hold back, and not ravish you on the spot," he said, having a hard time concentrating from doing just that.

"You have a condom?" she whispered in his ear, kissed his neck.

"Look in my pant pocket," he breathed, rubbing her butt cheeks while she bent over, reaching for it in his pants. She gasped at the sight of the gun that was hiding under the pants.

"Why do you have a gun?" she hollered, shocked over the sight of his weapon. "Are you gangster?"

"Yeah, but not the ones you are used to. You will only know the love and gentle side of me. As a matter of fact, I want you to call me *Pashou*. That's what my mother calls me," he told her. Shoty held on to her for a while, assuring her that she was safe in his care.

Joanne had a hard time opening the condom wrapper. He took it from her and ripped it with his teeth.

"Put it on," he said. She looked at him, nervous because she never held one before. He recongnized her dilemma. "Start at the head and slide it down."

She followed the instruction. He flipped her under him and took position between her legs.

SHOTY

"Open up for me, Jo. I need to be inside of you now, baby." My voice was shaky from the emotions I' was feeling. As she spread her legs wider, I guided the head of my rock-hard penis to her dripping wet pussy and rested at the opening.

"Look at me." I pushed the head in and felt her barrier. "This is going to hurt a little. I'll try not to go too fast. You ready?"

She nodded yes. I moved my hand and traced her nether lips, playing with her bud, getting her more aroused, the urge to bury myself to her unclaimed cave with the suspense of me claiming her is killing me. She rotated her hips while passion built inside of her. She moaned, I leaned into her and penetrated in slow motion, giving her a little at a time, breaking her hymen.

"Ahhhhhhh, Shoty it hurts," she cried, pushing on my chest.

"Shhhhhh, it will pass." I continued to work my pelvis into her slow and steady until she relaxed under me, and I want to feel more of her and have a deeper connection on loving her. I bent down and whispered in her ears. "Joanne, I need to feel you, baby." My voice was shaky from her response, as she caressed my buttocks. I pulled out of her, took the condom off, entered her, little by little, until I was buried deep inside her tight, juicy pussy. I was overwhelmed with pleasure.

"Damn, you feel so fucking good. Your pussy is delicious!" Holding onto her hips, I started to move a little faster in and out of her, over and over again. She whimpered under me and held tight. And I was holding back the desire to plunge deeper.

"Open wider. I need you to take all of me," I cried. The sounds she was making did a number on me.

"Shot! Ummm! Ooooh…" she moaned, reaching up and kissing the side of my face and neck. I continued to pump inside of her.

"Call me *Pashou*. Fuck, you sweet!" I hollered, enjoying the ride. "Wrap your legs around my waist." She followed the instructions. "Yes, baby!" I looked down at her The sensation was unreal. I've never been with a woman that felt so fucking good, she was incredible. She arched her back gave more access.

"Just like that," I plunged farther into her core.

"Pashou, I coming!" she screamed, digging her nails into the bed sheet as intense sensation overtook her.

"Wait for me! I'm not there yet!" I sighed, moving my hips faster, holding the small of back. Bringing her closer, I plunged back inside her over and over. Her body started to tremble and shake. I watched her eyes roll to the back of her head. I arched my back and roared with pure pleasure and drained all my passion inside her. I bent down kissed her, hard and rough. I still pumped her juicy pussy, which felt like a heartbeat around my dick.

CHAPTER 10

Shoty was enthralled with making love to Joanne, but the added bonus of her being his virgin made him the happiest man alive.

The sensation he felt being inside her was indescribable. The way she moaned and fixed her face as pleasure coursed through her body made him want to hold her like that forever.

Joanne finally understood why her therapist wanted her to have a relationship with a real man, to feel and be embraced by one. She wrapped her arms around him, and became lost in his eyes, returning his kisses. Joanne realized that she was in love.

"Oh, my!" she sighed, running her hand up and down his back.

"What?"

"Nothing. I just thought of something," she said, smiling at him. She loved this part of being with a man and couldn't wait to do it again.

He raised his right eyebrow and stared at her, waiting for her to elaborate. She reached up and kissed his lips, ignoring his questioning look. Feeling him so deep and hard made Joanne feel hot and ready for seconds. Even though her muscles were sore, loving him was worth it.

JOANNE

The sounds of bells ringing in the distant woke me form slumber. I looked at the clock, which read 8:30. I missed the 7 a.m. mass at Saint Gerard. I tried to get out of bed, only to be held back by Shoty, with his arms around me. I felt like every muscle in my body hurt from my late-night activities. I lay back down and willed my body to cooperate. Then, taking his arm off me, I sat up and dragged myself off the bed.

I noticed the condom on the night stand and threw it in the trash can, making my way to the bathroom to get ready for the ten o'clock mass.

Water fell on my body from the showerhead, the warm waters massaging my skin. I lathered my arms and chest with scented soap, washed my body, and thought of Shoty making love to me all over again. I rested the shower hose between my legs, letting it relax and sooth me. After I finished I walk back in the room, Shoty was still asleep on his stomach with the sheet covering only his buttocks, his upper shoulders tight with muscles, which traveled all over his perfect frame.

I sat on the bed, shaking the thought of seducing him to make love again. I start to lotion my body when his arms snaked around and pulled me back into his embrace.

"What are you up to? Smelling so good! I thought I would have carried you in the shower, and loved you there too this morning," he exclaimed, kissing the back of my neck.

"You should be sore! I wasn't very gentle, and I took you like three times this morning. Why are you not exhausted?" He traced my back with his finger, kissing and nibbling his path.

"I have to go to church. I have sinned, after all." I reached for the bottle of lotion and applied it to my body, and then I put on my clothes.

"Honey! Are you serious? Church! But baby, I'm tired. I want to sleep."

"So go to sleep. I'll see you later! I never miss church."

I continued to get dressed, putting on a simple, one-piece, short-sleeve little black dress that reached above my knee. I finished it off with a red belt, high heels and matching hand-purse.

I was sitting at the vanity, doing my hair and make-up, when Shoty rolled out of the bed, not looking happy.

"Church," he mumbled, making his way to the bathroom to take a shower. I grabbed my purse, ready to go out the door. "Joanne, I need a towel," he yelled in a grouchy voice.

"Look in the cabinet by the mirror," I yelled back. "I'll see you later, I'm leaving."

I'm coming with you." he said while walking into the room, drying off.

"Oh, you don't have to! I can meet with you later if you like. Maybe we can go see a movie or have dinner if you don't have plans."

"I said I was coming!" he said as he got ready. I could tell by the way he was putting on his clothes that he wasn't in the mood to go. I saw him strap his gun on the back of his pants then pick up his keys and sunglasses.

"You really going to church with that on you?"

He ignored me and continued to get ready. "Let's go!" he said, going out the front door.

"*Pashou!* You are not going into church with me wearing that thing under your clothes." I stood in front of him, waiting for him to leave his gun in the room.

"I don't go anywhere without it. You want to go church, let's get going so I can go back to sleep." He walked past me to the stairs.

"You don't care for church," I said, following him.

"No, I don't care for church, but you do, so I guess I'll be going from now on."

When we reached the corridor, he stopped to talk to a group of guys in a SUV. I started to walk in the opposite direction.

"Joanne! What are you doing? Let's go!" he called out to me, but I continued to walk.

"Joanne!" he roared and ran to catch up with me.

"Fuck are you doing! You didn't hear me calling your name?"

"I'm walking to church, and I don't want to be late."

"Baby, I have a car. We can drive there."

"Yeah! I saw you with your gangster friends, but I'll walk. I do this every Sunday, around 3:30 in the morning."

"Jo, I can't walk these streets. Driving around is a risk as it is."

Oh! I thought you were a gangster, that walked around with a gun? Besides, I told you to stay in bed. It will only take an hour, so I'll see you later." I finished making my way to rue Bernard en route to Saint Gerard.

SHOTY

I watched her big booty bounce as she walked away from me in that tight dress that hugged her frame like a second skin. I looked at my security team who had camped out all night in front of her house. I signaled them to circle the block and follow my "pain-in-the-ass."

I caught up to her as she turned onto Michelle-au-rest.

"In the future, if I say I'm taking you to church, believe that I'm taking you. Since this is our first time together, I'm going to let all that shit you just pulled slide."

As I reached out my hand to her, she fastened her hand on top of mine, I drew it to my lips and kissed it. "I wear the pants in this relationship, remember?"

She didn't say anything and just looked on the path to her church. We continued our walk, with security not far behind. Earlier, we had some issue with some of the business owners in this block. I watched every face that passed us, holding my gun firmly in one hand, Joanne in the other.

"Shoty?"

"Uh, what!" I said as I turned to look at her.

"You're not even listening to me. I called you three times."

"Sorry, honey—just preoccupied, what?"

I was still watching my surroundings.

"I was trying to understand you," she said. "I thought guys your age usually run away from commitment."

"I don't know about all guys," I answered, "but some of the ones I know jump in without even thinking, I think I'm a jumper too."

"You want a relationship?" she whispered in a small voice.

"Baby, I just made love to you, with the added bonus of being your first. What you think I want? And you have me out here walking this street. I think we have more than just a relationship, don't you think?"

"I wasn't thinking. We only shared one night. I didn't think you wanted more."

I had to stop and stare at her for a moment. "So let me get this straight—you held onto your virginity for twenty-three years of your life, and just like that, you let me pop it—and not expecting anything in return."

"Well…" she didn't get to finish her thought, as she was cut off by the roars from motorcycles coming our way. There was AK, on red

Kawasaki Ex250, followed by Cage, on his 1300 Yamaha, and next came Sic, on his jet-black Honda Goldwin Navi XN.

On the north side of rue Bernard, Simi, Teck and Chopper were in a black Yukon Denali. To the west, Magnum, Riffle, Tank and Bullet were in a black SUV. To the south, four more bikers approached, Mac, Caliber, Pistol and Rocket.

My phone vibrated, and I picked it up. It was Nock.

"Man, I'm in the delivery room, operating. I got a call that you are walking in enemy territory. What the fuck you doing?"

"Relax, we're cool. Joanne just wanted to go to church. I'll tell you about it later. Go back to operating, Dr. Mangrass. Besides, all the guys are here." I hung up the cell phone as AK approached while cutting off his BMW 750 engine.

"You just lost your damn mind!" AK said, pointing up the street. "What are you doing? I was enjoying my date, ready for a second round when Wilkins called."

I looked up the street and saw the head of my security blocking traffic, closing the whole block to pedestrians and cars. With all the commotion, I didn't realize Joanne walked off until security scrambled after her.

"See what I have to deal with? The woman is stubborn. Let me take her to church. We'll talk later." I rushed after her, leaving the crew to follow behind.

Joanne never said a word to me. During the mass, she went to confession, giving me a weird look cuz I was on an important phone call. She got on her knees and prayed the whole time.

After Mass let out, everyone walked out the church. I held her hand when we reached the exit. The Crew was chilling on a high wall outside the church, which caused some of the churchgoers to be uncomfortable.

"Really, Shoty? They couldn't wait for you off the church grounds? This is embarrassing."

"Well, get un-embarrassed, because this is me, and that's how we roll. If you going to be with me, my family is very important. There's no discussion."

She looked around, counting. "All these people are your family?"

"Yeah, all the ones on the walls except one—my doctor—he couldn't make it. But there's fifteen of us, plus a few close friends." I pointed to Baptist. "He's my head of security and close friend. Tech is a member and part of the family. We're still fifteen members, but we lost one before Tech joined."

"One of your friends died? I'm sorry to hear that. He must have been special, since you're still grieving the loss."

It took me a minute to compose myself, remembering Mich. "It was a long time ago. Come, let me introduce you to my family."

We walked over to Cage, who leaned on his bike with no expression, just staring at the crowd around him.

"This is the son of Satan, Oliver Santiago. We call him Cage. Next to him is Rocket—you met already. Here, you have Bullet, Riffle and Caliber—Cali for short. Chopper... Sic... Big black guy in the truck is Magnum. Sitting in the passenger seat is Pistil. Simi and Tank were in the other truck behind them. The three by the steps are Mac, Tech, and AK, who are preoccupied—it must be something he likes over there. You'll meet Nock later, when he gets out of surgery, but this is my family—the A15 CREW."

Finished with the introductions, I walked over to AK, who was lost in watching this pretty little thing in yellow.

"Don't you think she's a little too young?"

"Na man—she just what I want. I been trying to see if I can approach her without adding to her distress. That lady don't like her— she snaps and blames her for things that have nothing to do with her. Like this little boy who dirties his clothes, she's yelling at her, not the boy."

"Well, you know how these people are when it comes to someone they don't like, but let me help you out."

"Yo Mag, pass me that football in the back."

Magnum threw the football.

"AK, go long."

Flying in the direction of his girl, the football hit her on the forehead.

"Sorry!"

AK retrieved the ball and helped the girl. She was pretty, with a natural look of the Taino peoples who were indigenous to the Island. She kind of reminded me of that singer, Ashanti. She held her forehead and looked at AK, pissed.

The older lady who might have been her guardian cursed at her for being hit by a football. AK apologized while slipping the girl his number.

Meanwhile, Joanne was left alone with Rocket and Cage. Joanne mean-mugged them, still not saying anything.

"So, you have Shoty walking these streets?" Rocket teased. "You do know if anything happens to him, I'm coming after you, right?"

"Last time I checked," she answered, annoyed, "he was a grown-ass man who walks around with his gun. I suggest you take your concerns with him," she snapped, rolling her eyes.

"I'm taking my concerns to you," Rocket said and approached her, with his gun under his vest, visible for Joanne to see.

She looked at him from head to toe, not backing down from his intense stare. Rocket got down to her nose level.

"I didn't forget that you put your hands on me, and now you have my brother following you like a puppy. Trust me, I will come at you with everything I got," he threatened, pounding his chest.

Joanne returned his stare and didn't even flinch from his outburst.

"Cage, can you tell your bitch-ass friend to get the hell out of my face? And if he ever threatens me again, it will be the last thing he'll do on this earth, cause he's going to meet with your father! Soon."

Cage, observing the scene in front of him, turned to Rocket, who was grumbling over the fact that Joanne had stood her ground with him.

He used an animated voice, seeming pissed off, really wanting to hurt Rocket. "Rocket," Joanne said, "stop playing. Are you going to meet Satan?"

CHAPTER 11

By the time Shoty made it back to Joanne, the war between the two came to a halt. Rocket approached Joanne and gave her a hug.

"You did good. Not too many people can stand toe-to-toe with me. If it's you and Maddy—a word of advice—don't try to fight with her. She fights and plays dirty. But tomorrow, we are going on a shopping spree. Take Shoty's credit cards. Call me if you want to go!" he said and jumped on his Honda XM.

"Yo Shoty—later man, see you at Mag's." He pulled off, jumping eight of the church stairs and into traffic.

Cage watched him flying on the bike, pushing 90 miles an hour in a 25-mph residential zone,

"That's crazy! He's nuts," he said, turning to Joanne.

"It was nice meeting you under normal circumstances. I'll see you guys later. Mag, I'll be at your house."

"You always in my house! She off for the next couple of days. She left this morning."

Magnum paid attention to his friend's body language, but like a trained soldier, he showed no sign of emotion. It was hard to tell if he was happy or upset.

"Good, now I don't have to muffle her cries for a few days. You know where to find me." He too took off, doing over 100-mph on his bike.

Joanne just shook her head at the display of power and wealth. She felt a little out of place, not enjoying being around all the guys. She turned and looked up at Shoty, who sensed her discomfort.

"It's okay, they will protect you if I'm not around," he said, pulling her into his embrace and kissing her on the forehead.

"Come on, get in the car. We're driving back—no more walking," he said.

Reluctantly, Joanne followed Shoty to the waiting SUV with Magnum. Before entering into the vehicle, Shoty wrapped his arms around her waist and brought her closer to him. He kissed her on the lips.

"Listen, I know you're sore. We are going to spend the afternoon with my little niece. She's three and a little pain-in-the-butt. On Sundays, I usually spend time with her—we all do… when we're not away on business."

Joanne just stared at him, not knowing what to say to yet another demand.

"Is this your way of asking me to spend the afternoon with you, or are you telling me to?" she asked, crossing her arms over her chest.

He cast her a pitying glance. "Yes, I'm telling you what we are going to do. Why? Do you have more important plans?"

"It would have been nice if you had asked. I usually spend my Sundays at home with a book... and peace and quiet!"

"Now you get to spend it with your man. It won't be quiet," he warned her with a straight face.

Joanne frowned and took a deep breath. "I... uh... I don't follow orders—never have, and I don't plan to in the near future, Mr. Shoty. So next time, ask me first before you include me in your plans." She broke away from his embrace then climbed inside of the truck without saying another word to him.

Shoty watched her sit in the back, wondering if he pissed her off. He shook his head, thinking how wonderful it would be to tame her. A smirk creased his lips as he walked away toward A.K., who was in a deep conversation with the girl's aunt.

"The girl is very stupid, so you don't have to apologize to her. I tell that damn girl every day to pay attention to everything! Do you think she listens to me?" the lady vented, still blaming the young woman for getting hit with the ball.

It was obvious from A.K.'s body language he was frustrated with the conversation. He itched to put the fat lady in her place. When he took a step and closed the gap between himself and the lady, Shoty noticed his demeanor and held him by his arm, addressing the lady.

"Sorry Madame, we don't want to cause any trouble," Shoty said while pulling A.K. away, his eyes staying on the girl as he wanted to make eye contact with her. She kept her head down and stared at her toes.

The lady continued with her verbal abuse before getting physical, smacking the young lady on the head while the other children cheered her on. The young lady never looked up or complained about her abuses.

The crew sat back, watching the family of eight make their exit out of the church parking lot on foot. It took a lot of convincing for A.K. not to get involved.

"Look man—she's not your girl. You can't interfere in her life like that. When she's yours, I will help you take that witch down, but for now, we walk way. Let Tech do his job. By morning, you will know all there is about your lady in yellow."

Shoty pushed him in the vehicle next to Joanne, who had her arms crossed, staring at him, not very happy. He signaled Pistol to join him.

"One more minute and we will be on our way," he pled and walked to his remaining friends. He shouted the order to get everyone off the church grounds en route to Magnum's house.

Joanne sat in silence throughout the ride, ignoring all the occupants in the vehicle, focusing on the congested street that was full of merchants. More exotic canvas paintings and wooden mementos were displayed on the corners of the streets. And there were merchants, carrying round baskets on their heads, chanting the price and value of goods offered to customers. The steep roads, with its high carved walls wove alongside narrow roads, covered with hurried, frenetic pedestrians while cars climbed a mountain, speckled with uniquely-designed homes with high colorful gates. Whilel Joanne was lost viewing the activities of the streets, the vehicles took a turn into a vast green space covered in vegetation and coconut palm trees lining a long white sand road.

The truck pulled up to a driveway, its lavish wide gate embellished in the center with the letters: MICH. Soldiers were posted throughout the area, guarding the Mediterranean-style mansion, which was surrounded by a lush landscape of green grass and wild orchids.

"I see Cage left his soldiers over here," Shoty commented to Magnum as they drove through the open cages.

"They're staying here permanently—until I can get Maddy out of my house," Magnum sighed as Shoty shook his head and sucked his teeth.

"He really lost his mind! Who would have thought the son of Satan had a heart!" Shoty stated.

Magnum parked and looked over at his friend. "You're not having any regrets, are you?"

"Man, please! That was two years ago. I haven't thought of her in that way. Besides, look in the back seat. I'll do it all over again for that," I said with a big smile on my face, looking at Joanne.

"Alright man, hope this don't bite you in the ass, cuz you know how Santana take shit seriously. And do me a favor—keep my name out of it! I'm still feeling tense over that shit with Wilkins," he said as he remembered the night Maddy was attacked, when Cage lost it and questioned Magnum about his competence as a guard, and why he felt the need to fire him. He almost killed his friend and head of his security for not being able to handle the situation.

There was total silence as the vehicle's occupants collected their thoughts over the incident. Shoty was chasing Madeline, and he never told Cage he saw her first.

"I found my wife," Shoty said above a whisper, looking straight at Joanne through the rear-view mirror. Magnum turned and stared at her, causing Joanne to roll her eyes and continue to ignore them both.

"When are you going to make it official? Hope you didn't forget your…" He stopped, remembering Joanne was in the back seat.

"Yeah, right! Guess later, we need to come up with a solution. Man! Nothing is never easy with you," Magnum complained while reaching for the door handle.

He exited the car and helped Joanne out the back seat. He offered his arm, escorting her to the front door.

"Welcome to Blanc Villa, Mrs. Celestin," he stated while leading her into the front foyer and entering the house. "Please make yourself at home. I have to go check on my daughters. We'll come down shortly to keep you company."

Magnum signaled for Shoty to show Joanne around as he went up the stairs.

"Beautiful home. I like how it's open and airy," she mumbled as she looked around the high stone wall with matching tiles. In the far corner, two oversized sofas formed a circle large enough to sit more than twenty people in a space leading to the outside terrace. There was a high glass wall, separating the two.

"The view here must be wonderful at night." She looked at Shoty, who was staring at her.

"What?"

"Nothing!" he said as he leaned on the wall with his hand on his pocket.

"Then stop staring at me! I feel like there's boogers in my nose or something," she said with irritation.

Shoty left his post, pulled her to him and rested his hand on her bottom. "I was enjoying the view. I didn't know it was a crime for a man to stare at his wife."

"I'm not your wife!"

He smiled at her and kissed her nose, rubbing her hips and that bodacious booty, which he loved. He leaned in to press her to his hardness.

"See what you do to me? I can't think straight," he whispered near her lips and continued with his caresses. The door opened and the rest of the crew entered the room, killing the mood.

CHAPTER 12

"Man, get a room, there are children here!" Sic shouted at the entranceway.

"Leave him alone! He's in love—it's the stage where he can't keep his hands off of her or that booty," Tank joked as he entered, laughing at the sour look on Shoty's face, hiding behind Joanne.

Before long, the house was full of people—all men. Joanne, the only female in the room, felt a little uneasy as she watched them interact with each other.

"Is there a reason why you're hiding behind her?" Sic asked, causing the room to erupt in laughter.

"Fuck you, Sic!"

"Wow, the almighty Marlon Celestin can't keep his man in check! What are you, Joanne? Wonder Woman?" he asked, watching her from the corner of his eye, suppresing his laughter.

Just then, Magnum entered the room from the opposite side with two little girls, one on each arm. The older girl, excited to see all her uncles, flew to greet each with hugs and kisses.

"Joanne, these are my daughters," Magnum said. He faced them, studying Shoty's demeanor, noting that he was not moving away from his date. With just one look from Sic and the rest of the room, Shoty's ailment became clear.

"Oh, you just need to move away. Walk it off," Magnum observed, while presenting his daughters to Joanne. "This one here is Brianna, and 'Miss Social Bird' over there—her name's Claire." He handed Brianna over to Joanne and led her toward the couch.

"Here, have a seat while your man gets himself together," he said while pointing Shoty to the exit.

"They're so beautiful. They have your dark eyes," Joanne said. admiring their beauty.

She saw both girls were equally gorgeous, with their distinctive dark eyes, inherited from their father. She couldn't help but fall in love with them. Brianna settled on her lap, looked up and touched her face.

"Look at that! She likes you," Magnum commented. "She's allowing you to hold her and not screaming her head off!"

"Why do you say that?"

"She doesn't like people touching her!" Claire said, eying Joanne with curiosity. Displeased with how Brianna was taking to Joanne, she immediately caught an attitude towards her daddy's new friend.

"Daddy, it's Sunday! I thought it's *family* day! Who's this?" she asked with much attitude, which got everybody's attention.

"Watch yourself, and that tone!" Magnum's voice warned, chilling the air as he stared at his daughter. "Now apologize." The staring contest continued until Magnum shifted his feet to get off the couch.

"I'm sorry!" Claire blurted out, contemplating her father's next move.

"Rephrase your question!"

"Um, I just wanted to know who your friend was, Daddy, since today is Sunday," she said, staring at the floor, avoiding looking at her father.

"Eye contact! I can bring who I want in my home! That does not give you the right to question me! Do we understand each other, Claire?"

Father and daughter stood their ground in a silent conflict that ended when Shoty entered the room.

"Uncle Shoty!" Claire exclaimed. She ran in his direction and flew into his arms.

"Yeah, Bear, what's up with the frown on your face?"

"Daddy's being mean, and he yelled at me," she whined in a small voice.

"Because?" Shoty paused and searched her eyes, waiting for an explanation, knowing Claire had done something to piss-off her father, since Magnum never raised his voice at his children.

"I asked about his lady-friend over there," she said, pointing to Joanne.

"What's wrong with her?"

"See how Brianna's taking to her? She's not crying. What if he marries her?" she said in a frightened voice.

"I thought you wanted a mother?"

"Not this one!" she whispered in her uncle's ear. "She looks like a psycho."

Shoty laughed at his niece, pinching her nose and setting her down.

"What you know about psychos?"

"Uncle Roc says it all the time, especially after your car got blown up. And a few weeks ago, he said something about a psycho, choking him half to death. He saw Uncle Cage's dad coming for him."

"Tell Uncle Roc he talks too much," Shoty said toward Rocket, who smiled at him.

"Come on, let me introduce you," he said to Claire, taking her hand and walking her toward Joanne on the couch.

"Claire, this is your new aunt. Her name is Joanne, and she's not a psycho." He raised his voice to get the point across, looking directly at Rocket.

'What? I didn't lie," Rocket insisted. "Just because you can't see what we all do."

"Keep me out of this. I don't want any part in it," Sic said from across the room, while the rest of the crew followed suit.

"Yeah, keep me out too!"

"And me!"

"I got your back, Shoty," Tank shouted."

"Hold up! Did you hear what he just said?" Pistol hollered, staring at Shoty in disbelief.

The room grew quiet as everyone looked from Pistol to Shoty, triying to see what they missed in the conversation. Pistol turned to Magnum for elaboration.

Shoty then walked over to Joanne and dropped to one knee. Soon after, the whole A.1.5 crew were at a standing salute, waiting on Shoty to continue. The entire room was focused on Joanne's reaction.

The room was in total silence, in anticipation of welcoming the second wife of an A.1.5. crew member. Their order demanded a ritual, in which all members were required to accept, protect and salute the chosen wife, "who must be a virgin." That ritual went back centuries and was passed down through generations.

Joanne watched as all in the room dropped to their knees, not understanding the significance of the ritual. Setting the baby on the sofa, she tried to leave. She shot up to her feet and searched for an exit, eyeing Shoty with suspicion.

"Okay, I don't know what is going on, but I'm leaving," she said, making a bee-line toward the door.

He quickly grabbed her hand and brought her back to the sofa.

"It's nothing to be afraid of. You're the safest person in this room." he assured her. "In my organization, there are things that must be complete before we go any further, and one of those is that when we find a life-mate who is pure and innocent, it's our job to protect and welcome her into our circle. So without further ado, Miss Joanne

Castillo…" He fastened his right hand over his chest while the echo of 15 voices loudly welcomed Joanne to the family.

"Today, you became the wife of an Arsenal 15 Member. On Your Honor, We Lay Down Our Lives."

Joanne, on the couch with Brianna in her arms, was confused as to what had just occurred. She looked to Shoty for an explanation. Instead, he rose from his knee and disappeared with Magnum into his office, closing the door, leaving her with unanswered questions. Everyone went back to their previous activities without any further clarification.

"Okay, is someone going to say something about all that?" she asked. "What do you mean by 'you'll lay down your lives?'"

She paused, waiting for someone to say something. Nothing! It was as if she wasn't even in the room. Her heart sped as her imagination ran wild. She scanned the room for signs that would connect the group to a cult or some other kind of evil. She took a deep breath, willing herself to remain calm.

"What the hell did I just get myself into!" she whispered softly. She stood and walked toward the front door to leave, and she almost reached the handle when she heard someone call out.

"Shoty, your wife is leaving. You better come and explain yourself to her."

CHAPTER 13

JOANNE

I was holding onto the door, about to run out of that loony bin, when Shoty came out of the office and charged toward me. Now, I don't get scared easy, but his actions, along with the earlier group display, was over-the-top. I was shaking in my shoes with fear.

He stood there, hand in his pocket, a frown on his face as he watched me. My hands were on the door handle, as I was ready to dash out.

"I'm trying to figure out why would you think I want to hurt you?" he asked, seeming confused, waiting for a response.

I took that very moment to analyze the man who was in front of me and realized he wasn't someone you wanted to play with. It appeared he wanted to hug me and kill me in the same instant. My time was running out. I needed to answer his demand.

"I just want to go home. I didn't plan for this here. I just wanted to get you out of my system. I figured that if I had sex with you one time, then you would forget I existed and move on to the next—not this mumbo jumbo that just happened here. I mean, you're talking about me being your wife!" I threw my hands in the air for dramatic effect and poked my left finger at his chest, which caused him to take a few steps back.

"Hell no!" I said, continuing to vent. "I don't want to be your wife or anybody's else." I faced him, angry, nose-to-nose with my finger still poking his chest. "You didn't even bother to ask me what I wanted! You just assumed I would be okay with being your wife. Well, hate to bust your bubble, Mr. Shoty, as they call you—I won't be your wife, so undo all that mumbo jumbo you and your friends just did, cuz the answer is No!

"I don't even know you! You could be a mass murderer for all I know! And what type of cult are you involved in? You worship the Devil? What kind of ceremony was this?"

As I lashed out on him, he just stood there, listening, staring at me like I had two heads. An eerie silence fell over the room as its occupants watched the show I was putting on, but all that attention was wrecking my brains. I didn't know if I needed to run for my life.

The seconds felt like hours at the front door as I waited for a reaction or some response. Instead, his chest moved forward, pressing me back against the door. His lips were on mine before I could even blink. All the feelings of wanting him came right back, and all I wanted at that moment was to wrap my arms around him.

SHOTY

Watching her in her moment of rage, I sensed that she feared for her life, not knowing what to expect from me. I admired her courage for standing her ground and loved the way her nose flared every time her finger connected with my chest. *Damn, this woman was so beautiful!* She made my blood boil! I had to kiss those sexy lips of hers!

I moved in and did just that, though I felt her resisting me as I took more control, pinning her to the door frame and deepening my caress on her lips. I moved to her throat and nibbled.

"Ahem, ah, ahem! There are children in this room," I faintly heard Sic say in the background. I forgot I had an audience and came to a stop.

By then, I had her where I wanted her. She had her arms wrapped around me, enjoying the display of affection and was kissing me back.

"Now, can we stop being melodramatic! It's family time, and this is your new family. See how the girls are looking at us—like we just lost our mind. You got me kissing you like I'm ready to have you against this wall right now," I whispered in her ear, pulling her closer to my raging hardness, making her feel my desire to rip that dress off and bury my throbbing member into her sweet cave.

"Uh!" was all she could say. I loved making her daze?

"Come on, lunch is ready. Can you take the girls for me?" I pulled her away from the door and guided her back to the girls on the couch. "I'll be back soon. I need to wrap up some things in the office. Start without me, we'll join your after," I whispered close to her ear, kissed her temple left the room.

I need to finishing talking to Mag regarding Stephanie, my psycho ex, who blew up my car a couple years ago—who also has a very rich father that's waiting on a wedding date, to merger our operation division and communication, with Magnum.

It didn't help that I also bursted her cherry. I just couldn't see myself with that witch. I had been putting it off and making excuses for the past two years. Magnum interrupted my thoughts as I walked in to the office.

"Are going to share your troubles with your new wife?"

I thought about that question for a moment, closed the door to his office, leaned my head on the frame and imagined telling Joanne about Stephanie. Joanne had anger issues—she'd rip me and Stephanie to shreds

"No, not right now. I have to think on how to handle it before this blows up." I finished, picked up my glass from earlier and took a sip of rum. "I need something to calm both my anxiety and sexual desires. I still want to bed my wife," I chuckled, liking the sound of that.

"Let see how long you keep that smile when Constant hears of this. You know he's been pushing for this marriage to take place. He's not going to like this!" Mag said, letting me know he doesn't like this situation.

I looked up at him and shrugged my shoulders, sinking deeper into the couch. At that moment, all that mattered was that I found my wife, my one and only. I really loved this woman. She wasn't like any other—not even Madeline, who I thought I had feelings for until she crushed mine like I didn't matter. She found Cage, and they are happily in love with each other. Now I've found my own, and I have to fight to keep it forever after.

My first war is with Constant, our benefactor, who oversees our organization and maintains control in the specific chapter in masonic law. A couple of years ago, we thought it was a good idea to merge with the northern chapter to gain more power and prestige, but the north didn't want to merger businesses. They wanted something more committed, like a marriage contract, which was not easily broken, and heirs would rule the empire.

Out of fourteen candidates I had to choose from, I got stuck with the short end of the straw. I didn't mind it in the beginning, not until Stephanie my bride-to-be started showing signs of unstable nature, like showing up at the office or my house un-announce, disrupting my meetings with investors and making a spectacle of her.

To make matters worse, I couldn't get out of the contract for the simple fact that I had tasted the forbidden fruit. I should have known to run. In loyalty to my comrades, I tried to make it work until my dear bride-to-be started hurting women she saw in my company and destroying my personal affairs.

"Last time I spoke to Constant was to get me out of that contract," I reminded Magnum, who was swinging his chair around by the window.

"Yeah, your sleeping with her didn't help. As far of her father is concerned, you consummated your marriage then."

"She climbed into my bed after I left the club drunk, I might add. Back then, I couldn't resist a beautiful woman in my bed. Shit, I still can't! Look what's in your living room with your daughters."

'I thought you climbed into her bed?"

"Mag! Did you see her in that dress, and when she came close—her perfume. Then she put those lips on me! Mag, your brother is weak, cuz I was done then. Took everything in me to hold back as long as I did to go to her crib.

I never wanted a woman that much, Mag." I breathed deeply, thinking about all the time Joanne made me wait and beg for her attention. I can't wait to take her home and make sweet love to her some more, but business first. *Take control man. These feeling are new. Breathe and take control.* I willed myself to cool off my broiling desire to rush out and take my wife home.

"You know you're going to have a face-to-face with Constant. I'll back you up, but it's not going to be easy, I can promise you that. Her dad was set on this merger, and there's a lot of money at stake," Magnum complained, concern in his voice.

"I know we all pledged our alliance tonight to protect her, and that's without a doubt! You need to make amends with your brothers. You have to talk to all of them and see who has your back against Constant." Mag finished and headed to the door to join his daughters.

Feeling the weight of my decision, I realized that it could damage our circle financially. We're not in the position to break away from our benefactor, and his happened to be Simi and Rocket's dad. *The shit I get myself into!*

"I'll talk to them on Monday's meeting," I informed him, heading for the door. He turned to me with a stern, murderous look, that made our enemies run for cover.

"Stop sleeping with Stephanie!" he commanded.

"Well, I haven't really been with her…" I could see he wasn't fooled by my answer. I felt like the little brother being chastised by his older brother who was only six months older.

His eyes grew dark and he sighed, annoyed with the situation. I nodded "yes." We left it at that headed into the living room."

"Besides, I think I need to get this one out of my system. The call for her is strong, man."

"Let's hope she can make you into a respectable husband. and keep your dick in your pants. That way, I won't have any more messes to clean," he said, annoyed.

"I'm not that bad. I can barely keep up with Rock and Riffle, you know it. And Cage just give up his Siamese twins."

"Thanks for reminding me. Stop sleeping with them too," he whispered as we approached the dining room.

"Shit! I forgot about them."

"Oooh! Uncle Shoty—cursin! Daddy, did you hear him?" asked Claire, her finger pointing my way.

"Yes, sweetheart, I heard. Go get your jar and tax him." Magnum sighed grilling me for using profanity in front of his children.

"Okay, Daddy!"

I smiled as Claire rushed up the stairs to get her jar. We had established a system. A while ago, when Claire started repeating our every word, that whenever we conducted ourselves in a negative manor around the children, we would then donate to their college fund by emptying out everything in our pockets into the jar.

Claire came running back down the stairs with a full jar from a week earlier

"Wow, Claire-Bear! By the time you turn eighteen, looks like you'll be one of my investors! That a lot of money you got there, Missess," I said while flipping my pockets inside out.

"You know!" I continued, "you need to tax Uncle Roc for using the word 'psycho,' cuz that's not a very nice word to say to people, especially a family member."

I finished watching Roc mean-mugging me, his face saying, "I going to get you for that!" as Claire approach him.

Her jar was filled to the very top with hundreds of dollar bills spilling out all over the stairs on the way back to her room.

"Hey Claire, you need to come back and pick up you money, sweetheart, Sic called before whispering to tease Roc. "Uncle Rock can't go on his date tonight, cuz he's broke until the morning.

"I can't get any money from your till then? Seriously? You're going to let me spend the night with no cash?" he scolded Shoty, who was doing the same to him. Rocket then turned to Joanne.

"Your man is a bitch-ass, and I'm going to get him later for that." He walked over to his friend and punched in the stomach. Shoty blocked and they continued on their brotherly conduct of affection. The room exploded in a roar.

"Roc!" He came to stop looking toward the stairs.

"What? She's still upstairs," he explained as everyone point to Brianna on Joanne's lap.

"Man, she do not know anything. All she do is cry her head off. Besides, we started that with Claire because she was repeating everything Simi and Riffle were saying."

"Now she repeats everything you say," Shoty threw back at him with right hook to his side.

"You just mad cuz your girl is a psycho," Rocket said while play fighting with Shoty, circling around him, ready to box.

"That's why you just dropped 10-Gs in the jar. Keep it up and you're gonna go broke. And you thought Simi has a problem! What's that? Your third drop for the month already?" Shoty laughed.

"Yeah, you are right. Damn, I really have to watch what I say around this little girl." He paused with his hand on his hip thinking of all the money he had to put in that jar.

"Yo, why is it you always have to bring this girl up? Can I have a moment of peace?" Simi protested from across the room, not wanting to think about his psycho whatever she was.

"You check your statements for the day yet, or is it to early?" Mag asked. Simi just looked up and gave his phone to Magnum with the bank ledger for the morning showing he spent $150,000 by noon. Rachelle, his wife, had devised a plan to get him back in his villa by spending his money, which he refused. Their love story was comical. Rachelle wanted to give him her love, and he wanted to run away front it. He claimed she's too young for him, and she was determined to have him.

"Well, at least Mac and Rif are working on it if you can't get any result," he said, pausing for effect.

"Your niece can support you," he finished between chokes of laughter as the room erupted with condolences to Simi's misfortune.

"Ha, ha. Laugh all you want, it's funny how you've turned the tables on me—when these two clowns started the whole thing." Simi said angrily, making them laugh even harder. Joanne could not help but join in.

She sat back and observed the circle of men interacting with each other. They were a close-knit family who enjoyed each other's company. There was no tension or ill feelings toward them as they lived life and enjoyed every minute of it. And they had unlimited access to money, but it didn't define them or control who there are in any way. They all acted as equals. It was hard to pin-point who was the leader.

Feeling comfortable being around so many men was not an issue for her any longer. It was as if the anxiety just went away and she relaxed and dropped her guard around them. They would protect her, and that made her happy—the fear of men has disappeared.

CHAPTER 14
JOANNE

The day slowly came to an end. I had a wonderful time with the girls their the most precious thing on earth, and I fell in-love with both of them. After lunch, the girls and I went to the park that was located right in their back yard. It was a very lavish park, with themes that complimented the girl's names.

Claire Bear Park is a small amusement park with all her favorite rides, like a mini-train that circled the entire park. In the center were go-carts, with which she raced her uncles. Brianna was still a baby, so most of her themes were under development. Brianna Banana Park would include her favorite animals and fruits.

Diner was served around five, and everyone came to the table. As I looked around, I noticed I was the only female present, so I leaned toward Shoty, whispering.

"Where are the other females in this family?"

He gave me a funny look about my question.

"You and Madeline. She's away for a couple of days! Not all females make it to this table with our little ones—only family," he stated proudly.

Now I was giving him a funny look. "Well, you're gonna have to explain that to me, cuz I don't know how I'm family. We just met and fucked once," I whispered in his ear so only he could hear, cuz I was not trying to get taxed by Claire.

"Later for all that. I explain it to you again—when I have your legs wrap around my neck tonight," he mumbled, kissing the top of my nose.

Diner was delicious. Blanc Villa had a wonderful cook. It was the first time since moving to Haiti that I felt a little joy, where I didn't have buried myself in work. Holding Shoty's hand, we said our goodbyes and went to the front door.

"Again, Joanne," Magnum said as he came over, "welcome to the family. The girls and I love you already, so that tells you were meant to be here."

He and Shoty shared a glance and a silent understanding.

"I got it man, it's done, no more. At tomorrow's meeting, I'll address the other issue."

Shoty ushered me out the door and into a black SUV that sped off before he could even close the door.

"Well, that was rude" I frowned. "I didn't finish saying my goodbyes and you just push me out the door."

He ignored me, reaching up and press a bottom and a front middle window came down, revealing the driver, who happened to be Rock. *Great! Now I got to deal with this fool too!*

"Are you two always together?" I asked.

"No, not always. Most of the time though. Why?"

"Nothing. Just asking," I said annoyed.

I looked out the pitch-black window with just of my reflection staring back at me, and she looked and felt happy. Lost on my own thoughts, I wasn't paying attention to my surroundings when the truck pulled up on a long stretch of road, climbing a mountain.

"Where are we going now? cuz I have to get home."

"In a few, baby, we almost there," he answered.

"But that's not my way home. There's no mountains where I live."

"Yes, honey. I live on the hilltop. In about two minutes, we'll be home," he explained, pulling me to him.

"Can we do this another night, cuz I have to get home. I have work in the morning, and I didn't prepare anything for tomorrow."

His demeanor changed, and he grew quiet as he stared at me.

"Is there a problem?" I asked, "cuz you just staring again?"

"Well, my wife don't work. We have enough money, and you have access to my banks. Well, you'll have that once Mac does all the paperwork. But working is not one of your job titles. I'm a very rich man, if you haven't noticed."

"Who says I work for money? Besides, I love going to work and doing something with myself," I answered. "Now can you take me home, please? It's getting very late and I need some sleep."

Just as I finished those words, the doors to the truck opened to four soldiers standing, making a path to the white doorway of a foyer with beautiful multi-colored wild orchids. They waited for me to exit the vehicle.

I calmly closed the door and announced to Rocket, "Please take me home. It's getting late, and I have to be in bed by nine."

He simply turned and faced forward. Mr. Shoty gawked at me again—this time without talking. Now we were 25 minutes into the staring contest, and I was ready to walk home, if I knew where I was. The darkness didn't help my sense of direction. When I checked the clock on the dashboard, it read 8:30 p.m. This had gone far enough. I was reaching for the door handle to open it when his chill voice stopped me.

"If you walk out this truck, its to go in that house," he said, pointing toward the soldiers. "Under no circumstance do you walk down that hill."

I stopped and leaned back on the seat, reverting to the three-year-old dealing with her uncle.

"I want to go home! I want to go home! I want to go home!"

I kept that going, and by the fifth try, he gave in, without another word.

"Take her home, Rocket."

The silence in the SUV was killing me on the ride back to my uncle's house, so I got up and sat on his lap and kissed the side of his frowned-up face. He ignored me at first, so I continued with my caresses that felt right. I loved the feeling I had with this man and wanted more. I rubbed my nose to his and bit his bottom lip. Finally, his hand snaked around my buttocks with a firm squeeze.

"So, you've taken pointers from your little niece," he stated in a low grouchy voice. Our eyes connected it became clear he knew what I was doing. "She gets away with it cuz it's cute—it's not that we don't know what she's doing. Remember, she's only three."

Holding me tighter on his lap and I could feel his hardness trying to poke out of his pants.

"You have me out all day," I said. "My poor uncle is probably sick with worry. He might even think I was kidnapped. And I told you I have work in the morning. You're on some macho bullshit."

"Watch you mouth," he interrupted coldly.

"Why?" I said, wiggling myself off his lap, only to have him tighten his grip.

"We don't tolerate disrespect form our wives. There's a technique we use to deal with things like that, which we've passed down from many generations. You wouldn't like it, so continue… without the bullshit."

I just sat there and glared at him. Was he for real?

"Um, now I lost my train of though. I just need to go home, get showed and go to bed."

"You going to get your things for work and some personal stuff you need, and we are going back home. I'm not sleeping at your uncle's house," he stated.

"You can do what you like, but I'm going to bed—my bed!" I screamed at him. I could feel the tension of willpower in the SUV circling us. I took a deep breath to calm myself and slide off his lap.

As he rotated his hips, I felt the full length of his hardness, wanting to come out and play.

"Why are we fighting about this, Jo? I just want to take you home to our house, because I have a house that is now yours too… and make love to you all night. Why are we arguing about this?"

"I don't know about your house being mine. I didn't choose any of the things in it, and I will not sleep on a bed that you have used with 'god knows how many females' you've had in it."

"I don't bring females into my home! It's against the rules for the simple fact that we never know how or when we will meet our wives. Case in point."

"I'm sleeping in my bed tonight and off to work in the morning, and you can't stop me."

I let that statement sink in for a moment, as he finally left me off his lap in deep thoughts.

"It's a security issue. It's not safe for me to be around your uncle's house, and for him too." He paused, looked out the window and rested his head on the headrest with his eyes closed. His left arm went around my waist, pulling me to him and his kissing and rubbing my nose to his.

"I have to keep you safe. I do business with a lot of shady people who would hurt you to get to me, so please, love, follow my orders," he begged, with kisses on my neck. The SUV came to a stop in front of my uncle's driveway.

"Still not sleeping on your bed. We can go to hotel for the night."

"Alright!" he roared and bit my neck, tapping on the dividing window. "Take us to Bull's-Eye for the night," he asked Rocket, who gave a skeptical knowing glance in the review mirror. It became clear what this Bull's-Eye was.

"Is that where you take all your female companions?"

"Well, I might have used it in the past, cuz I've never brought company into my home. It's a club and a hotel that belong to Simi. And they have like over a hundred rooms," he explained.

"It sounds more like a brothel to me," I said. "A hundred rooms, and you've probably used them all." Watching the guilt on his face was worth a thousand words.

I crossed my arms on my chest and I stared at him. Rocket kept looking back a forth to see who was going to speak first. He shook his head.

"Look, I'm going to make it easy for you. You two can take my house. I'm never there, and my bed is still in a box. I'm always at Cage's fortress, and he stays at Magnum's."

"Why? Cuz he has the whore house." I could see that blood drain from their faces. He turned gray hearing the truth.

I came to my senses and reached for the door to go in and get some personal belongings.

"Fine. I'll go because it's not safe for my uncle. Thank you for your home, Rocket," I said, feeling agitated that he might be a playboy with money and that women just threw theirselves at him.

I walked inside the house, looking for my uncle, who was not there. I went in my room to gather all my belongings, ready to leave. When I opened the door, two soldiers were there to take them from me. I saw my uncle talking with Shoty as we approached the SUV.

"Sorry, uncle. I didn't mean to worry you today. I just didn't get a chance to call you to let you know where I was all day."

Emilio Costello was a six-foot-one-inch, muscular slim man in his late 50s. He was of bronze complexion, a loving family man who had four children with his wife of twenty-five years, and a devoted brother who looked after the Costello real estate and business in Port-Au-Prince and in Jacmel.

"It's okay. I knew where you were and in whose company. I spoke to your dad already. He's waiting for your call. He wants to make sure you're happy." He finished brushing the hair on the side of my face as I whispered the events of the day to him briefly. "He says I'm his wife," I finished.

"Yeah," he told me, and he has my blessing. He says whatever you do to him, he could handle it, and his people understand that, cuz he's been warned. I explained the same thing to your dad today."

"How do you know all of this?" I asked.

"His lawyers were here all day today about his intention, and he said that he needed to talk to your father first. I believe he spoke to him this morning while in church," my uncle said. I hugged him one last time before climbing in the truck.

We sat in silence the SUV in route to Rocket's house, which was now my new home.

"Is there something wrong? Your mood has changed," Shoty said.

As I glanced his way, he appeared to have genuine concern for my well being. "Why didn't you tell me you spoke to my father this morning?"

"Why? That's man-talk. If you must know, I needed to make him aware that I was your daddy now, and he didn't have to worry about you any more."

"But how did you get his info? It took my uncle weeks to get in touch with him, and I still haven't been able to talk to him," I confessed with tears running down my eyes.

He pulled me into his embrace, rubbed my back and kissed me on the forehead. "Come on, baby, don't cry. Here." He reached in his pocket for his phone, which looked like a project I worked on with my dad a couple of years ago—it had the same exact design and logo. But dad scrapped the project because of security issues that made it unsafe to the public.

"Hello?" I heard my dad's raspy voice coming from the speakers.

"Daddy!" I shouted with joy, missing that sound for months. "Daddy, are you and Mommy okay?"

"Yes, we're fine. I'm so happy to hear you voice," he answered. "Cathleen, come on the phone. Jo-Jo's on the line." I heard my mother running in the background to get to the phone.

"Jo-Jo! my sweetheart! How I miss you!" she cried. "I've been so sick with worry about how things are going for you down there." She took a deep breath to control her racing heart. "Until this morning, when your young man called and said the had taken you church... and he promised to call back so we could talk to you." She paused, sobbing, trying to recompose herself. "He also promised me... Oh Jo—he made me a commitment that he'll always do right by you, and try to take the time to understand you. Those words made my day, cuz my baby girl found someone who can understand her."

She took another deep breath. "Now, I told him a little about you, like things you like and what's make you act crazy. He assured me he could handle it, and that you have about 15 other people that would help him, because their job is to protect you at all costs, even from him. Other than that, how are you? Do you eat in the morning before you bury yourself in that lab like your father does? I can't never get over how your two could ever forget to eat. You finally fall in love?" she asked.

"Yes, mommy. I did!"

"Is it all that I told you it would be? He makes your heart beat fast and you can't get him out of your system?"

"Yes, mommy, it is."

"Oh, I can't wait to tell your aunties! We've been waiting for this day to come! My baby finds her love," she whimpered, and the crying started all over again. I could hear her and my dad fighting over the phone. They pause for a moment where I couldn't hear anything

"Hello?"

"Yes, yes, I'm here honey," my dad said, coming back on the line.

"Oh, my baby girl! You all right? It killed me that I couldn't talk to you all these months, but I had to make sure no one was capable of finding you. And they tried—they bugged the house and our phones. The police were stationed at my door for weeks. Now, they just circle around every two hours. But let get off this line just to be on the safe side. I've got a feeling you're in very good hands. May I talk to your husband in private?" ge asked. I handed the phone over to Shoty.

"Yes, sir. I understand," Shoty said to him, "but don't worry about it. I'll take care of it. When I'm in the city next month, I'll talk them face-to-face. Good night, sir, and tell Mama good night." He put the cell phone away and held me tight as I fought back my tears.

"Thank you for doing that! I needed to hear from them."

"That is my husbandly duty, to put a smile on my wife's face, even though she's crying right now," he said, wiping the tears away.

"Can I ask you something?"

"What? Don't ever be afraid to ask me if something's bothering you."

"Where did you get this phone?"

"The cell phone? From our benefactor. He has a company that makes them—new ones come out every six months, but its not for everyone. My organization is the only one that uses them. Why does it interest you?"

"It's my design," I said. "All the features and coding belong to me. Dad got rid of the program three years ago because it wasn't safe. Things that I thought were innocent—someone was spying on my dad and the coding on the phone. It became scary when the military came for the codes.

"Alright, honey, I'll look into it, but for now, we're home."

The vehicle turned onto a pebble road curved in the shape of a snake, with a wild tropical garden of palm trees and orchids in each side, leading to a French-style Chateau in the distance.

CHAPTER 15

He pointed to this massive automatic security gold gate that arched like a piano in a crest with the word "MICH" in the center, where the C was split in half with it sides on each end of the entrance. It was exquisitely landscaped, with luscious green grounds, a tree lined driveway leading to a circular courtyard on the side. The continuous garden reached up to an 11,500 square-foot chateau with ten bedrooms, multiple pools, bathrooms and resting areas.

The vehicles pulled up on a side service door, where the soldiers again formulated a line waiting, for the couple to exit the SUV. Shoty consoled his wife, opened the door and led her into their new home. Rocket took the lead in showing her around.

"This is a ten-bedroom, with a bathroom for each room, and more in the pool area outside," he said, leading her the front entrance where there was a better view of entire design of the house. He stopped abruptly, looked at Shoty walking in with Joanne. "You need to carry your wife over the threshold."

Without hesitation, Shoty bent down and carried her inside, gently putting her feet on the ground and kissing both arms, showing off his muscles. Joanne gave him a questionable look.

"What! I work hard to get them! I bench press 250 pounds every day," he said, still flexing.

"Forgive him. We dropped him on his head a couple times," Roc explained to her as he took her hand, leading her further in the parlor room. It was an open area, with beautiful gold titles and sparkles, with diamond chips. A hundred people could have easily fit in this space.

In each corner their stairs leading to the upper floors, a total of five altogether. The most amazing amenity was a water fountain that sat in the center of the room, a circular structure with cushion all around. Rising toward the glass ceiling was sculptured fish, ten feet high, emblazoned with "MICH" in LED lights, spitting water into a half-tilted ceramic bowl. Shocked at the display, Joanne blinked twice at the massive sculpture, lost for words.

Shoty waved her off. "Don't even—he was dropped on his head a lot growing up. He thought he was a fish once upon a time." Shoty told her the sculpture reminded Roc of his past.

"And you thought you were ET and wanted to phone home. That's why yours is full of stars."

The two friends shared a quiet combat in which Joanne was unaware of hidden threats toward each other. Shoty composed himself and continued with his story about the fishes that were all over the chateau.

"So he built this house to remind him of that time."

Surprised to hear he build it, Joanne began to feel guilty about living in his home.

"Oh no, you built this? I can't stay in your house! Please take me to hotel, and tomorrow we can look for a place."

"It's okay—he's outgrown this place. He's been trying to get rid of it for years. If you like it, that's fine with me, but I just want to go to bed. I hardly slept last night," he said, reminding her of their late night and early morning activities. "You can see the rest tomorrow," he said as he began pushing her toward the stairs in route to their new bedroom, leaving Rocket to say good-bye to his fishes.

"That was rude. You didn't even say 'good night'," Joanne scolded as she reached the room.

"He'll be alright. Besides, he wanted to leave. He has a date and he's already an hour late."

"Wow! This is amazing!" Joanne shouted, captivated by the spectacular view in front of her.

They were in a room with a view on to the balcony, which overlooked beautiful beaches and towering palms, extending out to crystal clear blue waters. The architectural style of the home is truly magnificent.

Joanne glanced out, admiring the beauty of it all. Shoty was preoccupied with the soldiers who were helping him open all the furniture that was still in packages—Roc never bothered to unpack them. Within minutes, they had assembled a king-sized bed at the center of the room, under the skylight, and then the soldiers left with the empty boxes.

"Now we're alone. Come here, Mrs. Celestin. I have you all to myself," he said while taking off his shirt and motioning for her to join him.

She took his hand, leading him into the bathroom with all-white walls, dark-wood cabinets and black frame mirror mounted light fixture. Sterling silver hardware on the cabinet added a natural light throughout the bathroom. The frosted glass above the mirror and around the tub further illuminated the room. The simple shower doors bearing a leaf design accented the gold, wall-to-wall tiles inside the shower.

Shoty undressed his wife and pulled her in the shower, onto him while raising her hands to his lips and kisses them, feeling the love for this woman, his woman. He traced the side of her face and kissed there too… then her neck, her collar bone and in between her breasts… down to her bellybutton and resting at her hips. He was on his knees, worshiping her figure, her flat stomach, her full body with a high, pear-shaped butt. He lifted one leg over his shoulders and proceeded to kiss her there.

As his lips made contact with her center, the warmth of he's breath, the motion of his tongue—like a kitten, lapping milk for the first time—sent an electrical shock that traveled to her brain and made her senseless. She tried to hold on, grabbing the handle on the wall for support while resting her head back. Eyes closed, a moan escaped her mouth.

"Ooh, Mmm!" she sighed, loving the feel of his tongue. "Shoty, this feels so good!" she stuttered between breaths, using her other hand to rub his head, pushing to get closer to his mouth.

Sensing she was ready to peek, Shoty took hold of both of her butt cheeks and pulled her to him, deepening his kissing and sucking at her essence with a three-step motion: lick, lather and suck simultaneously.

Joanne body jerked, and she screamed with a forceful release that trembled her to the core. Shoty slowly rubbed his hands all over her abdomen and thighs, leaving gently kisses everywhere he touched, waiting for her to bestill her racing heart and control of her body.

After a few minutes of worship, he lifted Joanne and carried her to the bed. Lying on top of her, he parted her legs. With one hard thrust, he was deep inside her with a groan and a sigh, whispering in her ear.

"You take my breath away," he said, kissing the side of her neck, nibbling on an ear lobe, pushing himself into her with great force, insatiable.

She wrapped her arm around his neck, urging him on, enjoying the strength of her man, moving inside of her, opening wider to receive his powerful penetration, wanting to satisfy him in return. She remembered her mother and aunts coaching on that subject. She thought they were annoying and that she would never use their advice because she didn't have time for man, but now all that instruction flooded through her mind.

Not holding back, Shoty pumped harder into her, near his peak in the sack of his balls, crying out her name. "Oh, Jo-Jo! You're so sweet, my darling. Ahh, baby, you feel so damn good!" He continued to enjoy his wife, palming her hips to drive further into her.

Joanne stopped him by putting her hand on his chest. She flipped him over and straddled him, running her hand down his stomach and reaching for his penis, caressing the head and stroking it up and down, admiring its length and width.

"It's so big!" she cooed, adding a little pressure as she stroked it faster.

Shoty loved watching her—the innocence in her, and her lack of fear turned him on. He wanted to be inside of her again, so he moved his pelvis, drawing her closer, urging her to put it back in.

"Baby, please put it in. I need to finish inside of you," he begged, his voice shaking with emotion and anticipation of her meaty sex.

After one last stroke of the head, Joanne lifted her hips and inserted him, locking her muscle around his penis, finding a grip as she rotated her hips and pelvis in a slow circular motion. She closed her eyes, following all the instructions she was given. Shoty couldn't take his eyes off of her as she rode him, and reaching up, he grabbed her left breast and flicked a nipple with his tongue, teasing it with his teeth.

She started slow, and then she moved at a faster paste, and when he started to breath heavier, she waved him off and paused. After waiting for him to regain control, she continued with her lessons. By the third round, Shoty was in the verge of losing his mind with intense pleasure, wanting to explode.

"*Cheri*, please! Let me cum!" he hollered

Joanne heard his plea and only rode him faster. Shoty felt an electrical shock wave that curled his toes and legs. His arms stretched out, his eyes rolled to the back of his head, and he screamed his satisfaction before falling into a deep slumber in the middle of the bed.

She bent down and kissed him on the side of the neck, then his lips, and finally on top of his nose. She poked at him and wiggled her body off him and made her way into the bathroom to finish her shower.

At 10:55 p.m., the bash-board of Rocket's phone buzzed with emergency call form Shoty's head of security.

"Yeah?"

"Sir, we need permission to enter the compound. Mr. Celestin appears motionless," the man stated, waiting for a response.

"Is he in danger?" Rocket asked while sending an alert about the situation to all team members.

"That's why we called, sir," the man continued. "We couldn't determine if he was okay. He's just in the middle of the bed, motionless.

"Where is his wife?" he asked the soldier, making a U-turn, headed back to his former home.

"She's in the shower, sir. That's why we called before going in."

"Alright, sit tight. I'm on my way."

Rocket finished and switched to intercom with the whole team.

"Yo, who's closer to my house?"

"I'm two minutes out, I got the call," Santana stated, rushing down rue St. Pierre, making a left turn onto avenue St. Anne as he reached the gate.

Going to the back of the estate, he climbed the balcony and popped open the sliding door. Waiting, he heard the shower running. Shoty was still in the same position, with no change. He walked into the room and checked for pulse. Without warning, an object came flying at his head, which he blocked with his left arm, but the other piece of the lamp hit his forehead.

All he was saw was the blur vision of a naked woman, yelling about staying away from her husband, as he hits the ground.

Joanne had walked out of the shower, unable to find a towel. As she turned and walked toward the bed, she came to a halt as a black figure hovered over Shoty. Without any hesitation, she picked up the lamp and swung it at the intruder. Before she had time to process what was happening, the lights came on, revealing all of his friends in the room.

She was stunned at seeing how many men were in the room. All were at a loss for words, except Riffle, who was having a hard time taken his eyes off Joanne.

"I don't even like them big," he whispered to Rocket, "but damn, that's a goddess!"

"And she's your sister," Rocket reminded him.

"I know! That's what makes it so hard, I didn't know she was that fine," Riffle said, scratching his head, looking for something to cover her with.

"What happened? Why are you're here?" Joanne yelled at them, still holding onto the lamppost, confuse about why they were all in her room.

No one answered; they were preoccupied with their two motionless comrades.

"Talk to me, Nock—are they hurt?" Magnum asked.

"Well, Shoty vitals are fine. He's in a deep sleep, like a sated sleep," he said while looking at Joanne. "When I get a wife, you gonna hafta teach her how to do that!" he added, bewildered, "because that's some lethal shit! And then you knocked Santana out?" Sensing no foulplay, he called out orders. "All right, let's clear the room. Get Santana out of here. Nock—let the hospital know we're coming."

After everyone left, Joanne wondered what the commotion was all that about. Standing alone in an empty room and holding the lamppost, exhaustion overwhelmed her. Climbing in the bed next to her husband, she drifted off to sleep, thinking about of what kind of people she was involved with. Sensing her closeness, Shoty snaked his left arm around her, pulling her closer to his heart.

CHAPTER 16

The clear blue of the ocean met the early morning sun, cascading a brilliant tableau of orange and blue, spilling inside of the room. Shoty yawned and stretched, looking out the glass wall. He searched the room, recalling of the events from last night, making him smile, remembering the image of her on top of him. His gaze fell on Joanne, lying next to him. He could hardly breathe, looking at the most beautiful creature he had ever laid eyes on. Another smile crept on his face as he bent down and proceeded to wake her up. He rolled on top her and planted small kisses around her neck and cheeks.

"Wake up, sleepy head, its 6:30." He continued to wiggle his body between her legs and enters her slowly. "You got work this morning," he said, inhaling deeply, pushing further into her core flex, his butt cheeks moving in and out.

The sensation was unbearable, so holding back the urge to bury it deeper in her, he instead whispered in her ear. "Wrap your legs around me so I can take you in the shower."

Joanne moaned and stretched, feeling the fiction of his penis sliding in and out her. Opening her eyes, she connected with her husband's nose, their lips locking with passion. She followed his instruction, securing her legs around his waist with her arms around his neck. He carried her in the shower.

Against the shower wall, he pumped all of his strength into her. As she felt the momentum of his movements, a convulsion overtook her and she screamed out his name as water streamed all over them, leaving both husband and wife breathless.

By 7:30 a.m., Shoty noticed his wife's mood had changed. She wasn't talking and appeared distant, like something was troubling her. Joanne was gathering her things and fixing the bed when he approached her.

"You okay? Something wrong? Your mood is different."

"Your friends scare me. I can't determine what they are. One minute, I feel protected, and then in the next, my life is in danger."

"Your life is not in danger," he assured her.

"Well, you weren't there last night. You wouldn't know!"

"Last night? What happened? We went to sleep!"

"Right… Come on, I need to get in the lab before 8:00 this morning."

"Yeah, I need to get in the office too. But listen—you have nothing to fear from my family. They will protect you."

"So *you* say. I've seen different."

"So I *know*! Did something happen that I don't know about?" he asked.

"I don't like Santana. He scares me. He's a monster!" she said in an emotional voice.

"Well, no one likes Santana! But it's better to have him on our side, though. You'll love Cage—he's my brother and best friend."

Shoty sat on the bed, thinking of her statement for a moment.

"He won't let you see that side of him unless you're his enemy. He is a very private person—even with us. Maddy is the only person that he truly opens up to."

"Guess I'm his enemy then…"

"Why do you say that? Santana hasn't said two words to you!?"

"Can we go, please?" she asked while heading down the stairs.

He followed her to the side door and stopped her, pulling her into his arms.

"Don't be afraid of anything. I will always be there."

He caressed her cheeks planted a soft kiss on top of her lips. She returned his affection and headed out of the door to the waiting car.

"Morning! Can you drop me at Tenth Avenue, Mabroise, to the university, please?" she asked the driver before settling back in the seat, lost in thought. Shoty observed her silently, trying to figure out why her mood had changed. The car approached the university, pulling to the front.

"Can you go around to the back?" she asked, searching in her purse, looking a little frantic. "I need the lab area down there," she said, pointing to a "Restricted RD" area. "You can stop here. I'll walk to the gates… as soon as I find my badge."

As she checked her pockets, Shoty motioned the driver to continue, and the car moved towards the gate.

"Please stop," she insisted. They're very psychotic around here! Besides, I don't have my badge. I can't get in. I have to go back and get it. I can't remember where I put it."

A security guard tapped on the window as she was speaking.

"Morning, sir. We're on a 'no-walk-through' schedule for today," he informed Shoty.

"My wife needs to get to work. Is Tech around? I need him to clear her."

"No sir, he's not in yet, but if you get out of the vehicle, I can clear you, and you can take her in, sir."

After he waved toward the tower for the scanner, three more security officers join him, all eager to shake Shoty's hand. Joanne watched the scene shock to see the guards had another side that didn't involve hurting people. She looked over to the driver for some type of clarity, but he just shrugged his shoulders and look forward.

A fourth officer came with the computer scanner, and Shoty inserted his thumb, shook officer hands with the guards again and climbed back in the car.

"Okay, you're all set. Tech will clear you later today so that you won't need a badge anymore," he said. "Markus, take us to building B121."

"You know my lab?" she asked.

"Yes. They just told me," he said looking at his phone, dialing numbers on the keypad. Putting it down, he dialed another and finally hit intercom, which was just static. Annoyed, he put the phone back in his jacket pocket.

"Sorry, honey. I'm just going to drop you off. No one is picking up their phone this morning I have to get in the office."

He pulled her onto his lap, kissing her forehead and rubbing her bottom as she opened the door.

"Have good day! What time should I pick you up?"

She was still dazed from his interaction with security, his access at the facility and his ability to provide personal information that was stored in the most secure place on the Island. She was more confuse than ever about who he was.

"It took a lot of effort for my father to get me in here, then I had to wait two weeks before I was allowed to walk through the gates," she said, looking into his eyes. "You just walk in with a hand shake?"

"Nan, they fingerprinted me and did a full body scan. No one can get in this facility without proper paper work and clearance. This is a research facility for both science and medical, which I know you know, being in the field you're in. Are you a scientist?"

"No."

"Then what are you? And who are you?" she demanded, a silence filling the car for a long moment as the couple share a battle of wills.

Shoty considered her questions for a moment and decided not to reveal too much to her just yet.

"I'm your husband and a businessman. I make millions everyday, and I have a lot of powerful people in my pocket from all over the world. That's all you need know for now. But come on, honey—I really have to go. What time should I pick you up?"

Joanne just stared at him, not knowing what to say. "But I just asked you a question." She repeated in a no-nonsense tone.

"And I gave you an answer," he said playfully, kissing her lower lip. He slouched his body on the seat and squeezed her butt cheeks to bring them closer to his erection.

"See what you do me? I can't think straight with you near!" He breathed in her ear while rubbing her bottom to his penis. He closed his eyes, remembering the feel of her as he gyrated his pelvis into the fat of her derriere.

"I don't know what kind of female your use to…"

"Shhh," he said, putting a finger on her lips while angling her to exit the vehicle. "Can this be done later? We can pick all that up when I pick you up, okay?"

She closed her eyes and counted to ten, not ready for their first fight, which he would not win. She mustered all her strength not to explode, so she changed the subject.

"I don't have my badge. I can't open the door."

Shoty lifted her off his lap, got out of the car and insert his thumb in the panel to open the lab door, leaving Joanne speechless yet again. He kissed her cheek, ran back in the car and directed his driver to pull off. Joanne watched the dust rise as the car speeds down the road.

As Shoty got off the elevator, he was greeted by his secretary, Marline Deltus, a thirty-three-year-old mother of three who'd been happily married for the last five years. She started as a temporary employee, five years earlier, when the company opened. She was such a wonderful worker, capable of keeping up with him. Shoty wanted her to stay and even hired her husband to work on his cars.

Marline, running to catch up with him on his way to Magnum's office, handed him some folders.

"Why is it no one is picking up their phone this morning, Mar?" he asks, coming to an abrupt stop so she could catch her breath.

"Well, hello to you too, sir. The boys had an emergency last night. Just got off the phone with Mr. Constant. He says they're on the way. And I put the investors in the gaming room. They been here since 7:30 this morning."

Shoty looked at his watch, which read 8:50, and gave her a questioning look.

"So, what time you get here? I was not supposed to meet them until now."

"I was here at 6:00, getting your files ready," she said as he opened the door and entered his office. "Everything is in order for the meeting. But you're late. I thought you were with the rest of them."

"What's going on? Did they say anything to you about their whereabouts? I was even able to get through on the intercom."

"No, sir. They just said they're on their way. I'm going to move the investors to the conference room, so you can start on time.

"Yeah, do that. I'll be right there. Thanks, Marline."

No problem, sir, and congratulations on your recent marriage. Is this the young lady that was wrecking your nerves over the last two months?"

"Yes, that is her, Marline, and thanks—you'll love her," he answered, still smiling, with Joanne in his mind. He shook it off, ready to make some serious money.

It was 11:30 a.m. Shoty spent the last two hours in a closed-door meeting, working with 15 international investors to revolutionize communication towers in the island as well in their countries. The goal was to collect fifty million dollars to start the project.

Marline sat at her desk, answering the phone. "MICH Enterprise, how may I help you?"

"Hold on!" a strong male's voice stated, addressing someone else in the background. "Here you go—this is the office. He's not picking the personal line."

"Hello?" Joanne was on the line, trying to contact Shoty all morning. She didn't know how to get in touch with him, since they never exchanged numbers. Thank God, Allen, her assistant, mentioned the unusual number of soldiers stationed by her lab door.

"MICH Enterprise—how may I help you?" Marline said again.

"Yes. Good morning. May I please speak with… shoot! Sorry, Marlon, please?"

"Mr. Celestin is in a meeting this morning. Can I take a message?"

"No, I need to talk to him now!" Joanne said, a little annoyed because she didn't feel well. Her body ached all over.

"I'm sorry, but that's not possible, and I have no idea when his meeting will end. You can leave a message., I'll have him call you or you can try calling back later this afternoon. What would you like to do?" She paused, waiting for an answer.

"Guess I have to call back," Joanne said with much attitude before hanging up.

"Wow, wonder who that was? I hope for his sake that his new wife doesn't find out about all these women always wanting him," Marline mumbled to herself, continuing her work.

When the door finally opened, Shoty shook everyone's hand for the participation and assured them on a safe return on their investment before escorting them to the elevator. After the elevator door opened, the rest of the crew walked in, greeting the investors waving them goodbyes.

"You got everyone on board?" Mac asked while motioning for Shoty to follow him. They walked down the hallway toward the gaming room.

"I need something to drink. It was a long night!" He opened a bottle of rum, and within minutes, half the bottle was gone.

"Why you're just coming in now?" Shoty asked. "What happened last night? and everyone turned off their phones? I couldn't reach any of you this morning."

He seemed angry, because their phones were never turned off. He studied their faces as they all sat around the gaming room with their preferred drinks, but he noticed someone was missing.

"Where's Santana?"

"He went straight to his office. Maddy been blowing up his phone all night. That's why we all turned ours off. She didn't call you?"

"How would he know?" Riffle commened as he drained his second bottle of whisky.

"Why didn't anybody contact me?" Shoty asked.

"You know, you were asleep, and we didn't want to upset your wife any further." Tank explained, patting his back in sympathy.

"What?" Shoty asked, confused about the statement and the way they were acting, searching his memory about what might have went wrong. All he remembered was making love to Joanne and waking up in the morning to and making love to her again. He had no activity on his phone since he spoke to her dad.

He had stood up to demand an explanation at that exact moment Santana walked into the room with bandages wrapped around his head. Shoty was in shock. In the eight years he had known Santana, no one had ever gotten a hit on him. He was an assassin, and a very good one. He carried the title, "Son-of-Satan" for a reason.

It took a moment to get his thoughts together, to realize that it was a serious matter that needed to be addressed right away, before word got out.

"Okay, so what are we waiting for?" Shoty asked. "These people are still on the island, or they've left already. Where is Tech and Josh? They found them? Somebody say something!"

No one was moving. Santana just sat down next to Riffle on the couch, grabbed his bottle and rested his head back. The room was silent as they watched Shoty go into war mood. He opens the back-panel wall that revealed the artillery cache in that office. Shoty choose a couple of different weapons, ready for revenge.

"Marline," he said on the phone, "cancel all my afternoon appointments. I have an emergency."

"Yes, sir."

"Are you sure you want to go to war with the person who did this?" Santana, said, sitting up. "Cuz I don't." He looked around the room. "Do any of you want to?"

One by one, they shook their heads, indicating "no."

"What the fuck is wrong with you?" Shoty demanded.

"Man, just show him last night's heat signatures, and then he'll understand," Magnum suggested. "Put it up on the big screen."

Shoty observed the monitor displaying two bodies on top of each other, which he determinged to be him and his wife in bed last night. Then one of the orange colored images walked to another room. The second figure lay on the bed, motionless.

A few minutes later, Figure 1 came back into the same room. The lights come on a couple of seconds later to reveal Santana on the ground, with Joanne, naked, holding a lamppost. The crew had formed a circle around the room, observing Nock who was examining the still body on the bed.

"Now I don't know about you, but I'm just a mortal man. What I look like going up against a goddess? Santana joked.

The image of his fearless wife holding onto that lamppost burnt into Shoty's brain, he put the weapons on the table and fell onto the couch, scrutinizing the image further. Finally, he connected the dots about what had occured last night.

"Fuck! Joanne hit you?" He exclaimed, above a whisper, not really wanting to come to terms with what the ramification of this act.

Santana looks over at his friend, understanding what he must have been going through at that moment. "The way I see it, your goddess was protecting you, and she didn't know it was me. All she saw a someone in black, hovering over her husband," he said while closeing his eyes, trying to will the pain away.

When Madeline walked in the door, Santana's injury was the furthest thing from his mind. She was upset that she hadn't talked to Cage since she came back last night. Unable to reach him on the phone only made her worry more, because he had never "not been in contact with her." Then she found out in the morning after the hundredth call that he was in the hospital all night!

"*Cajou*, honey, what happened?" she said, fearing for him. She rushed into his lap and searched his head. She removed the bandages and planted kisses where she touched.

"Ooh, baby! There's a big lump right there."

"Yes, I had a minor incident. Doctor said the swelling will go away in a few days," Gage assured her. He was touched that she was so concerned.

However, she punched him in the gut, demanding answers. "How did this happen? Where was Jocks?" she demanded.

"Ouch! That hurts! It's a long story. I'll tell you all about it later," he answered, caressing her back.

"What can I do to make it better?" she asked, knowing she would walk on fire for him.

Gage saw the occasision as an opportunity to try and get her to come home. He had been trying for the last two years to persuade her to move to the chateau he brought next to Magnum's, which he had remodeled to suit her taste.

"Well," he said, kissing her nose, "you can leave Mag's house and come home so we can start our life together. I've been waiting to long for this. I need my woman to take care of me."

Madeline considered his request about moving in together. She had always refused because she believed that Cage had no in trust in marriage. They been together for three years without the slightest mention of it from him, nothing about marriage or starting a family.

Seated on his lap and worried about his injury, she realized that life was not wroth living without him. She finally came to terms with the fact he might never be ready for marriage.

"Okay," she whispered faintly, kissing him passionately on the lips.

"You said okay? You're moving in?" he asked in disbelief.

"Yes, I'll go and get my things. What time are you coming home?" she asked.

"Wow! Home! I like the sound of that! I'll be there as soon as I'm done here, after lunch. There's nothing to do here today Shoty cancelled all his afternoon appointments."

"Oh! Hi guys," she said, finally acknowledging the rest of her other friends.

"Yeah, we know you have eyes for only one person in this room, Rocket joked as he watched the two sick lovebirds.

"Shut-up, Roc, you always have something to say. Ain't nobody's fault if you can't find the kind of love we have," Madeline retorted, sticking her tongue at him. She looked over at Shoty, noticing the gloomy look in his face. "What's wrong, old man? Why the sad face? And Claire told me she met someone, and you called her your wife! Please tell me she's the one who chocked Roc, cuz she's already my bestie."

"Damn, I forgot the situation with Roc. And now Cage! What the fuck did I get myself into?" he mumbles, more to himself than anyone else.

"What you mean your new wife did this to Cage?" she said with urgency in her voice.

"I said later, Maddy," Cage responded, raising his voice to let her know it wasn't an issue up for discussion.

"Excuse me, sir," Marline said as she entered the office, "but I have a caller who's been asking for you all morning, and she's getting more agitated with me on each call. She won't leave her name. She just asks and then hangs up when I tell her you're unavailable."

"Just call the number back. Please and patch it through the intercom."

"You know," Madeline said, "you have a wife now. These calls have to stop. And what are you going to do with your psycho chick—the one who blew up your car?"

"Maddy, leave him alone. He already has enough problems," Mag warned

"Fine. I'll leave you alone, for now!"

"Alpha Two Commander Felix."

The security detail on Joanne came the intercom.

"You called the office?"

"Yes, sir. I couldn't reach you on your personal line. Your wife wanted us to reach out to you, sir."

"How did she make you?" Shoty asked. These were the best military personnel money could buy. They were supposed to be invisible.

"I don't know, sir, but she's been approaching us since 10 this morning, and we couldn't ignore her," the commander answered.

"Put her on," Shoty said after taking a deep breath while shaking his head, bewildered by the events of the day. He could hear chattering in the background. "Madame, your husband on the line," "Felix, call me Joanne," and "Ma'am, please, here's the phone."

'*Cheri*, my co-co hurts!" she blurted when she got on the phone with her husband.

It took a full minute for Shoty to register what she just said over the intercom—for the whole room to hear. Maddy can't hold back her laughter. People in the room had mixed reactions as Shoty scrambled to turn off the intercom and pick-up the receiver.

"Okay, I just have to wrap up something's here, and then I'll pick you up around three this afternoon.".

"It hurts. I can't even sit on the stool to work. I haven't looked at anything. I just want to go home and to bed so you can kiss it to make it feel better," she said in a tiny voice.

"All right. Put the soldier back on the phone," he said, waiting for the commander to come back on.

"Yes, sir, Felix here."

"My wife knows your real names," Shoty asked.

"She demanded it of us, sir! Again, there was no way of ignoring her. We all had to go through her interrogation, sir."

"She interrogated you?" he repeated in bewilderment, not understanding how trained killers, who would die before revealing any type of information were now freely submitting to a woman.

"You're going to have to explain that to me later, but bring her to me," Shoty said before hanging up. "Can you believe this mess? She knows her detail!" he explained to the room, "and by name! Freaking trained soldiers talking about she interrogated them! They had no choice but to reveal their identities? I know she's my wife, but she just a woman!"

"She's a goddess, man," Riffle commented. "The faster you understand it, the easier your life will become. Straight talk!"

Riffle knew why the soldiers caved in. Shoty was not seeing his wife for what she really was.

"Well, goddess or not, she's my new best friend," Madeline added, "even though she hurt my honey. But she was protecting you. She's alright with me. Can't wait to meet her, but I have to run. I'm excited about moving today." She turned and kissed Cage. "I'll see you at home."

"Home. I like the sound of that! See you there, my love," Cage responded, watching her walk away, feeling the joy of having her again in his life.

CHAPTER 17
JOANNE

She was riding in a Hummer with an eight-member highly-trained security detail, in route to Shoty's office. Ralf, Leo and Richard were in the front. Connor, Jake and Rick sat in the middle, while she sat between Denis and Gary. All men were heavily armed.

The entourage was a bit overwhelming, causing an ongoing scene, making people stop and wonder. *Who were they guarding? Was she a superstar? The president wife? Or some queen from Africa who was visiting Haiti?*

The gawkers were there at every stop sign or light that they passed. Crowds formed of people trying to peek into the Hummer, but those eyes were quickly averted when they see the heavy artillery the soldiers are carrying and the death masks on their faces.

"Guys, relax—the people are afraid of you," I said while observing the look they gave to the crowd, making some run for cover.

"That's the whole idea, Mrs. Celestin. That's how your husband wants it."

"Joanne—" I said, "please call me by my name, Jake. If we're together 24 hours a day and 7 days a week, you've got to loosen up a bit, and I don't think your daughter would like you to be so mean to people.

"No, she wouldn't, but that's my job, and I get paid a lot of money to do it," he explained.

I understood them wanting to do their job the right way. In the last three hours I've learned a little about each man. They been following me since the incident at Fabiola's house with Rocket. Each guard had a unique story—most relating to why they left home and joined that organization that paid good money for security.

The majority had been employees for more than two years at MICH ENTERPRISE. Most of were family men who didn't want to kill innocent people, but did because they were ordered to do so. Sitting back, I tried to figure a way to help with their family situations without getting them into trouble where they would lose their jobs.

After the Hummer reached its destination, the soldiers, in twos, formed a line so that I was in the center, while exiting the vehicle and walking into the office building. After entering the large office building and going up in the elevator, I was greeted by this nice-looking woman in her early forties. She had light brown skin, long natural curls to her shoulders, and she was about five-feet-four-inches tall.

She came around an old oak desk with carvings of all our leaders, fighting the Haitian Independence war of 1804. It was the most beautiful detailed piece of art I had ever seen.

"Hi, dear. My name is Marline. I must apologize about this morning. I didn't know that was you on the phone. I would have patched you through right away."

"Really? So how many women does he have calling him?" I asked in a serious tone, and I could tell by her face that she wasn't ready or didn't know how to answer. She struggled to find the right words. I continued. "It's just you said that 'if you knew it was me.' That kind of tells me he gets a lot of calls from females."

Despite her being a brown-skinned woman, I could see the color drain from her face.

"Don't worry about it! I'm new. He'll get used to me. So where is Mr. Marlon?"

"He's his in the conference room with the others. He asked me to put you in his office, so you could get some rest."

"Our orders were to bring her to him!" Denis interrupted, aggressive, not willing to let anything deter him from his mission.

"At ease, soldier!" Marline countered. "Your mission is complete. Please leave your charge and be invisible. Those are your *new* orders from you boss, and he wants to meet with your before he leaves. He'll give you the signal to approach."

With a bow, each soldier disappeared and left. Marline motioned for me to follow her down an off-white marble hallway that was decorated with exotic art of Haitian and African style—some of the pieces are strikingly beautiful.

She came to a stop in front of a huge, white-oak double-door with war figures from history that covered the entire frame. She opened the door to a humongous office that looked like a mini-apartment.

In the center of the room was a couch in the shape of a circle, which sat 20 people. There was an ottoman of the same shape that was big enough for all occupants to rest their legs. The couch was facing a wall of a monitors that played random picture of cities all around the world. Shoty's desk sat on the other side of the room with its back to the high glass wall, overlooking the city. A full bar, with other various art items, sat off to the side.

"This way, Mrs. Celestin. You can rest in here until he's ready."

She guided me to a side-door that had a hidden entrance. I went through the door and into an extravagant masculine bedroom that was both simple and elegant.

"Why does he have a bedroom in his office?"

"Well, on some nights he works very late and then has early morning meetings. It's easier for him to stays here on those occasions. He has everything he needs here… in case he doesn't make home. Once you get to know him, you'll see Mr. Marlon does not like to wake up in the mornings. He's very grouchy."

"Well now, let's try and get him home for now on, and I'll take care of the grouch," I mumbled with a fake smile. I didn't know what it was about Marline, but I didn't care for her vibe. Its okay. I can rest on the couch for a little while. Thanks for your help."

I dismissed her, walked over the couch and rested my head on the armrest. My body ached, and my legs were sore. I needed to elevate them. My thoughts ran wild with all the events leading to that moment. Feeling a bit overwhelmed—not knowing what to expect next, I had a hard time keeping my eyes open. I was fighting not to fall asleep right away.

SHOTY

As I was leaving the conference room, I walked past the secretary, who gave me skeptical look while shaking her head.

"That was two hours ago, sir. You're lucky she fell asleep. I opened the door to the office."

Joanne was asleep on the couch with her left leg propped up on the headrest and the other leg bent. Her position stopped me in my tracks. That posture on the couch exposed her co-co so that it was saying "hello" to me. I couldn't help but to crawl between her legs and kiss it, leaving little bites where I kissed and searching for her clitoris through her pants.

Joanne moaned as I took her right leg and pushed it back farther to gain more access to my heaven. She opened her eyes and glanced toward me intensely, with heat and hunger.

"My legs are sore," she meowed, rubbing my head. I used my chin to massage her center, caressing her thighs to rub the pain away.

"How does that feel?" I asked, wrapping one leg around my shoulder and stretching it out, then pushes it back and repeating that motion over.

"Ouch! A little softer! it hurts," Joanne complained.

"So tell me, what did you do to my men? They're not acting like the soldiers I hired," I said, moving a little closer to massage the small of her back and her abdomen.

"I didn't do anything to them. I just asked them some question," she responded.

"You just ask questions? And they freely give you answers, and that just it?"

"Yeah, they knew all about me. I needed to know all about them. Besides, they've been following me since that party." She paused. "Why did you hire them to follow me?"

I thought about that for moment and decided to tell her the truth.

"I knew I was going to take you one way or the other, because I get what I want," I mumbled, rubbing her inner thighs. "But you can kiss that team goodbye. I'll get you a different one in the morning."

I didn't get to finish those words before I was fighting for air in my lungs.

"Jo-anne! I ca-can't, can't bre-breathe! St-stop!" I gasped, fighting to get her hands off my tie. She pulled me to her eye level.

"You will do no such thing! These men have families to take care, and I like them. They will stay on. You got that?" she demanded before releasing me. Then the office door flew open.

"What the fuck is going on? Your vitals are all over the place—like you fighting to breathe, man!" Tank complained as he rushed into the office, monitoring Shoty, which provided a link to Shoty's health and all members' physical fitness.

Within minutes, all the members had formed a circle around Joanne, waiting on my command. I was still trying to catch my breath, grasping my neck.

"I'm confused," Sic commented. "Is he having sex, or is he being attacked, because he's in-between her legs."

"Nan, it's cool, guys. We just had a misunderstanding," I said to defuse the situation. I looked at my wife, sitting there, looking so innocent, displaying no emotion about what had just occurred.

"But we'll finish this at home. Give me a few more minutes and we'll be out of here."

I walked out the room, leaving her with the crew. I could read what was going through their minds, but I didn't feel like talking about it. I wanted to deal with the soldiers, and I needed some time away from her to collect my thoughts. Maybe I needed to get away from psychos altogether—except for one problem—I had just married one.

I walked down the wall past the mirror and stopped to look at myself for a moment.

"What the fuck did I get myself into?" I uttered as I continued to the conference room.

When I opened the door, all eight soldiers were on their feet, awaiting their fate. In that business, it was hard for a soldier if he lost his post or was traded into a different camp. It was a life or death matter, or a soldier could end up in prison for life.

"At ease!" I called while standing in front of the men, trying to figure out what to do with them. I couldn't be intimated by a woman, even if she was my wife. She didn't run my business, but my brain was running a mile a minute, walking back and forth, hearing her words in my mind—that these men were family men. I could have sent them to Cage for the rest of the contract, but I would have definitely killed them.

"Sir, let me explain," Felix, the commander of the unit, begged.

"You don't have to explain. My dear wife was abundantly clear that you are under her protection, and that you all will continue as her detail," I announced, caving in to her orders.

The soldiers were elated to hear that their lives had been spared. They clasped hands, celebrating their good fortune.

"Sir, please let the Mrs. know that we will follow her to the gates of hell and back!"

"I bet you will, but you can take the rest of the day off. See your in the morning."

"But sir, we just pledged…" someone called out as I headed for the door.

"It's okay. I have her tonight. Besides, I need to show her who's boss. Dismissed!"

I reached the office and was standing by the door with my mean face on as I signalled her to come to me. I noticed all the guys faces were showing concern for her, because they knew I was upset.

"Uh-oh! Someone's in trouble! What did you do to get *that* face?" Rocket whispered under his breath.

"Nothing!" she explained out loud, looking for and finding her shoe. She eyed me, afraid to approach, while I just stared at her, waiting for her to reach me.

JOANNE

I don't know what I did to get this man so upset. We were talking about security for one moment, and in the next, he was looking at me like I had horns coming out of my head. Then his friends all surrounded me, wanting to know what happened.

Now he was standing in the doorway with a grim look in his face, like he had a score to settle with me. I turned to Rock for support.

"Don't look at me! That's your husband," he repeated, shaking his head. I could see pity in his eyes. As I looked about the room, all the men had the same concern in their faces.

"I thought you were supposed to protect me—even from him!"

"Ooh, he's not going to kill or physically hurt you, but you will wish your never crossed him, from the looks of him. You did something very bad. He's not talking to us either," Sic whispered.

"You better go. He's not going to call on you again," Cage said, nudging me in the direction of the open door where Shoty was leaning.

"Bye, goddess. It was nice knowing you," someone teased.

"Fine, I'll go," I said as I walked to him.

He turned and left, motioning for me to follow. We rode to the house in silence. As we entered the foyer, he slammed the door, went to his office and slams that too, remaining there for the rest of the afternoon.

The house was lonely. Its residents occupied different rooms into the late hours in the evening. Shoty was in his office, drinking the day's events from his mind. He was having a hard time accepting that his wife manhandled him and was trying to decide what action to take with her. He was on in his second bottle of rum, so he did not trust himself around her.

She was in her room, waiting for her husband to walk in and talk to her. She watched the clock every ten minutes since being home. She paced back and fourth and decided not to wait any longer, so she made her way to the bathroom, undressed and wrapped a towel around her body with shaving cream and razor in her hand. Then she marched to his office and opened the door.

He heard her at the door and closed his eyes, not ready to deal with her yet. He didn't trust himself around her. Being drunk would only make matters worse.

"Go away, Joanne! Not right now," he bluted out, focusing on the view of the beach, with its still waters floating above the glow of the moon.

"I need you to do something for me. I can't do it myself. It's hard to reach," she responded as she entered the room and stood right behind him, dropping the towel to the floor. He turned and froze, seeing a glowing figure in front of him, rubbing his eyes to look again.

There she stood, with the moon as the only light in the room, which reflected on her skin, giving a magical glow to her naked body.

"Fuck, I'm too drunk! Joanne, go away, please," he pleaded, though not able to take his eyes off her beauty. He scanned her body, head to toe, and rested at her eyes, swallowing the lump that formed in his throat. He released a deep breath, feeling the liquor's effect dissipating from his body.

She handed him the shaving cream and razor, moved closer and sat on the desk, spreading her legs apart, showing him where he needed to shave.

"I can't reach here," she pointed, "and there." She softened her voice, watching the battle within, which raged between his anger and his urges.

"Look, I'm too drunk to be doing this right now. Can we do this another day? I don't want to cut you," he pleaded, trying to hand the razor back to her.

"No! I started already. It will annoy me all night. Please just finish it," she begged, spreading her legs wider for him.

Shoty had no choice but to bide her request. He applied the shaving cream in his hand and rubbed it on her nether lips, his hand tracing the form of her sex. The room temperature raised as he started with the razor.

Sweat popped out on his forehead as he concentrated on his task, wiping the razor off with his sleeve and continued. As the temperature grew hotter, he put the razor down and took off his shirt and undershirt before and returning to his task.

She stretched her body, moaning. "Mmm!" She arched her back, loving the feel of his hand.

"Why are you moaning?" Shoty asked, not in the mood to be intimate with her right then, even though his dick betrayed him. It was poking out his pants, ready to jump in. He took a deep breath, closed his eyes and traced her form again, wanting to rip off his pants and satisfy his urges.

"I love your chest," she said, reaching up and caressing his abs and biceps. She sat up to kiss his chest between his rib cage and ran her tongue all the way his neck, noticing the red bruises all around his neck.

"Oh, honey—your bruise, does it hurt? What happened?" She asked, concerned.

Shoty closed his eyes and counted to ten, mustering the determination to refrain from choking her in return.

"Are you serious right now? You did this to me!" He pounded on his chest to show her the anger he had inside over this situation.

She did not let his mood stop her from her mission, so she got off the desk and stood in front of him, continuing to kiss his neck and under his chin.

"*Cheri*, I don't remember," she whispered softly, her lips on his throat, working her way down to his heart. She kissed that too.

"I'm too much in love with you to want to hurt you, my love."

Hearing her say these words changed his mood. He watched as she slowly slid down his body and forced him to lean against the desk.

"You never said that you love me! Why now?" he asked while she kissed his belly.

"I show it to you with my body every night. If I didn't, you would never get close to me. Whatever it is you are," she said as she unbuckled his pants, reached into his boxers and pulled out his throbbing member. She caressed the length of it, while looking up at him. She used her closed lips on the head and opened her mouth, tracing it with her tongue.

She remembered her aunts' instructions and relaxed the back of her throat and accepted the length of him into her mouth, moving her head back and forth, until she heard him hiss.

"Shit, Jo. It feels like your pussy!"

He sucked in his breath, enjoying the sensation of her mouth, riding the waves, as she massaged his balls, sucking each one at a time and back to the head on his penis. Not ready to ejaculate, he focused his mind on other things, like how she was so good at it. Wanting to know, he opens his eyes to ask her just that, when she stuck her tongue out, swirled it all around his penis, moaning.

"*Cheri*, fuck my mouth!"

Shoty lost all resistance, and taking hold of her head, he pumped his dick in and out of her mouth until his body jerked with a force of electricity surging through them. He sprayed all his frustration in the back of her throat, which she swallowed.

He kicked off his pants, gathered her in his arms and they moved their lovemaking to the bathroom, where he worshiped every inch of her body into the wee hours in the morning.

CHAPTER 18

Joanne opened her eyes, blinded by the glare of the sun. She blinked to gain focus of her whereabouts, realizing she was in the bedroom, with her husband's arms wrapped around her. She smiled and kissed his chin, tucking her head a little closer, snuggling on his chest. Shoty kissed her on the head, tightening his arms around her

"You going to work this morning? It's about that time to get up."

"I thought you where sleep," she said, sitting up.

He removed his arm and rolled onto his back, givig her room to move her body.

"Nan, I didn't want to wake you. I've been up for a while.

"Why are you not tired? My body is exhausted and my throat hurts," she said as she stretched and yawned.

"Are you going in the office, or can we spend the day together?" she asked as she headed for the bathroom.

"We can, if that's what you want," he answered. "I'll just call Mag to let him know I'm home today." He watched her bottom bounce on her way out of the room. "Beside there are something I need you to explain."

"Like what!" she called, poking her head out the doorframe while brushing her teeth.

Shoty rose and joined her in the bathroom, grabbing his toothbrush.

"Like, how did you know to pleasure me like that last night?" he said in a serious tone.

"Is that what keeps you up all night? That I pleasure you and you like it?" she asked, noticing the grim look on his face.

"My aunts—remember I told you about my aunts? With vibrator and a banana… but my throat never hurt with the banana."

Done brushing her teeth, she turned to him, noticing that his body language seemed more relaxed after hearing her explanation. She walked toward him, wrapping her arms around his neck and planting a big kiss on his lips.

"Morning, my husband," she whispered.

"Morning my wife," he said, returning the embrace.

"I'm still a little confused as to why a bunch of old women would teach you the art of sex." he confessed, unable to comprehend their reason.

"Well un-confuse yourself, cuz if we have a daughter, they well teach her when she's of age."

"You will do no such thing, that is for her husband to teach—not a banana."

"Oh, you didn't like it? I did it wrong?" she asked, nearly in tears.

"No, baby," he said, concerned, apologetic, "you did it a little to well for your first time! It made me wonder if you really only used a banana. I enjoyed it, and I'm still getting electrical current when I imagine your lips on my dick," he said, caressing her.

"You liked it!"

"I loved it! Can't wait till we do it again."

"We'll have to wait until my throat heals. It really hurts," she complained

"Deep throat will do that to you, but let me properly say good morning to my wife." He bent down and felt her on her butt cheeks, then he headed for the bed.

Joanne and Shoty spent the last seven days, in bed not willing to leave each other arms. The only time they ventured outside of their home was to get groceries and for small walks on their private beach at sunset.

Joanne enjoyed the life she and Shoty shared, especially their lovemaking doing the day and long talks at night. Their "good morning" sex was one of the things she expected to start her day.

Shoty was unable to pull himself away from his wife and made conference calls with his business partners every day, working from home for about an hour—usually while Joanne was napping. The only unusual accourrance was his late-night calls that he went to the balcony to answer.

Their morning usually started around 7:30 with Shoty whispering in her ear.

"Are you going to the lab today?" Joanne would ask.

"Are you going to the office.?" he returned, and after staring at the clock, they snuggled and went back to sleep.

On the 16th day, the crew invaded the house, banging on the door

"Yo Shoty, we're here to rescue you. Yell so we know where you are," Tank teased

Joanne came to the door wearing only a t-shirt that Shoty was wearing by the pool. Tank took two steps back upon seeing her at the door. Riffle picked up a flowerpot, ready to attack.

"You kidnapped our friend, and we came to rescue him," Riffle explain holding the flowerpot over his head. Mag smacked him behind his head.

"Stupid ass! What's a pot going to do?" Mag said, shoving him out the way.

"Well, I don't know what we'd walking in to. I had to have something for protection." Riffle mumbled

Mag just shook his head. *Sometimes being the oldest is hard*, he thought. *Them fools have no sense!*

"Excuse the intrusion, Mrs. Celestin, but we came to see your husband. It will only take a few minutes."

"Sure, I'm sorry. Please come in. We were by the pool. I left him in the water." She moved away from the door so that they could enter. Riffle, SIC and Tank circled her, ready for action. Magnum's eyes rolled heavenward. *The stupidity never stops with these three!* Joanne look toward Magnum, inquisitive.

"That's your family," he said, "you have to deal with them."

Then the rest of the crew entered. Santana and this beautiful, dark-skinned petti lady, with deep dimples. She smiled, giving Joanne a hug.

"Maddy be careful! She might be armed., and we don't know the whereabouts of Shoty yet."

"Tank, you're in this foolishness too?" Madeline said. "You better cut it out before Shoty catches you. Please don't let them upset you, Joanne," she continued. They're children in a grown man bodies. Idiots!"

"Wow, you're Madeline? He talks so much about you. He never said you are so beautiful," Joanne said, excited to finally meet her.

"You're 'wowing' me? Have you looked in the mirror? You're the beautiful one, and look at this body! No wonder he can't leave this house."

Maddy admired her beauty. The guys had said she was beautiful, but seeing her made people feel they were in the presence of a goddess.

Shoty entered the house at that exact moment, looking for his wife.

"Bae, where you'd go? I miss you already," he called and when he turned the corner, his whole family was in the front room.

"Shit!" he hissed, knowing they'd never to let him forget the occasion.

"You're wearing a speedo? She's even got him wearing a Speedo." rumbled Riffle, not believing the sight of his brother in a Speedo. He left and went in Shoty's office to look for a bottle of rum.

"Hi guys, give me a minute—you know where to go," he said, taking his wife up the stairs.

Everyone gathered in the office, waiting for the lovebirds to return. Pistol tapped Caliber on the shoulder, whispering.

"Bet he's upstairs right now having sex before he comes back down."

"Man, shut-up with all that! But if he takes more then ten minutes to come down, I'll bet you all next week profits and that he comes down cheesing."

"Enough of this! You're in this man house—respect it and his wife. What they do upstairs is their business," Magnum growled.

"Right! Being silly," Madeline co-signed.

"What? He took a bet on you and Cage just last week," Pistol admitted.

"Magnum!" Madeline was shock, realizing how many times she and Cage had sexual exploits in unusual places. She blushed for the simple fact that they knew—when she thought they were being discreet. She looked over at Cage, who wasn't fazed by any of it. He merely patted Caliber back and put up two fingers, taking some of their bet.

After ten minutes as passed, Magnum joined in, "I give him 20 minutes and that cheesy smile of his."

"You're really doing this? Betting on a man loving his wife your all dummies? He's with a goddess. Thirty minutes and all your profits for the month!" Madeline wagered.

Simi laughed at the look on their faces, knowing they all just lost a lot of money to Madeline. She always beat them. It never failed. Nevertheless, he accepted Madeline's bet and waited for the turn out.

Thirty minutes and twenty-nine seconds later, Shoty walked through the door, wearing white pants and a white button-up shirt, along with a light blue jacket. He was smiling from ear to ear in a silent room that bursted out into laughter. After looking over to Maddy, he knew exactly what just happened.

"You just took all their money, didn't you?"

"Yep, that's because they're fools. Where's your wife?"

"Oh, she wanted to rest for a while. She'll be down."

"Damn! Shoty's the Man! Puts his goddess to sleep!" Sic taunted before turning to Cage. "Do you put yours to sleep?" He was afraid to turn in Madeline's direction, but wanted to know if his brother capable of shutting her up.

"All the time!" Cage said, looking at his beauty, blowing her a kiss. He motioned for Shoty to sit next to him and high-fived him in the process.

"So, you need to come back. Your absence has been noted, and some of your business associates are concerned about your being away for so long. The situation with Stephanie getting serious. She keeps sending her people to check on you. We have to deal with this right away, and your marriage contract needs to be stamp before you talk to her, or your 'Mrs.' upstairs will be your mistress."

"I know this girl keeps calling my phone every night," Nock said, "and it won't stop ringing until I pick it up."

"Let me guess—you missed date night!" Tank called out. "That's why she's acting extra crazy."

"Shhsh, shhsh! Lower your voice, man!" Shoty insisted, waving him off, not ready to explain these things to Joanne.

"Sorry to cut into your nap time, but there's a lot more we need to address," Mag interjected. "I have to be in Italy tomorrow. The girls will be with Cage and Maddy until I return."

"Yeah, I was telling Jo this morning," Shoty commented. "I have to go in the club tonight. It's the calendar moon." Twice a year, when the moon was high and near the planet center, they had to preform a ritual on the sacred ground that was located under the club.

The group then discussed all manner of urgent business and scheduled things for the next three weeks. They agreed that Shoty would go to work that very afternoon.

"Marline did a great job keeping up with your appointments in past weeks," Magnum added. "Also keeping Stephanie at bay."

"Yeah, I spoke to her this morning too. She's great." Shoty said as he looked over at his lawyer across the room. "Mac, can you give her bonus and a raise?"

"How much of a bonus?" he responded over his shoulder while counting Madeline's winnings.

"You can give her half her salary."

"Okay, she'll have it by the end of the day," Mac nodded.

Joanne entered the room, greeting everyone, before sitting with Madeline.

"Cute dress," Madeline said, admiring the ankle-length, crisscross dress with a beautiful design draping in the front that matched Shoty's vest.

"Oh, thank you. We bought it yesterday. I didn't think I was going wear it anytime soon, but Shoty said I had to go to the club tonight. You think its okay? Not overdressy, cuz that's not my area. I'm a jean and T-shirt kind of girl."

"You look fabulous! You two are picture-perfect."

The girls continued their mutual compliments while the guys were busy with their business affairs. Shoty had a hard time concentrating and kept glancing over at his wife every few seconds. He loved the way she looked—simple and classy—and the way she fixed her hair, in a simple bun that accented her face and brought out her eyes and full, rosy lips. The blue dress hugged her big, luscious breasts and accentuated her curves perfectly.

"Man, are you listening? You keep ogling over there!" Chopper remarked, snapping Shoty from his thoughts.

"Because my heart is over there," Shoty said, smiling at her and blowing her a kiss, which made Joanne walk over to him and plant her full lips in his, and sit on his lap.

Cage, not wanting Madeline to feel left out, signaled her to come to him, but she just rolled her eyes.

"Later for that, honey," she said with a wave of her hand.

"You 're not coming?" Cage said in a low voice.

"Fine! Madeline sighed, realizing he wasn't going to let it go.

"Just because Shoty did it doesn't mean we have too," she complaind before sitting on his lap.

"No, we don't, but my heart was there too."

"Ooh, I love you," Madeline purred, kissing him.

"And I'm going to be sick," Roc complained, "Now there's two of them! We'll never get any work done!"

"We *are* done, Roc. We're going to have lunch and meet in the office," Shoty assured him.

"Not yet," Mac countered, reminding Shoty about finalizing the marriage. "I brought the papers for Joanne to sign. I need to file them right away."

"What papers?" Joanne asksed.

Mac placed a folder in front of her and pulled a block of papers that had both Joanne's and her husband's name at the top. She started to read and realized what it was.

"It's the marriage contract and some other legal stuff," Mac explained. "Let us begin." He arranged the papers, pointing to the lines that required her signature and handed her the pen.

"This is the actual contract for the courts. Sign here… and there…"

This one is for the businesses. It means you have access to all your husband's investments, money and power. Don't abuse it!" he joked.

Joanne paused and stared at her husband.

"What kind of power?"

Mac cleared his throat. "Well, you have a great deal of money, Mrs. Celestin."

"I don't need money," she responded

"Regardless of whether you need it or not, you have it. Now let's continue. This one is in case at anytime, during the marriage, you and your husband have irreconcilable differences, you can separate and live in different homes, but there's no divorce. This is a 'life contract.' You are bound to each other. Your husband is and will be the only man in your bed," he read aloud and continued. "You agreed to that condition three weeks ago." He stopped talking after seeing the look on her face.

Joanne stared at him, not understanding all of what he said. She turned to Shoty for help.

"What?" she said, seeking clarification.

"It's okay, honey. I plan to be very old with you. It's already done. This is just paperwork for the courts."

"What does it mean I can't divorce you? What if I fall out of love with you? Should my life be miserable because at this point in time, I like your dick?" she demanded while wiggling off his lap. "Madeline— please tells me you didn't sign this bullshit!"

"No dear, I didn't. This is the first time I'm hearing of this practice," Madeline answered in a sad tone while trying to leave Cage lap, but he held her in place.

"Don't!" was all Cage needed to say. Madeline knew the matter was not up for discussion.

"Um!" Joanne began. "Well why do we have to be married? We could just be together, in case it doesn't work."

"It too, late Joanne. It's already done. Sign the papers so we can go have lunch."

"Well, Madeline, why didn't you sign the papers?" Joanne asked.

"Because we're not *married!* We're just boyfriend and girlfriend," she replied sarcastically in Cage's direction.

"Enough!" Shoty roared with a mace face that indicated he was displeased. "Just sign the papers," he commanded, pointing to the spot where she needs to sign.

"I don't follow orders! More of a reason we can't be married."

Shoty lost his temper and grabbed his wife to his side, hugging her to his body, whispering into her ear. "One: I will not tolerate your disrespect in front of my people, two: you're upsetting Madeline—there are reasons why Cage can't marry her that I don't want get into, and three: I need you to sign these papers so that Mac can file them today. Got it? If you want out of this marriage, I can put you in a body bag!"

Shocked by his words, Joanne went to the table, signed the document and left the office.

"Sorry, about that," Shoty apologized before the whole house was shook by a powerful door-slam that vibrated the pictures frames on the wall.

"So we're not going to talk about what happened in the office last month?" Sic asked, reflecting on an earlier incident.

"Man, that's old! I'm over it," Shoty answered, dismissive.

'What! What happened?" Madeline asked while moving away from Cage, who only stared at her.

"You mind as well tell them," Mag mumbled, "we all been wondering about that."

Shoty took a deep breath look around, noticing everyone was waiting for an explanation.

"We were talking about security, and I told her I was getting rid of her detail because they broke protocol. Well, the next thing I knew, I was fighting to regain my breath."

The room was in shock.

"You mean she choked you!" exclaimed Chopper.

Shoty lost it, having to explain the situation to them.

"Yes, Chop! She choked me—with a good grip I might add! Now, can we drop this?" he yelled as he watched Roc walk to the door.

"Did she just break the door?' Roc asked, examining it. "Damn! She broke the door!" he called out.

"I needed to work-up her security background," Tech said, glad he didn't have Shoty or Cage's problem. From the looks of things, those two weren't getting no pussy any time soon.

"Do it at the club tonight. Hopefully she'll be in a better mood," Shoty suggested, headed out the room to look for his wife.

Eventually, he found her at the beach, screaming at the ocean

"You do know the ocean roars back, right?" Shoty whispered softly from behind, pulling her into his embrace.

"This is not going to work!" she screamed at him, pushing him away.

"Stop with the screaming! I'm right here in you face. *What's* not going to work?" he asked, realizing he needed to stay calm in dealing with her.

"This sham of a marriage!"

"What's makes you think it's a sham? It's as real as if I stood before a priest and declared my love to you. I declare it to you before my whole team!" he reminded her.

"You threatened to kill me! That's not love!"

"I did not! Threaten to kill you? You asked a question that I answered truthfully."

"*To put me in a body bag*! Your very words!

"To protect myself and my family! Those rules where place centuries ago. It's our way of life. It's one of the reasons Cage can't marry Madeline!"

"What reason could there be for him not the marry the woman he loves?" she asked, crossing her arms. "According to you, that's what you did."

"You where a virgin! Madeline was not. That's their business. I don't want to get in to it!"

"You didn't give me a chance to want that life."

After along moment of silence, Shoty came to a conclusion.

"Okay then! I'll tell Mac not to file those papers today. You want out, you can leave! If you choose to stay, guess I'll see you later when I come home. At any rate, enjoy your life, Joanne," he called back before walking away

Joanne watched him walk toward the house, wondering if it would be that easy to end the madness. In her heart she knew she didn't want to spend one night without being in his arms. The small amount of time they shared together seems like a lifetime. She didn't not want it to end.

She tried to imagine what life would be without him and didn't like the outcome.

He had disappeared inside of the house, so she ran after him, wanting to jump in his arms and never let him go—only to watch all their guests at the gates, leaving the property. She sat in the house for a minute, not knowing what to do next, but she needed to be with her man. She decided to walk and catch a cab on the road, but within minutes on the road, security surrounded her.

"Madame, we were told to bring you wherever you want to go!" Ralph said as he opened the door to the SUV, waiting for her to enter.

Joanne was happy to see the guards and hugged Ralph before she entered the vehicle.

"Where to, Mrs. Celestin?" Jeff called out from the driver seat.

"Take me to my husband," she repeated with a broad smile in her face, feeling her heart ready to burst with anticipation.

Security was also very delighted to hear her destination for the simple fact they liked the new change in their boss, that life for him was much better with his goddess by his side.

CHAPTER 19

Shoty was not sure if he had made the right decision, but he wished she would stay. Brute force did not seem to work with his wife. His thoughts consumed him. He walked away from her, fighting the urge to look back. As he turned the corner, he saw family waiting on him and his wife.

"Where's Joanne?" Madeline asked as he approached the vehicle

"She's figuring out what to do! I told her she could leave," he grumbled as he opened the back door and got in the car. He leaned his head back on the headrest, lost in thoughts.

Cage, in the driver's seat, watched his body language through the review mirror, understanding his tormented feelings.

"Are you sure that was the wisest choice?"

"No, but I need her to be happy. She has to make her own decision to stay." He hoped that Joanne would be where she belonged when he made it home, in his bed, welcoming him with open arms.

Madeline was in her own world, staring out the window, traveling back in time to random faces of men on top of her. She could hear their shouts and moans of satisfaction, spraying their semen on her thighs. The penetration didn't hurt as much as her favorite cousin, coaching them to go faster. She lay motionless for three days and he and his friends raped her virgin 12-year-old body. She closed her eyes, fighting back the teas that she never allowed to surface. Finally, understood why she and Cage were not married, and why they'd never be married.

After all the years, she never understood the reason why she was raped. Lost in her own self-pity, she never realized Cage was holding her hand the whole time, their eyes connecting as he kissed her palm.

"I love you," he whispered, holding her hand to his heart.

She smiled at him, remembering that fateful day at Blanc Villa in the bathroom, where she was supposed to stock it with fresh towels. The crew sent her in there under the impression it was empty—only to come across a naked devil who broke through all her walls and claimed her as his. She'd been happy ever since.

Her conversation with Joanne affected her deeply, though they never talked about marriage. Cage noticed the change in her mood. It wasn't that he was unwilling to marry her. Instead, since joining the A.15, eight years earlier, they were certain rules that governed their lives. As far as he was concerned, he married her on the day he allowed her to control his life.

They reach the office, Cage parks the vehicle in the buildings private garage. Madeline unbuckled her seat belt, ready to leave. Cage pulled her into his lap, kissing her on the lips. Shoty exited the car, following the rest of the crew in an elevator that led to their office.

"Why the sad face?" he said as rubbed her bottom, kissing the side of her neck. He loved being close to her, addicted to the softness of her skin, her smell and the way she responded to his touch.

"Stop! You know I can't resist you when you do this," she meowed, kissing him, running her hand through his hair

"So don't resist me," he muttered.

He reclined in the seat, lifting her up so she could straddle his body, his palms pulling her derriere closer to his throbbing member as he gyrated his pelvis into the fat of her butt. His head dipped into her cleavage, planting kisses all over her breasts, in search for a nipple that he bits through her clothes.

"We can't do this here. They'll bet on us," she warned, caressing his head kiss his face. "They already have!" he explained, loosening the clip to her cat-suit around her neck and unfastening her bra, squeezing her breasts, putting both nipples in his mouth, sucking on them while working to take the rest of the suit off.

"*Cajou*—not in the car. You know I hate it in the car," she complained, helping him with the rest of her clothes. She fought the urge to respond to his touch, but she never had the strength to stop him. He always scrambled her mind.

"My dick's too hard right now to go in the office," he stuttered, working on his zipper, teasing her with the head on her thighs.

"See? He wants to come out and play," he whispered softly in her ear. He pulled back, taking off his shirt, working on his shoes and pants.

"He didn't play enough this morning," she cooed as she petted it.

"When it comes to you, it's never enough. Now stop complaining and ride it," he growled, inserted the head of his shaft into her soft pearl.

Madeline adjusted her hips, descending on the full-length, rocking her body back and forth, beginning her ride. Cage closed his eyes, enjoying the feel of her meaty sex close around his penis as her juices started to flow. He pushed his hips up to bury himself further into her core. Madeline held onto his shoulders, moving her hips faster to the sensation, the wonderful heat she felt every time she connected with him.

"Mmm, *Cajou*," she moaned, not being able to resist the passion growing in her loins. "Cajou,". she screamed, reaching the point where her eyes rolled to the back her head, losing control of her body.

"I'm cuming!" she stuttered, digging her nails in his shoulders.

"Cum for me baby," he encouraged her, holding onto her hips, forcing her to collide with his pelvis. He loved to watch her as she reached her peak. He slid his hand on her flat belly, caressing her muscles, rising up, kissing her between her breasts, shoulders and neck.

"Yes! Ummm, baby, you feel so good," he mummed, feeling he was about to lose control before she came "Stop!"

"Wait! Wait!" he stuttered, pulling her off him, sitting her on the back seat, adjusting the recliner to an upright position, joining Madeline in the back. With one swift move, he pulled her under him, entering her sweet cave, pumping his passion.

Madeline closed her eyes, fighting the memories that threatened to surface. He concentrated on loving her man, running her hand down his spine and up to his head, kissing the side of his neck.

Cage felt the shift in her mood, her body tensing under him. He leaned up on his elbows, watching the tears in her eyes. For the past three years, it was always the same—whenever he took control of their lovemaking. She always appeared to be in torment, fighting some kind of torture she refused to talk about.

He slowed in his movements, kissing her lips, sensually caressing her to sooth her worries away, only to her have tense some more, freezing like a rock under him. Over the years, he had learned to let her take control by flipping her back on top. He had enough of it and stopped to watch her.

Madeline struggled to regain time and space, concentrating her breathing, willing herself to be in the present. She realized that Cage had stop and was observing her with a curious and menacing look on his face.

"This needs to stop!" he growled in a low tone, fighting not to lose his temper. It had been too long, and getting the same answer again finally struck a nerve deep in his brain. He couldn't understand why she refused to trust him with whatever she was going through.

"You need to tell me what happened to you, and why you act like that when I'm on top of you? You act like—" He didn't finish his sentence, as a thought just occured to him, then he continued. "Did someone hurt you? Have you been raped?" he asked as he watched her lie emotionless under him—like the good trained soldier he taught.

Madeline froze, hearing those words for the first time they been together. He had never asked her those questions before. She searched for a quick way to defuse him, moving her body by rotating her hips, wrapping her legs around his waist to pull him further into her, which he quickly stopped by pinning her down. She remembered his instruction when dealing with an opponent—to never show any kind of emotion or fear. She lied.

"No!" she whispered in a faint voice, hating herself for betraying him on something they swore they would never do to each other. Madeline did not want to deal with her past. She did a good job of burying all those feelings away, refusing to invoke the pain by giving them voice.

Being a good lie detector, Cage closed his eyes forced himself not to react, controlling the anger that was building inside his heart.

"You know what? Until you are ready to explain all this to me, we are taking a break!" he said, coldly pulling away from her. He exited the vehicle walked toward to elevator doors, leaving all his clothing behind.

Madeline scrambled to gather his clothes and got dressed.

"Cajou! Come back! You're naked!"

He continued pretend not to hear her get in the elevator before finally turning to look at her. After the door closed, Madeline noticed he was consume by darkness and that Santana was back. could not stop the tears from falling She couldn't explain her past to Cage.

Joanne was at the front desk, talking to Marline, and she stopped in mid-sentence and froze when the elevator doors opened, and Cage emerged. He exited the elevator like a mystical creature out of the history books, with broad naked shoulders all covered with unique tattoos across his chest. Six pack abs ran to his flat stomach, while muscles wraped around his waist, continuing down his hips and his man-part, which was semi-hard and long.

He gives you the impression of a god, with the likeness of Anubis, Shango or Ogu. Time seemed to slow as he passed the desk on his way to his office and slammed the door.

"I've fantasized about how they look under their clothes, but this is beyond my imagination," Marline said, hyperventilating and fanning herself look as the door closed.

Joanne, too, was staring with her mouth wide open, having a hard time to blank the magnificent figure out of her mind. Shoty appears behind her, unamused. He bumped her shoulders.

"Oh hi," she smiled, turning and facing him as she wrapped her arms around his neck, look into his eyes, dreamingly—all thoughts of "naked God" fading away.

"What's this? he asked, not wanting to seem too excited.

"You left me," she mumbles on his lips, "and missed you the moment you left!"

"I gave you a choice, you can leave. It will be like it never happened, like we never meet," he said while removing her arms from his neck and stepping away from her. He wanted to think with a clear head to get a better understanding of what she wanted.

Joanne noticed he backed away from her took it offensively and yanked him by his shirt again, but this time, there was no tie to choke him. He immediately lifted her by the waist and carried her into the office.

"Do you want me to leave? You want to end this?" she screamed at him as he closed the door, leaving his secretary in shock.

"What is wrong with you?" he screamed, throwing her on the couch.

"You are confusing me!" she yelled back. "One minute, you're calling me your wife, and the next, you're telling me to leave! So which one is it?"

"I'm confusing you?" he said, taking a deep breath and closing his eyes to keep from wrapping his hands around her neck.

"You know what? You figure it out! I have to check on Cage."

"Yes, Cage! Wow! I wonder how Madeline get out of bed? That's a lot of eye candy," she said, fanning herself with her hand as she glanced at Shoty in the doorway.

"I imagine the same way you do," he responded as he closed the door.

He knocked on the office door, but there was no answer.

"He hasn't respond to any of our calls, and neither has Madeline," Sic said as he stood next to Shoty, worried about Cage's state of mind.

Without waiting for a response, Shoty opened the door and walked in. Cage was sitting at his desk, staring out into the street.

"You still naked?" Shoty asked, his voice echoing in the room. He read his friend's body language and was not happy with the change.

"Shoty—go back to your goddess. I'm not in the mood," Cage answered in a deep gloomy voice that Shoty knew too well.

"I'm going to have a hard time getting your image out of her head," Shoty said while carefully approaching the desk. "What did she do this time?"

"It's always the same bullshit with her, and I'm tired of it!" Cage complained. "Something happened to her and she refuses to talk about it. I can feel that whatever she went through was deep, and she's in a lot of pain from it!"

When Rocket opened the door, a crowd of women had formed in the hallway, trying to get a glance inside the office. "Man, put on some clothes!" he said. "You have all the women outside this office with their cameras!"

"Why doesn't she trust me?" Cage asked.

"It's not only you she doesn't trust," Roc explained. "She hasn't said a word to any of us. You have to understand that if she went though a trauma, she has to talk about it when she's ready. We can't force her." He threw a towel in his Cage's direction, standing next to him, looking out the window, and continued.

"I have noticed sometimes that she spaces out and forgets what were doing. I have a lot of love for her. Sometimes, when I've caught her in a private moment, I see great sadness in her eyes, but she covers it with that smile of hers. You can't force her, man. She'll come to you when the time is right," Roc says, looking over at Cage, whose anger was growing by the minutes. Roc walked over to the bar for a bottle of rum.

"Nothing, came back from the investigation either," Tech interjected as he came in the room. "It was only her and the godmother. All she provided was that Madeline's parents died when she was a baby, and she had raised her out in the country." Tech had spent three years searching for answers to Cage's concerns about the woman he loved and always reached a dead-end. She had grown up in the countryside, where there were no paper trails.

"Maybe I'll take a trip there to go see that godmother myself," Cage grumbled.

"And what? Scare her to death for your answers?" Magnum called out while coming through the door. "I was on the phone when my secretary barged into the office, demanding I go see what my people are up to," he said to Cage." Look, I can't deal with Santana right now. I have to leave this country in a few hours, and we have this thing tonight!"

Magnum hated dealing with Cage's alter-ego, Santana, who was very unpredictable and unmanageable. Wherever he went, bodies were sure to drop.

"Besides, you and Maddy are taking the kids, or did you forget?" Mag reminded him as Sic chuckled on the other side of the room. "What wrong with the hyena over there?" he says pointing to Silencer, who bursts into a roar of laughter, fighting to control it so he could answer him.

"He broke up with her," Silencer managed.

"Yeah, right. You wouldn't last an hour. You must have forgotten—when you flipped those tables at Suc Madeline, she didn't speak to you for two months, and that was a very dark time for you. Now fix the problem so I can leave in peace." He walked toward the door. "Shoty, I need you in my office. You too, Tech."

Everyone exited Cage's office, leaving him with his naked thoughts of staring at the sky and missing what he cherished most in this world.

In Mag's office, Shoty and Tech walked in, and taking one look at Magnum's face, they put all joking aside.

"What?" Shoty asked as he sat.

"This thing with Stephanie has reached its boiling point," Mag explained. "I was in the phone with her father, who's demanding a date to announce the engagement, and his flying in next week and wants to set up a meeting with you and Constant. He claims the faster we merger, the more money we can make by the end of the year."

"Why can't I just tell them I'm not interested in their marriage—that I'm already married?" Shoty responded, knowing the truth of the matter—the contract was set up so that neither party could rescind.

"Shoty, you jumped into this marriage with Joanne without thinking. You completely forgot you were practically a married man," Mag explained. "While you were on your honeymoon, Mac and I have been trying to get you out. We might find a way, but you have to meet with Stephanie tonight after the ceremony and discuss her terms."

"You told her!"

"Yes, I had to. She's the only person who can get you out, unless you want to go to war with Constant and her father. And this is going to cost you a lot of money." Magnum handed him the paperwork with the negotiated amount.

"Five hundred million! Is she out of her mind?" he yelled, breathing heavily.

"No, you're out of your mind when you pull out of the contract," Magnum screamed, fighting the urge to knock him upside his head. Instead, he calmed himself to think more clearly. "That's where you come in. She wanted a billion," he said deliberately to let Shoty know that he had been fighting the terms on his behalf.

"Don't worry about it!" Tech interjected. "Semi and Riffle are working to turn that into an investment, like they did with Rachel. Rachel was spending all Semi's money, and as a result, he's a very wealthy man."

Shoty took a deep breath, relaxing a little after hearing about their plans to help him out of the mess he had created. He was all for it—to marry Stephanie... and add billions to his capital. But that all changed when he crossed paths with Joanne. He then realized that he really didn't want to be with Stephanie and never had any feelings for her. It was all about money.

"Make sure you get her where we need her to be tonight!" Magnum continued without missing a beat. "I need you on your A-game. Now, lets talk about your wife... All the reports came back form the investigators, and I don't know why your wife is not in prison. She's been terrorizing boys to men since she was in high school. The girl has a stack of complains filed against her in three states. Plus, an assault charge in Canada that's still open. Mac is working on sealing them now."

"Yeah, she told me about those," Shoty said while examining the many folders on the desk.

"Before or after the ceremony?" Mag asked.

"It was before. She has a problem with men forcing themselves on her. We talk about it."

"We couldn't find any psych paper on her. Has she mentioned being institutionalized?"

"No! She has not!"

"Do you think she needs to be?" Magnum asked, his question hanging in the air as Shoty considered how to respond. He analyzed events from the last week and answered truthfully.

"I can handle her."

"Bet you can. I heard you almost got choked in the hallway."

"Almost, but didn't," Shoty smiled, amused by Magnum's annoyance.

"Let's hope so—with me gone in the few weeks. I need you focus, not you jumping into things without thinking. Now, you have to deal with two psycho women in your life!"

"I'm focused, Mag, don't worry about it. I'll get it done!" Shoty stated and walked out of the office, leaving Tech and Magnum to wonder about upcoming events.

CHAPTER 20

Fifteen members formed a circle in the middle of wide plain grounds above the highlights of the moon, chanting their creed toward the heavens in centering the earth, restoring balance to their circle. With arms clasped, holding their Ankh in their right hands, the chants continued until the energy vibrated throughout the ground and could be felt miles away.

The second ceremony of the year as came to an end, and its members returned to their underground lair, located at Magnum's club called PLIZE NWEM. It was a place were all members had their high-value trinkets, along with artifacts they collected were stored in security vaults. One thousand seven hundred and sixty yards underground, the crew rode in a private elevator, secured behind a secret wall next to Magnum's office.

The whole compound had a state-of-the-art security technology that was lights years ahead of its time. Not even a mouse could take residence anywhere throughout the facility.

Once the elevator reachd the top, the doors opened to the club area, which was a replica of the Coliseum in Rome. There were open areas, with its many private balconies, and a huge stage that circled around a dance floor capable of holding a maximum of 5,000 people. When there was rain, the whole structure transformed into a covered dome.

Cage was on the phone, desperately trying to reach Madeline, who refused to answer. He was becoming more agitated by the minute as he exited the elevator. "Roc, did you call her?"

"She's not picking up for me either," Roc answered. "I haven't talked to her all afternoon."

Shoty went straight to his balcony, where he left Joanne with her security. He couldn't wait to get her home and into his bed. He walked with a sense of urgency to have her in his arms.

Magnum called out to Shoty after seeing Stephanie approach the office door. Shoty ignored the warning, dwelling on his wife instead.

Joanne saw him and rushed into his embrace, their lips locking in a passionate kiss, like two lovers who hadn't seen each other in years.

"I missed you," Joanne whispered as she came up for air while wrapping her arms around his neck. His hands gravitated to her bottom as their tongues continued to dance in a sensual passionate kiss.

"I miss you more," he breathed, nibbling her ear lobe, forgetting they had an audience.

Across the way, Stephanie observed her future husband in the arms of another. With a heavy heart, she sighed aloud, to no one in particular. "My, my—he has never kisses me like that before!" She looked over to Simi, fighting back the tears that threatened to fall.

Simi then realized that Stephanie really loved Shoty and was looking forward to the wedding.

"Why don't you go in Mag's office?" he said. "I'll bring him in."

Stephanie just smiled, took one last look of her lost love and walked away. Feeling lost, angry and betrayed by the man she though was hers, she wanted to spend her life with him, have his children and care for his home.

They should have been legally married by then. She paced the room, getting her thoughts together on how to deal with Mr. Celestin.

Shoty was still locked with his wife, and they were chitchatting love words to each other when Simi approached them, moving up close to Shoty.

"Forgot about that meeting, man?" he whispered in a low tone for him to hear, and then he turned to Joanne, offering his arm.

"I would love to dance with the most beautiful woman here tonight. Will you do me to honor Mrs. Celestin?" he asked, bowing.

"Ooohh, you are such a charmer! Of course I will dance with you… if my husband says it's okay." She noted the annoyance on Shoty's face. "What's wrong? Is everything okay?"

"Nan, Cherie. It's okay. You go dance with Simi. I have to finish this meeting. I'll see you in a bit. Save me a dance," he said, smoothing her concerns way, kissing her nose before being pulled away by Tank. He turned and blew her a kiss, which she caught with her heart.

He closed his eyes to focus on the encounter, taking a deep breath and turning to his friends, noticing they were ready to support him in whatever decision he made. Tank cornered him on the right before he entered the office.

"Look man—I will ride with on whatever you do today, but before you go in there, I just want you to tell me if she's worth it."

"Absolutely!" Shoty answered without thinking. It was all that needed to be said.

"Okay, then that's all I needed to hear. Let's go and get you out of this marriage contract!"

Shoty, walked into the office to find Stephanie pacing back and forth, talking to herself about killing Joanne.

"You will do no such thing! You touch a piece of hair on her, and I'll kill—"

"Enough!" Magnum roared as he entered the room to witness the state of Shoty's anger. At that moment, he decided to take over the meeting.

"Now Stephanie, I spoke to you, and we negotiated terms we both agreed on. We are willing to pay you what you ask, but this plan has to be in motion before a single cent comes your way."

"Your willing to give me a billion dollars to get out of a contract?"

"We contracted five hundred million for you to be pregnant by another." Magnum recounted, and then he sought to clarify the statement. "That way! We don't have go to war. We won't react on our part… it'll be just a simple void contract." He paused and approached her, motioning for her to make direct eye contact. "No misunderstanding with your father. And you can finally get away from him," he reasoned.

"But I needed Shoty's protection," she yelled.

"Well, now you'll have his money to protect you."

The office fell into a deep silence as everyone waited to hear her decision. She looked at Shoty, unable to understand why he was just sitting there, saying nothing.

"So, you let your friends do you dirty work? After all these years, I never meant nothing to you?" she asked Shoty.

"It's not that I don't care for you, Stephanie. We never really connected. You want a big wedding, but all I want is a declaration. I know you knew it would never work between us," he explained.

"Why did you take my virginity then if you felt that way?" she yelled, feeling herself getting emotional.

"It was never my intension to take it there with you. You climbed in my bed while I was drunk. I'm not using it as an excuse, but you knew what you wanted. I'm sorry if I hurt you in any way."

"I remember that night like it was yesterday," she reminded him. "And I enjoyed our late-night dates every month. I looked forward to them."

Her father had contracted a marriage between her and Marlon Celestin, a light-brown, sexy, fierce black man that she fell heads over heels in love with. It took three years for her to get just a kiss from him. With luck, she climbed into his bed in that same year.

He was everything a woman wanted in a man. It would be hard to find a replacement, but one thing was for sure: Stephanie Lion-De Senat would not beg for a man's love. *If he doesn't love me, then good riddance! I just need to play with him for a little bit.* She contemplated ways to keep him by her side.

"Okay, I'll agree to it, but you must do something for me."

"And what would that be?"

Well, next week, I have to go to a gala, and there's a fashion show in the following week. Tomorrow night is the Children's Fund for Neglect and Abuse. I need my devoted fiancé by my side for the next four weeks, starting tonight here at your club."

"Are you crazy? My wife is outside!"

"No, she's in here. I have dibs on you first. She has nothing."

"Come on, Stephanie," Tank intervened. "This is a bit much. His wife is not that reasonable."

"It's non-negotiable!" she interrupted. "He can take it or leave it. His choice—I mean the least he could do is *act* like we had something."

"No! Forget it. We go to war!" Shoty shot back.

"Wow! You love her that much? You would crumble your whole organization to keep her? I wonder if she would stay if you had no money."

"Why are you being vindictive, Stephanie?" Shoty asked. "I'm willing to pay you the money you've asked for."

"Yes, the money I asked for. I get that you have no problem of paying it, which is why my father wanted this merger. Now, I'm to dishonor my family so you can keep your bitch? Or when you decided to put this little plan together, did you forget that I have to wear the whore badge?"

"What the fuck she said?" Shory asked, seething, ready to explode.

"Focus, Shoty" Mag said. "Now there's no reason for you to call her names. You don't even know her, and she hasn't done anything to you."

"She took my man! She done plenty," she said, resenting Joanne. "Where the fuck she came from?"

"You know—enough of this! If you pull out of the contract, those are my terms, starting tonight—or I tell my father about this little gathering here," Stephanie said, eyeing Shoty.   And I see you have my favorite band playing… I want to dance with the man who was supposed to be my husband… at least for one night."

"We need a minute to go over something. Please excuse us," Magnum said as he stood to leave.

"And another thing," Stephanie insisted, "no one outside of this room must not know about it."

Magnum motioned for everyone to meet on the other side of the office, not liking the direction the discussion was going.

Shoty in turmoil with his money and company on the line, felt forced to choose between his wife and his circle. He scanned all their faces to see that everyone had his back, but they were not ready for war. He closed his eyes and prayed that Joanne would forgive him, that he could come back into her good grace.

Without any hesitation, he looked at Cage, who understood what must be done, then on to Roc.

"Roc, can you take her home," he said in a low sad tone that tore his heart, knowing Joanne wouldn't stand for any of it.

"Yeah, I'll stay with her until you get back."

"I'm going to cancel my trip," Magnum announced.

"No, go on your trip—it will keep me busy, and it's an excuse to stay away from her," he exhaled. "Alright, lets do this! Oh, I have something to add." He returned to the office and faced Stephanie.

"Absolutely no sex. It's only four weeks and we are done—pregnant or not."

Enraged by his words, Stephanie lashed out and added restrictions to the agreement.

"You better not be sexing her either. She just might have an accident." Upon hearing those words Shoty lost it and grabbed her by the throat,

"This is the second time you've threatened my wife, I don't tak…

He didn't get the finish that sentence. Cage reached over and lifted Stephanie up to his eye level.

"She's under our protection. You so much look her way, and I will slit your throat. I don't give a fuck who your peoples are!" Cage warned and shoved her on the couch, like a ragdoll.

She stumbled and caught her balance, fighting a sexual energy that took over her body.

"Oooh! If only I wasn't in love with this one here, I would take you for a spin! Cuz…" she paused, scanningh his body up and down. "You make my blood boils. Damn, you're a fine specimen!" she declared, staring at them standing side by side, fantasizing about both of them in her bed and how much fun they could have.

But one look in his dark eyes caused her fantasy to vanish. He wouldn't hesitate to kill her.

"Forgotten! She doesn't even exist. Come on, Shoty. They're playing my song," she finished, heading for the door.

Joanne was enjoying herself, loving the live band. She noticed Roc behind her, whispering in Simi's ear, and then she saw Simi take off, leaving her alone with Roc.

"Sorry, Mrs. Celestin, but Shoty had an emergency at one of his businesses. He asked me to take you home." He motioned for security to form a barrier behind her while Shoty got dragged onto the dance floor.

Joanne took that moment to turn and only caught a glimpse of her husband with another woman on the dance floor before they were engulfed by the crowds.

"I thought I just saw Shoty with this woman!" She pointed, trying to look harder.

"No, Madame. He left already. Shall we go?"

"Do you know what time he might be back?"

No Ma'am! I don't, but he asked me to stay with you until he returns."

"Can you get him on the phone?" Joanne asked angrily, knowing that she just saw Shoty.

"Not at this minute, I can't, but soon as I can, I'll give him a call," he answered, making his exit from the club, dragging Joanne with him.

She pulled away from him, angry. "Why are you lying to me?" she protested while she stopped walking, crossing her arms over her chest.

Roc ran out of patience and threw her over his shoulder, headed for the SUV.

"In the future! Please learn that when I say we have to go, we have to go!" he said, shoving her inside of the waiting car, climbing next to her and motioning for Jeff to drive off.

"You son of a bit.." her words was cut off by Roc, who put his hand over her mouth.

"PSK, PSK! Don't say it, cuz my mother won't take kindly to that, and she won't never let you forget it. He removed his hand, only to have her scream at the top of her lungs.

"Shoty!" she screamed, fighting to get out of the vehicle, pushing Roc against the car door, contining to yell Shoty's name.

Roc grabbed her by the arm and pinned her to the seat.

"If you stop screaming, I will tell you what he told me to say to you."

That got a quick reaction from her.

"What did he say?"

"He says to go home. They're something he has to take care of. He says he loves you and he has to be away from you for four weeks. Everything his doing is to be with you for a lifetime. And listen to Roc's instructions… and no goddess stuff."

"He did not say 'listen to Roc's instructions!'"

"Yes, he did! Those were his words!"

"And how do I know that?" she yelled at him.

"I just told you."

"I'm suppose to take your word for it?"

"Well! Yes, I speak for your husband. Those words came out of his mouth! Not mine. Trust me! I don't want to be here either. But the goddess stuff—I added that one, cuz me and you are not going to have any craziness! I don't have patience for that, okay? Friends?" Roc finished, extending his hand as a peace offering.

Joanne paused a moment, staring at his hand, not sure what to do.

"You're not going to shake my hand?" Roc asked, pulling her out of her trance.

"It's not that! I just never had a friend before"

"Well! Now you have one, and a best friend at that! You know Madeline and me are besties! Oh, let's go get her," he said, calling to the driver.

"Jeff—to Magnum's house."

"Isn't it late? "She's probably asleep by now," Joanne said.

"No! She and Cage aren't talking. She's wide awake."

"How do you know she's wide awake?

"Because she can't sleep without her pillow."

"Where did the pillow go?"

"They not talking. Joanne—keep up," Roc insinuated.

"What? She talks to her pillow?" she repeated. Roc just stared at her until the truth hit her.

"Oh! You mean *Cage*! Yeah, I wouldn't go to sleep without him by my side either," she said fanning herself form the image earlier.

"Is there something I need to tell Shoty?"

"Nope! My man is very sexy."

"Well, don't let Madeline catch you looking at her man," he warned.

"I'm not looking at him. Her man walks butt-naked into an office building. I'm not the only one with eyes. Every woman there was staring and fainting, from what I heard."

"Stop staring. Maddy will cut your eyes out."

They remained mostly in silence for the remainder of the ride. When they reached Blanc Villa, Roc exited the SUV and offered his hand.

"So how does this 'friends' thing work?" Joanne asked while using his hand to assist her exit from the vehicle.

"You really never had a friend?" he stopped short and observed her for a moment.

"Oh! The goddess in you beats them up! Is that the reason?" he asked sarcastically.

"No! I don't beat anyone!"

"Right! Let's just go inside. Maybe Maddy can help you with the 'friends' stuff."

He opened the door and walked in, making his way to the stairs.

"How do you just walk in someone's home without knocking?"

"Knock for what? It's Mag's home. Come on, friend, let's go find my bestie. Hope those girls are not up.

Roc walked around the house, going from one door to the next, checking on the girls, who were sound asleep. Finally, he knocked on one.

"You do have manners!"

"Sssshush!" He turned to the doorknob and knocked again.

"Come on, Maddy, open up."

"Is he with you?" she answered from within. "I don't want to talk to him. "You can go away."

"No, he's not with me. I'm actually on a mission. Shoty has an emergency, and I'm babysitting his wife. I brought you a shoulder to cry on."

"Are you sure his not with you?"

"Now, why would I lie to you? He's not here."

"That's what you do. You lie to protect each other."

"Uh! I *did* see Shoty! You lied to me!" Joanne shouted, punching Roc in the arm.

"Ouch! That hurts! Remember no goddess stuff? Damn, Joanne!" Roc complained, massaging his arm.

"You lied! Who was that woman with Shoty," she screamed, poking him in his chest, backing him to the wall, continuing her assault on him.

Madeline heard the commotion and opened the door to find Joanne abusing her bestie. She took action to protect him by shoving Joanne aside and standing in front of Roc.

"Take! Your hands off of him!"

Roc airlifted Madeline with great speed—before she could land the punch that was promised for Joanne. Ready for the attack, Joanne countered with a left hook that landed on Roc's eye, and when he stumbled to the floor, both women froze and rushed to his aid.

"Roc, are you okay?" Madeline asked, reaching over to nurse his eye. She looked over at Joanne, ready to tear her apart.

"Chill, Maddy!" Roc pleaded, recognizing the murderous look in her eyes. "We talked about 'no goddess' stuff in the car, and you shook my hand on it," he said to Joanne.

"You lied to me! You said he left! But I saw him with that woman!"

"What woman?" Maddy asked.

Roc waved off the question. "No, he left. He was already gone."

Madeline, on the other side of the hall, watched Roc's body language, aware that he was lying.

"Where did Shoty go, Roc?"

"Not now, Maddy," he answered, rising from the floor.

"Why you lying?" Madeline persisted.

"Right!" Joanne cosigned. "And he thinks I'm crazy!"

"Yes! You are crazy," Maddy agreed. "You attacked my best friend. Don't do that again!"

"Sorry, but you tried to punch me.

"Because you where hurting my best friend!"

"Well! He's my friend, too, and his lying to protect Shoty," Joanne protested, focusing her attention on Roc again.

"So, what's going on? Why did we have to leave the club in a hurry?" she said, cornering him against the wall. "Why is Shoty saying I won't see him for four weeks?" Joanne backed him to the wall again.

"Four weeks!" Madeline interrupted. "What the hell is going on?" Shoty had no plan on leaving the country! I only wanted some time to think this afternoon. What is going on?" Madeline looked at Roc for answers that he wasn't willing to give. She, too, was in his face.

"Answer the question, Roc! Where is Shoty, and who was the woman?" they poked at him, repeating their demands.

"A minute ago, you were ready to kill each other," he said. "Now, you want to gang up on me?" He tried to maneuver out of the area, only to be blocked by a goddess and an assassin.

"What! Are you doing?" a chill dark voice roared from behind. "The whole house could hear your screaming up here! I'm surprised the girls aren't up with all that noise!"

"Thank you, Mag." Roc said, slipping from his attackers and taking refuge behind Magnum. "These two ganged up on me because they wanted to know about Shoty."

"What happened to your eye?" Magnum asked him upon reaching his side.

Goddess stuff!" Roc answered in a low tone before clearing his throat.

Magnum focus his attention on Joanne. "All you need to know is he's taking care of business!" He looked over at Madeline, letting her know that it was a closed issue. "Did Roc provide you with the message from your husband?" he asked Joanne.

"That's not good enough for me! He just can't leave and say, 'I'll see you in four weeks.'"

"It's going to be, for now. You won't see him for four weeks. I suggest you go back to your lab and do some work," he stated coldly while watching her reaction. "That's an order!"

"I don't take orders!" she replied angrily.

"And I'm not you husband!" he countered. "He's the one you can twist and turn. My orders get carried out, Mrs. Celestin." He turned to Roc.

"Make sure she goes to the lab tomorrow—unless she wants to spend time with Maddy and the girls." He turned back to Joanne.

"You're more then welcome to stay here if it's more convenient for you. Now, I must leave and get ready for my trip. Madeline—in my room!"

"Ah-Ah!" Roc teased as Madeline followed behind Magnum.

"Now! What was that all about out there?" Magnum asked about all the yelling coming from up the stairs.

"Rocket was lying. I didn't know why, and Joanne was beating him up," Maddy answered.

"So, you and Joanne ganged up on him?"

"Yes, he said Shoty's away for four weeks, and I know he didn't make any plans to leave. Why? What's going on?"

"Stephanie's going on! But I need you to keep all that away from Joanne. Keep her busy while I'm gone, and keep an eye on your knucklehead brothers for me—especially the ones that like to get into trouble. Don't let a day go by without touching base with them."

He took a deep breath, glancing at all the suitcases lined up by the door. His staff had packed them earlier, but he needed to go through them. He looked up at Madeline while she was on the bed, examining one of the bags.

"Now, you are going to fix this thing with Cage? All his asking you is to talk to him about what you're feeling. You keep shut him out."

"There's nothing to tell! He keeps hassling me about it, and I get so frustrated." She pulled out a black speedo and waved it at him.

"Give me that!" he said, leaping and snatching it from her

"Wait till I tell the boys you're a speedo man, too." She laughed.

He growled, which made her laugh even harder.

"You know, when my business partners see this face, they run for cover," he said.

She stuck her tongue at him, and then he went over and puts her in a headlock. They laughed and hugged each other. He took a moment to observe the woman she had become and the role she played, feeling bless to have her in his life.

"Fix it, Madeline," he said, serious. "I can't deal with dark Cage right now. Too much is going on. When you came into his life, it was a blessing for us. That's why you're our little sister. No matter what happens, nothing can ever change that."

"I know why me and him can never get married…"

"That won't change the fact that you're still our little sister and a best friend to some. That fool out there can't go a day without talking to you. "

"Alright, I'll try and fix it! But this time *he* said it was over."

"Because he was angry. Talk to him, Maddy."

"Fine! I'll watch over Joanne and keep them in line until you return."

"Good! I can always count on you."

"Have a safe trip, speedo man!" Madeline laughed as she closed the door, checked on the girls and went to the game room where Joanne and Roc were still arguing.

"You said we were friends! Well, friends don't lie to each other."

"Oh yeah? Well, friends don't choke and punch each other the eye either!"

"Your two sound like children!" Maddy interrupted. "Girl—save the argument. He lies to me every time to protect his brother. They're thicker than thieves." Maddy went to the linen closet to get some sheets. "So, what are you doing tomorrow?" she asked Joanne, handing her a sheet cover, and snuggling on the big couch.

"Guess I'll go to work. After all, I was ordered to," she answered sarcastically.

"Yes, Magnum takes his orders seriously. You want to spend some time with me and the girls? We'll be out tomorrow."

"Sure. When I get off, I'll come by.

"Don't sweat it. Before you know it, the four weeks will be here. In the meantime, let's have some fun! Want to be friends?"

"Yes! I would like very much!" Joanne answered, feeling at ease with Madeline.

"But no more beating Roc. That's my best-friend, and I'll to war for him—Shoty too by the way."

"You and Shoty are best friends too? I should have known! He always mentions you."

"Jealous?"

"No!"

"Good! There's no reason to be. Only one man for me!"

"You might lose him if you don't talk to him," Roc interjected.

"Be quiet, Roc!"

They stayed up until the wee hours in the morning, becoming fast friends.

CHAPTER 21

Joanne kept herself busy for the two weeks that Shoty was gone. She spent most of her days at the lab, or goofing around with Madeline and the girls in the afternoons. She had bonded with Magnum's perfect little angles. Between their father and uncles, they had everything life had to offer, except for a mother, which Claire was desperate to have.

Joanne had settled nicely in her new role has a wife, and she tried to understand the people around her and how they operated. They were very secretive about Shoty's whereabouts, and he still hadn't called to check on her. Even Maddy dodged the questions when asked about Shoty. Joanne counted the days until she would be able to give him a piece of her mind, when he came home.

The sun cast its brightness on the window, temporarily blinding Joanne as she stretched, getting out of bed. She felt dizzy again—the third time that week she had experience extreme discomfort.

Lately, her body ached, he breasts hurts, her nipples were tender and certain foods and smells turn her stomach, making her want to throw up whatever she had eaten.

It was Sunday, and She promised Claire she would take her to the park and stay with her the entire afternoon. When she tries to get up, the room spun, forcing her to lie back down to stop the dizziness.

By mid-afternoon Roc, knocked on the bedroom door, worried after she didn't show up for Claire's play date at the park.

"Joanne! Open up. Are you okay?" Roc yelled, knocking on the door more forcefully. He turned to the security force that surrounded him.

"You sure she's in there?"

"Yes, sir. She went straight to her room last night. She hasn't come out."

Roc tries one more time calling her name. With no answer, he lifted the panel on the wall and overrode the codes to open the door. He relaxed when he spotted her on the bed in a deep sleep.

After relieving security, he walked to the bed and shook Joanne awake.

"You okay? Security is worried about you. They said you haven't moved all day, and Claire was waiting on you." Roc joined her on the bed and helped her sit up.

"Can you tell Claire I'm sick, please? The room won't stop spining and I keep throwing up."

"Well, that's what you get when you don't listen. I told you not eat that griot on the streets. But no, 'Roc I want some Griot now.'" he mimicked in a female voice, reminding her about how she had him riding around town for some fritay.

"Yeah, I know! I think I'm sick from all that griot I ate on Friday."

"I'll call Claire and let her know, but Mac is out of town until tomorrow. I can take you to the hospital now, or you can wait until he comes back."

"I'll wait. If I don't get any better by tomorrow, I'll go to the hospital. Right now, I just want to go back to sleep," she yawned and snuggled back on Shoty's pillow.

"I'll get you something to drink. That will help settle your stomach." He got up to leave and remembered. "Oh yeah, listen—I have to take a trip tomorrow. I'll be back in the evening. I need you to behave yourself while I'm gone," he said. All he got in return was a wave of her hand as she fell back into a deep sleep.

Joanne slept the remainder of the day. The only time she got out the bed was to use the bathroom and drink plenty of fluids. The hours grew late. She felt much better. The nausea had stopped after she took the medicine that Roc brought. The only thing that concerned her was that some parts her body ached and muscles were weak, probably because she hadn't eaten anything since Friday.

She was famished, and have a taste for everything, wants to start right away, she rushes to the bathroom to brush her teeth.

Within minutes, she made her way to the kitchen and pulled all of the food out of the refrigerator. She fixed a plate with all different kinds of foods. Before she sat down, she turned on the television monitor to watch the news.

"Hello and Good morning. Today is Monday March 22, 1999. In Entertainment News, we have Carline Mattellus covering the fashion show from last night.

"Good Morning, Carline, from the looks of it, the show was spectacular.

"Good morning, Dean, Andrea—and what a show it was, everyone in the industry came out last night. It really was a fabulous display. The designer outdid herself with that spring collection—so many high-end designers showed up last night—like the beautiful and talented Stephanie De-Senat, accompanied by her billionaire fiancé, Marlon Celestin."

Shoty's picture flashed on the monitor—the image of him standing by a tall, slim white woman who kissed him on the cheek, showing off a huge diamond ring on her finger. Joanne blinked twice before returning her attention to the monitor.

"...whom I'm told, from a reliable source, that there's talk of a wedding as we speak," the reporter continued. "Did you see that rock on her finger?"

"Well, ladies take out your tissue, because billionaire bad boy himself is off the market. Stephanie is finally dragging him down to the alter," the anchor commented.

"I didn't think it was possible. This engagement was announces eight yeas ago, but we had never seen them in the same circle, and need I remind you that he's been connected to all kind of scandals over the years, not to mention the twins he was caught with in the nude two or three years ago at Bull's-Eye," Carline said, amused by the turn of events.

"So it's pointless for women to cry. When you're a billionaire, the world is your playground when you can have any woman you want," the anchor commented.

"Yes, Mr. Celestin has a track record. Stephanie will have a lot to deal with, but if you look back through the last few months, a lot of the bad boy stuff has stop. Until last week he really hasn't been part of anything—its as if he went cold turkey. When he started to venture back, it was with her by his side, so I guess we can safely say that Mr. Celestin is making an effort to make his upcoming marriage work."

"You heard it here, ladies. One bad boy is retiring, fourteen more to go in the billionaire club. Newscast Entertainment would like to wish the newly engaged couple blessings on their wedding day. I'm Dean-Andrea Jean-Pierre. Thanks for watching Newscast for your entertainment news."

Mouth frozen open, Joanne was unable to chew. Images of Shoty with all those women were burned in her memory, and there was all the stuff they said about him marrying someone else!

"Shoty's been here all this time, and he never checked on me, he's in town, he..."

The walls in the room closed in on her and she fell to the floor.

Blackness consumed her as security scrambled to reach her, but they had strict orders not to involve Shoty on any matter for the next four weeks. They rushed her to the hospital without notifying anyone and remained at her side.

Joanne opened her eyes to white walls and bright lights.

"Where am I?"

"At the hospital. Some men in military dress dropped you off this morning. Glade to see you up. You where very dehydrated. We took your blood to run some tests. They're not back from the lab yet, but as soon as I get them, I'll let you know what's going on with you." The nurse continued to check on her IV. "The people that brought you in didn't give us a name. You have one for me?"

"No name!" Dennis shouted from across the room while approaching the nurse. "No name. I told you that already." He was definitely irritated.

"It's just hospital policy," she explained.

"We paid you with cash."

"Okay, no name," she agreed, turning her attention to Joanne, making sure all her vitals are correct before walking across the room.

Dennis relaxed a little as he stared at nurse from across the room, moving closer to Joanne's bedside.

"How are feeling, goddess," he asked.

"I feel fine. It's just my body hurts all over. What happened?"

"You fainted and fell on the floor."

Joanne scratched her head, wondering what she was doing before she fainted. The memories flooded her mind.

"Dennis, is my so-called husband here on the island? Has he even left? she asked.

"I'm not at liberty to say, I don't know."

"You don't know, or you won't tell me."

"I don't have that information."

Joanne ran all the events in her head, from the time she met Mr. Celestin until that moment in the hospital. She decided that she must leave immediately.

"Dennis, can you excuse me for a moment. I need to use the restroom." She called the nurse to help her.

"I need your help. I have to escape them. Please help me," she begged.

"I don't know how! They're all over the hospital, and I could lose my job," she protested.

"You can't lose your job. You don't even know my name. Just show me an exit... and I need a diversion to run," Joanne suggested.

Feeling sorry the young woman, knowing what's it like to be trap in a relationship, that you have no control over your own life decided to help her out.

"Okay. I'm going to the front desk to pull the emergency alarm. I'll try to get him to help me," she said, pointing at Dennis by the door.

"Now, you will have about two minutes to make it down that wall by the elevator. There's a side door the employees use that goes all the way to Main Street. You can catch a cab there. I'll bring you your clothes." She went out and talked to Dennis, who posted himself at the front door.

Joanne hurried to dress herself and waited until Dennis moved away from the door. When the sounds from the alarm rang throughout the hospital, she made a run for the side door and slipped outside.

She quickly found a cab and cried all the way to her uncle's house. After waiting an hour, she was able to book a flight and head out for the airport.

In the meanwhile, security flipped the hospital upside down looking for their charge, scaring everyone in their path. Dennis interrogated the nurse, trying various tactics to get her to confess her part in aiding Joanne to escape. Unafraid, she stuck to her story while the search continued.

Shoty was in his office, staring at his wife picture. He wanted to hold her in his arms and missed kissing her full pink lips and hearing that dorky laugh of hers. Two weeks was too long for a man to be without his wife.

"Fuck, Joanne! I love you, baby," he cried in agony, kissing her picture.

His office door flew open, and Tank walked in, carrying his computer.

"Man, today's flight manifest!" he said, hurrying toward Shoty. "Look whose name's in D12! I had to check it twice and search the passport to make sure."

"Joanne Costello, what?" Shoty picked up the phone and called his house. It rang, but there was no answer.

"Shoty! That plane is boarding now! It will take us 30 minutes to get to the airport."

"She can't leave. She still has an active contract on her head. Where is security? Why the fuck are they not picking up the phone?"

"We're here, sir! She bolted on us while we were at the hospital!" Jeff answered from the doorway.

"Hospital! Why were you at the hospital?" Shoty shouted.

"She fainted this morning and we rushed her there."

"You didn't think to call me and let me know my wife is in the damn hospital!" he snapped.

"We were told not to call you for the next four weeks, sir, but because the seriousness of this situation, we decided to let you know we can't find her.

"That's because she's on a plane, leaving for the States in the next 30 minutes. Ground that plane! Now!" He yelled, rushing out of his office.

"You can't ground a plane! Just take the jet and meet her in the States," Sic yelled after him.

"She can't be allowed to go to the States, Sic! She'll either be arrested, or they will kill her."

"Okay! We're going to ground a plane," agreed Sic calls the tower.

Shoty had reached the garage and rushed to his car when Simi and Tank pulled up in a compact vehicle they used for emergencies.

"Come on, this will get us across town faster, plus it has a siren," Tank suggested, exiting the driver's side and motioning for Sic to drive while he and Shoty climbed in the back.

Sic was on the phone, unable to get any results from the tower. All his calls came back with the same answer: *they can't ground the plane.*

"I think we might have to use a bomb scare on this one, Shoty."

"So they can call us terrorists? I don't need that kind of heat right now. Who's on the ground, controlling traffic."

"They're the first ones I notified. They are working on it already. The problem is the plane in the middle of the runway, ready to take off. They might be able to stop the plane, but getting inside and pulling Joanne out is a whole other issue."

Simi, on the passenger side, called his dad, who picked up on the first ring.

"Constant, I need you to ground a plane right now!"

"You haven't spoken to me in months, and you call me to ground a plane? Plane run by a different set of rules. They don't get grounded."

"This one needs to get grounded now!"

"I need to jump, just because you say so?"

"Dad, please! Just do it!"

"It's going to cost you."

"Yeah, I know!"

"That little missy of yours up here? Cuz…

"Bye, Constant." He hung up.

Shoty sat back, overwhelmed at the length they would go for one other. The ringing of Sic phone drew him back into reality.

"That was the tower. The plane is grounded. They are awaiting our orders."

"Tell them we're on our way to get a passenger off the plane," Shoty commanded.

The car reached the front gates, which opened immediately, and airport security accompanied them to the plane. As Shoty ran up the steps, the captain opened the door.

"Hello, sir. What can I assist you with?" the captain asked.

"Sorry for the inconvenience. This will only take a moment, and you guys can be on your way. I'm looking for a passenger in D12."

"Sure, sir. Right this way." He pointed in the direction of the assigned seat.

Shoty, eyes lied on her, sitting by the window with her head down. He closed his eyes, preparing himself for the encounter. He walked a few paces down the aisle until he reached her row. She was seated next to an older woman who was trying to figure out what was going on. She stopped midway through a conversation when Shoty paused by her seat.

"Oh, you handsome man! You know what going on?" she asked.

Shoty ignored her, staring at his wife, seeing the hurt and tears on her face. It broke his heart.

"Look, I don't want to make a scene. Please get off the plane," he pleaded with no reaction from her. She just stared at her feet. After a few minutes went by, the passengers were getting antsy.

"Joanne, honey—get off the plane. I don't want to put you over my shoulders," he threatened.

The older woman noticed the tension between the couple and decided to move out of harm's way.

"Joanne, these people have to go. Please, get off the plane now," he silently roared, close to her ears. He made an attempt to left her from her seat, but she shoved his hands out of the way, grabbed her bag and exited the plane. He followed her, but he stopped to address the displeased passengers.

"Ladies and gentlemen, thank you for your patience in this matter. Your next flight is on me, just mention the date and time of this flight, and I'll will pay for your next trip. Thanks again have a safe flight," he said, shaking the captain's hand and exiting the plane.

He met her at the bottom step and grabbed her bags while she climbed into the car. He places her luggage in the trunk sit next to her, the vehicle speeds off the runway making its exit out of the airport.

Joanne sits in the middle between shoty and Tank on the silent ride back, to their house. She notices the direction they were going and requested.

"Take me to my uncle's home." Was all she said the car remain in silence throughout the drive until it reaches her destination, and parked.

Shoty holding is head down, trying to figure what to say, and what to do.

"Cherie say something," he sums up the courage to look at her.

She turns and gives him all her attention and roar

Say what?" Her voice vibrates throughout the vehicle

You lying son of bitch! Fuck you want me to say?" She punched him in the gut before delivering an upper cut to his chin.

Consumed by anger, she trashed the car finding any way she could to hurt him. She raised her right arm to struck another blow, but it collided with Tanks ribs, putting him in agony.

Shoty tried to clam her by taking a hold of her hands, only to have her body twist upside down, leaving her legs to attack. She kicked with her left foot, striking the ceiling, which caused a huge dent on the roof of the car. Her legs thrashed, out of control, with one foot landing a blow to Simi's left temple, rendering him unconscious.

Sic tried to help Simi, but he received a punch in the face that resulted in a broken nose and four missing teeth. He received a second between his eyes.

Still kicking, her feet damaged the roof, doors and windows of the vehicle and the frame.

"Shoty! Open the door let her out! Simi's hurt!" Tank gushed while holding his side, having great difficulty moving.

As Shoty opened the door, he received a kick that threw him out of the car and into the street.

Johanne emerged from the vehicle and slammed the car door, shattering all the bulletproof glass windows. Then she walked over to Shoty and kicked him multiple times

"I don't ever want to see you again, lying sonbitch!" she screamed, kicking him. She turned and ripped the door off the vehicle and attempted to slam it on his head. At last Cage appeared to have pinched a nerve on the side of her neck, putting her to sleep. He lay her on the ground

Shoty groaned on the tarmac, pain shooting throughout his body. Passing out, he watched as his wife fell in Cage's arms. He reached out to her, calling to to Cage. "Get her out here!" he pleaded, as the darkness consumed him.

CHAPTER 22

Alarms signal flashed out through the building at MICH ENTERPRISE, warning of immediate danger. Monitors served as automatic devices that buzzed, calling attention to danger.

Pistol came from his office and met Caliber and Bullet in the halls, who were also responding.

"What's going on? You see this, man?" Cali gasped while looking at his monitor. Pistol joined, bewildered about the readings.

"Is this thing right? It's saying that Tank and Sic are hurt. But look! The signature colors over Shoty and Simi!" Cali examined the monitor to see if was malfunctioning. Meanwhile, Bullet was on the phone, trying to reach them, but there was no answer.

"They didn't pick up! What where they doing this morning? When I came in, everyone was gone."

"Me too," Cali said. "I was going over the reports from the clubs last night. I didn't talk to anyone this morning either." He then dialed Tech's number, but again, no answer. "Tech's not picking up either. Can someone turn these alarms off? I can't think straight!" he complained as Bullet's phone rang. "It's Magnum. Mag, I don't know what's going on, but all the alarms are going off, and the system's saying Simi and Shoty are… Man, I don't know what it is saying!. No one is picking up their phones. Hold on. Let me put you on speaker."

"I know," Mag said over the phone. "I tried calling them. I'm getting the jet ready now to fly back. Find out what's happened and call me back. I'm cancelling the rest of this trip."

"I…" Pistol started to say something, but he was interrupted by Marline, who was running toward them, sobbing.

"It bad—they just air-lifted Shoty and Simi to General. They're both hurt pretty bad. Sic and Tank are on their way to the hospital in a ambulance too," she explained, her voice trembling. "Cage called. He had to leave the scene to take Joanne to Mag's house. He say's he'll see you at the hospital." Marline finally broke down, sobbing uncontrollably.

Pistol tried to comfort her, rubbing her back, giving her his handkerchief. "It's going to be okay, Ms. Marline. You know we're built from tough stuff. It takes a lot to keep an A.15 down. You know that."

"Yeah, but you've never got beaten by a goddess before."

"Joanne did this?" Pistol asked. "Damn she must have found out that he didn't leave town!"

"Mag? You're *hearing* this?"

"Yeah, I heard. I'm on my way. See your tonight." He hung up.

"Marline," Cali said, "tell my secretary to cancel all my appointments."

Cali and Pistol scrambled to prepare themselves and hurried to the hospital, not knowing what to expect or how badly their friends were hurt.

Across town, Cage pushed his 1969 Camaro ZL1, flying through traffic to drop Joanne off and rush to the hospital. He and the crew had gone through a lot of crazy and difficult situations, but this one took the cake. Never had he and the crew been part of a scene like this one: 1

gathered crowd; a dismantled car; Shoty, in the middle of a street bustling with traffic, unconscious; Simi, hunched over in his seat in the car; Tank, in agony on the sidewalk, Sic, holding onto his face and bent down in the driver seat!.

Helicopters flew all about, circling the scene. The paramedics and police were fighting private security to enter the scene. It was just too much chaos for one woman to inspire! he thought as he looked over at her innocent face, now unconsious.

He reached the gates to Mag's, drove all the way to the front doorand entered, carrying Joanne up the stairs.

Madeline met him halfway. Their eyes locked, and for a moment, their problems seemed non-existent; they longed to be in each other's arms.

Madeline scanned his body, noticing he'd lost weight, but he had bags under his eyes. She took a deep breath, rolling her eyes away from him."

"What happened? Is she okay?"

"Yes, she's just sleeping. I have to go meet the rest of the crew at the hospital," he explained while making his way to the game room, where he laid Joanne on the couch.

"Yeah," she responded. "I just got off the phone with Mag, and Roc is on his way. He says about two hours. Mag will be here by 2 in the morning. Soon as I get someone to stay with the girls, I'll be there… at the hospital."

"No, I need you to stay here with Joanne to look after her." He tried hard to stay focused, but he had missed her for the last three weeks. When he got up to leave, she blocked his path.

"Can you come to my bed tonight? or when this situation is over?"
She moved closer to him inhale his masculine scent, which she missed.

"I'm in your bed every night. You're the one who's not in it!" he
rebutted.

"That's because you said we were through," she whimpered,
standing nose to nose with him.

"Are you ready to tell me why you act like that, cuz that's not
normal."

"What do you want me to say, Oliver? I can't make shit up to satisfy
you!" Angry, she turned and walked away.

He held back all the rage he felt, not reacting to the lying game she
was playing. He exhaled and walked out the door.

"Then don't!"

Joanne, resting on the couch, drifted to a world of magic. The stars
floated around her and she was weightless in the air. Brilliant, colorful
light surrounded her body. She lifted her hand and waved some of the
stars away, removing them from her eyes. She looked around to see
miles and miles of stars and colors, feeling at home and at peace.

"Hello, beautiful!" a bright star whispered in her ear. "You're not
dreaming. You are where you need to be. This is who you are by nature,
a child of the universe, and I need you to go and help Simi. He needs
you to be by his side," the voice from the star commanded. "Get up and
go! Now, Go!" it kept repeating as it faded away.

Joanne jumped up, noticing she was in the game room at Magnum's
house. She looked to see if anyone was in the room. Madeline came
through the door see her in a state of shock.

"Ah, you up? Cage just dropped you off. Please tell me what
happened, cuz I'm getting all kind of crazy stories."

"I don't know, but I have to get to Simi," she said in daze, staring
past the door.

Cage arrived at the hospital to the scene of reporters lining the
street, trying to get the story. The police were upset because the crime
scene was cleared before they had a chance to investigate. All they were
left with was an alleged accident, and since the hospital was privately-
owned, there woulds be no press conference about the incident.

The side of the hospital with the operating rooms was secluded
from the public so that only those involved in their organization were
allowed to access the Pacific Wing.

When Cage reached the floor, the rest of the crew were in the waiting area.

"You spoke to the doctors yet? Have you talked to Nock?"

'No, they are working on Shoty. He went to observe them."

Cage sat next to Chopper, who was zoned out and in his own world."

"How bad is thing, man? I'm not ready to lose a brother—not like this, man," AK choked, not willing to believe the moment could be the end their brotherhood.

"Let's not jump to conclusions. We'll wait for the facts!" Riffle insisted, hopeful. "Let the doctors do their job."

"Facts, man, the computer says, it says… There's no color around SimiPistol said, freaking out. "It's all black. The report says there's swelling of the brain. And Shoty—there's no color. There's nothing! What does that mean?"

Cage sat back watching the agony on all their faces, remembering a time not so long ago when they were in a similar situation with MICH, when she passed away on the riverbank. Even though her body was never found, it was confirmed that she could not have survived that five-hundred-foot fall into the river's deep caves.

He also noticed Mac trembling on his chair, not participating on any of their conversation.

"You okay there, Mac?" Cage asked.

"I have two of my brothers fighting for their life over bullshit!" Mac responded, his voice cracking with emotion. AK patted his back to console him.

"It going to be okay, man. We're going to get through this. All four of them are going to walk out of this and laugh in our faces. You'll see, you'll see," he kept repeating as he walked to the other side of the hallway.

Minutes later, Nock came out of the OR with Sic and Tank. He assisted them to a chair, where the crew huddled together, concerned about Shoty and Simi.

"Shoty's in stable condition. He's okay—bruised up a bit, but okay. Let me run and see what's going on with Simi. I'll send one of the associates to come and take you to Shoty," Nock explains as he left.

Tank was treated for a fractured rib and a broken wrist. He would have to wear a support for his rib cage for a few weeks.

Sic a broken nose and lost of four teeth in the front gum line. He would have to see a dentist. He also had minor cuts and bruises from the shattered glass.

Hours later, and still there was no change in Simi's condition. The doctors used techniques to alleviate the pressure from his brain and ran tests to make sure his brain was not hemmoraging.

Suddenly the door flew open and Rachelle rushed in, demanding to see her man. Tears drenched her blouse, as she had been crying on the flight from Gonaives. Not long after her entrance, Marie and Reginald Constant, Simi's parents, came through the same door. As Marie looked around in the room, she noticed one of her children was missing.

"Where's Michael?" she asked

"He had a business meeting today in Jacmel. He'll be here soon," Tech answered.

Marie's eyes fell on Mario, sitting in the corner trembling. She walked over to him. "Can you move over?" She sat next to him and held his hand, at which time he lost it and cried on her shoulders.

"Where did Rachelle go?" she asked.

"Who was going to hold her down?" AK asked, shaking his head. "Not me! She went to find out what they are 'doing to her man.' Her words!"

"That poor girl! Since the moment she heard the news, she hasn't stopped. I hope Simi do something about her," Marie continued. "She worshipped the ground he walked on. You need to put some sense into his head. He needs to marry the girl already!"

"Simi going to do what he want to do in his own time," Roc commented as he came through the door and overheard his mother. "Father…" Roc walked over to Marie and kissed her on the check before punching his little brother, Mac.

"Man, cut that shit out and man-up!" he scolded.

"That's all for Marie's benefit," Reginald complained, watching his son, who always hit on his wife. "And he thinks its funny."

Roc's phone beeped for an incoming call. He kicked Mac a final time before answering.

"Yeah? Oh hey, Maddy."

"Joanne wants to talk to you."

"Not right this moment. I'll call you when I get a chance."

"No, Roc, she wants to talk to you now."

"Okay, put her on," he said coldly."I'm really not in the mood to deal with her." The room got really quiet, as everyone knew who was on the other line.

"Can you come get me? I need to be at the hospital, please."

"Why do *you* need to be?"

"I'm part of this family too. That's also my brother up there, Roc. Please come get me."

"I don't think that's a good idea. There are people here that might not welcome you."

"Fine. I'll get Cage to come and get me."

"Yeah, that's not going to happen. He's incapable of reasoning right now... not until Shoty and Simi walk out of this hospital."

"Okay, then I'll take a cab up there."

"Do yourself a favor, Joanne, and stay away and well-hidden." Roc shook his head and hung up the phone.

"So, can someone explain what happened, and why my sons are fighting for their lives?" Constant roared, unable to relax ever since he got the news. "While on the plane, I tried to figure out who the attackers were. The scene had been cleaned up pretty fast, which means you cleaned it up. Why?" he asked, speaking to the entire room. No one answered as no one was ready to share information with Constant yet.

"Not now, Constant. Later," Roc answered.

The doctors came in and explained what was being done to Reginald Constant in the operating room. They had relieved some of the pressure from his brain, and at that moment, they' were waiting to see if he would slip into a permanent coma, which was about 90% certain.

The doctor's exit left everyone in the room with mix emotions. Marie follows them to Simi's room, crying at seeing her child motionless on a bed with all kinds of tubes going in and out of his body.

Rachelle was beside herself with grief, sitting at the foot of the bed. The image of her child lying helpless, fighting for his life, rattled Marie to the point that she left the room.

Roc had no emotion as he stared off into space, upset with Joanne for calling him, and because she did not listen to his words.

At that very moment, Joanne entered the room.

Everyone in shock at seeing her standing there, her eyes are puffy from crying, her hair fizzled, looking like she had been zapped by electricity.

Bullet was the first to break the awkward silence.

"You came to finish the job?" he snarled.

"Shut-up, Bullet!" She approached Roc and pled her case.

"Please, Roc. I need to see him. I don't why, but I need to be by him."

Roc was angry because she came to the hospital after he just told her not to. He lost it.

"I just told you not to come here! Why can't you follow a simple instruction? he roared.

"Be careful, Roc," Bullet intervened, wary, circling around Joanne.

"Man, sit down!" Roc scolded. "You want do be in a bed next to them too!" He turned back to Joanne, who stood there with tears in her eyes, seeming innocent.

"Well, if the girl wants to see her lover," Marie interjected, "who are we to tell her 'no'?" As she glanced over at Joanne, she could clearly see why the boys lost their heads over her.

"She wants to see Simi?" Roc sighed, scowling as he turned toward Marie. "Your son, Mother, who *she* put in that bed in there in the first place." Roc was angry as he imagined a life without his two brothers. He wanted to hurt Joanne as much as her actions had hurt him. Thinking, he decided to let Joanne face his mother's wrath.

"Let's make this interesting. If you can get past her," he said, pointing in Marie's direction, "and make it through these doors, I'll take you in there myself."

"Michael, I'm confused. What does she have to do with all of this?" Marie asked.

"She's the one who did it! She beat up all four of them and demolished a car in the process!"

"I though your guys where attacked by your enemies! How is this possible?" Marie asked, confused. She looked Joanne over again to see a woman who was just five-feet-seven-inches tall, a 175-pound, beautiful girl, seeming to be incapable of hurting a fly.

"Michael, get her out of here!" his father, Constant mumbled, displeased with the boy's response to the woman.

"Since when do your put your mistress in the circle with family?"

"Be quiet, Dad, before I let her loose on you!" Michael threatened. "And for your info, she's not a mistress!"

"Somebody better start talking!" Marie insisted. "I want to know how this woman hurt my son!"

"She's a goddess, Miss Marie!" Bullet yelled from across the room, "and she has super powers." Satisfied with his explanation, Bullet went back to typing on his computer. Marie shook her head, amazed by the stupidity of it all, and spoke out to no one in particular.

"Is he smoking that thing again? Cuz I know you all have to be smoking!" She pointed her finger, going from one person to the next, but all the occupants just bowed their heads, refusing to make eye contact with her.

"He's not lying. He's telling you the truth," Cage confirmed.

"You, too?" she sighed.

"Marie!" Reginald exclaimed with excitement in his voice. He stood and approached Joanne to examine more closely.

"Your telling me you got beat up by a girl?" the older woman continued.

"Marie!" he insisted as he searched for his phone.

"What are you getting excited about, Constant?" she asked.

"Look at her... and feel around you..." he said as he dialed numbers on his phone.

"I need you in Port-Au-Prince now!" he said into the phone before turning to his wife for confirmation on what said the boys had said about the young lady.

Marie was speechless as she felt the intensified energy in the room. She had always thought her husband's obsession with demigods was a bit cuckoo. He had been researching them as long as they'd been together over thirty years.

Marie examined the young woman in front of her, who was crying her heart out, unfazed by any of the things they were saying about her. Her only focus involved what she needed to get done.

"It was never my intention to hurt your son, Ma'am," Joanne said, "but right now I have an urge to be by him. I've never felt so bottled-up. It's like I have ton of energy inside, and I need to get it out, and it's pointing me toward him. I mean him no harm."

Marie sensed the young woman's heartfelt love for her son and could not stand in her way. Yet before she was able to say a word, her husband called out from the O.R. door.

"Let's go, young lady. Come on. He's this way."

Joanne rushed to him, hurrying through the doors.

"Why is your husband acting extra strange?" Roc asked his mother as the door closes.

"He's research on demigods. I think he has finally found a female demigod," Marie explained to them. Moments later, Constant came running back.

"Marie, what are we going to do about Rachelle? I love her as a daughter, but Simi marrying a goddess is beyond what I ever expected."

"Simi can't marry her," Roc disagreed. "That's not his girl."

"Then who does she belong to?" Constant asked the silent room.

"Well, come on—tell me already, cuz we need to act quick before this gets out… Cuz they will try to steal her!"

Constant looked over all of the man he claimed as his sons many years earlier. He always made it a point to be by their sides, even though they hated him with a passion. No one spoke, so he waited, until finally Marie, figuring everything out, took hold of her husband arm.

"It's Shoty's girl," she whispered, low.

"Shoty's? That's impossible!" Constant countered. "He's contracted to a marriage already, and it was in the news that he was with that Stephanie girl! And you said she wasn't a mistress!" he yelled at Roc.

"She not!" he answered as he watched his dad pacing the room back and forth, deep in thought.

"Okay—minor set back, but we can make it work!" Constant said, talking to himself, trying to figure out his options.

"Okay Mac, get me the contract. Let's see what we can do to get out of it."

"We can't get out of it. You set it up that way," Mac reminded him.

"There's not a thing I can't get out of. Just get the contract."

"It's on my desk at the office," Mac responded.

"Good. Go get it. Where's Mag? He's my negotiator. He always knows the right way to talk to these hostile people."

"He'll be here in the middle of the night, flying in from Italy," Mac explained.

"Riffle, here's my phone," Constant continued. "Contact Stephanie's father and let him know I need to speak to him right away. I'm going back in the room. I just left Joanne and ran back for Marie. I'm glad its Shoty and not Simi, cuz I love Rachelle—even though she gets on my last nerve and is always in my personal affairs. I wouldn't have it any other way." Excited, Constant dragged Marie with him, motioning for everyone to follow him to Simi's room.

Rachelle watched Joanne crying her eyes out over her man, and immediately reacted.

"What are you doing? Get away from him, you bitch! He's my man!" She spat angrily and shoved Joanne away from the bed.

Joanne was dazed so she didn't really see Rachelle until she felt the shove.

"What are you doing?" Joanne asked. She looked at the pretty, light-chocolate, diamond-faced girl with big bright eyes that sparkles every time she blinked, a girl with long curls down to her shoulders.

"He's my man," the woman insisted.

"Well, good for you. At least one of us has one! Hi, I'm Joanne. I just need to be by him. I don't know what happened in the car," she confessed to put the woman at ease. She walked closer to the bed.

"Joanne? Are you really Shoty's wife?" Rachelle asked.

"I don't think so. But how do you know about me?"

"Shoty told me he got married, and we where planning a trip to come and meet you. We were waiting to get something situated before Constant got wind of it. Besides, I talk to Roc everyday."

Joanne stood by the bed, staring at Simi's lifeless body, crying all over again, laying her head on his chest, wishing he would get up and walk out of the hospital. She closed her eyes and thought of only that.

As the world closes around her, she saw herself in the air, the wind swirling, the ocean roaring, the room growing extremely hot, as if the Earth wanted to swallow them to its core.

Joanne saw many versions of herself floating above her and around Simi, and one of them opened her mouth cast a bright blue light into Simi's chest then follows it. All the electrical tops and sizzles in the room, the rest of her versions returned to their rightful owner.

Constant turned the corner to see the light that flashed in the room. He rushed in to witness the light that was transferred into Simi. Joanne stood there, her arms extended out while she was in a dazed state. Everything in sight started to blur. She was able to see Roc running towards her. She reached out her hands to him, feeling the world swallowing her.

"Roc, catch me," she whispered.

Everything moved in slow-motion—Roc running to catch Joanne as she was falling, Constant moving to action, trying to stop him, but he was shoved out the way and hit the ground.

Roc took hold of Joanne and got zapped to the nearest wall by electricity.

"That's what I was trying to stop. You can't touch her." He looked over to Cage, who was already at Roc side

"I need Santana," he said. With that, Cage transformed to his demigod self and picked Joanne off the floor into his arms.

"We have to get out of here. We can't let people see this. Get the security cameras and the clean-up team in here. We have to leave the hospital right now," he says, barking orders.

"Somebody shut Constant up, please! He's giving me a headache," Simi complained from the bed.

Everyone froze, staring at the bed. They saw a crown of light surrounding him while he sat up. Simi notices Joanne in Cage's arms, out cold.

"What happened? Where's Shoty? Come lay her right here," he insisted when he saw Roc on the floor, ready to jump off the bed

"Relax, man, we got him." Rachelle helped Simi with the tubes from the IV. "Santana, get Joanne out of here," Constant barked again.

He turned to his wife. "Marie, go with him. Whatever you do, don't touch her. Just let Santana deal with it. Chop, come with me. We are going to get Shoty."

He walked out the room yelling more orders.

"Nock, find the hospital staff. Tell them I wanted to take my sons to a private doctor. Let's go, let's go! We have to leave."

"Constant, where are we going?" Marie asked, placing her palm on his chest, not knowing where to go. "Where do you all meet?"

"Magnum's house," Bullet answered while helping Simi with the IV and off the bed.

"There you go," Constant answered. "We meet at Mag's house. I'll be right behind, darling," he says while trying to kiss her, but she dodged.

"I'm not your darling," she snapped.

"Marie, this is a happy day for me. I have one son who just became a god and another who's about to marry a goddess. What more could a man want in life but his beloved by his side? Can we put all that behind us and start fresh this day please, my love?" he begged.

"Let's go, Constant. We have to get out of here," she mimicked, following Santana out the door.

With all the events unfoldingh, no one paid attention to Rachelle, who hadn't moved form the wall at the foot of the bed. She blinked and replayed the images in her head. She had a hard time understanding what had just happened. Simi was conscious and not to happy to see her—he just rolled his eyes when he noticed her in the room… and again, when Constant asked her to help him, . he waved at Bullet instead.

Rachelle, stuck in time, stared at the empty hospital bed, thinking about all the time Simi avoided her presence, accompanied by the words he associated with her,

"She's too young," and "She's not the woman for me," or "I like freaky girls.") The list went on.

At that moment, Rachelle finally grasped that he had always disregarded her feelings. She would never be able to get him to fall in love with her.

AK poked his head in the room, noticing the tears falling from her eyes. He entered and took her in his arms.

"It's okay. There's no need for tears," he said, trying to console her. He hated when she got that way. "Simi is still recuperating. Give him a chance."

He reasons hugs her closer to his heart. He never liked the fact that she fell in love with Simi at first sight five years earlier, relentlessly chasing him—such relentless devotion, while he paid little attention to her.

"I made a fool of myself, thinking he could love me back," she cried into AK's chest.

"Yeah, I know, but you wouldn't listen to me, and I never got in the middle of it because you where too wild. I could never say 'no' to you. He was able to control you, and then you moved into his home. You had his parents to guide you." He hugged her tight, brushing her hair back. "You know—a mom and dad, like you always wanted." He took a deep breath and kissed her forehead, regretting not being able to stand up against the way Simi treated her.

"We have to go."

"Can you take me to your house?" she pleaded. "I don't want to be around them right now.

"Ah, you'll finally get meet Jolie. I just convinced her to move in. We're still working on something."

"Is she nice?"

"She makes me happy. It's all new. We're getting to know each other, but she's a very secretive person." He admited how his little lady in yellow refused to share anything with him.

"But come on before Constant yells about some other orders that you didn't follow."

"He called Bullet to help. He didn't need me."

"Right. Let's go, girl." He escorted her to his car and made arrangements to meet with the rest of the family after he settled his affaires at home.

Constant wheeled Shoty out of the hospital on the bed while Chopper pulle up in an ambulance and parked alongside of the queue of vehicles, ready to head for Magnum's house.

CHAPTER 23

Shoty, high on pain-killers, drifted in and out of conscious, trying to focus on the blurred shadow around him. He moved his head in each direction, searching for an exit. The ringing sound in his ears made it hard to hear the voices in the background. He closes his eyes, willing the ringing in his ears to go away, and opened his eyes.

His vision focused on a figure that was familiar to him. He tried hard to make out the voice, but the sounds he heard around kept him from concentrating until the shadow came closer. He recognized the person he had been bred to be around for the past two months and automatically rose to protect his lady.

"Constant! Get away from her! She's under my protection. You can't touch her," he screams to make his point as the ringing in his ears grew more intense.

"Yes, I know, but your mother is on the phone, and she wants to talk to you."

Constant held the phone to Shoty's ear, and he could barely hear what his mother was saying, but her voice relaxed him.

"Mommy, I can't hear you, but I'll call when I can," he said before pushing the phone back toward Constant "What are you doing here?"

"My sons are in trouble. You think I wouldn't come? I don't why you treat me like the Devil," he complained, frustrated that his boys hated him so much

"That's because you are," Chop called back from the driver's seat.

Shoty heard Chopper's voice, relaxed and dropped his guard.

"Chop, what's going on? Where's Joanne?"

"She's with Cage. We took you out of the hospital. We are on our way to Mag's," Chop answered, happy that Shoty was okay.

"What about Simi, Tank and Sic? Where are they?"

"Everyone's meeting at Mag's. I just got off the phone with him— he'll be here before 2 a.m."

Shoty lied back on the gurney, replaying all the events from earlier.

"Must have been a dream, Chop. It was crazy, man! Joanne ripped a door off a car and tried to hit me with it! Whatever kind of medication they gave her at the hospital put her on some kind of hallucination trip," he said, faintly laughing, thinking about the rage he saw in his beautiful wife's eyes.

"It wasn't a dream, Shoty. It really happened. That's why I'm here. You been out cold ever since the incident," Constant answered.

Shoty fell silent for a moment, contemplating his next move. He couldn't allow Constant to deal with his wife—her actions carried a death sentence.

"You can't kill her," he said to Constant. "Take my life instead, but promise me you'll protect her, Constant. Promise me!" he pleaded as he head began to spin.

"Yeah," Constant nodded. "The pain-killers are affecting your brain. Why will I want to kill my son? Besides, you just met this woman—and I might add that *she* just tried to kill you!"

"It was a misunderstanding. It had nothing to do with the organization. You shouldn't judge her befor you know her," Shoty mumbled, his body tingling from the meds.

"What misunderstanding could this woman have to want to kill you?" Constant asked, having a little fun with his boys, so he could understand the depths of love Shoty had for his woman.

Shoty fought to stay conscious, his body drifting further as the medicine swirled in his bloodstream. He was able to breathe final request before he fell asleep.

"She's my wife. You have to protect her!"

"You know, you could have just told him you knew already," Chop said to Constant.

"What? And not have a little fun? The boy is pissy-in-love, talking about, 'take my life instead,'" he laughed, mimicking Shoty.

"You see—that's why we don't like you. You do stuff like this all the time!"

"I not worried about it," Constant sighed."Besides, what son every truly likes his father? at least I keep you on your toes."

"By manipulating situations, and then you have us do your dirty work!"

"Call it what you want. For me, I'm my son's keeper! I'll always know what your guys are up to… except for this Shoty's wife business. You hid that one pretty well."

"Why? Your spies couldn't dig up any information? That's another reason we can't stand you."

The assemblage of car coming from the hospital flew past the gates, while security and staff made way to for them to enter. Madeline greeted

Marie and guided her to the playroom, where Cage lied Joanne on the coach and exited the room without a glancing her way.

Shoty came in on a hospital bed. He twisted and turned in a corner by the window in the front room, moaning for his wife.

"Jo, where are you? I can't find you," He groaned. Cage sat at his side, comforting him and helping him settle down, until Shoty ripped the IV from his arm.

"Man, calm down!" Cage complained. "Joanne is upstairs asleep, and you're at Mag's."

"The girls are also sleeping," Roc warned as he helped Cage settle Shoty down.

"Take him to her," Constant suggested, seeing how agitated Shoty was getting by the minute.

Cage and Roc held Shoty, each taking an arm, and they dragged him up the stairs to one of the guest rooms, dropping him on the bed. Again, he cried out his wife's name.

"Okay, I'll go get Joanne," Cage said. Moments later, he carried Joanne in and laid her in Shoty's arms.

"You not afraid of another beat down?" Roc teased. "You want to snuggle?" He watched the couple trying to get closer to each other in their sleep. After turning out the light, he and Cage left the room.

Joanne sensed Shoty's presence near her. She inhaled his cologne, moving closer to him. Shoty wrapped his arms around, her holding her closer.

Joanne's energy field filled the room with bright blue light that surrounded them. Absorbing it, Shoty could feel himself healing internally. He opened his eyes and kissed her temple, caressing the side of her face, adding additional kisses to her ears and cheeks.

"I'm sorry I didn't tell you what's was going on," he whispered in her ear, connecting his head to hers. "I wanted to, but I couldn't. I just wanted it to be over, so I could start my life with you."

"Shoty, you knew you were engaged, and you lied to me!" she screamed, but he quickly kissed her lips.

"Please don't scream. I fell in love with you. All I wanted was you! She did not exist to me." He ran his hand along her cleavage, lowered his head and kissed the side of her breast.

"It was a contract, and I been putting it off for the last eight years. It was only a business transaction," he explained, unbuttoning her pants.

His hand travelled up and cupped her left breast. He squeezed it, searching for her nipple. He teased and bit her though her clothes.

"All the things you heard were about me getting out of it,he said pulling her shirt off over her head and exposing her triple Ds before burying his head in her soft bosom.

"I only have one week left, and then I'm done," he sighed, begging forgiveness.

"What are you telling me?" Joanne asked, "to forget all this happened and go home and wait until you are ready to play house?"

She tried to push him off her, but he held her tight and pinned her on the bed by climbing on top of her.

"Cherie, I'm right here. There is no reason to scream. Let's just talk, cuz I can't lose your love!"

"Well, that's not talking. You're taking off my clothes!"

"That's because I miss you! I haven't had you in three weeks," he said, sliding his hand down her side to pull her pants off. He loosened his hold, easing further down the bed to kiss her stomach and belly button. He lifted her buttocks, slowly pulling her panties down, creating a trail of kissed all the way down until he reached her toes. Then he switched to the other leg and kissed back up. With every peck, he sighed.

"I'm sorry. I just want to love you." He nestled his body in between her legs, touched her knees and kissed, working his way to her inner thigh, leaving many pecks there too. His hands caressed her legs, wrapping one over his neck. He stared at his heaven, parted the lips and kissed her bud, using his tongue to trace the shape of it with the tip, sucking it in his mouth, moving his head to create friction. All the while, he stared at her, moving his mouth.

"I'm sorry."

Her body trembled from the heat building in her loins. She took hold of his head, rotating her hips, bringing his mouth closer to her clit, moaning.

"Mmmmm…Uuuuuhh… Mmmm… Cherieeee! Mmmm…That feels so good!" she cooed.

She forgot all about their earlier argument as her heart raced and the sensation intensified. Her body trashed back and forth as he continued to trace circles all around her pearl.

Joanne arched her back upward, elevating her lower body as waves of passion flowed into his mouth. He hugged her button, slurping and drinking every drop, lowering her slowly onto the mattress. He crawled between her open legs, pulled the hospital robe over his head and kicked off his shorts, slowly inserting his throbbing cock at the mouth of her sex. He stopped, while looking into her eyes.

"I'm sorry. my love. I promise I will never hurt you again." He moved his hips, pushing his cock in a little further, holding back. He kissed her neck, her chin and checks.

"I love you," he whispered, sliding both hands under her shoulders and thrusting inward. Using his hip muscles, he started to slither his way slowly deep into her core.

Joanne held on tight, enjoying the feel of his engrossed head, caressing her insides. The softness of the skin with its long length sends electric currants around her groin.

"Mmmmm...Uh, uh, uh. You're so... biggggg... Mmmmmm!" She closed her eyes and moaned, moving her hips to receive each thrust.

He twisted his body, lifting her right thigh over his shoulder, gently pushes it back to gain more access in her juice box and plunge farther, all the while whispering in her ear.

"Sorry, he breathed, kissing the side of her neck. "Sorry," her chin, "Sorry," on her lips. He parted them with a tongue that played a sensual dance with each even stroke.

He pulled out and rubbed its head against the outside of her neither lip, and then he entered her wet pussy, using only the head, with short stokes. He watched her face as passion overtook her.

"Mmmm...sweets!! Look at me," he shuddered with passion.

Following his command, she opened her eyes, sucked in his breath, holding her head to his, their noses connected.

"As long as I breathe, I will never let this happen again," he vowed, pushing back on her leg and shoving his whole length into her sweet cave, caressing her face with kisses. He continued with his promises until she screams out is name.

"I'll never let this happened again, my love," he stuttered, releasing his essence as if he was giving her his last breath.

Joanne held onto him, fighting to control her racing heart, running her hand down his back, kissing the side of his neck. Forgetting about their earlier conflicts, she rubbed her nose against his, gazing into his eyes, feeling the joy of having him in that position, still lodged inside her, their souls connects.

He kissed her, afraid to break the moment of peace between them. He bit her chin and kissed her throat travelling with more pecks on her breastbone. He lay his head there, savoring the tranquility of her heartbeat.

"We're not really married then, are we?" she finally asked.

"We are very married, both legally and within my organization. Remember, I declared my love to you with them. On our knees, we swore to protect you with our lives. Didn't they prove that to you today?" As he rose to his elbows and stared down at her, flashes of the car door in her hand ran through his mind. He looked at her, wondering was she truly insane.

"What about your business transaction?"

"It's done. I'm not going to continue with that. I'll just pay her what she asks."

"What did she ask for?"

"Money for breaking the contract! I'll pay it in the morning."

"Why didn't you just pay it before?"

"Because it's a lot of money, and I needed her dad to think she broke it off—not me violating the contract," he explained.

"Why?"

"It would start a war between her dad and Constant. Both had a lot riding on it, like new business ventures, property revenues and a whole lot of capital for generations to come."

"What happens now?"

"I'm going to pay her the money, and she'll tell her dad she broke it off."

"She would still do that for you?"

"I've completed the task she asked for. There was just one week left. She'll do it for the money."

"You slept with her?" she asked.

He hesitated, not sure about how to answer that question, but decided to tell the truth.

"Yes!" He paused to see the rage from earlier that afternoon return to her eyes and quickly tried to explain. "A long time ago! Yes, I was intimate with her, but from the first day I met you, I've had no interest in other women. The two months I was trying to get your attention, I couldn't look at any woman because they weren't you," he confessed, struggling to keep her in place. She tried to push him off her, but he grabbed both of her arms, locking them over her head.

"Relax, it was long before you I met you. I haven't had sex with anyone but you, and I only want you," he said in a sensual voice, bowing to massage her lips with his.

"Even after you beat me and my friends, I want you, Joanne. You're the only woman for me. I want to grow old with you, rock our grandbabies together. I want to die in your arms, because you're my heaven," he sighed, still entwined deeply in her, moving his hips, feeling her muscles clench around his rod,every time she struggled to get rid of him, causing his arousal to increase.

With her silky moisture all round him, he began to drive into her slowly, their eyes fused together while she fought to get out of her restraint.

Her tussling and wiggling built friction that rushes blood to his veins, giving him a full erection. Her chest rose and caved as he overpowered her. Angrily, she lashed out at him.

"Get the fuck off me!" she breathed. Without missing a beat, he pinned her down and pumped with all his of strength vigorously into her, all the while never losing sight of her.

"Remember, I wear the pants. That stunt you pulled today will never happen again!" he growled as she mean-mugged him, gritting her teeth, which he ignored. He used his knee part her legs wider, gyrating his waist in circles and plunging farther in her mound.

"F…u…c…k, oooooo, uh, uh…uh. What, what are you doinnnnng, to me!" she cried, her body shaking from the wonderful current that warmed her body, beginning at her center and leaving tingle sensations everywhere it travelled, causing her eyes to roll back, her breathing quivering while the waves started to crash.

"When you have a problem with me, you deal with only me—not my family. Number two, if I say I'm done with something, believe that I am. Number three, and this is very important, Joanne," he said, pausing to make sure she was paying attention.

"Don't… Do…n't Ssssstop!" she moaned, wanting that feeling back. She begged and pleaded for him to continue, moving her hips to guide him back.

"I need you to pay attention!" he said, waiting until she opened her eyes and was able to control her breathing. He fought his own desire not to succumb to her delicious heat.

"My job as your husband is to protect you at all costs. I will never do anything to hurt you or put you in an uncomfortable position. Do you understand those three rules I just gave you?"

She slowly shook her head, indicating *yes*, not really knowing what she was *yessing* to. He looked like he needed a *yes* answer.

Satisfied with her answer, he continued to move his buttocks in search for her juicy warmth. He forcefully devoured her, making her frantic. She stiffened from the violent pleasure coursing through her body. He released her hands, grabbing her hips to receive every powerful thrust of his pelvis. She dug her nails into the sheet to hold on while her body jerked and twisted with little lights exploding around them. His sweats drowned them. Steam rose from his body as he reached his climax. He held back, lowering his faceto suck on her breasts, putting small bits on her nipples.

He flicked with his tongue, causing a gush of fluid to coat his cock. He purposefully pounded her, vigorously, to the point of numbing her pussy, sending her over the edge as her body spamsed from multiple orgasm after orgasm.

CHAPTER 24

Uhh…uh…uh, wha… what was that?" she asked, fighting to breathe and gain control of her racing heart. She twitched, struggling to move lower body, which was numb due to ongoing spasms.

When he pulled out, she instantly missed his warmth and watched his throbbing, glistering cock, dripping with white nectar. He tapped it on her clit, causing her body to shudder more.

He climbs from the bed and stood aside to observe her agony before changing to his no-nonsense manner.

"Shower?" he asked, noticing that her legs were unable to cooperate with her attempt to stand.

"What did you do me? I can't move!" she complained.

He simply picked her up, walked to the bathroom, turned on the water and held her against the wall, easing her wobbly feet to the ground. He supported her by fastening his arms under hers.

"Who wears the pants?" he asked, gazing into her eyes, waiting for her to answer.

"You did that on purpose," she accused him, seeing the twinkle in his eyes.

"Who wears the pants?" he repeated, glareing at her to make sure she understood.

"Fine! You do! Happy now?" she sighed to him and kissed his lips. He pushed her under the water and turned the knob to cold.

"Aiiiieeeeee! You know I hate cold water!" she shrieked, pounding on his chest.

"Eh, Eh, Eh," he laughed. "Yes, I know., Put your feet down." She followed his instruction, planting both feet on the shower floor, standing erect.

"Now, you going to apologize to my family. I will have to deal with Constant in a little bit," he said, looking up, bewildered at how she could have caused so much damage.

"Who is Constant? And why does he matter so much," she asked, shifting her weight from one foot to the other.

"You hurt his son, Joanne. This is very serious."

"Oh my God! Simi!"

Joanne zipped past Shoty and darted out of the bathroom. Stunned by her actions, he called after her, and reaching out to catch her, he slipped and fell in the tub, watching her naked bouncy derriere exiting the bedroom.

Joanne forgot all about her mission physical condition and rushed downstairs to find Simi, never realizing she was still naked.

"Simi!" she called out, spotting him lounging on the circular couch. She charged in and knelt in front of him.

"I'm so sorry! Are you okay? Does your head hurt?" She examined his head for bruises.

"What's up with you godly people that you don't wear clothes?" Roc could not believe the scene in front of him.

The entire room was in total shock at seeing her naked body. Simi had a hard time concentrating on what she was saying to him and tried to keep it eye-level but he failed. He scanned her luscious body, enjoying a view of curvy watermelon breasts that sat high, their gumballs nipples pointing in his direction.

He then understood why Shoty was so obsessed with her. It took a minute to tear his eyes away. He glanced over to see his mother scowling at him before returning his attention to Joanne.

"I'm ok, goddess, but you need to get out of here before your husband comes," he warned. Leaning his head on the back of the armchair, he stared at the ceiling.

Constant observed the magnificent creature kneeling in front of his son and felt blessed to have, for a second time, be in the presence of one of the most beautiful woman he ever laid eyes on. He turned see his wife who scowled at him as well. Shrugging his shoulders, he returned to the scene.

Marie had enough of the boys' gawking, so she stood up and looked for a towel or jacket to cover Joanne

"Joanne!" Shoty's voice echoed in the room. "Get over here." He had screamed from the top of the stairs before limping his way down with just a towel around his waist, whiche he held with one hand.

Marie was gawking at the view coming down the stairs. *Ripped muscles, a tattooed muscular chest with a barrel of a smoking gun!* She used her hand to fan her face as she watched that chest getting closer… and closer.

"Really, Marie? He could be your son," Constant interjected, remembering when she used to gawk at him like that.

"Well, he's not my son," she reminded him and moved to a safe distance to watch the husband and wife showdown, because Shoty seemed pissed when he reached his wife, who was still on the floor, talking to Simi.

"Woman, did you just loose your fucking mind?" He placed a towel on her shoulders.

"What's that for? she asked, wondering why he was screaming .

"You're in a room full of people," he answered., She turned and look at him. standing there with just a towel.

"And you're in a room full of people with just a towel," she reminded him.

"Least I have one!" he snapped back, still staring at her.

"What?" She asked with a stank attitude.

"We just had a conversation upstairs," he insisted. "No more crazy stuff! What are you doing down here?"

"I had to make sure Simi was okay. I forgot! I had to be near him."

"Woman, you going to send me to an early grave! Let's go!" When he reached for her, she flinches, pulling back.

"What are you doing?" she demanded.

"Getting you up the stairs!"

"I'm not ready to go. I have a mission."

"The mission is over. Let's go!" he commanded, grabbing hold of her arm, helping her to her feet, half-dragging her by the stairs.

"But I wasn't ready," she protested, fighting him on the way up the stairs.

"Joanne! You're naked!" he roared.

She abruptly stopped upon hearing his words and finally looked down, realizing she was indeed very naked. In a state of shock and embarassment, she turned and ran up the stairs. Shoty couldn't help but to slap her butt cheeks as she took off.

Magnum opened the front door at the moment just before she fled and was greeted by the curviest derriere he had ever seen, bouncing up the stairs.

"I've must have missed a whole lot," he commented as he entered.

Shoty was happy to hear his voice and approached him in the foyer. He pointed Magnum toward the stairs.

"Man, I don't even know what that was all about. I had a rough day, Mag."

"I heard. Glad to see you on your feet. Why don't you go put your goddess to sleep and we'll talk in the morning?" he suggested.

"Yeah, alright. See you in the morning," Shoty said, glancing up and the going up the stairs after his wife.

Magnum searched the room and located the next couple who were a thorn on his side.

"Madeline and Cage—your man-eating child is outside, terrorizing security,"

"He got out!" Madeline jumped up run to find Santo a kitten that Cage gave to her after their first fight, three years earlier. But Santo had become a full-grown white tiger that terrorized people. She opens the door and call out his name.

"Santo! Come on!" she yelled as she scanned the perimeter.

Santo was on the other side of the field, and he was excited to hear his mommy's voice. He dashed towards her at full speed and knock her down, jumping up and down around her.

Marie, still not used to the great white tiger, flew into her husband's arms after his massive head entered the room. She did not understand how they were able to cohabitate with a vicious animal. She held onto him tighter, never realizing how much he was enjoying her closeness.

For years, Constant hadn't been able to hold his wife the way he used to. Ever since the birth of his younger child, Dianna, who was now eighteen years old and studying in France with her mother's family—his white mistress of twenty-three years.

Along with her, he fathered two other children, Mac and Dianna, but he adopted their older brother, Balthazar, and kept his stepson under his protection.

Marie never forgave Constant for his infidelity, and the they had been separated ever since. She abandoned her home and all the endowments she acquired throughout the years with only the clothes on her back. She had moved into Simi's home, after he purchased his first villa in their home town.

She only venture to her house when she wanted sex from him, and only then. That night was one of those nights. She had a lot of pent-up sexual energy that needed to be released. She yanked his collar, wrapping his tie around her wrist, pulling him to his feet and dragging him up the stairs. No one found that out-of-the-ordinary. *Those two had a strange relationship!*

"Madeline, dear," can you show us to our room? That is, if you can leave that beast alone for a minute," she said, referring to the tiger. She stood at the top of the stairs, still yanking her husband.

"Yes, Ma'am. I'll be right there," Madeline responded, pushing Santo on his butt in Cage's direction. "Come on, go to daddy," she coaxed, pressing her hand on his back and giving him a nudge.

Cage noticed her struggling from his seat in the corner. He whistled, causing the tiger to stop all at once and crawl on his stomach toward his master. Madeline was finally able to leave and show the awkward couple to the guest room and check on the girls.

Shoty walked into the room to find Joanne, pacing backed and forth, upset with herself.

"At least you're dressed now. Shall we finish showering?" he asked while moving closer and pulling her into his arms to face him. Immediately, he noticed the uncontrollable tears falling from her eyes.

"Why the tears?"

"I just made a fool of myself! Now your whole family thinks I'm crazy," she answered between chokes and hiccups. She pulled out of his embrace and began pacing the room again.

"Okay, they knew that already," he said. "You don't have to worry about them judging you. Besides, I'm the one who should be upset. You just ran out of the bathroom and didn't stop after I called you."

He suggested that her overall mood had changed, that she was getting more emotional by the minutes. She burst into tears when she saw the serious look on his face.

"Damn, woman, how many personalities do you have?" he complained while standing in the middle of the room with his arms crossed. He watched, helpless, as his wife crawled on the bed and buried her face in the pillow, crying uncontrollably.

"Joanne, why are you crying?"

She ignored him and put the pillow over her head. He came closer to her and sat on the bed, rubbing the sides of her legs to console her.

"Honey, tell me what to do. I've never seen this side of you! Please don't cry."

He tried being calm to see if that would help her, but she only buried her head deeper into the pillow and sobbed more.

Shoty lay behind her, whispering sweet love words in her ear and kissing the back of her neck. In time, she clamed and turned to face him.

"Your whole family saw me naked! Simi's mom—how am I going to face her?"

"It's forgetten already. Like the first time, no one will ever mention anything to you."

"Can we just go home now? I don't want to face them."

"We can leave in the morning, but right now, we are going to get some sleep. Too much happened today. My body needs rest." He snuggled her closer to him and rested his head back on the pillow. He closed his eyes, reflecting on all the day's events, wondering if he could have a life without her. He dismissed those thought unable to imagine a life without her. He slowly drifted off to sleep, entertaining happy, excited images of his eccentric wife.

In the next room, Constant was beside himself, keeping his wife, at bay. He hated when she went all "dominatrix" on him. It started a few years back, after Rachelle moved in with her. Rachelle had convinced Marie to use Constant for sex only, to satisfy her own urges, instead of punishing herself by not having any sex at all. At the beginning, Constant was very happy about being back in his wife's bed—until she gave him terms and conditions for when they would get together.

Marie grabbed him by the waist, pulled off his belt, twirled it in the air and whacked him on buttocks.

"Dance, Constant! Let's see you shake that booty!"

"Marie! Come on, honey! Is it because you know I can't say no to you that to degrade me like this?"

"You want to this taste this coco or not?" she teased, waiting for his response.

She loved to elicit the sad puppy-dog look in his eyes. He took a deep breath and started his striptease, unbuttoning his shirt and exposing his hard, muscular chest. Marie sat back on the bed, observing her husband of twenty-five years.

The man is still the sexiest she had have ever laid eyes on. He always had the capability to get her juices flowing. She looked at his naked frame, remembering the first time she saw him at a local restaurant, surrounded by a circle of friends. She knew he was the strongest of the bunch and ran into his arms for protection from a relentless suitor.

Now, she realized she had never stopped loving him. She just hated the hurt he put her through. In a moment of weakness, she motioned for him to come her, and she took off the rest of her clothes befoe he crawed between her legs.

She pulled him up to kiss him with all the passion she had hidden for the past years, not wanting his love, due to his infidelity.

She closed her eyes, taking in his scent, feeling his skin against hers, listening to the sound of his breath when he inhaled, His body heat clung to her body like the sun in the early morning.

Over eighteen years, they hadn't kissed each other so passionately, their tongues nervously clashing. Constant held her face, coaching her again, like the first time they ever kissed.

"Shhh, shhh! Slow it down, my love," he whispered gently, massaging her lips with his, slowly inserting his tongue inside of her mouth. Her tongue shyly met his, tongues in a sensual dance. He bitthe button of her chin and kissed her neck, making his way to her breast, sucking on them, moving form one to the other.

His hand traveled further down, resting on her hip, carressing her butt as he slid in between her legs and kiss her, loving her scent, missing her taste. He indulged in the feel of her bud under his tongue.

"Mmmmm... Honey I missed you," he breathed, coming up for air before diving back in, loving every inch of her, until her hands held the side of his head and she rotated her hips in synch with every movement of his mouth.

Marie heard his words, but they had a different effect on her. She remembered all the nights she waited up for him to come home, and sometimes, he didn't even bother at all. Tears moistened her cheeks, but she shook the memory off.

The wonderful heat built in her lower region caused her hips to have a mind of their own, getting closer to the source. The feeling intensified by the minute. She always enjoyed the way he worshipped her body, making her come to that explosive point where she arched her back upward. A tingly sensation began at her center and spread to her entire body, while pleasure coursed to soul, her heart thumping and ready to burst from of her chest.

He climbed on top of her, soothing the intensity of her orgasm by whispering sweet words in her ears.

"My beautiful creation, there's no other one like you! My addiction, my universe—I love you!" He guided his penis to her opening, reading himself to enter utopia, but she shoved him off her, using her right foot to kick him off the bed.

"You fucking liar! You promised to never lie to me, you asshole! Get out! Get out, fuck! Get your lying ass out of here! She continues to scream, throwing things from her dresser at him.

"Marie! Why are screaming? What did I lie about?"

"Get out! I don't want to see your face!"

"Baby, calm down, we are not in our home. You're screaming."

"Get out!"

He grabbed his clothes, put on his shorts and opened the door to find his three sons standing in the doorway, with grim expressions on their faces, and he bushed past them, bumping Mac on his way out.

"Oh, no nooky for you tonight, Constant!" he teased his father.

Constant not in the mood for his childrens' antics. He shoved Mac against the wall and whisperd to him

"That's why I always have a back-up! Now meditate on that, boy!" he growled, pushing him away

"Dad, that was a cheap blow!" Semi said, defending Mac. "You didn't have to do that."

"Don't worry about it, Simi," Mac answered, "he ain't going nowhere. No nooky for him there, either. I'm shutting that one down too."

"You three need to get out of my personal affairs. If I didn't have either one, you three wouldn't be breathing."

Mac looked over at his brothers and shook his head as he watched his father walk down the stairs out of the front door. "I'll be back. See you're later," he said as he left the house, right behind his father.

Rocket just stared at his mother on the bed, deep in sorrow over the mess of failed a relationship between her and her husband, who couldn't leave his mistress. He walked over to the bed and wrapped her in his arms, and takng off his shirt, he covered her nakedness and pulled the sheet over her lower body.

He sat next to her without saying anything, hating the way Constant treated her. Rocket could never understand how a man could say he loved his wife and hurt her so deeply. It was the main reason he did not have a relationship with his father.

Simi came and sat across from Rocket. Lost in his own thoughts, heard his mother sobs, which pierced his heart like a knife. He wished he could have done something to help her move on from Constant, but the rules were set: she was there until *death do them part*.

Constant, in the service car, took out his phone and dialed a number.

"Hello?" a sleepy female voice answered.

"What hotel are you staying at?" he asked.

"I'm not in a hotel," she replied.

"I thought I told you to go to a hotel," he said agitated, shaking his head.

"Yes, you did, but when I spoke to Mac, he said he couldn't understand why I would go there when he had a house," she answered.

"Uh! You people are fucking with my emotions! Be outside in ten minutes!" he commanded and hung up.

"Hello? What the hell is his problem?" Julisa mumbled as she rose from the bed, searched for a bathrobe and made her way to the front door.

Constant sat in the car's back seat, loosening his trousers to ease the heaviness in his ball sacks. He downed two shots of rum, back-to-back—one for his head, and the other for his balls.

Angry for not knowing what he did wrong, he glanced toward the front door and then at his watch, noticing he had been waiting for over five minutes. He called her back.

"What's taking you so long?" he breathed in the phone.

"I'm here. I'll be out in a minute," she said and walked out the driveway to the waiting car and tapped on the window.

"Why you not dressed? Where are your things? We are leaving!"

"Regi! I just got here. I haven't even seen my son. What do you mean, 'leaving?' and what happened at the hospital? Is Simi alright?" she asked. "And what is going on with you?"

"Get in!" he demanded after opening the door, temporarily blinded by the bright light shining from behind.

Mac had parked behind the service vehicle. He exited the car and walked toward his mother.

"Hi, my darling," his mother said, flying into his arms. "How are you?"

"I'm good, but what are doing out here in just your robe? You should be inside," he complains to his mother, rolling his eyes at his dad.

"Your grouch of a father didn't give me enough time," she answered. "But how's Simi? And boys are they all alright?"

"Yeah, mommy, they're good. We just finished at the hospital. Everyone's at Mag's house."

Constant became impatient. He leaned his head back, counting one to ten, and then he opened his eyes.

"Julie, get in the car. I'm tired, and I need to go to sleep." He tried to control his anger, but he failed.

Julisa was taken back by the force of tone he used. She looked form father to son, sensing there was something brewing between them... and she was in the middle of it.

"My son just got home, Reginald. I haven't seen him for the past two months."

"I don't give a fuck about you, you snotty-nose kid," he said to Mac, and then he turned to Julisa. "Get in the car and let's go!"

"Can you give me a moment with your dad for a minute?" Julisa asked Mac. "I'll be right in."

After Mac nodded and left, she climbed into the car.

"How dare you talk to me like that in front of your child?"

"That's not my child! He's your kid, and his trying to sabotage me!"

"And with good reason, from the looks of it! What is making you so crazy?"

He thought about her question for a moment and decided to tell her the truth.

"I need to be inside of you, and your child is purposely getting in my way. Shit, I need my woman!"

"Oh, poor Constant! Marie kicked you off her bed, and now you want your bitch to fuck you?"

Constant just stared at her, shocked by her words. "Why would you call yourself that? Throughout all these years, that was never our situation! And when did you start calling me Constant?"

"You're acting like the asshole you truly are right now! Besides, you smell like pussy. Good night, Constant. See you later. Go beg Mrs. Constant to finish you off."

She left the vehicle and walked toward her son, who just smiles at his dad, satisfied.

"Leave your dad alone. Our business is older than you are," she chastised him, making her way into the house, leaving Mac on the steps.

Hhe felt he just got punished for doing a good thing. He scratched the back of his head and followed behind his mother.

With nothing left to do, Constant instructed the driver to take him to Bull's-Eye, the hotel and club that Simi owned downtown. It was booked for the night by a big concert that the club sponsored that very night. Constant looked at the pretty young lady at the front desk and questioned her again about vacant rooms.

"No, sir. Everything is overbooked—even the special rooms in the third floor are all occupied, sir," she informed him while tapping keys on the computer."

"Alright, I'm going to my son's office," he said as he walked in that direction.

The hostess, not knowing what to do, picked up the phone and called her boss to inform him.

"Don't worry about it. I'll be right there." He closed the phone and watched his mother on the bed, gently wiping the tears away.

"I have to go and take care of Dad. He's at the hotel. All the rooms are booked. Do you want me to bring him back here or take him home?" he asked.

"Go take care your dad, Simi. Take him where he wants to go."

"That will be next to you. That's where he wants to be," Simi responded sadly.

"Not with the lies, my darling. I love your father, but I can't live with his lies," she reminded him.

"Alright. I'll see your in the morning," he said, kissing her forehead

"Later, Roc," Simi said as he rose to leave.

"No, *I'll* go get him. You stay with Mom," Roc said as he put on his vest.

"You, of all people? It's okay," Simi comforted. "I'll go get him. I'm not ready for World War VII from the two of you!"

"Not even going to talk to him," Roc said. "You just got out of the hospital. I still don't know if you're completely healed yet," he said as he closed the door.

Minutes later, Roc walked into Simi's office and found Constant at the edge of the balcony, deep in his bottle of rum.

"So, you finally come to kill me? Where's my security? These piss ants think they can control my life and hold my pussy away from me!" He was enraged as he thought about all the fight he and Roc had over the years regarding is mother.

"You think I would kill you?" Roc asked

"For your mother, you boys would do anything to keep her happy,"

"So stop hurting her. You love her, but you drive a knife into her heart everyday. It's the hardest thing, watching your mother cry over her husband!"

"Roc, all I want is to love her. I don't know what I did wrong tonight," he confessed with tears in his eyes. He sipped from the bottle.

Roc stood there and watched his dad in the rare form. They sat in silence for the long moment, neither wanting to break the peace. He approached his father and grabbed the bottle from him, taking a swig from it.

"Never thought I would see the day when you, of all people, would cry over anything."

"Why do your think I'm a monster? I cry! You're my eldest. I was in tears throughout your labor. I cried when you became a doctor, which was one of the proudest moments in my life."

"Maybe it's because you do monster stuff and people fear you?" Roc suggested to his father.

"People fear me because of my position and money. It should not be that way with my family."

"I don't think anyone in the family is scared of you. They just don't like the way you deal with certain things"

"Like what?"

"Like the situation you had a couple of months ago. You didn't have to annihilate that whole family over one mistake."

"One too many!" Constant countered. "Okay doctor—humor me. When you have a cancer growing in your body, do you negotiate with it or do you cut it out?"

Roc ignored his question and continued his argument.

"You didn't have to do it. You could have contained it. Then you turn around and dig a mass grave in their own backyard."

"Well, it was their land. Now they can be in it forever, one big happy family It was for the greater good."

"You kill children and have no remorse about it?" Roc complained angrily.

Constant considered his son's stance and body language and tried a different approach. "Tell me, how many attempts where made on you and your brother's lives over the years?" He paused when he noticed the change in his son's behavior—shoulders relaxed a little. "And they sent a very skilled assassin after you!" he continued. "He would have got the job done—killed you and your mother! He refused, shielded you with his life until he was able to deliver you to me. An assassin with a conscience! For that, I'm forever grateful to him and his family. They will always be protected. You remember Bernard."

Finished with the memory, Constant looked up the stars, lost in his own thoughts. "Everything I do is to protect the ones I love. You children were raised without seeing the ugliness of the world, because the monster in me kept them off your doorsteps. But I also trained you to be prepared for it," he explained.

"Guess in your world, you can justify the ugliness that you surround yourself with—while the real world suffers from your monsters."

"Heh, heh, heh ah ha. Oh, Michael, you have a lot of growing to do. I thought I did a better job getting you prepared. You're forgetting that you're billionaires, running a trillion-dollar business."

"Whatever, Constant. Let's get you home. You need a bed."

"What I need is my wife! I'm fine. I can sleep here and meet you downtown tomorrow."

You can't sleep here— not when all your sons have homes," Roc said.

"What's wrong with this place? Looks like a mini penthouse to me! Besides, I'm not welcome in my sons' homes, remember? I'm a monster."

"You're still my father, and I can't change that! But your wife did say to take you wherever you wanted to go."

Constant's face lit up. A smile crept up his face on hearing that Marie changed her mind and he could go back to her.

"You going to take me to her?"

"Nope! Not a chance—not after you just went to your mistress." Roc shook his head, watching Constant's happiness drains from his face, and laughed.

"If you knew you weren't going to take me there, why even mention it?"" he growled.

"I just wanted to see the look on your face when I crushed it."

"That was cruel!" Constant complained.

"Yeah, I'm being raised by a monster. What did you expect?"

"Give me my fucking bottle," Constant said, snatching it from Roc and making his way to the door. He complained that his children preferred their mothers over him. He turned toward Roc. "You're not my son either!"

CHAPTER 25

Shoty came out of the shower, wrapped the towel around his waist, looked in the mirror, admiring his frame, and flexed his biceps to make his breast muscles dance. When he walked in the room, his wife was still asleep with the covers wraps around her ankles, her naked button pocks out like two huge mountains he had to urge to climb.

He reached the bed and kissed each one, and then the small of her back. He kissed her ear kiss and the side of her temple.

"Hey, sleepyhead. I have to go in the office," he said, kissing her again. I'll pick you up in a little while, and we can go home," he whispered in her ear.

"Mmm, huh huh…" was all the answer he got back.

"Okay, later. I'll call when I'm on my way."

He slapped her butt left the room, making his way down the hall to dress in the game-room, where all their personal belongings were stored for nights they spent at Mag's.

A couple of female house staff stopped and stared with their mouths wide open, enjoying the view.

"*Mezammi, gade jàn gason sa yo sexy bó ici a!*[1]"

"*Epa blag non pitit, chak jour m preske pipi sou mwen la. Ou poko we enyan?*[2]"

"Morning ladies," Shoty said, greeting them as he passed and entered the room.

Sic, on the couch, heard the sound of the door and looked up.

"You're up early. On your way to the office?"

"Yeah. I have to get the money ready for Stephanie," Shoty grumbled.

"You not even going to try to negotiate? After you already completed all she asked? "Sic commented

"I just want to put that behind me now."

"That's a lot of money to pay off," Sic complained, counting the numbers in his head.

"It's alright. I can make more. Besides, I want my wife and my life in that order. Crazy situation wasn't pretty yesterday!"

---

[1] *"Girl, these guys over here are sexy!" (Creole)*
[2] *"You ain't lyin. Every day, I almost pee myself. You ain't seen nothin yet!" (Creole)*

"Please don't talk about yesterday," Tank said from the other side of the room. "I never want to experience something like that in my lifetime, ever again!"

"How do you feel this morning?" Shoty asks, rushing to his side, helping him up.

"Like a crazy woman with super powers puts a hole on my side," Tank snapped, examining Shoty, noticing he didn't have a scratch on him. "But how is it you and Simi are on your feet so fast?" he asked.

"I'm still trying to wrap my head around that one. It had to do with being near Joanne—she was on a mission last night," Shoty explained.

"Was that? What happened downstairs? The naked show?" Nock said, coming out of the bathroom, drying off.

"Who was naked?" Sic stood up from the couch, wanting to know what he missed.

"Joanne came down stairs butt-ass naked, hoovering over Simi." Nock began explaining the story.

"You mean like the first time naked?" Tank asked, looking over to Shoty for confirmation.

"Yeap, and Constant was there too." Nock stated, sitting next to Sic, who smiled, showing his four missing teeth on the upper front gum line, from the blow he received.

"Shoty, of all the psycho women you had in your life, this one takes the cake," he warned.

"Thanks for the storyline, Nock. Anything else you want to add?" Shoty fired back at him, reflecting on many situations he encountered over the years. Yes, indeed his wife hit the number one spot.

"Stop calling my wife a psycho," he muttered in a small voice while setting out his clothes, suddenly realizing the room was quiet after his last statement. He couldn't help but laugh it off.

"Man, she is crazy! What did I get myself into?"

"That's for the love of big booty gods! Now you have one." Tank celebrated with his friend, trying not to laugh, because his side was hurting.

"Roc left already?"

"Yes. He was going to meet with Mac and Constant on something about Simi and the beach. He rushed out of here—said he might come back for his mom before heading to the office," Nock said while getting dressed.

All done, Shoty searched for his gun in the wall vault.

"You know who has my gun from yesterday?"

"Probably with the scene of the accident, the car was demolished."

"I need it back. Which warehouse did they take it to?"

I don't know. I'll find out and let you know!" Sic said, looking in the mirror at his lost teeth.

"What time did you set this appointment?" he asked Nock.

"The dentist said he'll be able to see you around twelve today."

"Can't believe she knocked my teeth out—all the front one at that. You think I can still get a date like this?" he asked to no one in particular, making a face in the mirror, grinning.

"No! Not like this—not even if she's desperate," Bullet said flatly while rolling over put the pillow on top of his head

"And shut up, Sic. People are still trying to get some sleep," he complained.

"You shut up! No one told you leave the house, you should have slept where you where at," Sic countered, throwing a pillow his way.

Shoty just shook his head. *Those two will pick a fight at anything!* He walked toward the door.

"I'll see if I can finish by noon and meet you there. You guys need to have breakfast with Joanne and ask her to heal you."

"I don't want that nut of a wife of yours no where near me. I don't know about Tank," Sic complained.

"Man, stop being a punk. You afraid of getting beat up again?" Nock teased.

I have the marks to be afraid. Look at it all," Sic said, grinning. "My front teeth are gone over his obsession with psycho woman. She can't heal this," he said, pointing toward his mouth. "What? She going to make them grow back?" he asked in a serious tone.

Tank was having a hard time holding back his laughter. He held his side, rocking back and forth in the corner.

"Please stop, Sic! I can't. Its hurts too much to laugh. But I'd love to see those teeth grow back."

"You're some funny characters this morning," Shoty said as he headed out the door. "Tank, I'll call Jo later and tell her to come see you, man. I'm out."

Shoty walked off the elevator and stopped at Marline's desk, reading his messages. The floor was at a standstill, shock that he was standing there—not at the hospital in critical condition, as it was being reported in the news.

"Mr. Celestin, I thought you where in the hospital! Everyone has been grieving. We thought the worst. The stories we heard yesterday said basically you where at death's door," Marline said, happy to see her boss. She trailed after him on the way to his office.

"Tell everyone thanks for their concerns, but I'm okay. Get the bank on the phone. I need them right away. Also, call Stephanie. I need you to set a meeting with her today before eleven." He paused to open the door to the office. "Anyone here yet?"

"Yes sir. All the Constants are here."

"Alright. I'll be in their office when you take care all of this thing. Come get me," he commanded.

Shoty walked down the hall directly to Simi's office and opened the door to find Constant in the darkest side of the room with a towel over his head. He pointed in his direction in a questionable manner.

"That's a whole fifth of rum all by himself, because he got turned down, not once, but twice." Mac gloated, feeling proud of keeping his parents apart.

"Twice? You mean your mom is in town?" Shoty asked, but before Mac could answer, Constant replied.

"I never go anywhere without either one," he boasted, turning his nose up in the air.

Shoty walked into the room, idolizing the old man

"You know I want to say. When I grow up, I want to be just like you!" He wished he could have had two women… until reality hit. "I don't think that will be good for my health."

"Nope, I wouldn't advise you to! They don't make women like they use to. This new breed of women now acts like they don't know how fall in line."

"You don't have a bottle for him? Let him drown out his sorrows," Roc suggested.

Shoty sat next to Mac, watching Simi, who was lost in his own world, looking out the window.

"You ok there, man? You haven't said a word," he said to Simi.

"His been like this all morning—just lost in space," Roc explained, concerned for his brother's well-being.

"His fine! Just let him feel out his new powers. He'll be able to control his energy field," Constant assured them.

He witnessed this type of behavior before many years ago, when he first started his research with Julio Costello, his research partner on Earth's phenomenon of God's Theology.

Even though he succeeded on what he set out to do, he never shared that information with anyone, not even Julio.

"You've experienced this before, Constant," Shoty said, disturbing his concentration.

"Yes, many years ago. As a matter a fact, I should call Julio to let him know it happened." He patted his pockets for his phone.

The door opened and Marline walked in. "Mr. LeCase, your mother is here. I put her in your office."

"Thanks, Marline. I'll be right there," Mac said, excusing himself.

"I promised her I would have breakfast with her this morning before I ran out."

"What happened?" Shoty asked.

"Dad called! Your newest member of the god world was naked on the beach this morning," he said while holding the door handle

"By any chance, was he yelling at the water?"

"What?" Mac responded, confused over the statement.

"Never mind. Just go," Shoty said as he turned and watched his friend at the window.

Constant seized the opportunity and stopped Mac by the door.

"Look!" he said, trying to level with him. "Can you give me a moment to apologize to your mother properly?" he begged, noticing the expression on Mac's face. "No funny business. I just want to say I'm sorry, that's all. I don't like when she's upset."

"Only because you ask nicely," Mac said, not trusting the motive for Constant's apology. He called Marline over. "He's going to my office. Make sure you stay with my mother until he leaves," he said, pointing at his father.

Not in the mood to fight with his son, Constant quickly left the room to find Julisa.

Marline tried to keep up with his long strides, running to reach his side.

"I'll give you 50 *Gs* to walk away and keep them busy for the next hour," he whispered without missing a beat.

"I'll bring her to the gaming room for you," she whispered back. "There are no activites in there today." She pointed him in the direction.

"Would that be cash or a transfer?" he asked.

"Whatever you like, sir," she confirmed, overjoyed about finally being able to send her children abroad to study.

Marline escorted Julisa to the gaming room, under the pretense that she was meeting her son, and she quickly locked the door from the outside. Julisa watched the door close, feeling a little strange until she heard the voice she knew all too well.

"So, you're going to explain what was that all about last night?" Constant said in a voice that echoed in the room. He spun around in a chair by the window.

"I should have known this was your work! What you do? Pay her off." She hugged the wall, afraid to move. He rose from the chair within two strides, charged her and pinned her on the wall. He locked his hand on the frame, staring down at her. She inhaled his minty breath, her favorite aftershave, relaxing a little when their cheeks brushed.

"Smell better," she kissed the side of his face, loving the grim look he sported whenever he was displeased.

"You're avoiding the question," he groaned against her lips while she brushed his with hers.

"Our son called right after you pulled up. That's why it took me a moment to come out." She stopped, kissing his neck.

"And?" he growled.

"He didn't want me to meet with you. I should turn off my phone and go to bed. I didn't have it in my heart to refuse him." She kissed Constant's nose and caressed the side of his face.

"So, you'd rather refuse me," he growled again, pressing his body closer to hers. Jis hands slid down her hips, maneuvering under the skirt. With one hard tug, he pulled her to him and ripped off her panties!

"Constant, you ripped them?" she said in a mousy voice, loving that possessive side of him.

"Tell me to stop!" he grunted, freeing himself from his trousers.

"You ripped them already! What I'm going to wear? Mario will notice," she whimpered, taking hold of him, caressing the head.

"Say you want me to stop, or I'm going to take you right here on this wall," he groaned.

"Your son can't find ouuut…" She didn't' get to finish before he shoved his whole length in her, nailing her on the wall.

She dug her fingernails into his shoulders while he lifted her to meet his ferocious thrust. He pumped into her, thrust after thrust, sending electrical currents, hitting her G-spot. She wrapped her arms around his neck, succumbing to his powerful style of lovemaking.

She moaned his name, trying to keep up the movements of a starved beast. He noticed how her body quivered and held her in place, releasing her long blond hair. He slowed his movements, carrying her over the couch, where he sat her on top of him.

"You ignore the questions that I ask you."

"I'm not ignoring them. You where being a jackass last night and you hurt me to the point I had to call Belo and tell him you said Mario is not your son.

"He's not my son. He is yours, and he'll do anything to protect you. He won't even look my way," he complained.

"And Belo will do anything to protect you," she countered. "He defended you last night, explaining that's not what you meant, and that I took it out of context."

"That's because he is my son, and we're alike in many ways. I have nothing in common with Mario or Michael. Those two will kill me for their mother."

"You love all your children," she reminded him, moving her hips.

She loved the way he felt inside her. No other man was capable of satisfying her body the way he could. She had plenty of lovers before him—even a husband, twenty-three years earlier. Constant was the only one who could rock her world.

"That doesn't mean I have to like them," he said, controlling his breath, urging her to move on him a little faster. Her juices coated his rod as he leaned back, enjoying the ride. He imagined it was his beloved on top of him.

Julisa sensed the change in him. He was more passionate, kissing her all over, his eyes closed. He reached up and kissed her right breast before giving the other the same attention. His pumping was more sensual as he grasped both butt cheeks, squeezing them and pulling them closer.

After a few more strokes, her body spasmed with a great force that pulled her harder onto his cock. She fought to control her racing heart as more spasms continued to course through her body

Constant, in a trance, felt his dick, soaked by her juices mixed with her fatty meat, chocking him to the verge of exploding. He held onto her hips and pumped all his sexual frustration into her. With one last hard thrust he screamed. "Marie! I love you!" He continued to pump all his frustration away, ejaculating deep inside of her, holding her tight, kissing her and caressing her body, controlling the intense racing of his heart that pulsed in the middle of his head.

Julisa, not a jealous woman, knew what she was getting herself into. It was a first for him to ever mention his wife. She quickly hopped off his lap and looked for her belongings, preparing to leave.

"Cherie, that was wonderful," he said as she grabbed her things and headed toward the door. "What? Why are you leaving? We still have some time."

"I'm not Marie. I see that's where you rather be."

"I know you're not Marie. Why are you bring her up?"

"You just called me Marie!"

He lied his head back, realizing that he did let the name slip.

"Sorry about that. It was never my intention to upset you. "I'm sorry, my Ju-Ju. Please accept it and don't be mad."

"Goodbye, Constant. Go and enjoy your wife," Julisa said as she walked out the door.

Constant banged his head on the couch for being a jackass. He rose and went to Marline's desk.

"Can you get her twelve bouquets of roses? Six and six? For the first six, write, *I'm sorry, my Ju-Ju*. For the other six, put, *For Julisa Lecase, my reality*. She's staying at Mac's house," he said, unhappy about her anger. There was one thing on this earth he could not stand, and that was for her to be upset and him being the cause of it.

"Ok, sir. I'll get them delivered it right away."

He walked back in to Simi's office, only to be confronted.

"Where is my mother?" Mac asked.

"She left... upset with me for being a jackass." He looked over at Simi, who was still in the same position as before, staring out the window. Constant sat back, lost in his own thoughts, paying no attention to Mac and his gloating.

"Told you I got that on lock. He's not getting any at all," he boasted to the rest of the room. Constant ignored them, focusing on a way to fix this mess he just created.

In Blanc Villa, Magnum was cooking breakfast for his girls when Joanne joined them. She got out of the shower, craving coffee.

Fully-dressed in a bathrobe, she wrapped her hair with a towel before joining the Blanc family at the table

"Morning!" she addressed everyone, feeling shy from last night's events.

"Morning, Mrs. Celestin. What would you like to eat this morning?" Mag asked, sensing her uneasiness. "Come on in. There's plenty of food."

"No. Nothing for me. All I want is coffee. I can't keep anything down lately. My stomach's been acting crazy since yesterday and the world seems to be spinning," she said as she rose and sat on the barstool, resting her head higher than the table.

Marie also came down in her robe to greet the girls. She turned toward, Joanne who was trying to hide.

"Morning, dear. Hope you slept alright last night... and that husband of yours didn't punish you too much," she said, "cuz he was pretty upset with you,"

"I'm not worried about him. I'm so sorry that you had to witness all of that. I'm not that person," 'Joanne apologized.

"You mean you're not crazy like everyone around here are saying?" she teased, but Joanne just buried her face on the table.

"Sweetheart, you are fine," Marie comforted. "Stop worrying about what is proper and keep that man of yours on his toes, cuz the next woman will keep him entertained for you, crazy or not. But I heard you surpassed crazy and went straight to psycho. I know that will keep him on his toes." Joanne hated being called either. Ashamed, she refused to look up as Marie continued.

"If it will make you feel better, you can see my bosom—that way, we can be even."

Joanne faintly smiled.

"No one is taking any clothes off!" Mag roared, putting some eggs he just finished cooking on the table.

The smell of breakfast turned Joanne's stomach, making her jump up and run to the bathroom. Marie rushed after her, trying to help, holding her head over the toilet.

"It's okay, sweetheart. Just take deep breaths and wait for the nausea to pasts. How far along are you?"

"You think I'm pregnant?" Joanne asked, shocked, never thinking her sickness could be related to pregnancy.

"You're very pregnant," Marie said and turned toward Magnum in the doorway.

"Can you get a cold compress to help her relax?"

Joanne held onto Marie, feeling herself fall into a deep darkness. Mag rushed to her side, reaching out to grabbing her from Marie. However, at the touch of her skin, her energy field zapped him across the hallway. He landed against the wall in the kitchen with the wind knocked out of him. Dazed, he got up, reached for his phone and called Cage

"Get here right now. Joanne's passed out in the bathroom."

The kitchen staff cleared the area and moved the girls to the other room while they helped get their boss to his feet.

Cage ran in, wearing only his boxer briefs, to check on Mag.

"What happened to you?" he asked, noticing the smoke that surrounded his body.

"I just got electrocuted. Go to her. She's been out the whole time." Mag gasped.

"You called Nock, and Shoty?" Cage asked as he helped Marie to stand on her feet and scooped Joanne into his arms before exiting the bathroom.

Madeline went to the doorway, checking on the girls.

"No, I'm doing that now," Mag replied. Tank and Sic, on the top stairs, heard all the commotion and came to investigate.

"What is going on?" Sic yelled.

"Joanne's passed out. We're rushing her to the hospital," he said as he exited the house. "Shoty—meet us at the hospital!" he said into his phone. "Joanne passed out. We're on our way now."

He hung up with Shoty and dialed Nock's number. No answer. He dialed again with the same result. "Magnum—call his office."

"Come on. Miss Marie," Mag said, "you can help Cage with her."

.

"Dr. Mangrass's office—how may I help you?" the receptionist answered.

"I need to talk to him now!" Mag insisted.

"I'm sorry, sir. The doctor is in surgery all morning. If you leave your name and number, I can have him call you later on this afternoon," she suggested.

"It's a family emergency, and he's not picking up his phone. Please, Miss—go in there and tell him to pick up his cell phone."

"Sir, I'm not allowed in the surgery room. You'll have to wait until he comes out. Thank you and have a nice day, sir."

Magnum was taken aback by the secretary's behavior and was redialing the number when his phone beeped, indicating another caller.

"Hey," he answered.

"We in the truck with Shoty. We about seven to eight minutes away," Mac said on the line.

"I can't get Nock on the line. His secretary just hung up on me!" Magnum complained.

"We're down the street from the hospital. Where's Constant? This is his area of expertise."

"Yeah, hold on," Mac answered. "I'll get Nock to meet with you in the front. He has a new secretary." Mac turned to his father in the truck and handed him the phone

"Dad, Mag wants to talk to you." He gave him the phone and grabbed Shoty's to call Nock's office.

"Dr. Mangrass's office—how may I help you?"

"Hi, Shelia. I need you to get him in the front of the hospital now! Tell him his sister just passed out. We on our way now."

"It will be a bit difficult, but I'll get the message to him."

"Thanks, Shelia. We still on for the football game next week?" he asked.

"Whatever you need, Mr. Lecase. I'm here to please you," she cooed.

"Look I can't talk right now," Mag said, "but I'll call you after all this is over," he added before hanging up.

"New flavor of the month?" Shoty asked while zipping through traffic, frantic to know something about Joanne's condition.

"She keeps me entertained, for now," Mac replied.

Constant leaned forward to return Mac's phone.

"Bet ain't no one keeping that pussy away from him," Constant grumbled.

"Nope, not a soul! Besides, they can't anyway!" Mac answered his father. "I was raised by the best."

"Pissant!" his father vented.

"You two need to cut out this contest between you before it gets out of hand," Shoty warned.

"And mother or not—you shouldn't keep them away from each other."

"When it's your mother, we can talk," Mac responded.

"Okay, I'm not getting in your business. I'm just warning you to chill before your say something you can't take back."

"I hear you. I just want her to be happy and live her life—do all the things a normal wife do with her husband."

"What make you think she's not happy?" Constant asked.

"Is Marie happy? Mac rebuffed.

"My issues with Marie are *different* from your mother's. I don't have a problem with Julisa. Well, now I do," the older man confessed.

"What does that mean?"

"Nothing. Grown folks' business," he said as the truck parked behind Cage's Mustang, in front of the hospital doors.

Most of the crew was already there, blocking traffic at the entrance, while hospital security tried to reason with them to unblock the entrance.

Simi and Roc came around the corner after parking their vehicle in the hospital's garage. Tech controlled traffic, so he had his security move out all the cars from the entrance.

After Shoty gave his keys to one of the soldiers while entering the hospital, Constant stopped him, revealing the conversation he had in the car with his wife.

"Congratulations are in order. Marie told me your wife is pregnant. Now, that changes things, which means we have to take her somewhere else. The hospital can't do anything for her."

Shoty was in shock on hearing he was about to be a father, but he was more concerned about his wife's complications. "What you want us to do?" he asked. "You know where to go?"

"Yes! I already order the chopper. The place we have to go is near Port-salut. We can land in Chadonnieres, take a boat out to Port-A-Piment, and from there, we hit Rue departmentale 25. Once we get there, we have to walk the rest of the way into La Grotte Marie-Jeanne. That's where the caves are to her world!"

He searched through the numbers on his phone and dialed. *No service on the call.* "I wish I was able to find my partner from my earlier studies. I can't contact him."

"When do we leave?" Shoty asked.

"Let get everyone here. Her kind don't like being disturbed by outsiders. It would be like walking on eggshells dealing with them," Constant warned as his phone beeped. "The helicopter will be here in thirty minutes. It will land on the roof. Go set up things with Nock."

Just then, Madeline pulled up in her Mustang, identical to Cage's, with the girls and some bags.

"Good. You'll be leaving in thirty minutes," Constant said as she carried the girls from the car.

"I don't have anyone to watch Santo," she said. "The zoo keeper is on vacation."

"Well then, go pick him up," Constant demanded. "Hurry! The chopper is going to be here." He continued, "Tech, I need you to get some of these cars out of here. Call Jocks and tell him to meet us here." Next, he turned toward A.K. "Where's your sister? She's not picking up her phone."

"She's upset with a certain somebody. She's not even talking to me right now," A.K. answered. He said Rachelle was so upset about what Simi did that she locked herself in her room.

"Go get her," Constant demanded. "We have to go. I don't want to leave anyone behind."

"Going to war, Constant?" Simi asked.

"Gods are the best-kept secrets in this world, and we about to enter their dimension. If we approach in numbers and show unity, they're less likely to attack. That's why I want to enter as a big happy family. Go help Cage with Joanne and secure your affairs."

"Does that mean Julisa is coming too,? since you don't go nowhere with either one?" Roc antagonized.

In his urgency, Constant forgot about her, so he slowed his pace and gave her a call. After she refused his call, he tried and text her and waited for a response.

At the hospital, Madeline entered with the girls, carrying sport-suits for Cage and one of her own, for Marie. She also brought a change of clothes for Magnum.

'Oh, thank you, hun. I just realized I was only in a bathrobe the whole time," Marie said, thanking her and looking a bathroom so she could change. Cage still wasn't talking to her. He just grabbed the suit and kissed her cheek as he slid on the pants and shirt. She holds onto his arm, passed him Brianna and sat Claire in front of him.

"I have to get Santo from the house," she said, looking into his eyes, longing for him to hold her. "I was in bed last night. You didn't come."

"After I dropped off Santo, I had to go deal with something with Jocks. I had just got in this morning when Mag called. Why? You ready to talk?"

"You wouldn't know, cuz you wasn't there to listen," she answered, rolling her eyes and walking out the room.

"So now you mad!" he fumed, but she kept on walking. "Madeline," he called after her, but she never turned back as she left the hospital.

Magnum rest his back against the wall to give it support from the pain and discomfort he received when he slammed against the wall. He tried to hold one of the girls on his lap, but the pain made him cry out. He handed little Brianna back to Cage.

"You need to get that looked at. You're in a lot of pain," Riffle advised, taking the other girl and playing with his niece.

"I'll be alright. The way Constant's barking orders, we don't have time. I'll have it checked when we get back."

Just then, Constant walked onto the floor that they had secures with their own security, totally shutting down the hospital.

"We are drawing to much attention. Let's start moving everyone to the roof. The only persons missing are Rachelle and A.K. Simi—carry Joanne. Cage—stay with him." Constant glanced over at Shoty on the corner, watching his motionless wife lying on the bed.

"Shoty, as soon we get to the cave, you'll be able to hold your wife. Help the boys get her in the chopper." Constant searched for Mac and discreetly pulled him aside.

"Your mother is very upset with me right now. I need you to send her back to Gonaives until we come back. I asked Cage to keep his best team on her."

"You want Cage's guerrillas with her?"

"I don't know how they would receive me. I have a past history with them. Joanne will protect you. Me—it's a different story."

"Exactly what did you do? To have gods wanting your head?"

"I fell madly in love with one, and I had to have her after I was told I wasn't fit." He looked toward Marie and smiled to himself, remembering her flying into his arms.

"I made her give up all that she was to be with me. In her people's eyes, I stole her," he confessed to his son.

"If they find out about Julisa, they will take her away from me," he said, pausing to look at his son. "They'll kill her and Dianna."

"Then I should stay with my mother until you return?" Mac asked.

"I need you with me, cuz they know of you already," Constant insisted as he continued to dial Julisa's number, with no response.

"I'll call her now," Mac finally agreed, seen the concern on his fathe's face.

"Also, tell her to behave herself," Constant instructed, "and tell her to follow the directions they give her. She likes to dodge and escape if she feels she's a captive. I'll make it up to her when I get back."

After the helicopters landed on the roof, everyone secured themselves in their seats, waiting. A.K arrived shortly thereafter with Rachelle, kicking and screaming, and they boarded the chopper.

Rachelle came across Simi, standing face-to-face, acting like she didn't exist. She covered her hurt feelings, choosing to sit far away from him.

Constant positioned himself next to Madeline and her child-beast who lay his massive head on her lap as the older man instructed her on the proper way to hurt and mortally wound a god... in case the need arised...

CHAPTER 26

Military helicopters, looking like mini-cargo jets, reached Chardonnieres within hours of take-off. Constant rounded up all their belongings and the extras that he ordered for the excursion. He got everyone loaded on the boat and ordered his team to prepare the backpacks that they would need once they reached the caves.

They laid Joanne on a carry stretcher on the deck as the boat glided through the waters at full-speed, reaching its destination of Pot-A-Piment in record time.

The hummers dashed through Rue Departmentale 25, reaching La Goutte Marie-Jeanne to enter the cave before night fell. Tall trees, covered with vibrant green mosses and huge vines made a pathway to the clearing and camouflaged the creepers and snakes that inhabited there.

The hissing sounds of animals were everywhere, the crackling branches indicating the ever-present danger, predators hunting. The air smelled and tasted of prey being hunted in a forbidden place where mortal humans weren't allowed to venture.

Deep in the jungle of the southern peninsula, surrounded by massive green trees that led to the cave, arrows flew through the air, landing near their feet, serveing a warning not to go any farther.

Constant stepped over the arrows and continued, looking back.

"Give the babies to Marie or lay them by Joanne. Keep your heads up. We're not welcome past this place," he warned, and he covered another mile before the guardians of the jungle blockaded his party.

An army of strong warriors, dressed in their original Arawak tribal gear, aimed pointy sharp spears at their attended targets. A few feet before they reached the mouth of the cave, both forces came to a standstill, guns drawn, infrared lights pointed at the warriors' temples, arrows securing their marks at Constant's heart.

"Your bullets won't work here!"

A huge, fierce-looking savage with copper skin, rippling muscles and a signature bird Taíno headband covering his face, appeared to threaten the group. They could only see the opening for his eyes as he walked up and faced Constant. His booming voice alone made them shake with fear and terror.

"I know after all these years, you didn't just show your face here," he growled in Constant's face.

"Hello, Mannon. It was always a mystery to me how you, of all the fallen angels, would be the one who guards the gates to keep humans away." Constant stood eye-to-eye with his opponent, who hadn't changed of the past twenty-five years, when they first squared off. "I'm not here to quarrel. I have a very pressing matter."

"Eh! Eh, you have a pressing matter with the gods? I see you are ready to part from this world! I would welcome you anytime, Constant, the thief." Mannon turned and grabbed hold of his spear, launching it at Constant's throat, which forced Cage and Madeline to react. In one swift move, Cage was at Constant's side, ready to attack the fierce worrier.

"I would kill you right now, but I see you came prepared. This is not over. You will pay."

Constant didn't even flinch during the threat. He stood his ground, waving off the shooter, but Santana was already in action, and he charged at the warrior, knocking him off his feet. Santana was ready to take Mannon's life, but Constant got in between them to calm the situation.

"It's okay, Santana. His feud is with me." Constant turned to face Mannon.

"We can settle this."

Mannon stared at Santana's grim face, recognizing his origin, surprised by his audacity, while addressing.

"You bring *him* to their gate! You have crossed the line. They will wipe out your whole existence for this!" he grumbled, experiencing fear for the first time in a long while.

Santana, occupied with Mannon, didn't sense his life was in danger. Mannon waves his arm, ordering his Army to stand down, leaving his second-in-command to fire a lethal arrow at Cage's back.

Madeline heard the shift of the air and sprang into action, catching the arrow inches before it hits his target. She then snatched his bow and sent the arrow back to its owner, who fell from his hiding spot in a high tree. Santo leapt from behind her, opening his ferocious mouth and jumped on the warrior, mauling him on the ground.

Madeline rushed the fallen second-in-comand, wrapping her body around him like a python, pointing another arrow at his throat.

"You threaten to hurt what I value most in this world!" she snarled, raising her arm above her head, ready to drive the arrow through his chest.

Her opponent just smiled, unafraid for his life

"I'm immortal. You can't kill me," he taunted, loving the feel of her. It had been a long time since a woman excited him.

"No! But I know how to wound, being not from this world—and I know how to make you feel un-imaginary pain," she growled, striking her mark with vengeance, puncturing a hole in his chest with the poison arrow meant for Cage.

He screamed in agony as she tightened her legs around his neck and pushed the arrow farther into his shoulder blades. Mannon looked over at his warriors as he struggled in pain and succumbed, signaling his army to clear a path.

"Enough! The path is clear. You can go," he growled furiously.

"Let him go, Maddy!" Constant ordered, signalling for his people to move on and enter the cave, leaving Mannon and the warrior on the ground.

The crew was not surprised by Madeline actions. They had, after all, trained her to be the perfect assassin, What had them worried, however, was the level of evil surrounding her.

Cage walked over to her take hold of her hand and kissed it.

"Thank you," he whispered, pulling her into his arms passionately kissing her.

"I'll try to work things out between us. When you're ready to talk, I'll be there to listen," he promised.

Without any response, she grabbed Santo and walked ahead of him to catch up with the girls inside the cave.

The lush entrance of the cave was surrounded by vegetation and formation rocks and vines so thick that they created their own shapes, like trees.

The red sand covering the clearing appears like a red carpet, flittering throughout many mazes of caves—each with its unique pathway.

The deeper the traveler went inside, the colder the air grew, with high walls that resembled salt mines and sea reefs, almost taller than maple trees.

The farther in, the smaller the world appeared to be, the multi-size holes that covered the mine gave them the sense of walking in outer space, while the darkness that fell dropped the temperature even further.

Constant stopped and approached the caravan the soldiers carrying supplies and pulled out the backpacks containing the coats he brought. Everyone dressed accordingly, and he ordered the soldiers to camp at the entrance, while the rest of the group continued their journey. Temperatures eventually reached below zero degrees and dropping.

Magnum, in pain from his earlier blow, tried to ignore the cold and focus on other things, like Madeline. He hated the person she was becoming and the way she had changed over the years—ever since they started her training after the attack. At first, it was great teaching her the things they were experts at doing, but it had taken a new change. She had truly become a hard-core killer.

He watched his daughter, sitting comfortable next to Joanne without a coat, not understanding the science behind it. Constant explained that Joanne was protected by her energy fields from the cold and all other kind of potential dangers.

The sun hid on the other side of the mountain, casting its last rays through the hollow cave with its halo-shaped ceiling. The soft white clay walls, mixed with a natural color of bright fluorescent glows, created a path far enough for the eyes to see. A rainbow cast its spells on the top of a huge hole that was open to the heavens, pointing out a clear exit from the cave.

Upon reaching the mouth of the cave, rays of the sun started to peek through the holes, caressing their bones. Coats were shed, bodies welcoming the full blast of the sun's fingers penetratint to their frozen toes.

Most of the travellers lounged on the red sand, enjoying as their body was restored. Marie felt a familiarity with the high walls, huge steps which wrapped around the mountains, their turquoise blue waterfalls flowing from many caves to a magical pool on the ground.

She closed her eyes and listened to the sound of nature, feeling the wind caress her face. Flashes of a non-existence world occupied her mind with a sense of nostalgia. The path continued, dividing into four distinct directions, all reaching the other side of the mountain, covered with trees of all the same height.

Constant looked at his watch an hour before the sunset

"Come on. We can't rest or waste anytime we need to reach the other side before the sunset."

"Which way do we go?" Roc asked, pointing. There are four paths," feeling a definite impression they were being followed. "The warriors are back. They're following us," he told his father.

"No, they're not. They wouln't enter the cave. Those are the Guardians you're sensing. We go northwest past that clearing over there," he said, directing Roc to start walking in that direction.

Roc, Shoty, Jocks, A.K and Cali held one side of the stretcher carrying Joanne, following behind Constant. Fifteen minutes before sunset, Constant reached a clearing that appeared to look like an owl's eyes with turquoise water cascades dripping from the eyelids, giving it the elusion of a portal.

Constant stopped and admired the beauty of it—like the first time it took his breath away,

"Now what? Where do we go from here?" Roc asked.

"Now, we go southwest into the eyes of heaven."

They stepped into the pool, vanishing inside yet another cave, snf the journey continued. The crew was amazed by the wonders the caves, fascinated at not being wet after emerging from the weeping eye. They entered into a vast plain with still blue waters and a hint of golden, crystal sand.

Beyond the coast sat two magnificent golden phoenixes atop of two white pillars. The phoenixes bowed to each other with their wings spread causing a barrier.

A trident launched, landing between Constant's feet, and then a couple of energy balls struck. He blocked one that explodes on the ground and caught the other.

Soon after, four giants with bronze gold skin appeared, wearing golden armor over their broad, naked shoulders, each aiming tridents at the intruders, who were surrounded.

"You must be the only human dumb enough to return to a place where he's not welcome. I wonder how you past Mannon. He's vowed to kill you!"

"I see you still like to play with your balls, Olodumare. I was prepared for Mannon. It's hard to kill me—you made sure of that years ago."

"A mistake that I will soon correct. What does a snake like you want? We have nothing for you to steal!"

"I've never stolen anything from you. If you remember, free will is very important to your kind. I just convinced her I couldn't breath with her." Constant look over to Marie who was following the conversation without understanding any of it, though she this new strange world felt familiar.

Recognizing his sister, Olodumare grabbed Constant by the throat.

"The deal was that she would never find out, and you would make her happy! You're bringing her back?" his he said with contempt, his yellow eyes intensifying

"She doesn't know! I never told her the truth! We are here on a different matter, and I still can't breathe with her." Constant explained, peeling the fingers away from his throat.

Olodumare shoved Constant to the floor and picked up his trident.

"Whatever is your business, it doesn't concern us. Leave, before my father finds out you here. He's very testy this days."

"It does concern you. We have someone special with us. She's one of your kind, and she's pregnant with twins—boys at that."

"That's not possible! We only have one demi god on Earth, and you stole her!"

"You and your father *gave* her to me for helping you maintain the balance of good and evil… and I've kept my promise to you, helping you keep your secrets well hidden." Constant continued. "Yes! There are many of your kind on Earth, living as humans, and I've been searching for them. I recently came across her. She has no idea who or what she is," Constant whispered.

"There's talk of a war brewing. We've been noticing strange occurrences on Earth," Olodumare admitted while scanning his entourage. "You claim to be keeping our secrets, so why did you bring so many here?"

"They're my family and my most trusted allies. If you go to war, you would need everyone of them to keep your way of life. They would never harm your kind," Constant assured him.

Olodumare looked at his sister, genuinely happy to see her. He looked back toward Constant, conceding for a moment.

"I have to council with my father. I'll check your story. As he turned to leave, he called a group of naked goddesses to attend to Joanne.

They walk in formation toward the crew—six identical beauties, naked, with only gold scarves covering half their waists, fastened with diamonds belts that draped like a bow in the front

All the men stood, entranced, not wanting to blink in fear of losing sight of the vision before them. Madeline crossed her arm across her chest, watching Cage, at lost for words—and rolled her eyes at him.

The Oracles picked up the stretcher and carried it to the entrance where the Golden Phoenix's wings were spread and all mythical creatures disappeared behind it.

Constant peers as the gates closed and walk toward Santana.

"Whatever happens, do not show them your true self—the war they're talking about has to do with your kind."

"You have quarrel with my kind too, Constant?"

"Why do you think I've always kept you around? I knew who you where the moment you took Marie out of the house."

"And here I thought it's was because you thought of me as your son!"

"That, too! You grew on me, and I love you like you are my son. I'll fight both them and your kind to keep you safe."

"Well thanks, Dad."

"No problem, Son."

"I would do the same, to keep you safe," Santana said.

"I know. You have proven that over the years, but now, it's very important not to react, to show what you are."

Sic was still staring at the closed gate.

"You think those monster birds back there killed us, and we just don't know were dead yet?" he speculated not wanting to disturb the image of black goddesses in his head.

"I was thinking the same thing," Bullet commented. "I keep pinching myself!"

"No, you're not dead, and you're not dreaming," Constant answered. "This world needs to be protected. If I thought you couldn't handle it, I would have never brought you here."

"How long have you known about this?" Simi asked.

"When my angel fell into my arms and then disappeared, I had to search for her. Eventually, I came across things that were not possible and kept searching until I landed here. I had to travel the world, looking for her, while she was in my backyard the whole time."

"Who would that be, Constant?" Mac asked, even though he knew the answer. He always thought of her being more than just Constant's wife.

"You know who you she is, though I cannot reveal it to her. It was a deal I made with her father."

"So, we're demi-gods?" Roc asked.

"No! She was stripped of all her powers. She has no claims to her father's world. Her brothers can't even look at her."

"That was my uncle?" Simi asked, astounded.

"Yes! Olodumare is your true uncle, but he would never acknowledge you."

"Why would you make her give up everything?"

"I did not. By the time I found out, it was already too late. She wanted to be with me. I fell in love with her. At the time, I was too selfish to understand what she did, and what it meant. I tried making her happy, but life has way of putting obstacles on your path."

"What now?" Mac asked timidly.

"We wait until they come back."

"What if they decide to keep her and refuse to return her?" Shoty asked, voicing his fear of not being able to take her home with him or raise their children together.

"That would happen only if Joanne didn't want to come back. Constant answered. "Then this would be her sanctuary. Being that she's pregnant, and after what she did to you and your crew, she will raise hell to be with her husband."

Constant longed to hold his wife, watching her as she played with the girls while sitting on the ground. He left momentarily to search the caravan for supplies he thought that would come in handy. He removed the tents and set one up for his wife while motioning for Simi and Cage to do the same, and then they started a fire.

They camped close to the mouth of the cave, their backs toward the wall for safety. Everyone sat by the fire, lost in the own thoughts.

Magnum lied flat on the ground, still suffering from his injury, willing the pain away. Tank secured his arm around his ribs for support, since he forgot to take his pain medicine earlier. Sic played with his gums, moving his jaw in all directions, daydreaming about the wonders of God's creations.

Colossal stars twinkled on the multi-color skyline of faded purple and gray that merged with celestial blue and a touch of pink, mirroring the still crystal waters, shimmering off the coast. The men looking up experienced the illusion that they could reach out and touch a star.

Hours passed with no change to the climate or sense of night or day. The atmosphere remained cool and comfortable, and the sounds of the waterfall splashing on the steps descending the mountains soothed the campers into sleep.

Shoty fought against the effects of the calming sound. He sat up, refusing to fall victim to its lure, though his eyelids grew heavy. The flames from the fire dances shadows onto his face. Slowly, his body hunch over, but his ears recognized the sound of a bird call. Suddeny, he jumped to his feet, searching his surroundings.

When the phoenix opened its wings, a cluster of the naked wonder emerged. Females appeared by the fire, with fruit baskets and water jugs. Some of the women knelt over Magnum and began taking off his clothing, while others worked on Tank and Sic.

"What are they doing?" Sic asked.

"Relax, boys. They're going to heal your pains," Constant said, raising his head to explain, and then he lied back down with his wife, returning to his dream.

The Oracles helped Magnum to his feet and walked him a short distance to a translucent pool under a waterfall and next to an evergreen tree.

They formed a circle around each, taking hold of body parts and submerging each under the luminous crystal water that dripped from the roots of the tree of life.

Seven Oracles circles around, offering drinks from their hands until the last offering. They remained in a circle, clasping their hands again, bowing their heads.

A thousand little stars appeared, covering the mens' bodies, all grouped together to create a bean of light that pulsated, exploded around them. When the men emerged from the pools, all the pain they suffered from earlier in the day was gone.

Sic kept looking for the missing gap on his gums, even biting himself, feeling out his new front teeth. He grinned his teeth at Bullet for confirmation, dazed from the events in the pools at lost for words.

Tank could finally stand straight and take a deep breath. He was totally stunned, being worshiped by a group of the most beautiful women in existence. He jumped up and screamed for joy while doing the Michael Jackson's moonwalk.

Madeline lay in her tent next to the girls, clueless about the miracle events taking place at the campsite. She noticed a small piece of yellow lent on the corner of the tent, growing by the minute. It formed into a yellow star that she seen many years earlier. She closed her eyes, listening to the familiar voices that gave her the hope to survive.

"Wake up, sleepy head. Come on, I need you outside," the yellow start urged before circling around and giving her a shove in the back.

Madeline follows it and witnessed all the men being captivated by the nakedness of their hosts. She stood, watching as they engaged, noticing that three of her brothers were also naked, all standing there like it was the most common thing for them to do—especially Magnum.

She shook her head and looked off in the opposite direction while she was being pursues by other naked women. As they took hold of her hands, her first instinct is to fight her way out, but Constant intervened.

"It's okay, Maddy. They see something that needs to be healed. You can go with them," he said.

The oracle circled her, removing her clothing and fastening a gold sash around her waist while dragging her to the edge of the pool.

Cage's heart skipped a beat, his eyes glued to the scene unfolding right before his eyes. He counted as seven naked beauties in a circle undressed his woman. As their hands travelled all over her body, he scratched his head, letting the scene develop.

Madeline was not confortable letting people touch her, so she slapped their hands away, protesting with every moment. She felt the hand of the last oracle on her shoulder when she was at the edge if the water. It gently shoved her toward the pool. Before she could fully enter the water, a high-pitch voice vibrated through them, causing the Oracle to fly out the water. They bowed their heads, facing the floor.

"She cannot drink from the tree of life! She full of evil! Who brought this woman here?" The voice vibrated. Its energy shook the platform, knocking everyone off-balance.

Constant knew by the sound of that voice who was speaking, so he quickly pushed Cage inside on the cave's mouth and out of sight. He ordered him to stand his ground, reminding him of the talk they had earlier about "not reacting."

"Shhh… Stay quiet! You don't want to anger him right now," Constant warned in a low tone. He signalled for Jocks to help him in keeping Cage at bay.

"Maddy's in danger!" Cage argued, fighting to go to her, but Constant and Jocks had pinned him against the wall.

The tiny yellow star rising high above circled Madeline's head, and in a tremulous female voice, the answer came.

"*I did, Olorun. She's my charge, and I failed her. I couldn't keep her safe. She's not evil,*" the voice said.

"*I want them out of my realm! Their presence agitates me!*" the male voice shouted, penetrating throughout the realm, echoing in the distance.

Madeline stands stood inches from the pool, searching in the direction of the voice,

"Show yourself," she demanded.

A bright light shined through the tree a dark shadow, emerging as tall as the sky above, covering all with shimmery stars in a rainbow of colors.

"Who are you?" Madeline insisted, unafraid of challenging the supernatural force.

"*You are in my realm and you are asking me who I am? I am everything of all-knowing. I am Lord here and creator of all things. Now who are you? How did you get in my realm?*" he bellowed, descending to her eye level.

In his eyes, Madeline witnessed a violent galaxy of stars colliding with each other, forming whirlpools and vectors of cosmic blues, sapphire, teal and magenta, with bluish-white dust from colors scattered from shattered planets scattered about the Milky Way. Billions of stars exploded, and the galaxy was left in bereavement in darkness.

Deep in the twilight, twin starts were born, illuminating the galaxy and restoring the balance of light and darkness. He opened his mouth the distance of vast worlds beyond the nebula, full of bright starts and new planets.

"*Now, that is my purpose. What is yours?*" He turned to an exploding sound, deep in the city.

In Otherworld, past the gates of the Golden Phoenix City of origin, Orun Aye (heaven and earth), bluish-white bricks lay in the path stretching to the top of the mountain. Fully armed giants accompanied the Phoenix guarding the gates from the inside.

Mountains covered in white sandstone extented beyond the horizon, with lush evergreens harnesses—sixteen branches on each tree that surrounded Olorun's kingdom.

The spirals of white marble steps reached the top of the mountain, under a halo ring suspended in the air. Clear turquoise water gushed out from seven different opening from the caves deep in the mountaintops into a pool that ran throughout the city, casting eerie light.

White pillars dripped a rainbow from many bridges that connected to roads and streets. It citizens fluttered, never touching the ground. Vegetation and palm trees seized the city, bearing fruits on every corner. Thick white clouds covered each and every shingled roof home with natural earth-tones of soft white and lush green. The place flourished, lightening and bluish-white of sapphire brick roads.

Joanne was a guest in Olorun's home, resting on a bed of crystals to absorb their energy. Her field was the second strongest to ever enter the city. Because her powers were so intense in this realm, Olodumare order servants to restrain on her arm and legs. She began to stir, turning her head side to side, opening her eyelids.

CHAPTER 27

Olodumare walked away in search of his father, who was usually hard to find unless he wanted to be found. He climbed the highest mountain and called out to him, waiting for a sign that he may enter the council.

In a place where time did not exist, Olodumare walked away with the sense that his father did not want to be bothered, that Olodumare would be in-charge until his father wanted to emerge from whatever world he was in.

He climbed off the mountain, making his way to a special friend he met eons ago. She had recently come back from Earth with no memory of their past.

She was a shy, slim girl with lighten sliver hair and a fierce attitude that blew up half the city when she woke up from her slumber. Olodumere learned his lesson then and chose to restrain the lady for her own protection... and for the safety of his city.

He reached her door and rattled it, but he heard nothing. He knocked and heard her faint voice.

"Please come in," she answered.

He opened the door found her where she sat every day, staring into space, dreaming about her lost love—with two identical twin boys sitting at her feet.

She grieved over a husband who didn't know how to love her supreme being. She climbed a high water tower and then accidently fell into the rush of currents. He quickly created a whirlpool that transferred her to the mouth of the cave.

She, too, was a goddess who was sent on Earth as a child to help humanity. Instead, she was treated cruelly by many people in her life until she crossed path with her husband. He protected her and provided all that she needed—except to truly love and cherish the woman in her.

Olodumare found her unconscious and took care of her. He tried his best to soothe the pain away. Being in love with her, he couldn't act on his feelings and found other ways of showing her his attentions.

He took on the fatherly role for the two boys, checking in on her and making sure she was all right, assisting her on some of the missions she was assigned to accomplish.

Michelle was the goddess of war, with a vast army all around the Earth. She was highly skill in the art of war, with a bonus because she had lived on Earth. Her earthly husband and his people trained her to become a deadly assassin.

"Hello, Michelle. I need your help. There are intruders at the mouth of the cave. They brought a woman with them, and she needs our help."

"How do they know of the passage?"

Her honey-soft voice vibrated in the chambers, caresses his ears. He closed his eyes, letting its effect course through his being, wishing he could indulge her sweet nature.

"One of the humans is an old ally who helped us before."

"Well then! They're not intruders," she said, finally turning to look his way.

"No, he's not, but the woman in the crystal chamber is with child. They fear for her health."

"She's a goddess, then?"

"Yes, a very powerful one. I can't sense her origin."

"If you can't sense it, it's because she's part of you, Olodumare," she explained.

"I don't know," he said, "but she should not even exist, and to bore children on earth… those are forbidding."

"You can say what you want, but free will still exist," she reminded him, kissing the two boys and walking toward the door.

Olodumare stared at the way her body swayed toward him, her movements synchronized with her body structure, her lightly-bronze face appearing annoyed from being disturbed from her dream world. She brushed her locks back, fastened a cape with a hood over her long robe, which was slit at the waist, exposing her unique tattoo on her inner thigh.

"One of this days, you are going to have to tell me—of all the weapons you have at your disposal, *why the tank on your thigh?*" he asked, wondering what would possess her to choose that particular artwork.

She smiled knowingly at him, holding the boys' capes joining him at the door.

"It is indestructible. I prefer it, over all."

"But you've never used a tank in your battles before. I read all your reports of combats."

"You don't have to use it to know that it's… ahhhh!"

"What is that?" she screamed. An explosion from the rooftop flew up in the air, taking the side of a building. Shattered glass flew, turning into missiles as it impacted the ground.

The city was in a panic, its citizens running for cover. More explosions occurred to centers in one area.

"Is this the Crystal chambers?" she asked while running in the direction of the burning building.

"Boys, I want you to go to the safe house until everything is cleared," she said, jumping in the air to discover the cause of the explosions.

"But you promised!—you said we could come on the next mission!" one of the boys shouted after her as she leapt to another roof.

"Not now! Go!" she commanded.

Joanne peered out, her eyelids open, her vision blurred. She blinked, adjusting her vision, noticing all the translucent colors that filled the room. She felt the hard surface on her back, surrounded by stones, and tried to move her hands and feet, but they were restrained. She fought to escape the restraints. She wiggled, twisted and called for help. Having no other option, she screamed

The vibration of the voice shattered the material around her as she fought on the bed of crystal, and she screamed again.

Michele reached the room, with Olodumare not far behind. When she opened the door to the chamber, she got blast on the wall from the powerful vibration.

"It's okay. We're not here to hurt you. We just want to help you," she pleaded, edging across the floor, moving closer to Joanne.

"Where's my husband? Who are your people?" Joanne demanded, her voice sounding brittle as she searched for an escape route.

Michele reached her and released her hands.

"Do not blow anything. I'm untying you. Now, I'll release your legs. Relax," she warned.

"Don't release her—not until we know how to control it," Olodumare yelled at the door as he came through the threshold with a dozen guards at his heel.

Joanne sensed he meant her harm and extended both of her hands toward him, sending electrical bolts from her hands, blasting the whole side entrance, and Olodumare and his guards with it.

"I killed them!" She sighed. Wide-eyed, her hands flew to her open mouth, in shock about what just happened. Joanne stared out at the open hole, and then she turned to the lady with silver hair for an explanation.

"Why did you do that? I told you to relax," Michelle complained, taking hold of Joanne's hands to help her off the crystal bed.

"Come on. We have to fly down. You blew the entrance."

Joanne peeked over the edge of the platform and froze. In a gush of wind swills around them, all she was able to see was the fog of clouds that surrounded the rooftops.

Olodumare emerged from the clouds like the mythical creature he was, whith his with the guards following closely behind. They hovered above the building's structure, suspended in the air.

Michelle raised her hand toward him to stop him from interfering.

"I'm, I'm dreaming," Joanne whispered as she turned to her companion.

"No, you're not! You're in a different world, but we have to jump to the bottom." She noticed Joanne backing way from the edge. "If you think your going to fall, you will. Just think of flying, like a bird." Grasping Joanne's had, she guided her backward.

"Ready?"

With great reluctance, Joanne closed her eyes and jumped, falling through the clouds, screaming, never opening her eyes. Michelle rushed after her.

"Relax. Think of yourself as a beautiful bird that loves to fly." She coached the guards to form a circle that would prevent Joanne from falling, and then Michelle grabbed her hands again, helping to balance her weight

"I'm floating!"

Joanne seemed amazed as she watched the city, from high above. The crystal-clear waterfalls gushes out, and the high mountain caves shimmered and sparkled under the white bridges.

"Your world is beautiful," Joanne said, amazed by all the wonders of the lush greens pastels, Earth-tone bricks and colored stones of many sizes that made up the houses in the city.

"Thanks," Michelle said. "Here—try and balance on your own. Think happy thoughts." She encouraged Joanne. After withdrawing her hands, Joanne was able to spin around without being knocked off-balance.

"Good! You're getting the hang of it. Come, let's get you on the ground."

Joanne followed her, planting her feet on the ground and then looking up to see from how high she had descended.

"I was all the way up there?" she asked, pointing to the half-blown building past the clouds. Happy to be on solid ground with her feet on the surface, she noticed she was the only one touching the ground. Everyone else was floating. She also noticed that some of the residents had on pure white robes or toga wraps around their bodies, and some wore only a sheet of fabric around their waists. She leans toward her rescuer.

"Why do some have clothing, and some don't?"

"The ones with clothing lived on Earth and still have the urge to cover their nakedness, while the others never been there. Plus, with the weather here—you don't need clothing."

"Wow! All these people never been to Earth before? Why?" Joanne asked.

"Because they don't want to, or they have no desire to leave." As Michelle told Joanne to reach the ground fight to gain control of her gravity, her robe opened exposing her thigh. Joanne notice the tattoo.

"You've been to Earth then?"

"Yes, many times," Michelle said, silently reflection on the past.

"Would you go back if you could?" Joanne asked, sensing regret on the woman's face.

"I don't know if I could ever go back," Michelle answered, holding out her hand to Joanne, beginning to walk down the path that led to her house.

With no machinery to congest the city, the roads were wide open, it citizens gliding or flying to the destinations. Joanne walked with her head held high, obseering all the curious infinite beings surrounding them.

Michelle stumbles again, exposing her right thigh displaying a huge army tank.

"Your tattoo is interesting. Is there meaning to that symbol?"

"Someone I knew on my days on Earth—and miss him very much," she answered, suppressing great sorrow.

Joanne froze, remembering the tattoos on all the guys' chests and the story Shoty told her about his fallen comrade, Tank, and his wife.

"MICH," Joanne whispered, and the she saw Michelle's body tense as she turned and look at Joanne.

"No one knows that name here. How do you know to call me that?"

"I'm Shoty's wife."

Stunned from hearing one of her brothers' names, Michelle hands shook and waterfalls fell from her eyes. She glanced up at Joanne.

"How are they? I haven't talked to or seen my brothers in a long time."

"Uh, they are fine, I think. The last time I saw them... well, we had some issues. I think I beat them up."

"You beat an A.15 crew member?" Michelle laughed, remembering how fierce they could be. "Of course you did! You're a goddess, after all! They always said that only forces 'out of this world' could get the best of them. 'Man' can't touch them, and they've proved it!" she laughed. "So Shoty have a Goddess? Is anyone else married? Did Tank marry his white girl?" she asked, but before Joanne could answer her, a tremendous roar came from above them.

"*Who is this woman? Why is she in my city?*"

"Dad, I needed to council with you. I waited for you, but you never came. She's sick and with child. She was brought here by one of our allies. They're waiting at the mouth of the cave," Olodumare explained.

Olorun hovered over Joanne, displeased with all the powers he sensed from her. The closer he got to Joanne, he sensed whe was able draw power from him. Feeling drained, he backed away quickly.

"*I want her out of my realm, now! I don't ever want to deal with her or her mother! I can feel she carries all of her mother's power. I hope it swallow her whole, along with those children she carries!*"

He turned toward Olodumare and whispered into his ear, who gave Joanne a skeptical look after his father's order him let them perish. Michelle overheard the whisper and discreetly pulled Joanne and started giving her instructions about what to do once she reached the gates.

"He's not going to help. He wants you and the twins to die. Since you are away from your mother, he would then gain all of the power you have. He is your uncle, so he can inherit them, which would make him more powerful then he already is." Michelle looked around to see if anyone paying attention to what she was saying.

"Once you reach the gates, take off your clothes andget in the pool. I'll send some the oracles to help you get all of the guys in the there with you. Concentrate on releasing all your energy onto them. Have Shoty in front of you to help you carry the ones for the boys. You must do it quickly before he comes after you. Go, now!" she said, hugging Joanne.

"Welcome to the family, Joanne. I wish I was there to live it with you."

"Why don't you come back? Tank would love to have you. It's hard for him to even say your name."

"If I could go back, it wouldn't be for Tank. Tell Santana I'm sorry—it was never my choice. I never meant to hurt him. It was my mission to kill him."

Michelle signalled the oracles to follow her out the gates, and she watched Joanne leave, though she still had a lot of unanswered questions.

"What are you doing, Michelle?" Olodumare whispered behind her ears, giving her a rash of goosebumps.

"Nothing. I just sent her out the gates," she answers and turned to walk away. Not satisfied with the answer, he grabbed her by the arm, turning her to face him.

"If he finds out you helped her, he will banish you from here! He might even send you to purgatory," he said, gazing lovingly into her eyes, gently brushing the side of her face, letting his true feelings show. "That would break my heart—if it came to that. I don't want to see you suffer."

Michelle stared at his hands on hers until he removes them. she smiled at him and reminded him of a very special person in his life.

"I sure your wife is waiting on you, Olodumare. Give her my love, would you?" She walked away, leaving him to worry about her well-being.

Joanne was confused about what had just happened. While walking toward the gates, she understood what she must do to keep her family safe.

When the phoenix opened it great wings, Joanne walked out to find her frantic husband at the entrance. They locked eyes and run into each other arms, starving for attention.

"I missed you! I was so worried when I heard the explosion. I didn't know what to do. Are you okay?" he said between kisses, checking her for cuts and bruises. He hugged her again.

"Man, move over! She don't belong to only you!" Roc voice echoed from behind.

"Roc!" she shouted excitedly and flew into his arms.

"Man! Even in heaven they kick you out? You had to raise hell in there, Joanne, for them to show you the door!" he joked, hugging her tight. Simi shoved him over so he, too, could crush her to his chest

"There's no time. We have to get in the pool," she said, taking off her shirt. She walked over to her husband and took of his shirt. The Oracles took the hands of everyone before undressing them and pulling them into the water. Joanne looked over at Madeline and Constant, sending the Oracles after them, while she positioned herself in the center the pool, facing her husband. She turned and searched for Cage, signalling him to come to her.

"She said you need to help balance the force by holding me down,". she told him.

Cage took his position behind her as Constant protested about not being worthy of entering the pool. Joanne waves him off.

"You have to be in here. I wouldn't be in this position if it wasn't for you. Please help me finish what you started."

"We must hurry!" one of the Oracles warned. "He knows what you are up to."

Everyone in position, Joanne concentrated on releasing all her power to them, envisioning all the different versions of herself, leaving her body and entering their new host. Santana's strength was needed to ground her, as the force of energy ripping through her vibrated and rumbled throughout the mouth of the cave, a shift that many on Earth felt.

All the celestial beings emerged from the pool with signs of electrical shock, in a freezing state. Sic's teeth chattered together as he searched for his clothing. Santana's hair spiked up in the air and his jawline twitched from the current still running through his system. Madeline couldn't find her footing and dropped to the ground, letting the sensations exist her body. Mac had the classic look of being electrocuted, with his pale turned skin and ash showing around his lips.

Constant was enthralled about becoming a god himself. He had always secretly wondered what it would be like to be one. He could feel the power in his veins, his mind processing so many things at once. He watched his sons' transforms and couldn't wait to rule, with them at his side. He smiled, imagining the realization of the dream he had ever since he met his first infinite being.

Constant looked around the camp and noticed that Joanne was still in the water. He rushed in after her and carried her out. Shoty was on the ground, still tossing from the currents. Constant carried Joanne over to Marie and lay her down. Then he rose to leave, Marie caught his arm and looked into his eyes. Sinking into his arms, she kissed him.

"Oh, my darling! I miss you," he said. "I haven't had a kiss like that from you since Simi was born. I miss it." He embraced her and held her close.

"I miss you, too. This place reminds me the reason I fell in love with you from the beginning. I feel like I know this world. I belong here, and in your arms," she confessed, caressing his face and chest, feeling the heat she had for the man.

"Let's get everyone out of here," he said. "Once we get home, we can deal with all this." He kissed her forehead as he finished putting on his clothes.

The Oracles helped everyone with their attire. The the men packed up the camp and placed Joanne on the stretcher waiting at the mouth of the cave. Shoty still wasn't in control of his body. Magnum supported him as he walked, and Bullet held the stretcher, ready to move out when Olodumare rushed in, which would be their signal to leave.

"Go, now! Before he catches you!" Olodumare warned, afraid of his father's anger, worried about the young lady and Michelle.

Constant rushed everyone toward the cave exit, but right before they got out, they heard the rumble of the earth under their feet. A tremendous voice blew in, searching for them.

"*Where is she? Where is the young woman? She couldn't escape without help! Olodumare! Go find your general and bring her to me! She will pay for this!*"

Constant, afraid to face Olorun in his fury, continued to run. They would not rest until they were far away from the city of Orun Aye.

Back in Otherworld, Michelle faced Olorun as he descended in his human form, a blaze consuming him from head to toe. He cornerd her at the mouth of the cave, demanding answers.

Olodumare walks through the gates with the identical boys. He had prepared them for travel. He pointed, directing them to enter the cave. He was conflicted, standing in a place between his father and the woman he loved.

"Father! Enough of this. Why are you blaming her for this people who came here?"

"She knew about them and she helped that woman maintain powers that were meant for my house. I can't sense her any longer. She harbored them there, hiding."

He extinguished the fire consuming himself. Destructively angry, he shoved his son out the way with unimaginable power and surged toward Michelle.

She held her breath, unafraid of the universal life force coming at her. Instead, she was transfixed by the alluring figure that appeared before her eyes. She forced herself not to blink, unwilling to lose sight of the divine spirit confronting her about her loyalty to him.

Olorun's massive biceps pinned her to the wall, his eyes glowing with the luminosity of a star cluster, his perfect jawline brushing hers with the smooth skin. Ripe muscles covered his whole frame, giving him the illusion of a black panther, ready to devour its prey. His long locks shimmered and stardust covered her chest—his mouth a brush away from hers.

"*Goddess of war—did you betray the house of Olorun?*" His penetrating voice shook every cell on her body, turning her to ashen gray and unable to respond. She reluctantly shook her head, indicating yes, *she did help the lady.*

"*You are banished from my world! You will never return! Everything that belonged to you is now mine!*"

He grabbed her by the throat and placed his lips against hers, sucking out her essence, leaving her mortal. Raising his hand, he threw her in the cave and caused an earthquake, sending a violent cascade sand and rocks to seal the mouth of the opening, never to be opened again.

Then he turned to his son still on the ground, watching his heart banished from his world.

"That was the last time you will ever bring her back!" Olorun warned. "Do that again, and there will be civil war in my house. Go home to your wife and love her for a change. Start looking for a new general. We may go to war sooner than expected, since we now have a new emeny." Olorun grumbled and changed to his non-physical from before disappearing in the sky.

Torn between following his father's orders or to follow Michelle, Olodumare sat in the one position, grieving his lost love. They been together since land was created on Earth, and they had walked every corner of it.

He had lost her once when she was reborn and lived on the earth for a long time. When she returned, she claimed to be in love with someone else and claimed not to remember the love they shared. Now he had lost her forever. He was doomed to be alone for eternity.

CHATPER 28

Constant had warned everyone that they might lose their memories after exiting the cave, after they passed the whipping owl. Tracing back their steps, only a handful of people who were privileged enough to remember all events they experienced the caves.

Marie was in love with her husband again. She couldn't keep her hand away from him. She smiled every time she looked at him and climbed onto his back, hugging his neck and showering his face with kisses. The girls laughed at them.

Rachelle wished that she and her beloved could be so affectionate. She was happy that the couple finally found joy in each other again. Simi had never looked with such affection during the whole time they had been together. She decided to leave him once they returned.

Shoty was unaware of what is happening or about what was going on with his wife. She had been asleep since they left the pool. Constant confirmed that she was fine and needed rest to regain all the energy she lost. He insisted she would come through at any moment.

They reach the whipping owl and assembled around it, each person focusing their thoughts, unprepared to forget all they had experienced.

"Is it me, or does it seem like we been walking all day?" AK asked Constant. "Can we camp here a little bit before going on?"

"If that's what you want to do, it's fine. We can rest before we reach the cold levels of the cave." He sighed and sat Marie down before he began searching for the camp gear.

A small fire was lit, and everyone gathered around, watching with wonder. Simi finally sat next to Rachelle, but he never said anything to her. Instead, he drifted in his own thoughts, while she pretended he wasn't even there.

When Joanne stirred in her sleep, Shoty flew to her side. She opened her eyes, looking around, seeing his face, relaxing to know she was safe.

"You okay? You've been asleep," he concerned. She shook her head and tried to sit up, feeling hunger pains making her stomach growl. Shoty got her some dry fruits, peanuts and a bottle of water from the caravan. Then he snuggled with her.

After resting, the traveling party continued on their journey. They broke camp and gathered all their belonging. They stood in front of the eye, ready to pass through. Roc was the first to go, followed by Sic and Chopper.

Simi waited with Rachelle while the line was dwindling down. He grabbed her hands, whispering.

"I need you start acting like a woman instead of a spoiled child., If you do, maybe I'll start coming around."

"You don't have to do a damn thing for me, I'm over you!" she said, pausing to let her words to sink in. "I'll be leaving your home soon as we get back. Have a nice life, Mr. Constant." She walked off, passing everyone, and entered the owl's eye, leaving Simi to watch her bottom bounce away. He smiled, knowing he would make her pay for does words.

Joanne approached Cage with the urge of something important to tell him, but she drew a blank and could not recall what it was.

On the other side of the eye, all the men's memories were intact, but the women were fuzzy and only remembered bits and pieces of events that occurs prior to exiting.

Marie ignored her husband and walked over to Roc, and taking hold of his arms, she rested her head to his chest. Roc kissed the top of her head while watching sorrow fall over his father's face.

Constant backed up to the wall and dropped to the floor, feeling his heart shatter again, He closed his eyes, remembering the few hours they spent together, making sweet love to her in the tent and again in a private area by the waterfall. He remembered promises to each other, the repetition of marriage vows as he bathed and worshipped every inch of her body.

Shoty felt Constant's pain and knelt by his side, offering him an arm, patting his back, encouraging him to move on.

"You got her to fall in love with you twice in a lifetime. Third time's the charm!" he said, hopeful.

Constant stared at his wife for long moment.

"Yeah! Thanks." He s grabbed his gear and moved along the trail leading to the freezing cold areas of the caves.

The cold winds swirled around them, pushing them back, making it harder to move. They took small steps, inching along toward miles of roads leading to the jungle.

Roc struggled to hold his mother, whose bones were to cold to move. Finally, he walked her over to his father and set her in his arms.

"He can keep you warm," he told his mother. She turned her nose up at him, not wanting him to touch her, but as the warmth of his body penetrated her bones, she relaxed, welcoming the heat, and buried her head under his chin. Happy to hold her again, he crushed her closer to his heart.

Simi notice Rachelle struggling with the cold winds and tried to help her. Instead, she moved away, rushing toward her brother and jumping on his back. He already had Claire tucked under his coat, with Rachelle on his back, so he had a difficult time walking forward with the winds pushing him back. Simi walked up and grabbed Rachelle from his back, crushing her to him, whispering in her ear.

"See what I mean? Stop acting like a brat!"

"Get you hands off me! I don't want you touching me," she spat.

"Shut-up!" he said before planting his lips against hers and sensually caressing her lips, jaw and chin. He parted her lips with his tongue in search for hers. Their foreheads touched and they rubbed their noses together as he enjoyed the woman side of her.

AK laughed at the display of affection from them and walked off, shaking his head.

Roc walk by and purposely bumped into them.

"Get a room!" he hollered before continuing.

Madeline walks on, unfazed by any of the elements and reached the exit access. There she waited for the entourage to catch up with her.

Magnum, the first to reach her side, opened his coat set Brianna on her feet. They gather around a small clearing to shake off the cold in their bones before moving on. Madeline heard a faint noise and assumed a battle position, while the rest of security team circled them.

The crew watched her, sensing a major change, though no one could determine whether it was good or evil.

"You think she's affected more by all this then we are!" Bullet asked, remarking on her military mood.

"Only time will tell. We have to keep a close eye on her." Riffle states observe her reaction to every noise.

"We're not alone," she announced, feeling tension in the air.

Five miles away from the road, sitting in a mobile unit, surrounded by highly trained military personnel, Beltozar watched the monitors of the last known place his father was before he and his brothers went missing.

For four and half weeks, he had been searching for them. Every time he entered the jungle, it seems he walks around in circles for hours to a dead-end destination.

His mother in the RV came out every day and sat on the trail, waiting to see if anyone came out of the jungle. With no luck, she cried herself to sleep every night for the last four weeks, worrying about her son and her lover.

The monitor beeped, and heat signatures came on line, showing all missing party as active in the jungle. Without missing a beat, Belo rushed to the coordinates area and tracked them with the GPS monitor, entering the heart of the jungle "that did not exist."

Within minutes, he was surround by Mannon's army, stringing him high on a tree, upside down.

The fierce warrior approached him and applied a machete to his throat.

"These parts are forbidden to white man. How did you get through?" his voice vibrated.

Belo froze at the grim looks from the warrior, and knew they would not hesitate to cut off his head for entering their sacred place. Yet he remembered who his father was and answered the warrior without showing any fear.

"I'm tracking my father. He went missing about a month ago. This place is the last thing that registers in the GPS."

"No white man ever come to this parts!" Mannon repeated while raising the machete, ready to strike.

"Cut him down, Mannon!" echoed Constant's voice, coming from the clearing with Marie still in his arms. He puts her down to face his friend and enemy. Once again, both armies squared off. Infrared lights beamed at the warriors' foreheads, while deadly poison arrows pointed at their intended targets.

"This is no concern of yours. You of all people know the rules," Mannon said, still ready to strike with the machete.

"It's very much my concern. This is my son," Constant huffed closing on his enemy.

"You have a white son?"

"I have two of them. Now cut him down," he commanded.

Mannon senses his new strength and power antagonizing him.

"Well, well. Well, aren't we almighty now, your highness!" He bowedand threw his machete in the air to cut the ropes, dropping Belo on his back. He winced in pain from the fall and fought to catch his breath.

"You didn't have to do that!" Constant complained, watching his son in agony.

Madeline walked over and helped him to his feet, using her hand the sooth the pain away and heal his broken bones. Her opponent from earlier witness her power and approached, her holding his arm, which had a huge hole in it with black and yellow puss oozing from it—he was paralyzed on that side.

Madeline used her finger to penetrate his wound and inserted another, masking her face, knowing she was adding pain to his agony. He screams from the horror of it all as she slid her whole hand inside of the wound extracted the ooze, twisting her hand very slowly, agonizing at his torment.

He hollered in excruciating pain that could be heard from miles away. Predators in the jungle took cover, fearing being next. Birds flew off for higher grounds.

Mannon watched her fierce, menacing face, rending a deadly warrior to kneel before her. He felt an erection for the petite dark chocolate, with deep dimples. Taking a step toward her, Constant quickly stopped him, sensing his excitement. He shook his head at him, pointing toward Santana.

She completely removed her hands and wiped the residue on his chest, while the hole closed. His natural color returned to his arms and shoulders, and all the previous pains magically disappeared. He bowed to her, and the rest of his Army to followed his lead.

"I've been on Earth for centuries. I've never felt any kind of pleasure or pain. I thank you," he said, admiring her courage, her strength and beauty. He signalled for followers to clear a path for her.

"I'm forever in your debt," he said, awaiting her instructions.

Santana looked on, noticing that the warriors were admiring his woman. He felt uneasy about the way they were looking at her. When he tried to reach her side, Roc stopped him, signalling him to chill.

Constant grabbed his gear, motioning for everyone to move out after he saw Shoty, carrying Joanne.

"Do you want to walk?" Constant asked Marie. "I can still carry you." She nodded, and he took her up in his arms, ready the leave the jungle.

"I almost forgot," Mannon called after them. "Olodumare sent you a message." His eyes fell on Madeline. He smiled. "His father is looking for a new goddess of war. He says that you need to keep yours very close. You just might loose her!"

Mannon watched as Santana picked Madeline up and plant a kiss on her lips before carrying her out of the jungle, with Santo jumping around them.

"That's a lucky devil," he whispered looking directly at Constant.

"Yes, he is," Constant co-signed, watching the couple.

"No, he's not, and he only loves her," Marie rebutted, defending Cage.

Constant said his farewells and began carrying his wife. Her words affected him deeply. He drifted back in time, realizing how much he had hurt her throughout the years. When he reached the final path that led to the road, he pulled her closer and whispered into her ear.

"I never set out the hurt you. Some things were beyond my control. I got trapped and couldn't get out."

"For twenty-three years you were trapped and still couldn't get out?" she countered. When she started to get upset, he dropped the matter, kissing her on the forehead.

"Can I kiss you?" his hoarse voice caressed her ears. Remembering his kisses, she melted in his arms and perked her lips.

He indulged, savoring the moment of barely brushing his lips to hers.

"I love you," he whispered

Julisa, at the end of the path—was on pins and needles ever since Bello ran inside of the forbidding jungle. The locals had warned that he must not enter it, but Hell couldn't have kept him away if it meant saving his father.

She paced. The sun was already too hot. In the early morning, the birds were flying high along the path and sounds of tree branches snapping were evidence of military personnel along the path. Julisa noticed a large entourage coming towards her and saw her sons side-by-side behind their father, who was kissing his wife. She closed her eyes in a silent prayer for thanks and for courage to deal with what was to come.

Marie smiled up at her husband, snuggling the side of his face, wrapping her arms around his neck in affection.

Roc walked past and bumped into his parents, directing his father's attention to the end of the road. When Constant's eyes locked on Julisa, he froze in place, unable to do anything. Marie followed his gaze see the white woman she met many years earlier, the other love of his life,

She fought to get off him her, but he held on to her, signalling Mac and Bello to take care of their mother before he could move on.

"Put me down," she screamed, wiggling her body in his arms, he lifted her and tighten his grip.

"No!"

He carried her as they continued down the road, to the hummer climbed in behind her. She stared at him, hating that he always messed-up a good moment.

"Why can't you just divorce me and go marry her?" she screamed, lashing out. He lied back, closing his eyes, regretting the pain he has caused both women.

In Port-Au-Prince, Nadege and Ronald sat around the table, figuring out what they're going to do for the day that involved finding their child. It had been weeks since Nadege heard the sound of her son.On the night of the accident, she spoke briefly with him and he promised to call her back.

She terrorized the office every day for the last week, asking investigators what they knew happened to f boys and what they were doing about it. She wanted to talk the person in charge, but the desk people told her that he only came in for the first day of the disappearance and left to find the boys, leaving the companies in the charge of its outside partners.

"Ronald, are we going back to the office? See if they have some news," she told her husband.

"They will call, dear. I think you scared his secretary enough," her husband said, reminding her of the show she put on at pashou's office

"Well, I was not alone. Cathleen did a pretty good job herself in that department. Did you see how she lifted that big security guard off the ground? Hope her daughter don't take after her, cuz when she's angry, she can destroy some shit. The secretary was running for cover from her, not me."

"The secretary was running form both of you." He told her not to bother looking up from the paper he was reading, watching the boys' company stocks go down since they had been missing.

Nadege burst in to tears for the hundredth time since the ordeal began. Her husband just ignored her and watched her weeping at the table. He closed his eyes, trying to concentrate on the numbers in front of him.

"I don't know if my baby's in a ditch somewhere!" she continued. Was he kidnapped for his money? What is going on with my son?" she hollered—*acting a fool, her husband thought.*

"Ronald, you're letting her cry again!" Cathleen said, exasperated, as she entered the kitchen. She hated when he ignored his grieving wife. Sitting next to Nadege on the couch, Cathleen rubbed her back.

"You're missing your daughter. You're not acting likes a fool," Ronald said, rising and getting out the kitchen.

"Where's your husband?" he turned and asked..

"He went down to the beach to clear his head," she answered, watching Ronald exit the side door.

"Best you ignore her, or she won't ever stop!"

Cathleen wagged her head, hoping his son would not turn out like him, because Joanne was a person no one could ignore.

"Come on, Nadege, let's not jump into conclusions and wait until we hear what really happened."

"But Cathleen, that's a lot of people to go missing without a trace, and no one brought anything with them.I can't even find Constant—he's always on top of what the boys are doing." How could I not think the worst. And… there are some people around him that I don't really care for—deadly characters. Pashou has too friends. They look and act scary."

"More of a reason for you not the worry," Cathleen insisted. "These friends have sworn to protect my baby, and I know they'll do the same for him."

"What are going to do today?" Nadege asked between sniffles

"I was thinking we should track the person who went after them and see if he has a new lead."

"That a good idea. I'm glad you're here, dear. Otherwise, I might lose my mind with grief."

"Same here. Thanks for inviting us over, I would have lost it, too—not knowing where to go," Cathleen said as she glanced around the finish kitchen. "We did a good job fixing the house."

"I know, right? They're going to love it, and the staff the secretary send over is superb," Nadege remarked, proud of her work. "It's a really nice home, but what up with that big fish in the front?"

"I don't know. This was not Pashou's home. The secretary said it was a switch-a-roo with one of his friends,"

"So, why don't we go back to the office and see if the secretary can locate this guy?" Nadege suggested.

"Yes, that sound like a plan! Are we getting our husbands?"

"So he can ignore me some more? Stupid fool! I wonder what he would do if I didn't give him son to glorify him."

"Probably be whoring around," Cathleen joked, causing Nadege to laugh at the idea of her husband doing just that.

"You're so right! Come on—lets go see what this secretary can do."

When the two mothers walked into the lobby of MICH Enterprise, office staffs ran for cover, leaving security to deal with them. Yet before the lead guard could say a word, Nadege turned to Cathleen.

"Look, were not here to choke personnel. We want to ask for their help." She warns then adds

I hoped your daughter's not like you. She better not put her hands on my son!"

"She is just like me, and your son said he could handle it. And these people have worked my nerves for the last time."

"I think I jinxed my son," Nadege confessed, "the way he always acted tough around his girlfriends, I told him he would find a woman who would beat the crap out of him."

"Well, he found one, and you'll love her," Cathleen said, sensing her friend's hesitation.

"Really? You think so?"

"Well, she is *my* daughter."

"Who says I like you?" Nadege teased as she turned to face the general who came out to talk to the women. "Good morning, sir, we came here today to speak to Marlon Celestin's secretary, please."

"We don't want any trouble from your ladies," the general answered, eying Cathleen. "We've been dealing with all the mothers, and I'm telling you what I told them: there are no new developments involving the whereabouts of the MICH owners. The search continues. If any new information comes to our attention, you will be the first to be notified.

"We know that already. Cathleen responded. "We just want to talk to the secretary."

"She does not wish to speak to you, not at risk to her life."

"Her life is not in danger…" Nadege countered," and then her face went blank, as if she had fallen into a trance. "Are you alright?" she asked, nudging her. "You spaced out on me?"

"I feel my daughter, and she's weak…."

Cathleen hit the floor, and Nadege dropped to her side, clutching her phone to call Julio.

"Julio! She passed out! We're going to the hospital!" she said frantically on the phone.

"No, don't bring her to the hospital. They won't know what to do for her. Bring her here. I'll be waiting for you at the door."

Twenty minutes later, Julio carried his wife out the vehicle laid her on the couch. "What did she say before she passed out?" he asked.

Ronald exited the kitchen with a cold compress for her head. He passed it to Julio, his face showing concern for his beautiful in-law.

"Um…She said something about feeling her daughter and that she was weak," Nadege explained, "and then she passed out."

Julio sighed and relaxed, putting the cold compress on his wife's forehead, anticipating the return of his daughter.

Cathleen was not on the hospital.

"It means our children are coming home," he said while watching the door.

Later that evening, Cathleen still lay in the coach, unconscious the entire time. Ronald sat at a nearby table, worried about her health.

"Julio, how long are you going to keep her here like this?"

"She'll come through when the time is right. She's fine. You don't have to worry about her," he insists, his eyes still glued to the door.

"You know, this makes no medical sense," Julio complained. "I don't know. There's something strange about that Costello family! "Man, I know she's your wife, but you can't keep her here like this. You have to take her the hospital!"

"She fine," Julio insisted again, now irritated."

Ronald stood, agitated. "You don't know that, you don't know what is happening internally. She could be bleeding!"

"Look," Julio said, standing and glaring into Ronald's eyes to make himself clear. "I appreciate your concern, but there are things you can't understand, so please let me handle it! I can take of my wife…" He stopped as the front door opened with the vision of Shoty, carrying Joanne in his arms, asleep from the long ride.

Ronald followed his gaze and froze witness his son, a strong man, holding the most beautiful creature in his arms.

Shoty's mother, who sat on the couch, her head down, trying to block the shouting match between her husband and Julio, did not hear the door opening until she looked up.

"*Pushou!* My baby boy!" she screamed while rushing to him. Her voice echoes in the house, causing both fathers to react. Julio ran and grabbed his daughter. .

"She's okay? he asked and kissed her forehead.

"She's asleep, but she's weak," Shoty explained.His parent hovered over him. He hugged his mother, while she pinched him to make sure he was real. She kissed him and patted his solid form.

"Oh, honey, she beautiful! Is she okay? What do you need me to do?" she asked, leaving her son to check on his wife.

"Nothing," Shoty answered. "I think her father got it. Let's give them some room. Why don't you tell me how long you two been in town? When did you leave the cruise?" he asked, realizing Julio now understand the truth, though he could not share it. He ushered his parents from the front room to the kitchen.

"And I'm hungey—don't know the last time I ate," he told his mother who rushed to make her son a plate. His father gave him a questionable look.

"Not now, dad!" he said, closing the door to the kitchen.

Julio laid his beauties side-by-side, watching his wife's inner light cover his daughter in a protective glow.

The two lied in the the light of healing, drawing energy from each other. Cathleen opened her eyes hugged her daughter close, not wanting to let go.

Joanne opened her eyes and hugged her mother, excited. Cathleen wipe away her daughter's tears.

"Now, none of that. Hi, beautiful."

"Hi mommy," Joanne sighed.

"You saw your uncle?" Cathleen whispered. In her mind's eye, she saw the ordeal with her uncle.

"Yes, and he's mean! He says he wants for me and the baby to die," she told her mother.

"Yes, Oloran would not want this to pass. He's consumed with wanting to know who's more powerful. We are twins—he has the sky, and I have the Earth. Then he sent his son to make the waters recede and grow vegetation to challenge me by occupying it.

"At first, I accepted his challenge. We were at war for many centuries, but finally, I grew lonely and didn't want to fight anymore. I gave up and took refuge in the sea, where he couldn't sense my power… until I met your father and got pregnant. I needed to stay on land to transfer all my power to you, because it lies dormant in you. I became a mortal, and I don't regret one minute of it."

She brushed her hair back, admiring her creation across the earth, her greatest accomplishment.

"Your uncle wants all the power, and that's very dangerous. It's only a matter of time before he destroys all of it, like before, now that he has your powers."

"No, he doesn't!"

"But I saw him drawing them from you!"

"That was me drawing his!"

"But where are your powers," Cathleen asked.

"I transferred them to my husband and his friends," Joanne answered, smiling at her mother.

"You're such a clever girl" her mother laughed. "I would have done the same, but I wouldn't have trusted a man with that much power, and I couldn't have put them all in your father. He wouldn't have wanted them."

"Well, I kind of didn't give them a choice," Joanne confessed.

"So what happens with uncle Olorun now?" Joanne asked.

"He's probably going to want war, but he won't find it."

When they rose from the couch, Julio rushed to their side, hugging his beauties, happy to have their daughter back.

"I'm hungry," Joanne complained, and Julio directed them to the kitchen.

When Nadege saw her friend, she hugged her tight.

"You had us worried all day. How are you feeling?"

"Great. Look, my baby's back!" Cathleen exclaimed.

"I know. Mine's back too," she said, pointing at Shoty. He rose from his large plate of food and walked toward Cathleen.

"Wow, Jojo! He's handsome!" she said, hugging him tight, weeping. "Thank you for keeping her safe."

"It is my job to keep what mine very safe, and you," Shoty said, hugging her.

"His such a charmer Nadege. Where did you get him?"

"I'm sitting right here, Cathleen," Ronald said, pretending to be jealous. They laughed at the thought that he might be serious.

"Yes, Ronald, you're very handsome too," Cathleen confirmed

"Don't know why you're saying, 'I'm here,'" his wife mimicked, making Joanne a plate.

"I did all the work. All you did was sit there and grunt."

"That's because you like to ride, honey. I let you have your way, but you can bet tonight it's all about me," he said, staring at his wife.

The room was in pure bliss, laughing at Shoty's parents. Cathleen, enjoying herself, hi-fived Nadege. "And put their asses to sleep!"

Joanne giggled as she looked at her husband, who didn't seem pleased, and Julio went quiet, looking at his wife, causing mother and daughter to laugh even harder.

"What's wrong with your two? Cuz ain't no one putting me to sleep!" Ronald proclaimed.

Julio, paying close attention to the newlyweds, noticed how uncomfortable his daughter's husband was acting while watching his wife.

"You taught her!" he roared.

Cathleen bit her lip, not wanting to have that conversation with her husband right then. He never wanted her to teach Joanne about men. He felt that when the time came, her husband would teach her. She timidly nodded her head while avoiding looking into his eyes. She peeked with one eye, and he seemed furious.

"And the banana!" Shoty added, shocking both Cathleen and Joanne

"You just said you would protect me," Cathleen complained, "and you just sold me out!"

Shoty seemed amused over her anxiety.

"Cathleen!" he roared again.

"But honey, look—he's happy," she stuttered, turning to Shoty. "You're happy, right?"

Shoty went over to his father in-law and whispered in his ear. Julio was impressed by some of the tactics he used. He couldn't help knowing.

"You do all that to my daughter?" he asked, bewildered.

"No!" Shoty said stunned that he would ask.

"But I do it to my wife! Especially when she's upset." Shoty laughed and whispered into Julio's ear.

"You alright, Marlon? You can take care of a goddess?"

"I told you that over the phone, and I'm learning every day," he said. Both looked at Joanne, making her blush.

'Okay, let me know when you ready to share all these secrets," Nadege said.

Cathleen whispered in her ear.

"Oh, I want to know how to do that!" she cries out. Everyone laughs in wonderment. The three couples stayed up late in the night, sharing stories of the past.

CHAPTER 28

Life in the Celestin house had been an uproar of laughter, with the three couples enjoying each other's company. Joanne was ecstatic, having two mothers at her beck and call all day.

She fell in love with Shoty's mom, a sweet woman who devoted her life to loving and cherishing her children. Now, she learned she'd be a grandmother and had decided to stay with Joanne until after the birth of the babies.

Cathleen also decided to stay and spoil her daughter more. Between her and Nadege, Joanne didn't have to lift a finger, and she loved the live conversation. Nadege didn't censor topics. She felt the kids were not children, so she pretty much talked about everything. She often caused Shoty to blush or cover Joanne's ears.

Nadege loved the bond her son had with his wife. They were very affectionate with each other and they discussed everything. Even when there was disagreement, they found ways to compromise. Arguments didn't last more than five or six minutes. The only thing that had her on edge was her son's defense mechanism, guarding his neck, during a disagreement. Other than that, she loved her daughter in-law.

It had been four weeks since the ordeal at the mountain. Shoty dealt with his newly inherited powers, which makes it difficult for him to sleep at night. But Joanne could put him to sleep and he woke up refreshed and took long jogs on the beach naked in the morning.

He loves having both mothers in his home. They were doing a wonderful job looking after his wife. They fixed the house and hired a staff to run it, though his mother cooked for him morning, noon and night.

At night, he sat with the fathers and had deep conversations about many issues facing the country, usually ending in a shouting match between Julio and his father. Shoty always stayed out of politics, which was not good for business.

He returned to work the very next day and buried himself in his work. With so much to make up after a month of absense, their stock had crashed, costing MICH millions in lost revenues. With most of his investors pulling out, his scheduled projects were at a standstill.

Riffle and Simi left town the day after their return to deal with international business on a twenty-eight-country tour and were not due to come back for six months to one year.

Sic and Pistol were doing the twenty-eight countries on the African continent. They would take a break for the birth of the babies.

Joanne stayed at home, being pampered by both of her mothers. She hadn't returned to the lab, though her father pretty much lived in the lab. He left early in the morning and didn't return until later in the evening, when he spent time with his in-laws. He needed to fly back to the U.S.A to retrieve his files and close loose ends. He was done living in the U.S. and wanted to be closer to his daughter

He promised Shoty he would help him in his technology department, testing new products for his company before they went out.

Constant, too, wanted to help. Since their return, he had been on his best behavior, trying not to hurt Marie, but he knew the boys needed help. He had asked Marie to accompany him back to Port-Au-Prince. Rachelle had left for the U.S. a week after they returned. It broke Marie's heart—it had only been the two of them in the house.

He hadn't spoken to Julisa. She refused his calls and flowers he sent every day. Bello had stayed with her for the past month, but he needed to return to France to run his birth father's companies. Constant helped him acquire them at the age of eight, and he had always been his own boss. Julisa felt she needed to go with her son, moving back to France.

Constant hadn't ventured in the godly-world stuff either. Their powers were dormant because they couldn't be accessed on Earth. They had a better understanding of the world, giving them capabilities of seeing good and evil in people around them.

He flew in late during the previous night. Marie hated hotels and refused to go to Bull's-Eye and called Mag to pick her up. She wanted to spent time with girls. With Madeline in training, she didn't have much time for them.

Marie wanted to talk to Mag about finding a permanent nanny or a mother for them. The girls were in desperate need of female guidance. If he could not find either, she asked him to consider moving to Port-Au-Prince in the next few months.

Constant and Marie were in the guest room at Mag's. He slept naked on the couch, leaving Marie on the bed. They had reverted to their old ways when Marie ignored him. Nevertheless, he tried desperately to get her to love him again

In the last week Constant fall back on doing things for her. He pretty much disappeared, living in the same house, staying in his office and eating his diners alone.

That day was the first day they were in the same room together. She stirred on the bed. Seeing him lounge on the couch, she scanned his naked body, taking her time to completely get the feel of him.

Marie fanned herself. The temperature rose in the room. Her body tingled at the sight of her sexy husband lying naked, staring off at the ceiling. He sensed her, turned and looked her way. Their eyes locked and he saw the heat in them, wanting nothing more than to climb into the bed and properly wake her up by making sweet love to her.

He closed his eyes, replaying the images from the caves—the way she rode him by the waterfall caused him to have a full erection. He patted it, trying to get it down, rubbing the head, but her image burnsed in his brain. He saw the way she set her face, her breasts bouncing, he heard her moans. He had no choice but to rub those memories away.

She heard his heavy breathing on the couch. His body responded to his touch as he remembered her wake-up calls in the morning before he left for the office.

She shook her head, exiting into the bathroom, leaving him to finish off his business. Sitting on the toilet, she wished she could forgive him and move on, but the hurt was too deep. *He had a whole other family!*

He walks into the bathroom, never bothering to look her way. He stood in front of her, to turning on the shower, his still semi-hard-on head poking-out. Her mouth watered, wanting to taste it. She moved forward closer to it, but he entered the shower, leaving her out of breath and starving. She had noticed lately that every time she was in his presence, she felt deprived.

Constant smiled in the shower after hearing the bathroom door slams. He enjoyed driver her crazy. He finished showering, dressed and walked down the stairs where he watched Marie with the girls in the front room. He quietly left without saying anything to her.

Roc had dropped off his Maserati earlier that morning so he could get around without security or the service cars that he hated. So Constant was at the gate, waiting for it to fully open, when his phone rang.

"Hello?" he said and paused, listening. "Why didn't you say you where leaving?" He closed his eyes. Her voice always affected him, so he took a minute, making sure his answer sounded cold and detached. "I didn't think anyone would notice, but I'm driven. I have to go."

"Why are you acting this way?" she asked.

"I'm not acting any way. Look, I have to get in the office, I promised Shoty I'd be there by seven. I have about ten minutes to get there. Have a nice day. We'll talk when I come back tonight. Goodbye Marie!" He hung up, smiling all the way to the office.

He parked in the garage and exited the car, removing his sunglasses. He was walking toward the elevator when he collided with someone from his past.

"Julio! man!" Excited to see each other, they clasped arms in a brotherly embrace after twenty-three years of absence.

"Oh Reginald!" Julio hugged him, happy to see his old ally again.

"I tried reaching you for months. All the numbers I had gave me a busy signal."

"Yeah, I had a family emergency a while back—had to leave country. But what are you doing here?"

"I told my son in-law that I would check out some of his work for him today."

"Hold on a minute!" Constant said, reaching for his phone to call Shoty, who answered instantly. "Yeah, look," Constant said, "I just ran to an old friend. I'm here in the building. Give me a few moments to catch up."

"You work here?" Julio asked.

Nan, I don't, but my sons own the building. I give them a hand when I can, but tell me—what have you been up to since we last saw each other?"

"Maybe we can get a cup of coffee?"

"Yeah, he's not expecting me until eight. We can grab a cup." Julio confirmed.

Constant led him to a side door that connected to the upper floor of shops and cafes. They walked in one of the lavish restaurant and were greeted by a pretty brown-skinned hostess, shape like an hourglass.

"Bonjour, Monsieur Constant. Your usual table?"

"I love watching creole women," Julio whispered, low enough for him to hear.

"They're the rarest pearls," Constant co-signed, while observing her figure jitters on the way to the table. *A bottom like that could make a man happy going to his death!* Constant thought as his head bounced with her movements.

They laughed, headed inside the restaurant like the young, free spirited youth they were so long ago.

"I see you still cause trouble every where you go," Julio joked. "Look this little caramel over here—she can't keep her eyes off you!"

Constant laughed and took a peek. The girl was indeed very beautiful. He caught her eye and winked, making her blush.

"Maybe she was looking at you, Julio?"

Nan, that's all for you, my friend," Julio said waving a hand. "So tell me: did you ever find that wife of yours?"

The friends had met when Constant was searching for his pregnant wife, who left because she was sick, like Joanne.

"Yes, after I left you in Egypt with the Shaman, he sent me on a different journey. It was difficult, but I found her. We have two boys together... although she's very upset with me now."

"You left your wife upset? You deserve an 'F, cuz your teacher taught you well. What would he say to you now?" Julio laughed.

"Shaman—now he was a character! He had like, five wives! and they all lived a few spaces from each other!"

"You remember his creed?" Julio guffed between laughs.

"Which one? He has so many!"

"The most important one, and I live by it everyday."

"Which on is that?"

"*Your wife must rise in the morning in pure bliss as you drink her nectar.*" he said, laughing.

"And he had a lot of nectars in the morning! I can't keep the two I have, now he was the man!" Constant said, confirming his admiration for the old African Shaman, they met years earlier.

"You have two? Damn, man—I'm still with my one."

"Yeah? what ever happened to that old Sea Hag who used to stalk you and mean-mugs all the ladies that fell to your feet," Constant laughed, not noticing Julio change in demeanor. "She gave me nightmares for years! I kept thinking she was going to drown me in my sleep. Everywhere we went, she was there lurking. Have you seen her since we left Africa? She was really in to you?" Constant asked, noticing that his friend was not laughing any more.

"I married her," Julio said, his face serious, "and we have a daughter."

"Oh shit! You married the mermaid and had a child? What, is she a fish?" Constant laughed sarcastically. "Look, don't be so serious. I'm just joking with you! All that matter is if she makes you happy."

"My wife is very beautiful," Julio said, "and so is my daughter. The Sea Hag was a disguise she used to run away from her brother."

"Well, I would love to meet her... and your daughter. As a matter a fact, I would like for you to meet my wife."

"That would be great. After all, you had me traveling the world looking for her."

"Let me see if she wants to go out, maybe tonight? Is that good for you?"

"Yeah, the ladies aren't doing anything but sitting at home and cooking."

"Wow! A home-cooked meal? We're coming to your house."

After calls to confirm dinner with their wives, Julio looked over the see the young lady crossing her feet, showing off her thigh. Constant smiled, nodding, signalling her to uncross her legs and open them wider. She obliged, showing off her pink panties and caramel thighs. Julio eyes, too, were glued to her offering.

"You know she's with someone?" Julio whispered, still watching her as she slid her fingertips along her crotch, her index finger inviting him to come and get it. Julio shook his head, remembering all the wild sex-escapades they shared. "You still got it man! You haven't changed."

"Yes, I have. I'm just having a little fun because you're here," Constant explained.

"You mean you were showing off? Oh, her companion is coming," Julio warned Constant while ducking behind a menu.

Stifling laughter, he sat erect as the tall, reddish-pale mulatto with light blue-gray eyes approached. He did not seem at all pleased.

"Shouldn't you be upstairs instead of being a perverted old man?" Mac asked.

"Oh look! It's my son," he said to Julio, and then the realization hit him, causing his face to drop. "Oh shit! It's my son."

Constant's son, Mac, was the young lady's companion.

"You didn't teach him the Shaman way?" Julio laughed.

"I teach! They just don't listen."

"We listen, but those rules apply to wives," Mac said as he glanced over to look at his flavor of the day. "She's just a plaything!"

"Plaything or not, she should only keep her eyes on you!"

"I'm over it," Mac shrugged, waving her off.

"Was that before or after you smelled those pink panties?" his dad asked.

Mac examined the girl at the table who had been flirting. He dropped a few hundreds on the tray and shooed her away. "That's my father!" he shouted as she left.

"You know you didn't have to do that," Julio scolded.

Mac took a seat, called the hostess over and ordered a bottle of rum. The two friends couldn't stop laughing at the expression on Mac's face when the young lady grabbed the money rushed out of the restaurant.

When Mac called Shoty, letting him know they were in the restaurant, Shoty decided to bring the entire office there for breakfast, and he left a message for his father in-law to join them. Everyone was assembled in the restaurant, save the four that were away.

When Shoty walked in, he saw his father in-law at the table with Constant. "Here I'm waiting for you upstairs," he joked, shaking his father's hand, and took a seat next to him. "What time you got in last night?"

Shoty was unaware of the tense atmosphere. Julio and Constant sat in uncomfortable silence while Mac threw back a shot.

"What's up with the bottle early in the morning? What's eating you," Shoty asked.

"Dad! Like he don't have enough women problems!" Mac said, still irritated.

During breakfast, Shoty decided to break the tension by being straight, asking the obvious question. "What is it? What's going on here?"

"How do you know Julio?" Constant asked.

"Oh, he's Joanne's dad. I thought you knew. Sorry for not making the introductions. Julio Costello, meet Reginald Constant… and over here is Mac—or Magnum. At the far end, that's Bullet and Cage, then you have AK, Cali and Nock. On the other side, that's Tank and Tech. Roc should be here soon."

Constant shook his head in shock, finding it hard to believe that his friend, Julio, was Joaanne's dad. "The Sea Hag gave birth to Joanne?"

"Excuse me?" Shoty complained to his father.

"Stop calling my wife a sea hag," Julio insisted. "It was a disguise. I told you she was hiding out from her brother!"

At that very moment, Rocket walked in the restaurant and came toward the table, removing his sunglasses, causing Julio to stand, his face tense.

"Olorun!" Julio breathed, confused and terrified. He stumbled from the chair, ready to flee. The last time he crossed path with Olorun's life force, he barely escaped with his life. If it wasn't for his wife, he would have died, never to be reborn.

At Julio's side, Shoty braced him, standing him up, grabbing the bottle from Mac. "Looks like you could use a drink!"

Taking the bottle, Julio took a desperate drink, his eyes never leaving Rocket's face. He collapsed in the seat next to his son in-law.

Roc returned his attention to the table. He was fed up with the stranger eyeballing him.

"Is there a reason why you keep staring at me?" he asks Julio in his stoic manner.

"Chill, Roc," Shoty said. "This is Joanne's dad."

"Okay. Nice to meet you, but why are you staring?" he asked.

"You remind me of a person who attacked me years ago. I do apologize. You just caught me off-guard," Julio explained, still staring. The resemblance is uncanny. *They were identical!*

Julio had the displeasures of battling with Olorun over his wife when he refused to help him find her. Olorun's solid form attacked Julio and killed him—by traditional medical terms. Olorun punched a hole in his chest and crushed his heart. Julio would never forget the look on his face.

"I was supposed to meet with you yesterday," Roc said, "but last-minute things came up. Hopefully, I'll be able to see my best friend Joanne today. Is she behaving?"

"She's being pampered by two mothers," Shoty said with a mouthful of food.

"You're her best friend?" Julio asked, stunned that Marlon would allow Joanne to be around Roc.

"Why? Is there something wrong with that," Roc asked, irritated.

"Well, it's just that he's a good-looking man. You trust your wife with him?"

Shoty raised an eyebrow, glancing up. "My wife only has eyes for me."

Constant gave Julio a thumbs-up. "I told you I taught them!"

Over the course of the day, everyone went about their normal schedules, though Shoty, before making his way home, cornered Constant about the morning's events.

"Are we going to talk about it, or pretend we know nothing?"

"For now, let's play ignorance."

"You think he doesn't know about his wife?" Shoty asked.

"From the way he reacted to Roc, he knows *exactly* who his wife is!"

"Why did he react to Roc like that?"

"I didn't notice it before," Constant answered, "but ever since Roc's grown out his hair, he's become the spitting image of Olorun."

"You've seen him?"

"Yeah, many times. He'll only reveal himself in solid form when he's extremely angry."

"You going to tell them the connection between them tonight?"

"Why climb up the family tree? Both sides have nothing to gain."

"Alright, see you at home then," Shoty said, but then he turned back to his father. "Oh, I forgot. System band is playing tonight at Mag's club. I want to take Joanne."

"I'll see if her cousin wants to go," Constant said. We'll meet at the diner party."

Constant entered Blanc Villa and went straight to his guest room find his wife already dolled up and fastening her heels while still in a bath robe. He scanned the room, noticing all the new shopping bags scattered on the bed. She was wearing a new matching set of diamond earrings, a tennis bracelet and a necklace.

"How much did all this cost me today?" he asked.

"Hello to you too, husband," she sing-songed, walking around, feeling out her new heels.

He grunted, knowing she was purposely avoiding the question. Whenever she went out shopping, she usually cost him a small fortune. "Hello, Mrs. Constant." He still stared so she would know he was waiting for an answer.

She rolled her eyes and walked toward the bed, picking up a dress and stood directly before him.

"Which one of these dresses?" she asked, showing him a short white dress that zipped in the back. "Or this one," she said, opening her robe, showing a white chiffon negligee with lace stockings, attached by a garter belt, all accented by the new white diamond jewelry.

Constant was instantly flabbergasted. It didn't matter how many time he saw her, she always had him at loss for words. He scratches his head, taking in the view.

"I need a cold shower," he mumbled to himself before exiting and slamming the bathroom door.

Marie stood in the middle of the room, staring at the closed.

"Two can play that game, Mr. Constant!" she whispered.

Shoty walks into his house, seeing the ladies had outdone themselves in preparation for the diner party. His house was truly transformed into a magical palace, filled with all shades of white and gold.

The smells from the kitchen were heavenly. He opens the door to find both his mother and mother in-law, busy at work, with last minute preparations.

"You ladies aren't dressed yet? It almost seven," he said kissing both on the cheeks while searching for his wife. "Where's Joanne," he asked, sneaking a piece of fritay to his mouth that was too hot.

"She was on her feet all day. We sent her upstairs to lie down," his mother answered, slapping his hand away

"Have I told you how much I appreciate the two of you here?"

"Ohhh... Nadege, his such a charmer," Cathleen announced while approaching Shoty and planting a big kiss on his cheek. His mother felt the urge to do the same, so both ladies kissed him. Shoty loved the attention.

"Your husband told you we're gong out tonight after dinner?"

"Yes, and we have our dancing shoes ready! Go find your wife."

Shoty walked up the stairs and into his room to find his wife on the bed, naked and a sleep. He felt the urge to wake her, undress her and climb in the bed behind her, kissing her neck, bringing his body closer to hers.

"How was your day?" he whispered in her ear, all the while guiding his erection, bending her knees a little, trying to find her opening. He wiggled his hips, pulling her to him. He was able to bury half of himself inside of her.

He slowly pushed in a little further. He loved taking her in that position because his rod felt like it being was choked by her meat.

He held onto her hip and started moving a little faster, her natural juice coating his dick, making it able to slide more freely.

"You think you can go on you stomach," he whispered, "I'll put a pillow under it. He straddled her from behind and caressing her butt cheeks, he slid his penis inside her hot wet pussy. He took hold of each cheek, rotating his hips and pelvis slowly and sensually.

He took his time, unrushed, afraid he might hurt her if he acted like the savage that wanted to fuck her right then. He bear-hugged her ass to bring her closer to the head of his cock. The sensation to bury his penis in her to the hilt her was driving him mad.

"Can you take all it, baby? I want to fuck you!" he breathed in her ear.

Joanne got on all fours, backing her butt into him, causing him to lie back in a sitting position. Then she took his whole penis inside her, jiggling her butt and making it dance by clapping it.

Shoty grunted and moaned, trying to hold on, but the sensation was too great. He felt his body ready to peak before hers, so he pushed her forward, making her get on all four again. He pumped, away hitting at her g-spot. Joanne felt a sweet warmth that kept building and building until...

"Oh! Fuck me! Oh! Ah, Shoty... Mmm!" she screamed.

Shoty gasped and groaned, spilling his seed deep inside her. He collapsed on the side of the bed, dragging her on top of him. "That was alright? I didn't hurt you, did I?"

"No, we're fine. We need to get up or we're going to be late."

They rushed out the bed and took a quick shower. Shoty finished and went downstairs to wait for their guests.

His father also came down, awaiting his wife, and then Julio joined them.

The three men were on their third shot of rum when the doorbell rang. Constant walked in, holding his wife's hand. She wore a simple white suit, with no jewelry. She looked like the goddess she truly was in the short knee-length white dress and white diamonds from head to toe. Her natural curls were in an up-do, showing more of the jewelry.

"Julio, may I present to you my wife," Constant said, and then turned to her. "Remember I told you about my research partner? This is him. We ran to each other this morning."

"It's nice to meet you," Marie nodded. "He's always talked well of you."

"Wow!" Julio flirted. "He said you were beautiful, and I didn't believe him. You a are a sight!"

Marie glanced over at her husband and walked away.

"Hi Ronald—haven't seen you in ages. See how our son is all grown up, with a wife and babies on the way? She turned to Shoty.

"I don't know who told him I was ready to be a grandmother," she complained.

"But you're already a grandmother—Mag's girls," Shoty reminds her.

"Yeah, but now its four times over. I wasn't prepared for that. I'm too young to be a grandmother. Maybe I'll have them call me 'auntie,'" she teased.

"You going to love it and you know it," he said while kissing her cheek.

Just then, the other beauties in the house walk to the platform The men are blown away, by the bombshell's coming down the stairs, beginning with Nadege. Each woman had her unique style—Nadege, in a soft teal gown with dark green rubies that matched her husband's vest, and Cathleen, in a light yellow, off-the-shoulder close-fitted dress that hugged her curves.

Joanne wore a pearl white dress, which was loose around the belly, along with a dark sapphire blue-ribbon strap purposed to hide her baby bump—Shoty wore same color vest. She accessorized with dark sapphire blue jewelry.

Shoty was the first to break the spell of admiration. He went to the stairs, and one-by-one, he took each woman by the hand, kissing it and then bowing.

Nagede gave Marie tight hug.

"Girl, look at our son—all grown up with a wife and babies on the way!" Nadege watched Shoty greeting the other women. "Ooh, he's so sweet, the perfect gentleman. I think we did a good job, don't you?"

Finally, Shoty greeted his own wife by holding her hand and dropping down to a knee, presenting her with a single red rose.

"To the most beautiful woman that the universe has put in my path. I don't know what I did to deserve you, my oneness! I love you!" He rose and planted a big kiss on her lips.

Joanne smiled and whispered. "I love you, too."

There wasn't a dry eye in the room. Marie and Nagede walked over to the happy couple and both mothers kissed Shoty, one on each cheek in a group hug. Cathleen felt left out and rushed to the group, hugging him from the front.

Ronald went over to break up the little hug-fest. "Come on, give the boy some room to breathe! Don't forget, we taught him all that stuff!"

"You know," Shoty said, loving the attention from the ladies. "I'm the luckiest man in this room."

"Little pissant!" Constant mumbled under his breath. "How you figure, Shoty?"

"I have three beautiful mothers and a gorgeous wife!"

"Yes, a Shaman Class 101 classic," Julio confirmed.

"And how did you teach my son?" Nadege asked Julio.

"I had to keep him up with the Shaman's teaching. He was always drunk," Julio said, laughing, tapping Constant on the stomach.

"Why am I not surprised, Reggie? You were always in the bottle," Cathleen reminded him.

"Hello, Sea Wit… uh!" Constant looked at Julio and smiled. "I didn't recognize you without the seaweeds in your hair. How's life been treating you, Cathleen? I can see you've changed."

When she punched him on the stomach, she made sure he felt it.

"I'm not going to let you get under my skin, you pestilence! I'm here to celebrate my daughter and her wonderful husband," she said, glancing toward the young couple.

Joanne noticed the intimacy between her mother and Constant and leaned toward Shoty. "They know each other?"

"Yeah, that your dad's research partner," he answsered.

"So that's how he has the codings!" at last realizing how Shoty and his company were able to use her codes and features.

"Yes, I meant to tell you earlier, but we got a little distracted. Your dad sent them to Constant for safe keeping when not just military, but also some other people in the industry, who heard the technology."

"Your two are such cuties!" Nadege commented. "You're always whispering, chit-chatting with each other."

The butler came to the door and announced that dinner would be served on thepatio and motioned for the diners to follow him outside. The luminous moon cast its reflection on the tranquil waters of the ocean, mirrored in the sky.

Everyone sat at the large round table, set with sixteen plate settings. The staff began with appetizers and drinks and soon filled the table with wonderful Haitian food.

The couples enjoyed the atmosphere. Shoty couldn't keep his hands off his wife. He kissed her and whispered in her ear every five minutes. He loved how the moon cast its light on her skin and the way the stars twinkled in her eyes.

The parents are at awed observing the interaction between the two. They smiled in admiration for the love witnessed.

Constant, too, was admiring his wife, but he could only see annoyance in her face. When he looked over to Nadege, it seemed that she too, could sense the change in Marie's mood.

"Well, we'd love to watch our children all night, but I need to go to the ladies' room. Marie, can you join me?" she said, and not giving her a chance to answer, dragged her in the house.

"What's going on with you?" Nadege asked while entering the kitchen. "You look like you ready to choke someone!"

"My husband!" Marie answered, a bit agitated.

"I've never seen him so comfortable around people. His guard is down, and that woman… he has a history with her, you know."

"Marie is jealous?" Nadege asked, surprised as they continued down the hallway. "You don't have to worry about Cathleen. She only has eyes for her Julio," she said, laughing. "You need to go and sex your man. Maybe then, you wouldn't be so tense, worrying about him being comfortable around other females."

Back at the table, Marie sat down and pulls her chair away from her husband. Constant look over to Nadege, who signalled him over to Cathleen. Nodding, Constant understood and pulled Marie's chair close to him. Wrapping his arm around her waist, he grabbed her butt, caressing her hips. Then he leaned his chair backward and leaned to her ears.

"Love it when you're angry," he whispered. "It gives me a hard-on." He took her hand and rested it on his crotch before returning to his conversation like nothing happened.

Marie looked over to Nadege, who is enamored with her man. Their passion rose. Constant smiled at their efforts and leans again toward his wife.

"Can I get a kiss?" he said, his loving eyes drawing her to him.

Marie stared at him, feeling herself being drawn in to his smoky eyes, and she puckered her lips, gently bushes his, though pulling away.

He stopped her. "Hun, hun!" he said, brushing his finger lightly on her jaw line and resting it on her chin, bringing her back to him. As his lips touch hers in a sensual kiss, Joanne and Shoty stare at masters at work.

Julio observed both couples. "You want us to show them the true way married couples kiss?"

Cathleen, with no hesitation, rose and sat on her husband lap, warpping her arms around his neck, their foreheads connected. She bit the bottom of his lips. Julio slowly stuck out his tongue and let her search for the rest of it with hers. Then his hand caressed her waist, travelling to her buttocks as he rotated his pelvis into her.

Joanne was in total shock at the display of affection from her parent. She put her hands over her eyes to block out the image. Shoty and Constant were beside themselves, laughing and high-fiving Julio and each other.

"Now, my dad and I are R-rated," Shoty commented. "You need to get at triple-X, cuz that was hot!"

Marie too, was enjoying herself, since all the tension had lifted. Shoty called his wife to him to softly kiss her lips, which created an infectious moment so that all the couples on the patio returned to kissing their spouses.

When Roc walked through the kitchen, he was greeted by a lip-locking session.

"This is a kissing contest?"

Joanne broke away from her husband and rushed to his side.

"Best friend! Where have you been? I missed you," she said in his arms.

"Been busy trying to catch up with a lot of things," he replied before walking to the table kiss his mother and Constant

"Man, get off me. It's probably a lethal kiss coming from you," Constant complained.

"Yeah, you'll never know, old-man!"

"You two needs to cut it out!" Marie intervened.

"What! He's your son?"

Roc walked over to Nadege and kissed her and Ronald, who stood up shook his hand and bear-hugged him.

"You've grown to a stronger man since I last saw you. How are things? You started the practice?"

Ronald was exited to see him, like a proud papa.

Julio held his wife in place. He had forgotten to warn her about the young man he saw earlier.

"It's okay. Take a deep breath," he whispered in her ear. "He's Constant's son, and yes, he looks just like him."

Constant and Shoty tried to lighten the mood by poking fun at Roc.

"More like a whorehouse than a practice," they laughed, giving each other more high fives. Marie heard them and commented.

"Thought he already had a whorehouse, isn't that's what Bull's-Eye is for?"

"No, dear. That's Simi with Bull's-Eye."

"Ha, ha, ha—very funny. How can you stand these two under the same roof?"

"Roc, where's our other best friend?" Joanne asked. "I can't get her on the phone all day. I need to tell her what colors we are wearing tonight.".

"I told her," Roc answered. "She's up front, fighting her man-eating child to cooperate with her. He wants to go in the bush. I left them alone," he said, turning his attention to Julio, who was still affected by his presence. He reached out to shake Julio's hand.

"Bonsoir, Mr. Costello. I hope this lovely lady in your lap is not your wife, cuz I'm in love,' Roc flirted, seeing how gorgeous Joanne's mother truly was.

Nervous, Cathleen allowed Roc to take and kiss her hand.

"You're such a charmer, like your father," she said in a shaky voice.

"You mean a whore like his father," Marie countered with and high-five to Nadege.

"Mother!" Roc said, in shock.

"Don't act all shocked, Roc," she said. "I know what you capable of."

Madeline walks in with her beast trailing behind her and greeted everyone at the table and taking a seat between Joanne and Shoty.

"Can't deal with him tonight. He needs his father. It took me twenty minutes to get him out of the bushes! And what's up with all the extra heavy-duty security you got going on tonight?" she asked stealing a bite from Shoty's plate.

"Joanne's security is always extra," Shoty answered. "They're here because we're going to the club in a little while. Where is your man?"

"I should ask you that question," she answered. "Don't you know each other's every move?" She switched to Joanne's plate, where they battled over the last piece of meat.

"I haven't spoke to him since this morning," Shoty answered.

"I had it first, Roc," she growled

"But you in Shoty's plate. Go back over there," he growled back.

"He doesn't eat meat!"

Roc shrugged and moved the whole plate to the other side, but he balked when Joanne tries to take it from him.

Nadege had enough and stood to place a plate of food in front of the four.

"That is ridiculous. There's plenty of food at this table!"

They looked at the plates and at each other before picking up their forks and eating, crisscross, from each other's plates.

Nadege threw her hands in the air. "Okay, I won't get involved in how you eat!"

"Oh honey, are you okay?" she said to Cathleen, who was in tears.

"I'm just so happy. My baby has friends," she said, resting her head on her husband's shoulders, watching, never paying attention to the beast down at the beach, terrorizing a bather.

Madeline jumped to her feet and called for her pet after hearing the agony of Santo's victim.

"Roc, do something," she pleaded.

"Don't call me. He don't listen to me. Call his father."

Madeline tried to jump of the rail to rush down the beach.

"You call him," she said to Roc before turning to Shoty.

 Shoty, help!"

"Help? Shoty asked. "What can I do?"

"Cage usually whistles. He won't respond to mine," she confessed.

Hearing the whistles from Shoty, Santo let his victim go and rushed back with blood on his mouth. He was antsy, pacing back and forth. Madeline hosed him down while Nadege kept her distance, afraid to come any closer to the cat.

"Why do you go around with a vicious animal like that you can't even control?" Nadege asked.

"He was fine until we came, and he heard something that set him off. When he gets like that, I usually leave him with Cage," Madeline answered, looking over the table at Roc.

"I'm going to take him back home. I see security has surrounded the beach," Madeline said, upset. She chastised the tiger. "Look what you did! Daddy is going to be upset you hurt someone," she said, scolding the white tiger who growled, pacing restlessly.

"Santo, we're leaving. Let's go!"

Instead of complying, the cat turned toward the table, walked to Joanne and laid his head on her belly.

"Well, looks like he's responding to you guys, so your can babysit him until his father picks him up."

When Shoty got off the phone, he told everyone that security didn't find any victim, but they came across a half-eaten fish on the beach.

"It's 10:30. We should start making our way to the club. Do you guys want to ride in one car, or should we each take one?"

CHAPTER 29

A black van containing six skilled assassins sat a block away from the club, awaiting their target—a 5-foot-6-inch black female, 175 pounds, with black or brown hair down to the shoulders.

They were doing surveillance before approaching the lethal organization. There had been pictures of her and her activities posted on van's wall for the past few weeks. They had been investigating her every move and had made attempts on her life, with no success.

Earlier in the day, they learned about the party at the club, and they had decided to form an alliance to quickly get the job done and leave the country. They were already on edge, with their number slowly dwindling from the eight at the beginning to six, since the surveillance person at the beach was mauled by a vicious cat.

The flash of lights alerted the assassins of their target's arrival. Five luxury cars pulled up and parked at the front entrance, followed by heavy artillery personnel who blocked the street, establishing a one-mile perimeter.

The professional killers took on disguises to appear as drunken partygoers entering the club. They watched their target while waiting on line. She was well-guarded with the vicious animal at her side.

The newly-combined force was concerned at the scene, wondering if the job was worth the effort or the risk to their lives. Each assassin, however, had his own reason for doing the hit, along the added incentive of splitting five million dollars.

Joanne grabbed her husband's hand after he pulled up to the door in his BMW i8. He smiled and took her into his arms, waiting for Santo to exits the vehicle—he refused to leave Joanne's side.

The couples entered the club, dancing to the kompas blasting in the speakers. System Band was due to perform in fifteen minutes, so the group was making its way to Shoty's private area on the lower level, closer to the stage.

The patrons at the club were excited to be in the presence of the wealthy, and afraid of the dangers that would accompany them. They saw the heavy arms on the surrounding walls and kept their distance from the entourage.

When Cage walked in, he noticed the extra manpower and felt more at ease regarding his previous activities during the day. He signalled for Shoty and Mag to follow him and whistled for Santo, who ignored him.

"What's with him?" he asked Shoty when they met.

"He's been like that ever since he got to the house," Shoty answered. "Madeline got tired and put us on babysitting duties, cuz she couldn't find you. Where were you?" Shoty paused, examining every exit and counting security on the wall. "Trouble?"

"I don't know yet, but its good you have the extra manpower. Follow me to Mag's office," Cage requested as he turned to leave, but he ran smack into a not-so-happy Madeline. He pulled by the waist and whispers in her ears. "Cherie, not right now. I need you to go check the back wall and keep your eyes open! I have to run in Mag's office." He kissed her on the neck and slipped away.

Shoty signalled Constant, letting him know he was off the floor. He watched his wife dancing with his dad, with Santo circling them, leaving a three-foot gap on the dance floor, since the partygoers were afraid to be anywhere close to the beast.

"I can't believe you brought Santo to the club," Mag commented, joining them.

"You must have forgotten who his parents are. He's just as stubborn as they are," Shoty said in a mater-o-fact tone.

"Remember last time he was here? He created mass hysteria, and Cage had to go to court for it. Back then, he was just a baby."

"He would not leave Joanne's side," Shoty said. "I couldn't leave him home. He terrorized the staff."

"This time, you pay the fines," Mag warned as he entered the office, turning his attention to Cage, who had been silent the whole time. "What's going on? You have on your serious face."

"I don't know how serious this is, but I've been following eight known assassins who flew in last week. I'm trying to figure out who's their target."

"You think they might want to infiltrate our camp? Cuz that would be suicide," Mag remarked.

"Yeah, but who in this country is important enough to send all those hit-men after one target?"

"You're thinking they're after Constant?"

"Maybe. I know he's rattled a lot a of feathers, but like Mag said, that would be suicide—especially for people I've trained to take a contract. To have me as an enemy would have to be worth it."

MEANWHILE, ON THE PLATFORM

Roc stood at the sidewall, watching the activities around him. Constant tried to get his wife to dance with him. Joanne was in the corner, holding Nadege's hands, calling security personnel. The Costellos were on the dance floor. A group of drunken, out-of-towners were close by. Santo growled at those in his way, backing up on Joanne.

Silencer approached, following Roc's direction and wondering what was going through his mind.

"You love her?" he asked.

"Of course I love her. She's my little sister and pain in the ass—also now my best friend. Why do you love her?"

"She's an incredible woman. She reminds me of Michelle."

"That is Shoty's incredible woman, and Michelle's was Tank's," Roc said.

"It' amazing what we went through this year, and its not even over yet."

"Yeah," Roc said, "and all because of one little woman, with the curviest shape that tempted our brother into her world."

Roc replayed all the scenes from the time they met Joanne, smiling. "And Simi warned him too, about her."

"But Shoty saw that butt jiggle turn to a zombie and follow it!" Sic said, feeling out his front teeth.

"You regret meeting her?"

"Nan, man. Beside you guys—she's the most important thing that's happened to me. I would follow her to Hell and back again!"

"You realize that she's choked me, she knocked Cage the fuck out, she knocked out your teeth and broke Tank ribs, Simi," he paused, thinking of that fateful day.

"I think Simi died that day, at least by medical terms—Shoty too," Roc reflected, taking a deep breath, remembering the tranquil life they had before Joanne.

"Don't forget—she zapped Mag against the wall and we had to travel in pain and freezing cold temperatures," Sic added, still trying to figure out how it all had been possible. "I got zapped too and beat up by an assassin and a goddess at the same time."

"Uh, when did this happen?"

"The night Shoty had to deal with Stephanie. Both of them wanted to know what happened, and I was their punching bag. Thank God Mag showed up when he did! Then we all got electrocuted for the love of Mrs. Celestin!" Roc finishes, looking in her direction again.

"And we wouldn't have it any other way!" Chopper said from behind with Bullet and Riffle. They all laughed in bewilderment, reflecting on how their friendship was tested yet again. They truly were a force to be reckoned with.

Nock had come over with his date on his arm, introducing her to his family. Sic pulled him away. "She's not crazy, is she?" he asked sneaking a peek over his shoulder. Nock sucked his teeth and walked away, talking to himself in Creole.

"I thought he had something important to say, punk-ass!" Sic screamed after him.

"I need to know if they're crazy from jump."

"You knew Joanne was crazy," he rebuffs when he reached Roc side.

"You're going to stop call my sister crazy," Mac warned with a bombshell date in his arms.

Roc moves away form the wall and extended his hand to her kiss hers.

"Who is the scrumptious strawberry blond with blue eyes that you have with you tonight?" he asked, flirting, finding her to be very attractive.

"Yeah, whatever, Roc! Look, I'm going to leave you with Mr. Flirt here. I have to look for Shoty," he told his date, kissing her on the cheek.

"Don't leave your woman around. I might just steal her," Roc yelled after him in Creole, smiling at her.

"That's your daddy's woman! You deal with him," Mac yelled back, headed up the steps.

Roc just stares at her, his mouth wide open

"You could have given me a warring."

"And what? Not be admired by the most eligible bachelor in Port-Au-Prince?" she asked, smiling. "From what I hear, you're quite a catch!"

"You growing out your hair? I like it. It gives you a very strong character."

"Thank you, you're gorgeous. I love what you did to your hair too—you took off, like twenty years!" Roc said, and all the guys agreed. She held onto Rocket's arm when a chilling voice from behind, stopping all the compliments. She froze, squeezing his arm.

"You cut your hair!"

Even though the music was loud, there was a silence surrounding them, She slowly turned, knowing that look all too well. Without a word, he signaled for her to follow him.

Julisa was glued in Roc's arm, her feet incapable of cooperating. Roc whispers in her ear.

"Your man is calling you," he said, giving her a little push.

She summed up the courage to follow her displeased lover.

Roc watched her go and glanced to his mother on the floor with Ronald. *At least she was smiling*, he thought. Sic, however, disrupted his train of thought.

"You see how your dad called her, man? I'mma say it—I want to be just like your dad when I grow up. And she knew she in trouble with man!"

"Who's in trouble?" Bello asked, greeting everyone with Dianna by his side. Dianna was looking for Carlo Mangrass (NOCK).

"Your mother?" sic asked.

"Man, stop playing, and if say 'yours,' then you're going to get sensitive on me,"

"No, man—your mother. Constant just called her like this…" he showed-off the finger motion and tries to mimic's Constant's face that went with it.

"Where were you when we had that lesson? Shaman law, dude," Bello said as he left in the direction of his parents. He met Mario by the steps and motioned for him to follow. They waited by the door.

In the private room, used for exclusive parties, Constant, using a low rough tone, asked, "Who told you you could cut your hair? And you left the country?"

"Last time I checked, I was a grown woman who could make…." In two strides he was on top of her.

"I don't give a fuck about what you though you are! At the end of the day, you're still my woman—until I say otherwise!"

"It's just hair. Constant. It'll grow back

"That's my motherfucking hair you cut! For what? To look like a two-piece whore?" he roared, furious. He did not trust himself, so he moved away from her.

Julisa's eyes were open wide in shock. Tears fell from her eyes, because the man she loved with all her heart was degrading her. His words were like a knife to her heart. She swallowed the lump that was large in her throat and countered in Creole.

"All this shit you say about me being your woman! You need to say those fucking words to your wife, cuz this whore is done!"

No sooner had she spat the words, she realized her mistake—she knew never to antagonize him when he was in a state of extreme anger. He balled up his fist, charged her on the wall and ran his fist into the concrete wall by her head, leaving a big hole.

"If you wasn't the mother of my children, I swear I would put you in a body bag! Take your fucking ass home!" He swung the door open to find her two children at the door.

"Take your mother home. Keep her there until I say otherwise." He walked away, leaving the boys to deal with their crying mother.

When Constant reached the spot where he left his wife and Joanne, he noticed that Joanne and Nadege were missing.

"Where are they?" he grumbles to his wife

"What's wrong with you?"

He ignored her question while he waited for her to answer him. Marie rolled her eyes, noticing the change in his mood

"Joanne wanted to use the restroom. Nadege went with her, and the cat followed," she told him, not liking the change in him.

He walked off to the direction of the restroom, leaving her to wonder what got him so upset.

Constant walks down the hall, noticing the two extra bodies on the team that was left to guard the ladies. He put his hand at his waist, not feeling the vibe, and then he heard the tiger growling. He took off running, with guns drawn, toward the restroom.

IN THE HALLWAY LEADING TO MAG'S OFFICE

Joanne's security in the hallway was waiting for their boss to inform him about the latest in their investigation. They knocked on the door.

"Sir, it's Jeff. I need to report on an, an ongoing investigation," he said through the doorway.

"Yes, come in!" Mag's voice answsered. He was sitting at his desk with Shoty, looking out the window, watching the crowd jam to the beat of System band.

"Mr. Celestin, we have new evidence that suggests your wife is in danger."

"What kind of danger?" Mag asked, examining the security footage for the club.

"There were three attempts on her life today alone. Yesterday, we found some explosives under the hummer. There was also an exploded vase at the shop. That was a bullet meant for her, sir.

"So far, we've been able to contain the threats, but now they're getting bolder. Your tiger killed a man on your beach tonight. That assassin was there to shoot her, and he did not show up on any of your surveillance."

"Vega—he's a ghost!" Cage confirmed, feeling betrayed. "You positive his dead?"

"His body is in the van outside, sir, with a headful of lead," Jeff said. "That was personal—nobody touches your goddess. We intend to send a message to the person who contracted these assassins. They're next!"

Shoty walked away from the window, checking his clip and fastening his gun around his waist.

"Let me take her home! Santana—I'll need you to stay with her for a couple of days. Mag—get one of the planes ready. I want to be in New York before the sun comes up!" He was reaching for the the door handle, when…

Pop! Pop! Pop… Pop! Pop! Pop! Pop!

The counter was *Bang! Bang! Bang!* from the restroom.

Shots had been fired from inside the club. Magnum checked the monitor to see where the shots were coming from.

"West Wing, lower bathrooms!" Jeff screamed, his team already exiting the office and down the hall.

Roc jumped the wall to get to his mother. Julio had both his wife and Marie and was shielding them behind his back. Roc reached their side at the same time security surround them. He saw Julio secure the ladies and give him his gun and car keys.

"Get them out of here! I going to look for my dad!"

"He went after Joanne and Nadege in the restroom," Marie told him, worried about her husband.

Roc ran into the bathroom, past dead bodies everywhere. Jeff walked in to see Richard and Danny on the floor, with their throats slit. They were collapsed on their knees, when a grief-strickened Connor came in, choking up to see his comrades lying dead on the ground. He heard the tiger's growling and ran to the ladies' stalls to find Constant, with two of the assailants. He smashed one of their heads into the mirror and the other on his back, with Santo desperately trying to maul him through his gear. Roc whistled to stop the tiger, and then he rushed to help his dad.

With his helper gone, Constant was able to bend his back and flip the assailant over his head, slamming him into the other assailant on the floor. Jeff quickly shot at their legs, rendering them immobile. Constant picked up his gun and aimed it on the ceiling.

Pop! Pop! Pop! He shot three rounds, causing the rope to drop. When he kicked in the stall, Joanne held her hand to her throat as Constant carried her out.

Roc checked on Shoty's mother on the floor and noticed blood on her was from the assassin who was on top of her. He had died from an animal bite and was missing half of his throat. Nadege only had a minor bump on her head. Roc lifted her from the floor.

Shoty flew into the bathroom, guns drawn as he watched his wife and mother being carried out. *"Bon Dieu!"* He lost it. He went over to one of the assailants on the floor, hoisted him up on the glass wall and demanded.

"Who the fuck sent you?" he screamed in the man's face. After the assassin refused to talk, Shoty became incensed, grabbing his gun.

"Who the fuck sent you, motherfucker, to kill my wife? And my mother!"

The man choked on the last word and could barely get it out. Shoty composed himself and asked again. Receiving no answer, he shot the man in his knee, and then turned to the other one, repeating the question, gun barrel in the bullet wound.

As Constant walked out the bathroom, Madeline was running in. He whispered something to her,

"There's someone in the ceiling. Make sure they're dead," Constant ordered as he heard gunshots coming from the bathroom. He handed Joanne over to Ronald. Ronald could hear the sounds of his son torturing the people responsible. He knew his son was involved with gangsters—he just never knew that his son was actually one of them.

Madeline rushed into the stall and flew up the ceiling. Shoty continued with his abuse. He pointed the gun at the man's abdomen, threatening to shoot out his guts and let him bleed-out on the bathroom floor. He aimed, but then the ceiling caved in on the assailant who was choking Joanne. The assailant winced in pain from the fall and the three bullets that hit him were from Constant's gun.

She grabbed him up threw him against the wall, pinning him by the throat with her heels.

Shoty looks over to his victim and gave him one last chance to die an honorable death. "I'm about to go war. I need to know who to bring it to."

Dying, the man complied and relieved his burden, saying the name shoty wanted to confirm.

"Andre Valbrune!"

"Now, was that so hard?" Shorty asked, looking over at Madeline, who understood what must be done. She removed her heels and stepped back, kicking the assailant with her right foot, lodging her heel in his throat. Shoty switched the gun to his favorite—a short-length, two-barrel shotgun, and blew the man's head off.

Then he walked over to the other assassin on the floor and put two bullets in his head. When he reached Madeline's side, he stood with her, staring down at her victim, inserting the barrel in his mouth."

"You came in *my* house and tried to murder my family," he said in a tight, choked voice.

"Tell Santana's dad I said 'hi.'"

Shoty pulled the trigger, and blood and brains splattered in a perimeter all around him. Madeline, standing there, removed her feet from her blood-soaked shoes as the man's body thumped on the floor.

Constant came in just in time to witness his son being the monster he had taught him to be, and he couldn't have been prouder.

Shoty stops in the door way, staring at Constant.

"I'm going to New York."

"I'm right behind you," Constant confirmed.

All three walked out the bathroom, covered in blood from the assassins who dared to hit... ARTILARY. 15. CREW.

CHAPTER 30

Cruising down Route Kenscoff in a black Aston Martin Rapide while observing the speed limit, Bello drove in silence while his mother sobbed in the passenger seat. Mac was in his Posche, following behind.

"I can't believe that over all those years, I didn't see that he never loved me," she wept.

"Mommy, how could you say that? The man was tripping tonight because he loves you. But I have a bone to pick with you. Why didn't you tell me Constant didn't send you to France?"

"Because I'm a grown woman. I don't have a husband. I live alone, I don't need to ask permission to go see my children. After you left, I was lonely, and I hadn't seen Dianna in over a year!"

"Mm, uh you escaped. That's what you mean?" he muttered.

"I don't have to escape anyone. I'm not married. I can do what I want."

"Not when you are tangled up with a man like Constant. You do what he tells you and when he tells you, you know that? What's going on with you? You're acting really crazy lately?" Bello asked his mother.

She glanced out the window, and considering what her son had just asked, decided to answer him truthfully.

"I want to marry again, to have my *own* man who can sleep by my side and wake up in the morning, cooking me breakfast."

"Aside from Constant not being there for you in the mornings, what else are lacking?"

"My own man, my own husband," she said. They sat in silence for a moment, Bello wanted to ease his mom's pain, but he didn't know what to say to cheer her up.

"Your father," she said. "He would have put me in a body bag, and he said I 'look like a whore.'"

"No, Mommy—he said you 'cut your hair' to look like a 'two-piece whore.'"

"He had me and whore associated in the same sentence!" she screamed, angry. "You always stick up for your father, even after he threatened to put me in a body bag!"

"Mommy, you angered the man. You left the country without telling him, and then you though it was a good idea to cut parts of your body that belongs to him."

"See! You're defending him! What? What are you doing?"

"Mac stopped. I'll see what's going on with him," Bello said, spinning his luxury car in the middle of the road as he reached his brother on the phone.

"Something happened at the club. Shots fired, and I think Dad and Shoty are in middle of it all," Mac informed him.

Bello pressed on the gas, his vehicle vibrating with a savage rasp, ready to take off.

"Put your seat belt on," he told his mother. He opened the glove box, grabbed his gun and took off, pushing the vehicle to its limits.

The roar of the engine could be heard from a mile away as it approached the club. He reached the gridlocked street where police were fighting private security over jurisdiction to enter the club.

Chaos was everywhere! People were running for their lives. The streets were congested from the number of guests exiting the club minutes earlier. Gunshots still echoed in the air coming from the club, private military had their guns aimed and ready to shoot at anyone who dared to pass through the barricade.

Bello lifted the car door, calling a question to military personnel.

"Where's my father?"

The employee noticed him as one of the owners and quickly opened the barricade, letting both cars through, which upset the police.

Bello parked across the street from the entrance and ordered his mother to stay in the car. Santana walk of the building out with a group of guerrillas, ordering them cut down all surveillance and light to the surrounding neighborhood. He turned to Bello.

"Good, your'e here. We're on total shutdown. Where's your mother?"

"She in the car," Bello answered.

"Take her to the fortress," Cage commanded. "What happened? You've seen Dianna?"

"They sent assassin after Joanne and Dianna. Last I saw, she was with Sic on the second floor."

"Where's my dad now?"

"Still inside of the club," Cage said as two shots rang out in the air.

"Why are we still hearing gunshots?"

"It's Shoty, doing interrogations," Santana answered.

Bello went inside the club to see Shoty, his dad and Madeline, covered in blood, exiting of the restroom. The clean-up crew was already on the scene, rushing to takes their clothes off, hose them down and spray them with soap-foam chemicals.

Joanne was on the floor, grieving over her two fallen soldiers on the ground. She cries her heart out. She screamed for Madeline, who ran to her. Madeline bent over the fallen soldier and shook her head. She hugged Joanne as the guerillas took her away.

Bello saw his father approach, done with his chemical bath, as he began commanding the soldiers. Constant, in military clothing, ordered all the deceased to be put on a bonfire, along with their clothes.

"Grab them and throw them in the pit. Then, I need you to find a grinder. Grind their bones to dust. Send it back to the Earth."

Shoty, half-dressed, gave the clean-up team a hard time. He couldn't stay put. Rushing over to a corpse, he proceeded to kick him in the face. Constant pulled him away.

"They put their hands on my wife and my mother, man! Where's the fucking plane?" he said, his speech slurred.

"Shoty, calm down! We need to think this through! We can't go in, guns blazing, on U.S. soil!"

"I don't give a fuck about the U.S. or their fucking politics! I want that motherfucker dead!"

"I want him dead, too, but we have to go in smart and level-headed!"

Mag approached Shoty, holding him at arms' length, trying to get through to him.

"Mag! They touched my mother! I don't care if I have blow up the whole fucking city! I want him dead!"

Shoty breathed in Mag's face, consumed by revenge, his eye pupils dilated, which indicated that the cool-headed brother Mag knew and loved was absent from this man's mind. Shoty picked up two shotguns and rested them on his shoulders.

"Let's go. We're going to the plane!"

"Constant—talk some sense into him," Mag said, appealing to reason. "He cannot go to the U.S. like that!"

"Mag, we're at war!" Constant whispered, looking up at the sky., Then he turned aggressively toward Magnum and slammed himself on the chest.

"Them motherfuckers brought this to my home!"

"We're at war? With whom, Constant?" Magnum said and lost it, charging back at him, continuing with his point of view.

"Because the mob has senators inside its walls! Are we going to knock off U.S. Senators now!" Mag asked. He couldn't get over the conversation his having with his own leader!

"If those motherfucking senators order a hit on my daughter!" Constant insisted. "So, yes! I will kill every last one of them!" He joined Shoty oin gathering things to leave.

Magnum motioned his security team over and watched the two in military gear, with a small army of eighty soldiers under their command, prepare to leave with no recon or strategy.

"Constant, reconsider what your doing and what it will mean for you and Shoty. Your both could wind up in jail! Even if you succeed!"

"They came to my home spraying bullets! I'm gonna return the favor!" he growled, his eyes glazed with revenge.

Magnum rubbed his forehead, calculating on what to do, contemplating his careful decision. With much reluctance, he called the order.

"Lock them up!" Magnum said to his team, and then he addressed Constant's Army. "My father is incapable of leading at the moment! You're under my command—unless you want to be in a cell next to him! Drop your weapons!"

His shrill voice carried a weight on the soldiers who were forced to decide to either disarm or follow their leader. Magnum tired of waiting shouts

"Take them down below and lock them up in a room until I return."

He turns around see the dumfounded look on the soldier's faces afraid to touch Constant and his army. It took ten soldiers to contain Shoty.

"Mag, what the fuck are you doing," Shoty screamed as he was being carried away. Constant stood his ground, challenging the soldiers that surrounded him and his army. Mag walked up to him.

"I need you to go with them, Father! Unless you want to kill me, you're not going anywhere," he said, turning to his team.

"Your heard me! Now move!" he yelled as he watched Constant slowly being walked away. Mag returned his attention to security and started giving orders to depart in one breath.

"Santana—I need you with me. Madeline—let's go. Bello—you riding?" he barked, leaving the club for the hummer waiting in the front. Bello climbed in next to him.

"You think that was a good idea to lock them up? He may never forgive you for that!"

"They're too far gone with revenge. We can't have those two hotheads, thirsty for blood, on foreign soil. Hopefully, we can get this job done with no incident."

"Man! I have to give you some! That was some gangster stuff back there! Did you see the look on Dad's face? I don't think he ever thought we could best him, cuz he was shocked!" Bello said with admiration.

"Let's focus on how we going to get all those dons in one place," Mag said, signaling Madeline to come to him so he could pick her brain. They sat in silence, thinking to devise a course of action. After a while, she mapped out a plan that they thought could work.

"Let's work this angle to our advantage and turn it into a hustle. We take over. We tell them we want to meet with all heads of operation introduce them to a new boss," she said.

Mag sat back, letting her words sink in. All the occupants in the vehicle were in bewilderment as the considered the ramification her words. Most felt they would get the job done without incident and a secret meeting.

Bello was the first to react, and staring at her, he calculated all angles to determine which course of action was best.

"Who are you?" he asked, noticing how much she had changed over the years—from the shy girl who hid behind Cage to this deadly force of nature.

"That's Mrs. Santana," Cage said, gloating at his star pupil. Of all the assassins he had trained, she was his greatest accomplishment. Not even Vegas, with his ghost capability, was as efficient.

He looked over at Mag, who had the same astonished expression on his face. He leaned silently, confirming that Bello and Cage were on-board. "Okay, let's get this emergency meeting underway."

The private jet flew over the Florida Keys, and the annihilators exited by parachuting onto a waiting yacht that Cage used when he wanted to enter the country undetected. Then the yacht cruised the waters into the Hudson River. They used a smaller raff to reach the shore, and then onto a white van, driven by his sister, Gina, who was pretending to take pictures of the coast while she waited for her brother. It was their normal routine every time he entered the U.S.

She heard the bang on the van's wall, indicating the package was delivered. She was happy that her brother came for a second visit. Last time, it was too short, and she wanted to talk to him about moving in with him. After she reached the brownstone on the upper eastside, she backs the van all the way to the garage, closed the door and entered the house.

Her aunts sat at same spot everyday, grieving over their little sister who passed away giving birth to Oliver twenty-five years earlier. Although they were two years apart, it seemed Oliver is the oldest by the way he commands her around and paid for all their living expenses. She could never understand why her aunts hated Oliver so much. They called him like the devil's son and treated him as such.

She had closed the door, walked into the room and made her way to the basement door, when one of them called after her.

"Gina!"

She rolled her eyes, not in the mood to talk with her aunt.

"Yes, I'm coming," she said, taking off her jacket and entering the living room.

"I saw you take the van out today? Why?" she asked.

"Because it's my brother's van! I can use it whenever I want to," she said, rolling her eyes.

"Well, I want to sell that van, because the police keep coming here and asking about it."

"It's not yours to sell, and the police can go to Hell!"

"Are you getting smart with me? In my own house? You forget who feeds your ungrateful ass! That's why your brother's eating shit in Haiti. You should go and join him, ungrateful little bitch!" her aunt said.

Gina closed her eyes and counted to ten, digging her nails in her skin to keep her from exploding.

"You know what? I'm not even going to waste my breath on you. I might just do that… and for the record—this is my *brother's* home! Now *you* look up the word ungrateful!"

She slammed the door to the basement and locked it, and then she lifted the panel and scanned her fingerprints and then the pupils of her eyes to enter a closet access to an elevator that dropped three hundred feet underground.

Oliver was at the elevator door, waiting on her. When it opened, she flew into his arms.

"What are you doing here? I wasn't expecting you until December."

"Business, I'm not staying long."

"Secret business. In and out?"

"Something like that! Miss you, sis. What took you so long to come down?"

"Your aunts! I hate them with a passion, they're so mean!"

"Did they do something to you!"

"No, it's not like that, They're so bitter. I'm tired of living with them. Can you take me back with you?" she begged, waiting for his answer.

"What about this place? There's no one I can trust with it."

"Ollie, come on, you can close it! You don't even do anything out of here, and I want to be with my sister," she argued. "She didn't come with you?"

He paused, let her sweat a little, because Gina loved Madeline unconditionally. Just then, Bello walked in.

"Man, I can't believe you have the ultimate cave! This is cool! Am I the last one to come here?" he said about Cage's underground lair that he built five years earlier under his home.

It was equipped with state-of-the-arts equipment that was necessary in case he needed to hideout. He could live there for more than five years, never having to go to the upper level for anything in his bunker.

"Oh, hello, beautiful angels," Bello said when he saw Gina in her brother's arms. "Please tell me you escaped heaven to be with me, because I'm in love," he declared, lost in her eyes.

Gina smiled, assuming he was joking when he took her hand, bowed and kissed it. Cage noticed how Bello was acting toward his sister and immediately shut it down.

"No! Cage explained and smacked Bello's hand away.

"You stay away from her!" he said, seriously not happy those two meeting.

"What? How come you never told me you had a sister? What else are you hiding from me, Santiago? I though we were family! I see you keep treating me like the step-child."

"You are a step-child!"

"Yeah, but you don't have to treat me like one. That's okay, though. Now, I'm going to marry your sister, and you don't have to treat me like that no more."

"Stay the hell away from her! You're a bitch. You can't have her!" Cage sneered.

"Now why would you go and put my business out like that?" Bello asked. "You forget who I bitched with! And I never told Madeline all the shit we did together," he reminded Cage.

"Like what?" Madeline asked form the doorway, coming up with Mag.

"Maddy! You came," Gina exclaimed. She looked at her brother, who had tried to trick her, and then she flew in the Madeline's arms.

"Hi, Gina."

"Mag, you're here too," she said, and then she grabbed her sister's arm and whispered in her ear.

"Please convince him to take me with him. I don't want to live here anymore."

Madeline smiles and hugs her. She had bonded with the five-foot-five-inch charismatic beauty who always fought to protect her little brother.

"I'll see if I can help, but let's hear more about all this shit Cage and Bello did together," Madeline insisted, looking from one to the other.

"Later! We have work to do," Cage said. "Gina—go back upstairs and stay there. If I need your help I'll signal you." He turned back to Bello. "Say your goodbyes, Romeo. Play time is over."

Cage headed for the computer room, and within two hours, he was able to secure the meeting at 7 a.m. on the pier in a secluded warehouse that was reserve for that purpose.

At 1:30 in the afternoon, they sat around, pulling images of the area from the monitor to ensure where they would position themselves, watch all the ins and outs of the place and devise a plan on how to disarm the mob's personal security.

Bello sat, studying all the floor plans. "You know, they are not going to let me and Santana in the meeting. Dad always fought them tooth and nail for him the enter, but they're too afraid of him."

"I know," Magnum said. "That's why Madeline is here. She'll be my secretary, while your two will take out the shooters around the perimeter. We'll take care of the ones inside. Now, they will also sweep for bombs. We need to find a way to put them in, undetected."

"Why can't we just leave them in the van?" Madeline asked

"We can't have any of this tracing back to us," Mag said as he watched the wheels spinning in her head.

"Okay, Bello needs to leave his post, set a security check-point there by that manhole, and Santana can plant the C4s on each car that enters the building."

"One problem with that plan is we don't have eyes. Their shooters could easily see us."

"Use Gina on surveillance," she said, noticing the displeasure written all over Cage's face.

"If I did that, I would have to take her out of the country," Cage said.

"She's ready to leave anyway. Don't you think she had enough?"

"Are we negotiating, or this an order," Cage asked, giving Madeline his undivided attention and waiting for answer.

"However you want to take it, but she leaves when we leave," she flatly told him. The tension in the room was so tense the air sparked. Magnum decided to be the voice of reason for the two lovebirds in their force of willpower.

"She can't fly back with us. She would have to take a commercial flight," he explained, waiting for the sparks to fade.

"Well, I guess you need to book her on the 9 a.m. flight back, Mr. Santana, and close your mancave."

Madeline walks over to the weapons room and chose two samurai swords with razor-sharp blades. Cage observed her. She always closed in when she was ready to do a job. He wondered if it was it a good idea to turn her into a killer. Ever since they left the jungle, her nature was more intense—hard and cold, with no laughter. Even when he mades love to her, she was somewhere else. He felt he was losing his goddess to his world.

They were on the pier by the Hudson River in New York at 6:30 a.m. Four members of the A.15.Crew took up positions, counting down the minutes for retribution for the ordered assassination to one of its members.

They needed to show those dominant world tyrants that they were not afraid to fight fire with fire. When they dared to touch one, they would have to deal with all its members who would annihilate every person that got involved.

Thirty tyrant bullies were schedule to attend the meeting, and not one would walk out alive. That day would go down in history as the Hudson River Massacre.

Madeline stood alone, looking at the waters over the coast. The orange color slowly faded away, while the rays of the sun reflected on the water. She closed her eyes, remembering her ordeal as she passed the riverbanks. Finally, she came to terms with the fact, understanding *that little girl died that day!*

The faces of men raping her, roaches crawling over her skin, feasting on her twelve-year-old body. She adjusted the knee blades that helped her slide on hard surfaces and walls. Magnum's two handguns were fastened behind her waist. She used a long trench coat to hide the swords in the inside seam.

She carried a briefcase with blank paper—her role was a nerdy secretary in high heels. She approached the Don's security, pretending to be nervous about losing her job. Papers falling out of her briefcase, she frantically fell to her knees, desperately trying to pick them up. Security didn't even bother searching her.

At 6:45 a.m., the convoy of cars began to appear with heavy personnel security. Madeline greeted everyone and show them into the conference room with a large table. The room and table were large enough to sit all thirty members of the mob and world organization comfortably.

Four guards were posts by the shattered windows with heavy machinery, placed on the old, stained floor.

"Now what is the meaning of this? Who are your people? To set an emergency meeting in New York! I had to take two planes to get here from Italy," one of the Dons said, irritated.

"Gentleman! Be patient! I won't keep you long! Like the message said, there's a new shift in power, but before we get started, I would like to personally like to congratulate Valbrune on a job well done! You have helps us by getting rid of Constant on the Costello shit!"

"See that! I told you it was going to work!" Valbrune laughed wickedly. "Got rid of that bitch! I wish I was there to see it—that stupid bitch broke just about every bone in my body."

"If Constant is dead, I get his power! Its rightfully mine!" Don Andre insisted.

"You little shit! Sit down! If I didn't give the green-light, you wouldn't even be sitting at this table," another Don hissed. Before long, the entire table was arguing about who would receive and control Constant's chapter.

"Now see here," a short, fat, ambitious greasy-looking Don stood to interject. "I don't know who and what you about! But you need to put in your time! Before you can claim things, you have to realize that the message read: *Meets the New Boss!* You black motherfuckers could never be my bosses! We tolerated Constant because he brought a lot of money into our business, and because he was a bully and kept people in check. His money belongs to this order! Unless we swore you in! You cannot claim it!"

Magnum forced himself to remain calm and smiled, fighting to control his voice.

"I actually wanted to give my support to Andre. Come up here, Andre," he said while looking at Madeline, who moved in front of him, placing the briefcase on the table and stepping back closer to Magnum.

"He didn't put any time in either!" a man with a heavy French accent shouted.

Magnum held Andre by the shoulder, congratulating him again. "So tell me! How many of you knew about the hit on the Costello girl?" he asked the entire table. They all began answering at once, , thinking there might have been a reward or bounty for killing the girl.

"Okay! Okay, quiet down, gentlemen! I just want to know! Why kill someone who was only defending herself!"

"What the fuck is this? The girl was a nobody," the fat man said, standing, pointing a finger at Magnum. "Don Carmine didn't see it that way! Because he got scared when Constant called about the girl, now that he's dead! With Constant gone, no one is going to stand in my way! Now that everyone is here, I can annihilate all of you!" he screamed, consumed by power. He pressed a button on a device to alert his people on the outside.

Magnum laughed, witnessing the expression on Andre's face. He grabbed Andre's face and knocked his head into the wall. "No! No!" he said, "sorry about that! But this meeting is called 'The Holocaust of the Mob!' Enjoy your ride to Hell, gentlemen!" He growled and took his position behind Madeline.

"Tell Santana's dad I said Hello!"

As Magnum snatched the two guns from Madeline's waist, time seemed to move in slow-motion as he he pulled the twin-triggers, shooting the guards posted on the far walls.

Madeline ripped her skirt off while simultaneously jumping up on the table and landing on her knees. She pulled out the razor-sharp swords and slid down the table on her knees—both of hands held to her heart in a prayerful stance. The swords were extended out past her forearm, slicing as she slid, decapitating all thiry members.

"Wow, this is rich! I didn't think you had the balls to pull this off!" a terrified voice echoed in the room, carrying a sinister laughter.

"Eh! Eh, Eh!"

Magnum, in panic, frantically searched for the source of the voice. Heart pounding and sweat tickling at his temple, he tightened his finger at the triggers, blinking to adjust the image.

The far wall was engulfed by a mystical fire that didn't burn or smoke. It grew closer to him by the second, sparking the shape-like figure of man walking toward Magnum, which caused him to back up to the nearest wall. His pulse raced, adrenaline rushing to his brain. He was distressed, have never witnessed that kind of phenomenon.

Time in that dimension froze, with only the orange and red glow of fire and the surprised expressions on the faces of the decapitated heads, suspended in mid-air, separated from the Dons' bodies.

Madeline at the end of the table with her swords slicing through the necks of her last two victims, her feet extended on the wall, ready to spins back around, her mouth wide open, appearing to be screaming.

"What the fuck is this?" Magnum said while pointing his guns at the intruders. A pure pitch-black figure appeared, muscle-hard chest, with red ceremonial beads around its neck. He was barefoot and his chest was naked, with a red toga wraped around his waist. Smoking a pipe, he was accompanied by a black hellhound with fire-glowing eyes, stood beside him, staring at the destruction. He picked up his straw hat and bowed to Magnum.

"That's a lot of damage you've created! God are going to want your head. You just bankrupted the world," the ancestral being said, and then he turned to look at Madeline still frozen at the end of the table.

"I see why Olorun wants her, even though I don't like her. But my son is in love with her."

"Y-you! Cage's dad?" Magnum said, stumbling back.

"Why does the surprise you? Every time your kill someone, you send them with a message, 'Hello to you, too, Magnum!' You and this little Missy here are making such a stir in my realm that I had to come personally. I would have expected that from Cage, but Magnum!" He shook his head walked to the end of the table, gazing at Madeline, from head to toe.

His chiseled form strikes back. He charged toward Magnum from the wall, his hand cradling around Magnum's neck. Magnum pointed the twin guns at his head, but with one swift movement, the weapons flew across to the opposite side of the room. The dark figure then lifted him up on the wall and hellhound jumped, growling his teeth on the side of Magnum face—so close that Magnum could smell death coming from his breath.

Magnum stayed focused on his maker, ready to reach the crossroads, so that he stared into the hollow darkness of his eyes.

"What-t dooo y-you want-ttt," he managed to breathed out

"You didn't have authority to take their lives. These people where protected. I have to report to Olorun that you murdered all his minions!" he screams in Magnum's face, annoyed with yet another human, and he had the urge to just snap his neck to make all his troubles disappear.

"Ca-Cage is outside," Magnum reminded him, struggling to breathe.

"He's the only reason you are still alive! I know he will come after me if I kill you and his precious assassin! Now hear what Olorun has to say to you and your little organization: *You aredropping too many bodies! We've endured three decades of your killing people that we put on this Earth for a reason. There are consequences for those deaths. You will not bear children from the goddess you love! You will watch her perish with the seed from your loins. You will not kill anyone from Earth. To do so will cause us to annihilate your whole association and rid...*"

A reflection he caught from the corner of his eye caused him to, in reflex, turn in the nick of time, changes to his fiery form... at the very moment that Madeline's sword came crashing down on the arm that was chocking Magnum.

He quickly snatched her by the throat, bringing her to his eye level, hoisting her up against the wall next to Magnum.

"Who are you, Madeline? And how you escape my time suspension?" he asked. She wiggled and fought to escape, digging her nails into his flesh. He was astonished, feeling the pain she inflicted.

"Who the fuck are you? How do you have power to wound gods?" he screamed, shaking her body to free himself from her nails.

"You know who I am! Now tell me who you are before I kill you!" she said, struggling in his grasp. She looks over to Magnum, who was slumped over and running out of air.

"Kill me, little girl? You have no idea who you're missing with. I am ESHU, the Elegba who communicates with Earth for the Heavens. Now tell me how you got powers to inflict pain!" he growls as the hound crouched tense at her neck, ready to strike.

Madeline closed her eyes and exhaled, releasing his arm and reaching behind her back. She grabed the two daggers from the side of her hips, unstraped them looked directly into his eyes.

"I gained those powers, because I'm the killer of gods!" she said, plunging both daggers in his arm. Elegba quickly released both her and Magnum, wincing in pain. Then Madeline jumped, landing on her feet as the hound launched at her. Pulling out the daggers embedded in his arm, she buried them in the hound's neck, digging them farther on both sides. Agonizing, his life-form escaped his body and dissipated into the fiery wall.

Her attackers stared in disbelief, his precious hound gone. He watched the assassin crouching on the ground, like a predator, with both swords in her hands, growling like a magnificent black panther.

He growled back, ready to avenge his hound, sensing another presence. He held his injured hand and hurried through the portal, returning to his realm, his hound's body, engulfed by the flames, disappeared without a trace.

The doors burst open to Cage and Bello, who entered, heavily-armed and ready to shoot. Right then, time, which had been frozen, began again. During the battle, heads dropped to the floor and blood gushed from the bodies that piled up. Magnum, on the floor, fought to regain his breath.

"Do I even want to know what that was all about?" Bello asked, pointing to Madeline, still in her stance as she focused on the wall.

Cage walked around, inspecting the room, blown away by the mass destruction and heinous crime. As he picked up Mag's guns, he discovered Madeline on the ground. He helped her to her feet and soothed out the frown from her forehead.

"You okay?" his voice said, penetrating through her body, causing her return to reality. She rushed to Magnum side and clutched his hands.

"Who was that?" she asked urgently.

"That was Cage's dad!" Mag answered, struggling to remain steady on his feet, feeling the muscles of his throat burning, hurting from the attack.

Madeline, shocked to hear that was Cage's dad, turned to him.

"Sorry I killed his dog. I think his going to come after me. He had that look in his eyes, like 'it's not over' before he vanished."

"Later for that," Cage said. We been here far too long, and we left Gina unattended. Let's go. We're off-schedule." Cage grabbed Andre, on the floor, and threw him over his shoulder.

The quadruplets exited the warehouse and ran a mile to reach the waiting utility van. One banged on the door, signalling Gina to drive off. Once they reached the highway on Battery Park, Cage pressed the detonator button and exploded the warehouse. The event was staged to look like a gas explosion, burring all of the evidence and sinking to the bottom of the river.

They dropped off Gina, with a promise to wait until she reached the plane for Haiti. With Andre as their hostage, they drove across two state lines to charter a private jet to the Florida Keys, where they would board their own plane.

Thirty-four hours from the time they departed, the enforcers arrived in Haiti in the wee hours of the morning. They transported Andre, with a black hood over his head, into another moving vehicle to his final destination.

They entered the club as discreetly as they left, carrying Andre to Shoty's cell and throwing him in."

"Yo! Shoty! Wake up! I have a gift for you!" Magnum said, still holding onto Andre by the collar. He waited for Shoty to fully awaken.

"Fuck you, Magnum! You locked me up!" he grumbled in the darkness, missing his wife in his arms.

"Can you blame me? I couldn't get either of you to listen to reason, but you need to hurry up and finish this job. Your wife is waiting for you,"

Magnum loved the element of surprise on both their faces when he simultaneously turned the lights on and removed the hood and gag over Andre's head, walking away.

Hears the pent-up anger being released by Shoty.

He reached Constant's cell, opened the door, walked in and sat next to him, offering him a bottle of rum. Both sat in silence, listening to the brutal thrashing in the next room.

"Least he gives him a chance to defend himself," Constant acknowledged, taking to bottle of rum to the head.

"Everyone is gone! They all sanctioned the hit on Joanne," he said above a whisper.

"All thirty of them. Guess they wanted war," he said, calculating all of the leaders that needed to be replaced immediately, before the world plunged into chaos.

"They wanted you out of the way. This fat, ugly-looking Italian got up and was like," Magnum got up to mimic the man's motions *"We tolerate Constant because he brought a lot of money into our business,"*) and he was like, *'You black motherfuckers could never be my boss.'* He was the first to go." He sat back down, noticing that Constant in deep thought.

"How did you get all of them in a room at the same time?"

"The only way we could!"

"Which was how?" he asked.

"We told them it was an emergency meeting, to meet their new boss, and we got rid of you," Magnum said flatly, leaning back on the wall, waiting on his silent leader.

"You came up with that?"

"It was a team effort. We all where in agreement with the idea. It was fast and served its purpose. We knew individuals in your organization are never in the same room at the same time."

"Reasons for that—case in point. I have to go to Europe before they're absence causes panic."

"What is going on with our girl? She has changed, and Cage is worried. I'm worried. You should have seen how she handled that Eshu guy. Even he was shock!"

"Elegba came to see you?" Constant asked, surprised.

"He appeared out of nowhere with a gush of fire! He said he's Cages' dad, but when Cage came in the room, he fled."

"That's because he's afraid of Cage! Well, his mother, for that matter. What did he want?"

"He claims we've committed to many crimes! We didn't have authority to murder Oloruns Minions," he laughed thinking about Eshuer's grim expression as he condemned them.

"And we can't have any children! We are to watch our wives perish with our seed." He took another sip from the bottle, with a mouthful, he continued about his encounter with the black god.

"We cannot kill anyone! On Earth, or they'll wipeout all of our existence." No sooner the last word can out

"*Pop!*" "*Pop!*" "*Pop!*" Three shotsrang out from the next room.

"Great!" Constant sighed, exasperated, feeling a headache in the middle of his head. He really hated dealing with celestial beings, if Esheur intervened, then their problems were just starting.

Shoty walked in the cell and snatched the rum bottle out of Mag's hands.

"Bitch-ass! Froze with gun! Then tries to shoot me when I turned my back. Why couldn't he just face me, fucking coward!" he mumbled to himself, upset he was not satisfied from killing that piece of shit on the floor in the next cell.

He watched Constant, noticing how extremely quiet he was.

"What going on? You okay? You seem lost. If you're worried about that thing with Mag, I think I would have done the same thing if I wasn't drunk with revenge. I don't think this carries any consequences. Magnum has my full support, and I back him on any decisions he makes."

"I'm glad you have each other's back. Simi called and gave me the same speech, as did Roc and the rest of your little crew, but I have bigger problems than A.1.5."

"Like what?" Shoty asked.

"Like finding out who Madeline really is! Deal with that entire leader that just disappear, answer to Olorun, Olodumare, and now Eshu. They are my bosses, and they're not very happy right now," he grunted, standing to leave, before being ambushed by the rest of the team at the doorway.

"We heard Shots fired!" Silencer said.

"I have to leave within the hour. Whatever happens, just always keep each other's back. Don't ever lose sight on what matters."

He reached the doorway, feeling the heaviness of the world resting on his shoulders.

"Oh yeah! One more thing—Madeline killed his hellhound, and she thinks he might come for her."

"You know what? Every time you open you mouth and report what happened, I feel a black hole swallowing the Earth, killing everything in it," Constant said as he walked out the club, calculating his next move.

He reached Cage's fortress, went straight to Marie's room and stood over her, watching her sleep. He gently touched the curve of her back, bent down and kissed the back of her neck.

"Don't touch me," she yelled in tears, "I fucking hate you! For the past twenty-three years, all you do is hurt me. Get away from me," she screamed.

"I'm sorry I couldn't love you the way I promised too. I just wanted to let you know I have to leave for Europe... if you wanted to go! I see that you don't! I'll call you when I can! Or *if* I can!"

He walked out from her room, headed down the hall, and finding Julisa's door, he entered and sat by her bed.

She felt his presence and flew to his arms, senses something was wrong

"What is it? What's matter?" she asked.

"You always knew how to read me. Something came up, and I have to leave the country for a while."

"Um, I don't have anything here. We have time to stop home, or are we buying things on the way?" she asked searching the floor for her shoe.

"I can't find my shoe."

"I'll carry you," he said and lifted her to him

"You're not mad at me anymore?" he asked, going out the door

"I'm furious with you, but I'll wait until you lose some of that weight on your shoulders!" She paused. "You call me a whore," she said, mean-mugging him.

He squeezed her tight and whispers in her ears

"My whore!" he said with a smirk.

"Constant!" She punched him in the gut, her face masked with displeasure.

"Oomph! Ok! My Ju-Ju! My best friend! My peace! My Lady!" he said, gazing into her eyes. As she wrappd her arm around his neck he reached the Hummer and sat her inside, and looking up at Marie's window, he felt one last regret before climbing in the vehicle and sitting next to his best friend.

Shoty walked into the fortress and searched for his wife. When he reached her room, she was sleeping in the middle of the bed, with a pillow tuck under her body—the way she like to sleep with him in bed. He took off his shirt made his way to the bathroom, took a shower and then climbed in the bed beside his wife.

Joanne stirred and felt his body near her. She was startled from sleep and looked around the room, surprised. He was back! She cried as he gathered her in his arms, showering her face with kisses.

"Why, my love? Why the tears?" he whispered, his lips on her temple.

"I didn't know what happened to you. They just throw use in here! It's been three days. I kept thinking the worst!" she cried, burying her head in his chest.

"I just had to take care of some stuff. I'm sorry to worry you. Everything is okay now! We took care of the problem," he said, releasing her and laying his head on the pillow. Joanne turned on the light, freezing in place when she saw his face.

Shoty! You're all bruised up! What happened?" she asked.

"The punching bag was able to punch back a little," he joked to lighten up the situation. "As long I'm breathing, no one will ever hurt you again. This I promise you!"

She stared at him, realizing he meant every word of it. He would never allow anyone or anything to hurt her and their children. She touched her stomach and smiled at this wonderful man. She fell madly in love with him in such a short time and looked forward the exciting future they were going to share. She smiled and showered his head with kisses, loving his scent.

Six Months Later

Shoty sat at his desk under a pile of paperwork, dealing with his own business, plus running Constant's while Simi was away. It kept him more at the office than at home with Joanne, who was due any minute.

Ever since Constant left, they hadn't been able to contact him, and the world was in chaos. The new leaders had no one to guide them. Many countries were at war, the financial market had crashed and the population was on edge. Order needed to be reestablished.

It was hard for him to think that it all that started because of his little lady. The godly world seemed non-existent for the last few months. Since the encounter in New York, everything pretty much went back to normal, except for Constant's disappearance and Madeline, who was on a quest to figure out who she was and pursue Elegba. She left Magnum with no choice but to interview a nanny.

In the jungles at La Grotte Marie Jeanne, near the mouth of the cave, three figures crawled along, careful not to disturb the guardians of the jungle. Her sons shielded her with their power that kept them invisible to...

J. Del. Chat

Born in Port-au-Prince Haiti, I moved to the States in the early 80's and settled in Asbury Park, New Jersey I attended Asbury Park High School and later went on to Brookdale Community College. I worked as a Teacher's assistant for over sixteen years. I am also a photographer, a restaurant owner and an. entrepreneur.

My books are about the role-play in relationships, offering a look into the duties of strong men and women, in search for the perfect mate, with traditions dating back to our ancestor from the beginning of time.

My books are written for young men and women, looking for the right the magic in love!